ANOTHER NEAR MISS

"Why are you giving me such a hard time?"

"You said it yourself; we didn't get off on the right foot."

"And I'm currently trying to correct that error, but you won't give me a chance."

"Maybe I don't want to."

"Why not? What did I do to you?" She opened her mouth, but he interrupted. "Besides the near miss with the car," he continued. She gave him a pointed look. "And the punching bag."

"Need I say more?" Monica asked.

"Come on, you know they were accidents."

"That's my point; I think you're a hazard to my health, Dr. Holmes."

"It's a good thing I'm a doctor, then." He winked. He was entirely too sexy for his own good. And he was definitely too sexy for a woman who had vowed to stay man-free for at least a year.

"If you'll excuse me, I'd like to get to my workout," she said, trying to edge past him.

"That's it? You're not even going to give me a chance?"

Did his voice have to sound so sensuous? A girl could resist only up to a certain point.

Farrah Rochon

Deliver Me

LEISURE BOOKS NEW YORK CITY

Dedicated to the memory of Lois Marie Pierre Sterling.
I know you had a hand in this.

A LEISURE BOOK®

March 2007

Published by

Dorchester Publishing Co., Inc.
200 Madison Avenue
New York, NY 10016

ISBN 0-8439-5862-6

Printed in the United States of America.

Visit us on the web at www.dorchesterpub.com.

The realization of this lifelong dream would not have been possible without the help of many. As with everything, I first give thanks to God for His many blessings. Thanks to my agent, Evan Marshall, and my editor, Monica Harris, for all your hard work. To my extended family for always believing in me. Thanks to my wonderful critique group and the members of SOLA. To my Dreadnaughts, I love you all. Lastly, to Chermaine, Donnie, Tamara, Donnie Jr. and Jasmine: your undying love and support gives me the courage to follow my dreams.

With God all things are possible.
—Matthew 19:26

Deliver Me

Chapter One

"You'll have to spread your legs wider," Elijah encouraged softly. "Don't be afraid. I do this several times a day, and I've never had any complaints."

Her breathing escalated, the hot breaths fanning his face. Eli tried to maneuver his shoulders into a more comfortable position. No easy feat in the backseat of the compact Nissan Sentra.

"Tell me your name again, sweetheart."

"Cassandra," the teenager let out in a rushed gasp. The hem of her sundress had rolled down her thighs. Again.

"This is in the way." Eli bunched up the material and pushed the dress over her shoulders. "That's better. Now just relax. I know it's scary, but it'll be easier if you stay calm."

Eli ran his arm across his brow. It was hot, but the summer storm raging outside the car prevented him from opening the door. A rivulet of sweat followed a path from the matted hair at the girl's temple, then sluiced down her jawline. The valley between her breasts glistened. Eli captured her knees and spread her legs as far as the small space would allow.

He had to open the door. He couldn't do anything cramped up like this.

Eli reached behind him and opened the back passenger-side door. The hot rain pelted his legs as soon as he stepped onto the slippery gravel. It wasn't the most ideal environment, but he'd have to work with what he'd been given.

The young girl who lay before him cried out in pain.

"Shh." Eli quieted her with calming words while his fingertips rubbed the area giving her the most pressure. Expertly he soothed away the ache, but he knew at any moment it would return worse than before. He could no longer wait. Neither could she.

He reached down between her legs. "This is going to hurt."

The girl gasped, her back arching. "Oh, God. I can't take this."

"A little more. That's it. It won't be too long."

Her earth-shattering scream pierced the air.

"Okay, Cassandra, I need you to push. We're almost there."

Where in the hell was the ambulance?

Eli freed one hand and reached into the pocket of his khaki slacks, retrieving the sleek cellular phone. He touched the speed dial for Methodist Memorial Hospital and waited impatiently for the operator.

As soon as he heard the click, he barked into the phone, "I requested EMS twenty minutes ago. Tell them to get to the 2700 block of Pine Street now," then slammed the phone shut and shoved it back into his pocket.

"Why isn't the ambulance here yet?" the girl asked between rushed breaths.

"They'll be here soon." He smoothed the damp hair back on her forehead. "I told you not to worry. I've delivered more babies than I can count. I won't let anything happen to you."

Eli rubbed the base of her torso with gentle circles. He felt the muscles contorting underneath his palm.

"Okay, Cassandra, this is going to be a big one. Grab on to the headrest and push as hard as you can."

She did as she was told, gripping the driver's side headrest and nearly pulling herself off the seat with the force of her push.

"That's perfect. Keep pushing until I tell you to stop."

The tiny brown baby entered the world riding a wave of fluid. Eli caught him in the palm of his hand and turned him over, quickly wiping away the film from the baby's mouth and nose. The baby's cry filled the car.

"You've got a son."

He heard the high-pitched shrill of ambulance sirens coming down the street.

"Great timing," Eli muttered under his breath. He made swift work of unbuttoning the white Bill Blass buttondown. He'd managed to keep his upper body out of the rain, but sweat still caused the shirt to stick to his back. He peeled his arms out of the sleeves, then wrapped the damp material around the newborn, placing the baby in the cradle of his mother's arms.

Eli backed out of the car. He stretched his six-foot-one frame and sighed as the muscles in his back loosened. He'd maintained that crouched position for more than half an hour.

He closed his eyes, relief washing over him like the late-summer storm beating down on his bare chest and shoulders. His pants were drenched, but it didn't matter. He'd helped bring another life into the world.

Eli raised his head to the heavens and let the warm rain

hit his face, opening his eyes to stare at the darkened New Orleans sky.

The ambulance pulled into the alley, its blue and white lights illuminating the bricks of the dilapidated buildings they were sandwiched between. Two paramedics jumped out of the rig, one carrying a bright orange box, the other pushing a gurney.

"Dr. Holmes? I didn't realize you were the one who'd called this in. Where's the pregnant woman?"

"She's not really a woman, and she's not pregnant anymore, either. She just delivered a baby boy. They're in the backseat of the car," Eli informed him, tilting his head toward the decrepit vehicle.

The paramedic with the box opened the car door and went to work.

"How'd you find her?" the other medic asked as she unfolded a sheet of plastic. She quickly spread it over the gurney and tucked in the corners.

It wasn't until she'd spoken that Elijah realized it was Abby Douglas. The low-slung baseball cap covering her forehead and eyes had prevented him from recognizing one of the first women he'd met when he started at Methodist Memorial. It hadn't taken long before Eli found himself breathing rapidly over her sweaty, naked body in an empty storage room.

"I was on my way to the little snack shop on the corner when I heard a scream coming from the alley. I found her crouched behind those garbage cans. She was at least six hours into labor."

"She's lucky you had a snack attack." Abby shot him the sly grin that had snagged him the first time. She was still pretty hot. Eli wondered if she was seeing anyone.

The two medics strapped the teenager and her baby onto the gurney, covering mother and child loosely with a sheet to shield them from the rain.

Eli leaned against the ambulance's open door. "I'm going to run home and clean up, then I'll go down to the hospital."

"Are you on tonight?" Abby called from deep inside the vehicle. She was hooking up a saline bag to the portable IV stand.

"Nah, but I want to make sure they're okay." He motioned his head toward the teen, who was staring reverently at her newborn. "Besides, they can always use an extra pair of hands at the hospital since so many still haven't returned since Hurricane Katrina."

"Tell me about it. Only about sixty percent of EMS is back." Abby pulled her cap more snuggly onto her head. "I'll tell them to expect you in OB recovery. I'm sure they won't be surprised that Super Doc has struck again."

Elijah smiled and gave the pretty paramedic a wink, then stepped out of the way as she closed the door.

A loud crack reverberated through the air, and the torrential rain poured harder from the dark sky. Eli hardly took notice. With a satisfied smile he watched as the ambulance made its way up the city street.

He should have known better. When had he ever come to this hospital and not gotten sucked into the never-ending wave of chaos?

One hour.

He'd promised himself he'd check on the teen mother and her baby, visit a few of his other patients, and be back home in *one* hour.

Nine hours later, Eli stretched out on a bed in an empty delivery room. His shift started in a little more than two hours. What sense did it make to go home?

"Dr. Holmes?"

Eli sleepily cocked open a single eye. One of the floor nurses hovered over him, half of her face illuminated by

the strip of light filtering in through the crack in the door.
"You asked to be woken at five."

"You gotta be kidding me." Eli groaned. Hadn't he just
closed his eyes five minutes ago?

"Five oh two, actually. I'm a couple of minutes late. We
need you. There's a breech in room six."

It was mornings like this that made him rethink his career choice.

Eli shook his head and threw his legs over the side of the
bed. He hadn't chosen his career. It chose him. The story
had made headlines: MEDICAL STUDENT DELIVERS TWINS IN
ELEVATOR." And Super Doc had been born. After that,
could he really choose anything but obstetrics?

The door opened again. "Dr. Holmes, room six."

Eli shoved his arms into a pair of scrubs that had been
left by the nurse—they took such good care of him—and
pulled them over his head as he left the room.

The patient's scream met Eli before he got to Delivery. It
was a surprise every piece of glass in the hospital had not
shattered.

"How are things going over there?" Elijah asked. He
spread his fingers as a nurse quickly slipped latex gloves
over his hands; then he made it to the wailing woman's
side. "I'm here now," he assured soothingly. "Everything's
going to be okay."

The woman's eyes opened wide with fear. One nurse
held her hand while another adjusted the fluorescent light
that extended high above the bed.

"The nurse said I'd need a C-section. I—I don't want a
C-section."

"Shhh . . ." Eli whispered. He checked her dilation. "I
wish this little one could come out naturally, but it doesn't
look like that will happen."

Her brows rose as concern washed over her face.

"Just trust me," Eli said.

Her lips pursed as she was gripped with a contraction. Eli waited for it to fade, gently rubbing the underside of the woman's stomach.

"Okay," he said softly, knowing the calming tone would put her at ease. "In a few minutes, you'll have a brand-new baby." Eli performed a precise five-inch slit and in less than three minutes pulled out a screaming, squirming baby.

"Is she okay?" the new mother asked.

"*He* is just fine. I told you to trust me." He winked. "Dr. Tanner will take it from here," Eli said, regulating the remaining duties to the first-year resident. "Nurse Robinson, let Recovery know that Mommy and her new baby are on their way," Eli called out as he shucked off the gloves and the gauzy light green drape. He slam-dunked them in the garbage on his way out the room. Methodist Memorial's highly capable nursing staff could handle the rest.

Elijah took off in the direction of the empty delivery room, hoping to catch a few more hours' rest. Otis, the janitor who'd worked in OB since Jesus was a child, walked toward him, pushing an industrial size load of linens down the hall. He held his hand up for a high five.

"Another success, Dr. H?"

"And"—Eli pointed at the clock on the opposite side of the hallway—"it's not even six o'clock."

Eli felt as if he'd walked a minefield when he made it back to the room without being noticed by anyone else. Just as he prepared to celebrate his feat with an hour of uninterrupted sleep, a high-pitched voice called out, "Dr. Holmes, room three!"

Elijah's head fell forward, his chin hitting his chest.

Sleep would have to wait.

Monica Gardner had stared at the mountain landscape hanging on the wall behind the chief of staff's desk for so long that she'd made up a pretend family for the snow-covered cabin nestled deep in the trees. She could practically smell the aromatic pot roast the mother pulled out of the oven as she called the family to dinner.

After Monica was sure she'd spotted a three-inch man skiing down the mountain slope, she forced her gaze away from the painting. She rose, walked over to the window, and watched as a fire engine red streetcar made its way up the street.

For the umpteenth time, Monica told herself this was the right decision. New Orleans was a city in dire need. It had been brought to its knees nearly a year before when Mother Nature had unleashed her wrath on the Gulf Coast. Monica remembered her obsession with watching CNN as the news channel brought Katrina's devastation to the world's attention. She'd written checks to the Red Cross and donated to the clothes drive at her church, but it had never felt like enough. She'd wanted to do more.

This job was the *more* she'd been seeking. To live here and take care of the people working tirelessly to bring their city back to its former glory was worth more than any checks she wrote.

Besides, St. Louis had nothing left to offer her—except the occasional bout of depression and heartache, of course. Occasional as in three to four times a day.

Monica took a deep, reassuring breath. She refused to fall victim to another bout of self-pity. If she tried hard enough, she could put Patrick Dangerfield and his lies out of her mind and out of her life. She would start an entirely *new* life here in New Orleans.

Monica jerked around when the door opened.

"Sorry to keep you waiting, Dr. Gardner." Dr. William Slessinger looked as if he'd gone three rounds with the world heavyweight champ. Monica felt honored that he'd even bothered to interview her personally. He could easily have foisted the hiring duties onto the human resources department.

Shaking his head, he continued, "I can just about guarantee something else will come up before we're done here. Take my advice: Stick with practicing medicine. Administrative work isn't worth the headache."

With an understanding smile, she said, "I plan to be on the shop floor for a very long time. I love the ER too much to give it up."

"Excellent," Dr. Slessinger answered, lowering himself into the high-back leather chair behind his desk. "I'm excited at the prospect of you joining the staff here at Methodist Memorial. This is one of the top hospitals in the Southeast. Our head of oncology, Dr. Collins, was in the running for the Nobel Prize in medicine last year for her research on abdominal cancer."

"I've read several of her papers in *JAMA*," Monica said, referring to the *Journal of the American Medical Association*.

"You would be an exceptional addition to our staff, Dr. Gardner. You've built an impressive reputation in a short amount of time."

Though not as impressive as it could be, Monica thought. In fact, her reputation would have been shot to hell if not for a fellow resident's stepping into a trauma and saving her behind. She wouldn't dredge up those memories today, either.

Monica gave him a gracious smile. "I owe a lot of that to the staff back in St. Louis. They've taught me so much."

"I'm sure they have. Carl Weller sings your praises."

"He's been a wonderful mentor."

Rising from behind the desk, Dr. Slessinger guided her out of the office. "If it's all right with you, I thought we'd go to lunch, then on a tour of the hospital."

"That sounds wonderful," Monica answered, her spirits

buoyed by the choice she'd made to move to New Orleans. She didn't need time to think it over; she was ready to accept the job here and now.

They walked a few feet down the hall to the bank of elevators. Dr. Slessinger turned to her, a knowing look on his face. "I hope I'm not being presumptuous in saying this, but welcome to Methodist Memorial, Dr. Gardner."

Monica couldn't help but smile.

Chapter Two

It was nearly four in the afternoon before Eli could finally tear himself away from the delivery wing. It had to be something in the air. Pregnant women didn't come sailing in one after the other like that on a normal day.

Peter Banyon, a second-year resident from LSU School of Medicine, met him in the brightly lit corridor.

"You left anything for me?" He hefted his backpack higher on his shoulder.

"Just the grunt work. I've taken care of the important stuff," Elijah said as he scribbled on his last patient's chart, smiling as Banyon socked him on the arm with a playful punch.

"Dr. Holmes, you've got three messages from Dr. Slessinger." One of the floor nurses handed him three separate pink slips of paper.

Not Slessinger. Not today. The man could drag out a simple hello into an hour-long account of how the word originated.

"He says it's important," the nurse added.

What isn't?

He did not have time for this. If he wasn't in his car in the next five minutes, he'd be late for his niece Jasmine's dance recital. Eli valued his life too much to let that happen; his mother would skin him alive if he showed up late to another family function.

Eli had no problem admitting he feared the slip of a woman who'd given him life thirty-four years earlier. Grown man or not, he'd rather go up against the Spanish Inquisition then answer to Margo Holmes. At just under five feet, she was like a little Napoleon Bonaparte, and not one of her three much-larger sons dared contradict a word she said.

"Stacey, do me a favor." Eli slung his arm over the shoulder of the nurse who'd started in OB the same year he began his residency. "Call Slessinger in ten minutes and tell him I've left the hospital. Let him know that I'm on tomorrow morning and I'll call him as soon as possible."

"You expect me to lie for you," Stacey said. Eli already knew she would. It wouldn't be the first time.

He gave her his signature lopsided grin. "I'll owe you one."

"I'll add it to your tab."

Eli slipped into his office and quickly changed into navy slacks and a moss green polo shirt. Ever since the time he'd once had to show up for a date in scrubs, he kept a fresh outfit at the hospital. When working in OB, you weren't guaranteed the opportunity to go home and change.

A few minutes later, he hopped onto the crowded elevator.

Two orderlies were debating a controversial call from last night's preseason Saints game. Eli had been able to catch a few minutes between deliveries. Just as he was about to add his two cents on the bogus penalty flag that had cost the Saints the game, the elevator came to a halt on the second floor. The doors opened, and Eli was momentarily lost as he stared at the most heavenly creature ever created.

She was beauty personified, a sweet caramel confection with soft brown eyes and lips like an angel. She was petite and slender, with rich brown hair stopping at her delicately shaped shoulders.

"Excuse me," she said.

Her voice. Hushed. Sensual. A sexy melody floating through the air.

Eli backed up a step to give her room, and the goddess wedged between him and one of the orderlies.

"Sorry. Someone spilled cleaning fluid at the entrance to the stairs," she explained. "Otherwise I would have taken them."

Eli opened his mouth to reply, but the elevator dinged, indicating they'd arrived at the ground floor. The doors opened and Pretty Eyes walked out.

She turned left. He was going right.

Big dilemma.

Should he turn right and miss out on getting her number, or turn left and face his mother's wrath?

He'd dealt with Hurricane Margo before. He could take whatever she dished out. Besides, with his mother, an apology and a kiss on the cheek would put him on the road to forgiveness.

But could he deal with disappointing Jasmine?

Just the thought of a hint of sadness on his niece's face sealed Eli's fate. He turned right.

He still arrived forty minutes late due to traffic on I-10, which was backed up nearly to the Mississippi River. Eli slid into the seat next to his older brother and whispered, "What did I miss?"

"The classical dance," Alexander answered.

"Did she notice?"

"Yep. Be prepared to buy half the stock at Toys 'R' Us to make up for it."

The hip-hop song Eli had heard every time he went to his brother's house for the past five weeks blared out of the speakers. Ten little girls, dressed in denim overalls with one strap hooked and the other dangling to the floor, stood in the middle of the stage. They started the routine Jasmine had demanded he sit through at least a dozen times. A huge grin spread across Eli's face.

"Look at my girl go," Alex said with pride.

"You'd just better make sure she's behind the camera directing videos instead of dressed in hoochie-mama clothes, dancing in them."

"Man, don't even talk that way. This is about as far as I'm letting it go. She's switching to piano lessons after this recital."

"Make sure her uncle Tobias knows that," Eli said, speaking of their younger brother, the ex–basketball pro turned aspiring music mogul.

The number ended, and the dance school's instructor came from behind the curtain, a microphone in her hand.

"Yo, Alex." Eli nudged him with his shoulder and nodded toward the instructor. "She's not that bad. You ever think about hooking up with her when you bring Jazzy in for her lessons?"

"No." His brother shifted in his seat. "Anyway, she's married."

"Find out if she's got a sister who's single."

"Not interested."

What else was new?

His older brother seriously needed some play. Eli knew it had been more than two years since Alex had seen a naked woman—other than on pay-per-view. He probably didn't take advantage of that, either.

And it wasn't as if the guy was hard on the eyes. The

Holmes brothers were known for their looks. People in the old neighborhood used to say they could open up a modeling agency and be their own clients.

Eli could not understand how Alex did it. If he went more than a couple of months without getting some, his eyesight went blurry.

"You need to get back on the dating scene, man. The way you live isn't healthy."

"Because I don't have a different woman in my bed every night like you do?"

"Because you don't have *any* woman in your bed. And it's not a different one every night. The one I got now is going on three weeks."

"Three whole weeks?" He could hear the sarcasm in Alex's voice. "Does she get a trophy?"

"Nah, that's not until the one-month mark."

"Would the two of you be quiet," Margo Holmes hissed from where she sat on Alex's other side. "It's bad enough you walked in an hour late." She shot the evil eye Eli's way. "You don't need another mark against your name."

Eli cursed under his breath. He could see Alex's shoulders moving up and down as his brother tried to stifle his laughter.

"You didn't think she'd let you get away with coming here late, did you?" Alex whispered.

Their mother leaned forward slightly and looked at them again. Eli decided to hold his comment.

After the recital ended, Jasmine came rushing from behind the stage, her Shirley Temple curls bouncing around her face. She plowed into him, wrapping her skinny arms around Eli's leg.

"What's up, Water Lily," Elijah said, ruffling her curls.

She stepped back. "My name is Jasmine," his niece informed him, a sassy hand on her hip. It was a game they'd played since the minute she learned to talk. Eli called her every type of flower except the one for which she'd been named.

"Did you seen me dancing?" Jasmine asked.

"See? Did I *see* you dancing?" He'd warned Alex about letting this girl watch so much television. "And yes, I did. You were the best dancer up there."

"I told you I was good."

He didn't worry about correcting her grammar again. There weren't enough hours in the day.

"I know you have a good excuse for being late, Elijah Marcus."

Eli turned to find his mother standing next to Alex. His brother dwarfed her, yet it was painfully obvious who held the power. Although her sons were grown men with jobs and lives of their own, Margo Holmes still ruled.

Eli shrugged. "I sent a memo that no babies were to be born today, but apparently three expectant mothers forgot to read it."

She pointed to her cheek and Eli obediently obliged, placing a gentle peck on the smooth skin. "You're lucky you have a career where I'm forced to accept your excuses."

"Number one reason I chose it." He grinned.

"Are you coming to dinner?" Alex asked. He stooped down and picked up his daughter. Jasmine wrapped her arms around her daddy's thick neck and held on as he swung her from side to side.

Eli shook his head. He knew the dinner invitation would be extended—the Holmeses never missed a chance to indulge in good food—but he'd already concocted a stellar excuse. He just hoped his brother didn't see straight through it.

"No can do. I'm giving a lecture tomorrow for the incoming medical students, and it needs a little tweaking."

Of course, his contribution was only five minutes long,

and he'd written his short spiel last week, but did Alex and Mama really need to know that?

His mother crossed her arms over her chest. "You will be there on Sunday." It was not a question. Unless there was bloodshed involved, Sunday dinner was not to be missed.

"Of course." Eli bent slightly to plant another kiss, this one on her forehead. "You need me to bring anything?"

"Just you will be fine. But be on time. And it wouldn't hurt to see you in church, either."

He was getting out of here before this lecture even started. The *when was the last time you went to church?* speech could give Slessinger's *hello* talk a run for its money.

"I'll try," he answered. Two lies in a row. He hoped they didn't show on his face.

"Bye, Uncle Eli," Jasmine called out.

"See ya later, Chrysanthemum." He winked and headed for his car.

When Eli pulled into the driveway of the two-story Tudor he'd bought a few years ago in the posh Old Metairie neighborhood, he found a sleek white BMW idling in his normal parking spot. He was thankful that his home had sustained minimal damage from the hurricane, and he'd been able to move back in months ago. Eli parked his Range Rover behind the BMW, and the doors to the two vehicles opened simultaneously.

A long, toned, honey-colored leg stepped out onto the brick driveway. An equally luscious body followed.

Alicia Taylor could stop traffic.

She was slim, statuesque and drop-dead gorgeous, and a dozen men would be all too eager to give her all she desired. Eli wasn't to that point yet, but he was close—

especially if it meant a repeat of what she'd surprised him with last Saturday night.

Whoever invented the phrase "men are dogs" knew what they were talking about. Alicia had had him howling like a bloodhound. He had been sure he'd hear from the neighbors the next morning.

Too bad her tenure was coming to an end. He'd miss her creativity in the bedroom, but when she started leaving messages on his work phone, cell phone, and home voice mail, Eli knew it was time to cut her loose.

Alicia leaned against the driver's-side door, her back to him. She put one hand on her hip and the other on top of the car.

Elijah pressed the button on his key ring, activating the Rover's alarm system. He walked up to her Beamer, stopping a scant foot behind her. He leaned over and placed his mouth next to her ear.

"Have you been waiting long?" Eli asked, his voice low.

"As a matter of fact, I have," she answered, not turning around. "You know I hate to be kept waiting."

The makings of a grin tipped the corners of Eli's mouth. "I guess you'll just have to punish me."

She relinquished her pose and reached inside the car, retrieving a tiny clutch. Eli heard her unsnap the closure on the small beaded purse. She pulled out a pair of chrome handcuffs and held them up.

"I guess I will."

Still facing away from him, Alicia reached back with her free hand and tugged the hem of Eli's shirt. She used it to pull him toward the front door, then turned and pinned him against it, plunging her tongue down his throat. Eli fumbled with the key and after three tries finally unlocked the door.

They never made it past the foyer.

Chapter Three

The blaring police sirens were giving her a headache.

Monica slumped her head against the steering wheel and tried not to scream.

In the true fashion of her unbelievably bad luck, she *would* get in a fender bender this morning, making her late her first day on the job. It didn't help that the granny she rear-ended appeared to be a pro at traffic accidents. The woman had the police on speed dial. Of course, the call to her lawyer had taken precedence over the authorities.

Great. Monica's insurance would go through the roof.

She really, *really* wanted to scream.

The officer, who had apparently graduated from the police academy ten minutes before responding to the accident, strolled up to her window.

"Are we done here?" Monica asked, not giving him a chance to speak.

"You're free to go, Miss Gardner, but you'll need to

make yourself available. I have a feeling you'll be hearing from Mrs. Gauthier's lawyer sometime today."

Wonderful.

"You people do realize this is a *minor* accident, right? Her car doesn't have a scratch on it."

"She says she's having chest pains from the sudden jolt she received when you rear-ended her."

"Chest pains, my ass," Monica muttered under her breath. She didn't have time for this. "Look, I need to get to work. Tell her lawyer to call away."

She put her car in drive and took off down Jefferson Davis Parkway. A flutter of excitement lifted Monica's stomach as the deep brown bricks of Methodist Memorial Hospital came into view.

Moving to New Orleans was the smartest thing she'd done in a long time. She'd already fallen in love with the city. Despite the trauma the city had sustained from last year's storm, evidence of its rich, colorful history poured out of every crevice, from the antebellum mansion she'd visited over the weekend, when she'd gone exploring up the Mississippi River, to Jackson Square, only a few blocks from her French Quarter apartment.

Monica had learned that the Quarter, as the locals referred to it, was one of the city's highest points, so the flooding that had devastated most of New Orleans hadn't reached it. Monica was grateful it had been spared. She adored the neighborhood's quaintness; she couldn't imagine living anywhere else in the city.

For the past two nights, the sweet music wafting from the funky little jazz club across the street had lulled her to sleep, leaving her with dreams of a tall, dark trumpet player ready to light her world on fire.

That was about the only place men showed up these days—in her dreams.

Not that Monica was complaining. Lord knows the one

man she'd allowed herself to get close to had ripped her heart out and stomped on it like an Indian rain dance.

If she wanted to be honest, Monica could admit that Patrick's departure hadn't come totally out of left field. Although they were together for six years, they had never shared the all-consuming, heart-stopping love Monica had witnessed between other couples. But Patrick had been a good social match. The son of a prominent businessman, he had the breeding and pedigree that made her mother's boat float. The fact that he didn't provide Monica with the happiness she wanted didn't really matter.

Despite their unfulfilling relationship, Monica still missed him.

Stop that, she chided herself. She did *not* miss him.

Patrick Dangerfield was a thousand miles away, living with his perfect new wife and perfect new baby in a perfect house in St. Louis. She had not left Missouri to bring thoughts of him to Louisiana.

Monica pulled into her parking space. The rectangular sign still read RESERVED FOR DR. MILLGRAM, the ER attending she had replaced. According to Dr. Slessinger, Charles Millgram had evacuated with his family to Houston, and like a lot of other people who left during Katrina, had decided to stay. Dr. Millgram's choice to remain in Texas had been Monica's saving grace. When her best friend, Nia, told her about an opening she'd found on an Internet job board for an emergency room doctor at a New Orleans hospital, Monica couldn't get to the phone fast enough.

Monica set the car alarm and started across the covered parking lot. She stepped out of the rows of cars and had to jump back when a black Range Rover turned the curve, going at least ten times faster than it should in a place where there was constant foot traffic.

If there was one thing about New Orleans that didn't

impress her, it was the driving. Everybody on the road should have had their licenses revoked a long time ago.

The ER's glass doors opened, and Monica headed toward the large square station in the middle of the emergency room.

"Good morning, Dr. Gardner," the nurse Dr. Slessinger had introduced as Patty on their tour of the hospital greeted her.

"Good morning, Patty. Sorry I'm late. I had a small fender bender on the way in."

"Are you okay?"

Monica waved off the nurse's concern. "It was hardly anything. But don't tell that to the sweet little grandmother I hit. I wouldn't be surprised if she came rolling through those doors, claiming I gave her a heart attack."

Patty grimaced. "One of those, huh?"

Monica nodded. She turned to the large dry-erase board hanging above the nurses' station. "I'll take the laceration in room three."

By midday, Monica had seen half a dozen patients. It was a good thing she'd been prepared for a full workload. Unfortunately nothing could have prepared her for the eight-year-old with stomach flu—thus the spanking-new pair of peach scrubs the charge nurse had so graciously loaned her. Someone had run upstairs to get a pair of green scrubs—the color delineated for doctors—but Monica didn't have time to wait. She could hear the wailing of the ambulance signaling the arrival of yet another patient.

Monica left the room she'd ducked into to change clothes and met the EMS team at the ambulance bay.

"What do we have?" she asked the driver as he came around the side of the rig. The other paramedic pulled the double doors open, and they lifted a gurney and placed it on the ground. A very pregnant woman lay upon the flat surface.

"Call came through about twelve minutes ago. Thirty-two weeks. Complains of severe abdominal pain. She has a good bit of swelling in her lower extremities."

Monica helped guide the gurney into the first available examination room, while the EMT listed the woman's vitals.

"Any meds?"

"Only your normal prenatals."

"Good job," Monica said with a nod, releasing the medics of their duty. "Get a monitor on the heart going and dip her urine," she called out. Monica quickly scrubbed at the large basin. A nurse slipped gloves over her hands, then Monica went around to the panting woman's side.

"I know it hurts," she crooned softly. "What's your name?"

"Sharon. Please, help my baby," the woman pleaded.

"Don't worry, Sharon," Monica reassured her. "Do you know the sex of the baby?" Monica asked, trying to gear the frightened woman's mind to more pleasant thoughts.

She nodded. "A boy. We're naming . . . him Andrew . . . Andrew Michael."

"Oh, I like that." Monica smiled as she checked the patient's vitals. She'd turned to check the black and green screen on the fetal monitor when a series of beeps sounded throughout the room.

"Doctor, her BP just shot up to 220 over 118."

"Sharon?" Monica positioned the stethoscope earpieces in her ears and made quick work of pressing the flat end to the woman's chest and stomach.

"Rapid heartbeat," Monica said. "Sharon, can you hear me?" She performed a deep-pain test by rubbing her knuckles at a point on the woman's sternum. Sharon responded with a jerk. "Sharon, is there ringing in your ears, or do you feel nauseated at all?"

The woman gave a weak nod.

"Any dizziness?"

Another nod.

"It's preeclampsia. Get OB down here. We need an emergency section." Sharon shook her head, tried to moan a protest. "I'm sorry, but you have a very serious condition," Monica explained. "We need to get the baby out as quickly as possible."

"He's . . . not ready," Sharon said in a meek whisper. "It's too early."

"Thirty-two weeks is more than enough time," Monica assured her. "Don't worry, Sharon, he'll be fine."

The woman's head fell back onto the table.

"Sharon?" Monica tried the pain test again. This time the patient didn't respond. "Okay, this baby needs to come out now. Prepare for a section."

The three nurses stopped. They all stared at her for a second before one asked, "Shouldn't we wait for OB?"

"Not unless you want a dead mother and baby on your hands. OB can take over when they get here."

A second nurse pushed over an instrument tray. Monica tore away the drape, unveiling an array of shiny chrome surgical tools. She had just made the five-inch horizontal slit across the underside of the woman's protruding belly when the room's double doors burst open.

"What do we have?"

Monica didn't raise her head. "Thirty-two weeks with preeclampsia. I'm performing an emergency C-section."

"Who the hell are you?"

This time she did look up, the hostility in the voice surprising her. "I'm—"

The man in green scrubs didn't give her a chance to finish. Instead, to Monica's growing astonishment, he pushed her out of the way. She stood still for a moment, suspended in shocked outrage.

He—whoever he was—barked out orders the nurses followed with unfailing precision. Monica couldn't help but feel a twinge of admiration at how quickly the doctor had taken control of the situation. She tore the bloodstained gauze gown from her shoulders and turned so the nurse could drape another over her, but when she took a step forward with the intention of assisting, the doctor shouted, "Stay back!"

Just who did he think he was talking to?

Monica watched as the masked doctor quickly but gently pulled the bluish infant from the mother's belly. He applied two clamps to the umbilical cord and snipped.

The baby was so small. The tiny ones always pulled at her heart.

A nurse took the infant and placed him in a plastic incubator that had been wheeled down from Maternity.

"Get her to the OR," the obnoxious doctor barked. He whirled around, facing Monica. His deep chocolate-colored eyes were blazing. "Are you out of your mind? What the hell did you think you were doing?"

"I was—"

He cut her off. "Do you think we allow nurses to perform surgical procedures?"

"Nurse?"

"Clean out your locker and get the hell out of this hospital. I'll make sure you never work at another medical facility in the entire country."

Monica tore the mask from her face, preparing for full combat. Her adversary took a visible step back.

"Dr. Holmes," Patty said, "meet Dr. Monica Gardner, the new attending in emergency medicine. Dr. Gardner, this is Dr. Elijah Holmes, OB attending."

He stood there staring at her. After a long moment, he stretched out his hand. "Dr. Gardner."

Monica refused to take it. Instead she crossed her arms over her chest and stared him down. "Exactly where do you get off coming into this emergency room with that kind of attitude?"

"Excuse me?"

"Asking me what I think I'm doing? Telling me to clean out my locker?"

"I thought you were a nurse."

"I've only been here one day, and even I know the nurses at Methodist Memorial wouldn't put a patient's life in jeopardy that way."

"I saw someone in nurses' scrubs performing a Cesarean. What was I supposed to think?"

"I would assume, as a doctor, you'd have enough common sense not to automatically conclude that it was a nurse performing the procedure."

"How could I—"

The doors burst open, interrupting his comeback.

"We need this room. We have a MI in full arrest."

Monica forgot about the pigheaded doctor with gorgeous brown eyes and focused her attention on her next emergency.

Dr. Holmes would hear from her later.

Monica gripped the paper gown at her neck and tore it from her body. She shucked the latex gloves from her hands and deposited them along with the gown in the disposal bin outside curtain three.

There had been an influx of patients in the past two hours, so many that she'd hardly had the chance to catch a breath before another injury rolled through the doors. Sensing that the fury had calmed, Monica ran to the bathroom—something else she hadn't had time to do in the previous two hours.

When she emerged from the women's restroom, she discovered Dr. Slessinger standing at one of the wall X-ray units, reviewing film with a resident Monica had met earlier in the day.

"Dr. Gardner," he called out to her. He said something to the young doctor, who nodded; then Slessinger switched off the light on the X-ray machine and started toward her. "I'm happy I ran into you."

Just when she thought she could have a few minutes to herself. Monica suppressed a sigh and pasted on a smile.

"How has your day gone so far?" the doctor asked. He had a cheerfulness about him she found endearing.

"It's been busy, but I can handle it," Monica answered.

"I knew you would jump in with both feet." He patted her on the shoulder. "You're going to fit right in."

A warm glow settled over her. Praise was always a welcome boost to her spirits, especially after a particularly long day. And even more so after being unfairly chewed out by Dr. Holmes earlier this morning. Honest mistake or not, Monica was still smarting from his high-handed reprimand.

Working in the same hospital, she knew she'd have to see him occasionally, but she hoped their encounters would be few and far between.

Yeah, right! the little voice inside her head taunted.

"Do you have any objections, Dr. Gardner?"

What? Oh, great. Thinking about that heartthrob in scrubs, she'd completely missed whatever it was Dr. Slessinger had been talking about.

"I'm sorry, my mind was on a young boy with cystic fibrosis I saw this morning."

Liar.

"I wondered if you would be interested in sitting on our charity board. Dr. Millgram was an active member."

"What would it entail?" Monica asked, already warming to the idea. Anything that kept her from sitting in her apartment, pining away for Patrick, was a treat.

"Over the years, the board has focused on raising money for our outreach programs. Because of our location, we have a unique opportunity to provide services to many who wouldn't be able to afford it," Slessinger explained.

That was a nice way of saying that although Methodist Memorial was a world-class facility, the neighborhood around it left much to be desired. Monica simply nodded.

"These days those programs are needed more than ever."

"They definitely are," Monica agreed.

A slew of nurses and paramedics wheeled a gurney down the hall, but before she could excuse herself to attend to the trauma, the other physician on call came from behind curtain one.

"I've got it, Dr. Gardner," Dr. Ray Carvel said as he followed closely behind the gurney.

"I didn't realize Dr. Carvel was here today," Dr. Slessinger said.

"He's on call," Monica replied. "He came in a few hours ago when things got a little sticky. I think he just enjoys being here."

"There are few as dedicated as he is. And speaking of dedication, Dr. Millgram gave new meaning to the word. He devoted countless hours to making Methodist Memorial's charity board the best of the area hospitals. I don't want to pressure you," Dr. Slessinger was quick to explain. "But it would be a tremendous help if you can spare a few hours a month. Are you up for this?" he asked, his eyes full of hope.

Could she really turn him down?

"I'd be happy to." What else did she have to do in this city, where she knew absolutely no one? "It sounds like a great program."

Dr. Slessinger's face brightened. "Oh, it is. Best in the city."

"Why don't we schedule a time when we can discuss exactly what I would be doing," Monica suggested.

"I'll go you one better. The monthly meeting is tomorrow. I'll e-mail you an invite." He pointed to her. "You're going to be an excellent addition to the team, Dr. Gardner."

Monica smiled to herself. There was that warm glow again.

Chapter Four

Eli passed his normal stop and instead got off on the seventh floor, which housed the neonatal intensive care unit. The preemie he'd delivered in the ER that morning was in excellent condition. He shouldn't have any complications from his eventful birth.

Unfortunately, Eli realized that *his* complications from this morning's run-in were just beginning. He had not made the best impression on the hospital's newest employee.

He'd experienced a temporary case of brain paralysis when she'd pulled the mask from her face. It had taken Eli less than a second to realize the "nurse" performing the C-section was Pretty Eyes from the elevator.

Eli had found himself thinking about that face more than once this week. Of course, he had no idea he would ever see her again. He'd pegged her as a random goddess put in his line of vision for a few minutes so he'd have someone to fantasize about in the shower.

But he'd been wrong. Tremendously, unbelievably, *painfully* wrong.

She was fantasyworthy, all right, but his running into her was not a random coincidence. In fact, they would have a multitude of chances to cross paths.

God help him.

He had an appointment in twenty minutes, but first Eli needed to see Otis. If anyone knew the scoop, it was Otis. Eli opted for the stairs back to OB. He found the janitor pushing a broom in the employee lounge.

"What's up, Doctor H?" Otis asked, the fluorescent overhead lights reflecting off his gold tooth.

Eli poured a cup of coffee from the carafe marked DECAF and got straight to the point. "Otis, you hear anything about the new doctor in the ER?"

The janitor's mouth cracked in a wide grin. "She's a nice-looking one, ain't she?"

Extraordinary hazel eyes, a head of luscious, silky hair, and a fit, nicely shaped body definitely constituted "nice-looking" in his book. Not to mention the confidence with which she carried herself. There was something undeniably sexy about a self-assured woman. But Eli refused to take the bait Otis dangled in front of him. He was sure it was none other than Otis who started half the rumors in this hospital. If he even hinted at what he really thought of Monica Gardner's looks, the rumor mill would have them getting married by the end of the day. Lord knew, if Eli had had as many engagements as he'd heard about over the years, he'd have spent the majority of his paychecks on diamond rings.

"Actually, I mistook her for a nurse this morning, and it didn't go over too well. I didn't realize they were getting a replacement for Millgram so soon."

Otis rested his hand on the top of the broomstick and leaned forward.

Jackpot! Eli knew all the old man needed was a little prompting.

"The name is Monica Gardner. From what I hear, she's from St. Louis. Came down and talked to the big boss last week, and he hired her on the spot. She got herself a place in the Quarter. I don't know which street, but I hear it's not too far from the river."

How did Otis always know so much?

Eli refused to question it further—as long as Otis provided what he wanted to know, he wouldn't think about how the janitor filled up his bottomless well of information.

"So, you gonna ask her out?"

Eli sent him a shrewd look. "You know me better than that."

It was common knowledge that Elijah Holmes did not date doctors. The reason behind it was no one's business, just as long as they knew the rule.

"Dr. H, you need to start giving some of the female docs here a chance. I bet you get some action if you do."

"I get enough action from the nurses." Eli made a production of looking at his watch, and pretended surprise at the time. "I need to get to my office. I've got an appointment in a few minutes." He grabbed a pear from the fruit basket someone had left on the table as he headed out of the lounge.

"I'll keep my ears open and let you know if I hear anything else about our new doc."

Eli gave Otis a nod, then shouldered his way out the door.

The Danielses were waiting outside his office when Elijah turned the corner. He'd been dreading this appointment all day. Since Katrina, he'd inherited a number of patients from doctors who had yet—or who had no plans—to return to the city.

In all his years of practicing medicine, Eli had never encountered a case like Amanda and Jeffrey Daniels's. Eli still wasn't convinced they were really married. The way the couple interacted, you'd think they were two strangers, strangers who didn't necessarily like the person they'd had just met. To add to the bizarreness, Amanda Daniels was being treated for bipolar disorder but refused to inform her husband of her condition. Eli felt it was morally wrong to keep such an important fact from her spouse, but patient confidentiality forced him to observe Amanda's wishes.

He shook Jeffrey Daniels's proffered hand and smiled at the man's wife as he held the door open for her.

Eli guided the couple into the office and motioned for them to take a seat in the two wing-back chairs in front of his desk. Amanda Daniels nudged her chair to the right, shoving it a few inches away from the one her husband occupied.

Here we go again.

"Okay, Mr. and Mrs. Daniels, let's see where we are." Eli opened the manila folder and splayed it flat on his desk. "This marks the twenty-eighth week, Amanda, putting you in your last trimester. How are you feeling in general?"

"Okay, I guess. I had a little dizziness yesterday, but nothing like that last episode."

"After you complained of the second dizzy spell, you know I had the lab to run a few more tests. Your anemia has gotten worse."

Amanda Daniels took a deep, solemn breath. "What does this mean?"

"I think you already know," Eli said apologetically. "I know you didn't want this, but I have to recommend putting you on bed rest."

Her face revealed nothing. "Is that really necessary, Doctor?"

"She can't leave the bed at all?" Jeffrey asked. Eli noticed Amanda's disgusted eye-roll. The tension between these two was as thick as seven-A.M. fog in San Francisco. And it was uncomfortable to witness.

"No, it's not that restrictive," Eli clarified. "She can move around some, but nothing strenuous. You're going to have to pamper her," he said, interested in the response that statement would provoke.

Amanda's face became as hard as stone. Jeffrey glanced at his wife and took a deep breath. Eli wasn't sure about the expression on the man's face, but it looked a hell of a lot like hurt. Homeboy was definitely in the doghouse. And he had been there for a while.

Since meeting the couple more than four months ago, Eli had never seen Amanda treat her husband with anything other than cold distaste. Eli wondered how the guy had managed to get her pregnant in the first place.

"Exactly how restrictive are we talking?" Amanda asked.

Eli walked over to the file cabinet behind his desk. He opened the second drawer and retrieved a set of stapled instructions. "Here are a few guidelines some of the doctors, myself included, came up with for the various stages of bed rest."

Eli stopped short, not sure to whom he should hand the packet. Both husband and wife reached for it, and he was willing to bet this month's paycheck that Amanda Daniels wouldn't invite her husband to share. Eli turned back to the file cabinet and pulled out another set. It seemed the easiest course of action to prevent the inevitable battle between these two. He didn't need bloodstains on the carpet. He had enough problems to deal with today.

"As you can see, the restrictions aren't all that inhibiting, but you'll need to take it easy. I don't want to see you back here any sooner then I'm supposed to," he finished with a smile.

Amanda returned the smile with a weak one of her own. Her husband had not said a thing since Eli handed him the instructions. He stared at the paper as if trying to digest the words.

God, they were unnerving. He was tempted to send the two of them straight to the marriage counselor in Methodist Memorial's counseling clinic. Eli could only pray for the baby, who would have to grow up in such a strained, tension-filled environment.

Eli sat back in his chair and folded his hands over his desk. "Well . . . I think that's all," he said after the uncomfortable silence became unbearable.

"One thing, Doc," Jeffrey asked, his eyes still glued to the instructions. He pointed to a spot on the paper. "Under the 'reduce activity' section, it says she should limit stair climbing."

"Yes." Elijah nodded. "Especially with such a severe case of anemia. Exercise is still important, but even a few steps can bring on dizziness. You'll need to cut out the use of stairs as much as possible."

"That's going to be difficult, Doctor. I live on the third floor of my apartment complex," Amanda began.

"You can—" Jeffrey started.

"No," Amanda hissed in a sharp, biting tone. Eli could practically see the ice dripping from the single word.

He'd had about as much of this as he could stomach. Eli had too much on his mind to worry about the Danielses and their frighteningly strange relationship.

"Umm . . . okay. Well, my advice is that the two of you either move to an apartment where there are no stairs, or request that your landlord put in a stair lift ASAP. You definitely cannot walk up two flights of stairs in your condition," he said to Amanda. "With your history, we have to cut out all risk."

Jeffrey rose and extended his hand across the desk. After Eli shook it, the man went to his wife's side and tried to help her out of the chair.

She flung off the offending hand. Jeffrey looked sheepishly over at Eli, his hands now resting at his sides as they both watched his wife struggle to rise from the chair.

"Thank you again, Dr. Holmes," Amanda said. She clutched her small purse to her side and turned for the door. Eli quickly made it around the desk and to the door, not wanting to witness what would happen if her husband attempted to open it for her.

"Thanks, Doctor," Jeffrey said again. Eli couldn't help but feel sorry for the guy. His situation was far beyond flowers and candy. Eli doubted anything less than having the O'Jays serenade his wife while feeding her chocolate-dipped strawberries was going to help Jeffrey Daniels get out of the doghouse.

"I'll see the two of you in a week," he said to their retreating backs.

Eli spent the last hour of his workday shuffling around the paperwork on his desk. If there was one thing about his job he absolutely despised, it was paperwork. As soon as the brass hands on the wall clock landed in a perfect vertical line, Eli shoved away from his desk and snatched his light windbreaker from the coatrack. He grabbed his keys, switched off the light, and pulled the door closed behind him, locking it and repocketing the keys.

There was a college football game on tonight, and Eli was looking forward to a quiet night at home. Alone.

Alicia had a business trip that would keep her overnight in Houston, and Eli welcomed the one-night reprieve. She was becoming a little too clingy for his taste.

Eli made it to the parking lot about ten minutes after six. If the gods were shining down on him, afternoon traffic would be clear and he'd be sitting in front of his big-screen television by kickoff.

He started up the Rover, pulled out, and had to slam on his brakes to avoid hitting a gray Honda.

His heart didn't know whether to lift or sink at the sight of Monica Gardner's angry face behind the wheel. She made a slight motion forward, obviously putting the car in park, and opened the door. One look at the fury in those hazel eyes and Eli knew this wouldn't be good. He got out and met her halfway between their two vehicles.

"Was the DMV stupid enough to issue you a driver's license, or did you buy it from Wal-Mart?"

She obviously wasn't looking for an answer, so Eli casually crossed his arms over his chest and stared down at her. She was at least a foot shorter than he was, and the view from where he stood was absolutely stunning. Her soft, flowery scent did crazy things to his senses.

"Well, say something."

He could tell by the strain in her voice that she was diligently working to contain a scream. Eli had an instant vision of her screaming under much more pleasurable circumstances. He tried not to smile.

"This is the second time you've nearly run me over today, Dr. Holmes."

"What?" Her accusation knocked him out of his lust-filled daydream.

"This exact black Range Rover almost clipped my toes off when I came in this morning. I had to jump a good three feet back to prevent getting rolled over."

"It wasn't me."

"Is there another employee with the same color and model SUV?"

Eli shook his head in the negative.

"I rest my case," she finished with triumphant sassiness. He loved a sassy woman.

"Whatever you say," Eli answered with a shrug. "I didn't see you this morning, and you must have come around that curve pretty fast, because I looked both ways just a minute ago before pulling out."

"*I* must have been driving fast?"

Eli decided he liked her angry—probably because that was the only way he'd seen her so far, but also because of the passion she exuded. Monica Gardner was an intriguing contradiction. Her eyes shimmered with blatant disapproval; yet Eli sensed she was enjoying this little tête-à-tête as much as he was.

He had to figure out just where she fit in his world. Her occupation was a solid mark against her. After that incident involving a fling with one of his professors back in medical school, Eli had vowed never to get romantically involved with another doctor. But he'd still rather have her as an ally than as an enemy any day of the week, even if he refused to date her.

If *he* refused to date *her*?

Man, he was getting cocky. This woman probably wouldn't agree to a date with him for all the money in Fort Knox. He didn't have to worry about breaking his rule where she was concerned. But, still, he didn't want her to dislike him.

"Look, we obviously got off on the wrong foot," Eli said, extending his hand again.

She crossed her arms over her chest. "You're just figuring that out?"

"Are you going to allow me to speak?"

She gave him a decidedly uninterested look, took a step back, and rested her hands on her hips. The stance caused her breasts to thrust forward.

The sight left Eli without a single coherent thought. Or maybe it was her action of running her tongue lightly over her bottom lip that snatched all thoughts from his brain. The unconscious act left her luscious lips glistening and unbelievably inviting.

"Dr. Holmes?"

Her snapping fingers finally caught his attention. He'd

never had a woman put him in a trance before. There was something seriously different about this one.

"I hope you don't space out like that during a delivery," she said.

"I'm sorry. It's been a rough day, and this conversation is not making it any easier."

"Well, your day would have gotten ten times worse had you run me over. You need to be alert when you get behind that wheel," she warned, then turned and headed for her car.

"Nice to know you're concerned about my welfare," Elijah called out to her, unable to keep his mouth from breaking out into a smile.

She opened her car door and stood with her hand resting on the window. "Don't flatter yourself. I'm an emergency room physician. You cause a five-car pileup, and they'll call me back to work. I've got a big night planned, and I won't have you ruining it."

She slid behind the wheel, and Eli chuckled to himself as he watched the Honda exit the parking garage.

Chapter Five

A jackknifed eighteen-wheeler held up traffic on interstate 10 for over an hour. A long, excruciating hour spent in insufferable silence in a car with the woman he loved more than life itself.

Jeffrey blew out a puff of air and tapped his fingers against the steering wheel in a nervous rhythm. He was nervous around his own wife.

If this isn't the most ridiculous thing in the world.

Not just nervous—he was afraid even to glance at her. These days, the littlest thing seemed to set her off. It had come to the point where he hated talking to her.

But, when he thought about it, Jeffrey realized this was probably the best place to bring up his concerns. Stuck in the car with him, she probably wouldn't listen, but she couldn't run away, either.

She sat with her back ramrod-straight. The rigid posture reminded Jeffrey of her sister, Regina: the terror who could have been his wife. Although, when he thought about how things presently were with Amanda, Jeffrey wondered whether he would have been better off with Regina.

No. He loved Amanda. *Loved*. He still loved Amanda.

The masochistic relationship he and Regina had once shared could never compare to the bone-deep euphoria he felt every time he looked into Amanda's eyes. He'd never truly understood the concept of breathtaking beauty before the day he'd met his wife. She affected him on so many levels. Physically. Emotionally. In every way.

Jeffrey could remember the feeling of tightness in his chest when she would look at him from across the table as they ate dinner. The satisfying contentment that came with knowing he would spend the rest of his life staring into that heavenly face.

As he looked out of the corner of his eye at her erect form sitting just inches away from him in the passenger seat of their Ford Explorer, Jeffrey couldn't believe this was the same woman he'd pledged to honor and cherish for the rest of his days. The woman he'd married was not this cold, unfeeling person. The woman he'd married would never flinch at his touch.

But this woman did. And he had no idea how or even if she would ever again be his Amanda.

Jeffrey let out a slow breath before saying softly, "Amanda?" She remained silent. Jeffrey gripped the steering wheel in frustration. "Can't you even acknowledge my question?"

"You didn't ask a question," she said in a soft, stoic whisper, as if she weren't aware she'd even spoken.

"Dammit, Amanda! I'm tired of this. Have we gotten to the point where we can't even talk anymore?"

She let out an exaggerated sigh and shifted in the seat. She still didn't look at him. Instead she stared at the crowded highway ahead.

"Exactly what do you want to talk about?"

This wasn't the time to bring it up. Not when she was in this mood. But when wasn't she in some type of mood? Even before she'd become pregnant, she'd made an abrupt metamorphosis into this person who wasn't receptive to anything he had to say. He might as well just come out with it.

"We need to talk about what Dr. Holmes discussed with us today."

"What about it?" she asked glacially.

"Don't do this, Amanda."

"If you want to have a conversation, you need to stop speaking in riddles. Now, exactly what about today's appointment is such a burning issue with you?"

"You need to move back into the house," he stated bluntly.

She was quiet for a moment before saying in a soft voice, "No, I do not."

"You heard what Dr. Holmes said. Stairs are out of the question, and you can't do anything strenuous."

"I don't plan on taking up kickboxing."

Her calmness pissed him off. Jeffrey would have preferred she show some kind of emotion—even anger. To have her remain so cold, so unfeeling made it seem as though she didn't care anymore. If she didn't care, then Jeffrey knew he'd lost her.

"You have to climb two flights of stairs to get to that apartment. You can't stay there. I'm not letting you endanger the baby."

She turned to him with the first gleam of fire in her eyes he'd seen in months. "Do you think I would intentionally put my child in danger?"

"I don't know. You weren't very excited when you found out you were pregnant."

Amanda sucked in a breath, her eyes wide and wounded.

"How dare you." Her fierce words were drenched in hurt.

It was a cheap shot and he knew it. Both he and Amanda had been floored when they discovered their one night of booze and memories had resulted in a baby, especially since years of fertility treatments had left them only with heartache.

"I'm sorry," he said quietly.

The traffic started moving again. Jeffrey bypassed the exit that would have taken them to the apartment complex Amanda had moved into when she'd decided she could no longer stomach living in the same house with him. Ten minutes later, he pulled into the driveway of the house they'd shared for eleven years as husband and wife.

"Just for a few days, Amanda. Let's try it out and see how it works."

She remained silent.

"Amanda . . ."

"I need some things from my apartment."

Jeffrey let out a rush of air he hadn't realized he'd been holding.

"A few days," she stated. "That's all I'm willing to give."

Monica sprinkled a few drops of balsamic vinegar over the exotic concoction of leafy vegetables and tossed them around the bowl with wooden salad tongs. She threw in a few croutons from the box on the counter and carried her dinner to the sofa to eat in front of the television.

The warm colors in her inviting living room helped ease the tension from her neck and shoulders. Monica loved her new apartment, with its faux brick fireplace and wrought-iron balcony overlooking a cozy courtyard. It was vastly different from any of the places she'd lived in St. Louis, and the more she thought about it, the more Monica realized this place was just her style.

Maybe that's why she'd been in such a rut for so long. She had been immersed in the wrong scenery.

Monica stabbed a leaf of radicchio and stuffed it into her mouth. She reached over, grabbed the remote from the end table, and flipped through a few of the sixty thousand channels on digital cable. The necessity for a channel dedicated just to game shows or golf was beyond her.

The phone rang. Monica pushed the mute button while reaching for it. She cradled the headset between her shoulder and chin.

"Hello?"

"What's up, girl?" It was her best friend, Nia.

"Just killing a few brain cells while I eat dinner," Monica answered. "What's up with you?"

"My life is as boring as ever, which is why I called. Give me some details, girl. How do you like it so far?"

"It's been great, except for the fender bender I had today. Other than that, New Orleans is wonderful."

"Meet any men?"

"That's not the reason I'm here, Nia. In fact, the male species is the absolute last thing on my mind."

Monica crossed both her fingers and toes after telling *that* lie. Ever since her run in with a certain obstetrician, the male species—one delectably fine specimen in particular— had taken up every crook and crevice of her mind. Not an hour had passed today when Dr. Elijah Holmes's image had not run through her head. Anytime his name was mentioned, Monica found herself straining to hear the conversation. It was pathetic.

She tried to tell herself that the only reason she paid attention to anything concerning the man was to make sure she wasn't around if he had to make another trip down to the ER. She'd had her fill of his arrogance at their first meeting.

Yet Monica couldn't deny the tingle of excitement that

had crept up her spine when she'd seen him at the end of the day—even though he'd almost mowed her down. Again.

"Just because it's not your number one priority does not mean you can't look," Nia chastised. "If not for yourself, you can find someone for me."

"You have a husband," Monica reminded her.

"I'm getting tired of him."

Monica laughed. Her best friend would never tire of her husband. Nia and Phillip were sickeningly in love. The fact that Phillip was Monica's older brother by four years made her relationship with Nia even more special. Their union had legally made them sisters, although in her heart she'd been Nia's sister forever.

It was because of her best friend that Monica and Phillip now shared such a strong connection. Although he claimed he'd never fostered it, Monica had been immersed since childhood in an unhealthy sibling rivalry with her older brother. Phillip had been the golden child, and Monica had spent her entire life playing catch-up. It wasn't until Nia had demanded Monica and Phillip finally talk things through that they had opened up to each other about their strained relationship. Monica was closer to her brother now than she'd been when they'd lived in the same house.

"I won't close my eyes to any romantic possibilities," Monica reassured Nia. "But I'm not actively seeking anyone out, either. I can use a little *me* time."

"I hear that, girl. Sometimes I'm ready to knock Phillip unconscious with a skillet upside the head just so I can have the house to myself for a few hours."

"Oh, shut up. You know you'd go crazy if he didn't call you at least five times a day."

"Nah, three's enough."

They both laughed.

"So, when do you think you can make it down here?"

Monica asked as she flipped silently through a few more channels.

"As soon as we're done with the union contract negotiations. After all the work I've put in, I'm not letting any of the imbeciles I work with close the deal."

"I agree with you there."

"Besides, Phillip would go ballistic if I left in the middle of the house renovations. He can't decide on a simple paint color without asking me a hundred questions about it."

"As if you'd let anything be done in that house without your approval," Monica snorted. Her best friend was nothing if not bossy.

"And you got that right."

Monica shook her head. Nia would never change.

"Well, handle your business. Just know that you've got a bed waiting for you in the French Quarter when you're done."

"I can't wait to sink my teeth into a hot beignet," Nia crooned.

"We'll have them fresh every morning," Monica promised.

"That's Phillip pulling into the drive," Nia said. "I need to go."

"Give him my love."

"Will do. I'll talk to you later, honey. You take it easy."

"I love you, girl."

"Love you, too."

Monica settled the cordless phone back onto its base and was suddenly overwhelmed by a surging rush of homesickness. She missed her best friend. To a certain extent, she even missed her family. Monica allowed a small smile to trace across her lips at the thought. She had spent most of her teenage years trying to get out of her parents' house. The fact that she missed her family came as a surprise to her.

The Gardner household had never been close-knit. They didn't have the time; everyone had been too busy pursuing their goals. Their parents had demanded excellence from the three children. Phillip hadn't disappointed them, becoming the youngest person to make partner at his law firm, a firm he now owned outright. Ashley, who had come as a surprise gift from the stork when Monica was eighteen, was a child virtuoso. She had mastered Mozart by the age of ten and had spent the past four years studying at Juilliard.

The fact that their middle child was a respected physician wasn't quite enough compared to the two geniuses. While Phillip broke records in the courtroom and Ashley played for foreign dignitaries at Carnegie Hall, Monica had missed out on being named chief resident and had taken too long to become an attending. If not for Nia there to keep her sane, Monica figured she would have long ago cracked under the strain of trying to live up to her family's high expectations.

Thank goodness for her best friend. Monica and Nia had been joined at the hip for as long as she could remember. Both thirty-four years old, they had a friendship that had spanned countless broken hearts, failed math tests, and Friday night sleepovers.

They had never lived more than a few minutes from each other. Both attended the same university and pledged the same sorority. The only time they'd differed was when it came time to choose a career. Monica had followed her dream of becoming a doctor, while Nia held fast to her pledge to take the business world by storm. But they had remained closer than blood siblings through it all.

And if Nia didn't get her butt down here soon, Monica would renege on her promise to stay away from St. Louis for at least a year.

Stop that! She was not going back to St. Louis, and she

refused to let a little bout of homesickness get the best of her.

With more determination than she'd felt in some time, Monica hopped up from the sofa and went into her bedroom. She changed into black spandex running pants and threw a T-shirt over her head to cover her sports bra. Twenty minutes later, she pulled into her parking space at Methodist Memorial. Monica grabbed her gym bag from the backseat and headed for the employees' fitness center—one of the perks that helped seal the deal when she'd decided to take the job.

She remembered the layout from the tour Dr. Slessinger had given her. She rounded the corner on her way to the butterfly press machine and had to crouch to the floor to avoid being pummeled by a red punching bag gone astray.

Monica righted herself and found Elijah Holmes trying his hardest to control the wayward equipment. She had to take a second to collect herself. He had the unnerving ability to knock every thought out of her head and replace them with thoughts of him.

Eli was sin wrapped in dark chocolate. His body was scandalously put together, with muscles that rippled underneath his brown skin. He was tall and lean and gorgeous. Sweat glistened from every piece of exposed skin. She had a powerful urge to lick him dry.

Monica quickly recovered from her plunge into lust-filled insanity. She plunked her hands on her hips and glared at him. "Are you determined to kill me my first day on the job, Dr. Holmes?"

"I didn't see you," he puffed out through labored breaths.

"That seems to be your favorite excuse."

"Honestly, I did not see you. You have this gift for popping up out of nowhere."

Monica tried to end the conversation by moving past

him, but he stopped her with a hand on her forearm. She looked down at the strong brown hand that held her; then she brought her eyes back to his face, sending him a look that had him letting go of her arm in an instant.

"Sorry," Eli said. "I was just wondering why you're even here. Weren't you on your way out when I nearly ran you down this afternoon?" he asked with a grin.

Monica returned his smile with a saccharine one of her own. "So nice to know you find attempted vehicular homicide so amusing."

"That was a joke." He grabbed a towel from the rack against the wall and wiped his face. Monica took the opportunity to glance at his chest.

She had to get away. Fast. It had been way too long since she'd had a man, and she was scant seconds from tackling him. The gym floor might not be as comfortable as a bed, but at least it was padded. It would work.

"So what are you doing back at the hospital?" he asked. "I assumed your shift was over."

"I didn't realize this facility was only for on-duty personnel."

"It's not. You know that's not what I was getting at. Why are you giving me such a hard time?"

"You said it yourself: We didn't get off on the right foot."

"And I'm currently trying to correct that error, but you won't give me a chance."

"Maybe I don't want to."

"Why not? What did I do to you?" She opened her mouth, but he interrupted. "Besides the near miss with the car," he continued. She gave him a pointed look. "And the punching bag."

"Need I say more?" Monica asked.

"Come on; you know they were accidents."

"That's my point; I think you're a hazard to my health, Dr. Holmes."

"It's a good thing I'm a doctor, then." He winked. He was entirely too sexy for his own good. And he was definitely too sexy for a woman who had vowed to stay man-free for at least a year.

"If you'll excuse me, I'd like to get to my workout," she said, trying to edge past him.

"That's it? You're not even going to give me a chance?"

Did his voice have to sound so sensuous? A girl could resist only up to a certain point.

"I think it's best our acquaintance be regulated to a friendly wave in the hospital corridor."

The corner of his mouth tipped up in a knowing grin, but he simply shrugged his shoulders and said, "It's your call, Dr. Gardner. I'll let you get to your workout."

Monica nodded her head in acknowledgment and walked past him to the butterfly press. She had to fight the urge to bypass the exercise equipment altogether and head straight for the locker room. She was suddenly in dire need of a cold shower.

Chapter Six

"Dr. Holmes?"

Eli stopped midstep and turned. "Yes?" he bit out.

The nurse shoved a metal clipboard at him. "You forgot to sign off on Mrs. Donaldson's chart," she said, clearly offended by his tone.

"Thank you." Eli accepted the proffered pen and scribbled his name. "I'm sorry for snapping, Stacey."

"Don't mention it." She smiled, satisfied.

"If anyone needs me, I'll be upstairs."

Taking the stairs two at a time, Eli realized he was more messed up then he thought. Forgetting to sign off on a patient's chart? Just a testament to the crap on his mind today.

Although he broke it to her as gently as he could two nights ago, Alicia was not taking the news that their fling was over as well as Eli had hoped. He'd been forced to sleep at Alex's house last night after he spotted her car in his driveway again. Something had told him to cut her loose when she started getting all clingy. If she had not pulled out that can of whipped cream last Saturday, Eli would have kicked her fine behind straight to the curb that night.

Alex had warned Eli that the player lifestyle would eventually catch up with him, but Eli would be damned if he'd admit to his older brother that he'd been right.

By the time Eli arrived at the administrative offices on the sixth floor, he could hear a barrage of voices coming from the conference room. He didn't feel like dealing with the charity board today. He peered through the door's slim rectangular window. Most of the members were seated around the oval cherrywood conference table, but a few pockets of people mingled in different areas around the room.

The door creaked slightly as Eli pushed it open.

"Dr. Holmes." Slessinger waved him in. "Good, now we can get started."

Eli went for his usual seat at the conference table, but stopped short. His breath caught in his throat.

Monica Gardner.

There she was, sitting in his chair, like a Nubian queen upon her throne.

Every time he saw this woman—and it seemed to be turning into a regular occurrence—Eli reevaluated his long-ago decision never to date doctors. It was a rule he'd held steadfastly since the incident back in med school that had jeopardized his credibility and nearly ruined his career before it had a chance to start. Getting caught with his head under his professor's skirt was not the smartest thing he'd ever done. But as Eli stared at Monica Gardner's deep-set eyes and perfectly shaped lips, he found two good reasons to say to hell with his rule.

The tinkling of silverware hitting glass disrupted Eli's train of thought. He rounded the table and took a seat next to Dr. Collins, with Monica directly across from him.

"I'm sure all of you are anxious to get this meeting under way," Slessinger said. "I promise it won't be long. If I happen to run off at the mouth, everyone in this room has my permission to tell me to shut up." His statement garnered the obligatory chuckles. The chief of staff allowed the laughter to subside before continuing. "Before we get down to business, I would like to introduce Dr. Millgram's replacement in the ER. Everyone, meet Dr. Monica Gardner."

Polite applause fluttered around the table as Monica pushed her seat back and stood.

"Thank you," she said.

That voice. Eli was tempted to close his eyes in order to hear it better. She had a voice as smooth as soft-brushed velvet, more suited to a nighttime radio deejay than to an ER doc.

"I want to thank Dr. Slessigner for that warm introduction, and for hiring me in the first place." Again, chuckles sounded around the table. "I also want to express how happy I am to join the staff here at Methodist Memorial. It is an honor to be part of such an outstanding group of professionals. I look forward to working with all of you," she finished, taking her seat again.

"We are all pleased to have you as part of our team, Dr. Gardner," Slessinger said. "Although Dr. Gardner asked me not to say so, I think it's important to note that she graduated in the top five percent of her class from Saint Louis University School of Medicine. The year she completed her internship, she was recruited more heavily than the Heisman Trophy winner."

Slessinger paused for more laughs, then looked over at Monica.

"I cannot think of a better replacement for Dr. Millgram. Your exceptional talent will only add to this hospital's impeccable reputation."

She accepted his praise with a nod of her lovely head before Slessinger continued, though Eli thought he saw a flash of uncertainty in her eyes. That was interesting.

Slessinger guided the board through the agenda. At the last bulleted item, he said, "As I stated before, Dr. Millgram was very active on the board, and we all know his favorite activity was heading the annual charity banquet. Now that he's no longer with us, I'll need another dedicated board member to step up to the plate."

The room became so quiet you could hear a grasshopper break wind. Just when Eli thought crickets were about to start chirping, a smooth, confident "I'll do it" came from across the table.

Monica Gardner sat even straighter in her chair, a swirl of determination filling the air around her.

"Wonderful!" Slessinger looked excited enough to do cartwheels. "I trust those of you who have played an active role in the banquet will provide your services once again."

Eli's heart gave an extra thump. He'd been Millgram's cochair for the past three years. He didn't know whether to get down on his knees and say a prayer of thanks, or run out of the room and look for another job. Getting the chance to work this closely with Monica Gardner could be either a blessing or a curse.

"Monica, could you stay a few minutes over to flesh out a few of the preliminary details?" Slessinger turned to address the others at the table. "That pretty much covers it, folks. I'm sure all of you have duties you should be getting back to. Thanks for coming, and, gang, let's start thinking of ways to make this year's charity efforts a hole in one."

A racket ensued as the majority of the room's occupants pushed their chairs back and nosily rose from the table. On their way out, many of them made their way to Methodist Memorial's new emergency room doctor. Eli sat back and observed as Dr. Gardner greeted them all with a warm smile.

He waited for the line of well-wishers to dissipate before he rose from his seat and made his way to where she stood at the large windows that ran the span of the left wall. Although he knew she could see his reflection in the window, she didn't acknowledge him. Eli smiled, tapping her on the shoulder.

She turned.

The woman had the most beautiful eyes. Deep brown, rimmed in a lighter hazel color.

Eli extended his hand. "Although we've run into each other a few times already, I don't think we've ever been officially introduced." She clasped his hand in a firm shake. Goodness, her palm was softer than silk.

"Actually, Dr. Holmes, you're the one who has nearly run into me several times. And one of the ER nurses did introduce us."

He acknowledged her barb with a smile. "You can call me Elijah, or Eli."

She nodded, but Eli noted she didn't give him permission to call her Monica. He sensed she was about to walk away, but he was determined to keep the conversation afloat.

"So, how do you like Methodist Memorial so far?" he asked as he leaned against the window.

"I've been very pleased, for the most part. There have been a few situations that left much to be desired." The look on her face left no doubt as to what she was referring to.

He was sinking. Fast.

"I do apologize about the near-accident in the parking lot."

"Both of them?"

Eli bit his tongue, took a breath. "Yes, even the one I don't remember."

"I remember it."

"I'm sure you—"

She held up her hand, successfully halting his rebuttal. "Before you go any further, Dr. Holmes, I should let you know I've heard about you."

That tone didn't sound good at all. Eli decided to play dumb.

"Really? After only a few days?" he asked. He hit her with a full megawatt smile.

"Yes, your reputation precedes you—both the professional and the personal one."

His smile dimmed a few watts.

"I can only hope you've heard good things." Eli tried to keep the caution out of his voice. He knew there was nothing untoward that could be said about his work in the OB. He couldn't be all that sure about the personal side.

"Excuse me, Monica," Dr. Slessingler called, capturing their attention. "Apparently this conference room is booked for another meeting. If you could meet me in my office in twenty minutes, that'd be great."

Monica turned her attention back to Eli, sending him a halfhearted smile. "Sorry, but I have to go."

Elijah caught her by the forearm. "Hold up. You can't just leave me hanging like that. So have you heard good things, or do I need to seek some people out for sullying my name?"

She shook free of his hold and took a step back, folding her arms over her chest. There was a playful gleam in her eyes as she looked him up and down. "I hear you're an exceptional doctor who has a knack for delivering babies in the most unusual places."

"I've had a couple of adventurous births, but they turned out okay," he said with a modest shrug.

"Yes, well, I also spoke with Dr. Johnson in Cardiology, and he says that with the trail of broken hearts you leave behind, he gets more business from you than from the nursing home down the street."

Ouch.

Eli leaned in close. "This may come as a shock, but there's something you should know." In a conspiring whisper, he said, "Dr. Johnson drinks. Heavily. You can't trust a thing that man says."

"Is that right?" Her mouth tipped up in a smile. It was about the sexiest thing Eli had seen in all his life.

"Very sad, but true," he answered with feigned sorrow.

"Well, since I know neither of you all that well, I can't be sure whom to believe."

"Between an upstanding obstetrician and a drunk like Johnson?"

"Stop that," she said with a teasing smile. "I do not believe Dr. Johnson is a drunk."

"No, he's not," Eli admitted with a laugh, "but you can't believe everything you hear. Did Johnson really say that about me?"

Her grin widened. "No, he didn't." She looked as if she was about to comment further; then something changed. Her silky brown eyes became lackluster. She checked her watch and said, "I want to look in on a patient we sent up to the OR before I go to Dr. Slessinger's office."

Before Eli knew what had happened, she was gone.

Monica apologized as she backed out of the wrong office and shut the door behind her. It was the second time she'd made that mistake.

It wasn't that she didn't know her way to the chief of staff's office—it was the one place most familiar to her other than the ER was. It was just that she had a hard time concentrating. After her encounter with Eli Holmes, her brain seemed to have taken the afternoon off.

Face it, the brain's completely fried.

Monica hated that he had that effect on her. Her senses became more scrambled every time she got near him, which had occurred way too often these past few days.

It had taken her a while to remember where she had seen him before, but when he'd smiled at her back in the conference room, Monica had realized he was the good-looking guy from the elevator the day she'd come for her interview. He'd been dressed casually then, slacks and a light-colored shirt. She remembered the way he'd smelled, like expensive cologne. She could recall with amazing accuracy the electrified tingle that had shot through her blood when she was forced to lean her body flush against his in the close confines of the crowded elevator. She had been fully aware of him that day. And the awareness was back with a vengeance.

When she'd seen him in the elevator, Monica had hoped he was just visiting someone—preferably his wife and newborn baby. She knew from experience that those men held no appeal whatsoever.

But Dr. Holmes didn't have a wife or a child—as far as any of the nurses in the ER knew.

His heroics from the week before, when he'd found a pregnant teen and delivered her baby in a car, were still the buzz around the hospital. Talk of his drop-dead gorgeous looks and incredibly fit body soon followed any conversation where his name happened to surface. In the few days she'd worked in the ER, Monica had heard his name at least a half dozen times.

Now that she'd gotten a dose of Elijah Holmes, Monica completely understood the hype around him. As her sixteen-year-old sister Ashley would say, the good doctor was all that and a bag of chips.

Not that she was in the mood for snacking. She was not going to renege on the promise she'd made to herself. No men. Not right now. Her breakup with Patrick was still too raw.

After another five minutes of ducking into the wrong doorways, Monica realized she was on the wrong floor.

Her mind was *really* screwed up today.

She tried to place the blame for her scattered brain on this morning's call from the lawyer of the woman she'd rear-ended Monday, although if she stopped kidding herself, she could admit to the real reason. The real reason was six foot three with an impeccable build and a heart-stopping face.

Why was she so weak when it came to men?

She bypassed the elevators and hurriedly made it down the flight of stairs. Dr. Slessinger was coming out of his office.

"There you are," he said. "I was just on my way to look for you."

"Sorry," Monica said as she walked through the door he held open for her. "I'm still learning my way around the hospital."

"That's quite understandable."

Monica only had time for a cursory glance of the spacious office before her gaze stopped directly on Elijah Holmes.

"I hope you don't mind my inviting Dr. Holmes to join us."

Oh, no. He was *not* on the banquet committee. Life could not be this cruel.

"Having worked with Dr. Millgram for years, he's a veteran at putting on an outstanding charity banquet. I'm sure Eli is more than willing to help you along."

Eli's mouth tilted up in an amazingly sexy smile.

"I trust I'm not speaking out of turn, Elijah."

"Not at all," Eli answered. "No use in Dr. Gardner

reinventing the wheel. We can go over what the banquet committee has done the last few years and build upon the things that have worked."

"Excellent." Slessinger clapped his hands together. He went around his desk and sat in the leather chair. "I'm really excited about the two of you working together. Being of the younger, hip generation, you can add a different perspective, something to draw in the younger crowd and get them interested in doing charity work. And—" He hesitated.

"What?" Eli asked.

"Well." Dr. Slessinger pulled off his glasses and started wiping the lenses with the tail end of his white coat. "There's something else." His voice had lost some of its jolliness. He looked uneasily at Eli, then at Monica, before blowing out a huge puff of air. Monica was instantly on guard.

"What is it?" Eli asked, the urgency in his voice telling her that he'd latched on to the uncertainty suddenly radiating from the chief of staff.

"The Parenting Center," Will Slessinger finally admitted. "The state has threatened to cut the program."

"What?" Eli asked, his hands poised on the armrest of his chair, as if he was seconds from jumping out of it.

"The word came down yesterday. Apparently the state believes its revamp of sex education courses in the area high schools will help curb teenage births enough to negate the need for the Parenting Center."

"You've got to be kidding me. That's the stupidest line of reasoning I've ever heard in my life. If the state thinks handing out a few condoms in health class will actually lower the number of pregnancies we see, then some of *them* need to go back to school."

The passion emanating from Eli was tangible. It was clear to Monica that this was a subject close to his heart.

"What about all the people who use the program who are not teenage mothers? What about the young couples just starting out who can't afford private physicians? With Charity Hospital still closed, these people have nowhere to go."

"You're preaching to the choir, Eli. I wish you were at the state capitol pleading our case to the people making the decisions."

"Well, someone needs to. There's no way they can shut down the Parenting Center, Will."

"There is a way we can prevent it," Dr. Slessinger said.

His calmly spoken words were apparently enough to quiet Elijah but not soothe him. The younger doctor pushed back in his chair. "How?" he asked.

The coldly spoken word hung in the air like a jagged icicle, frigid and deadly. Monica was grateful for the hum of the air-conditioning unit that kicked on, providing some noise in the suddenly uncomfortably quiet room.

Dr. Slessinger flexed his fingers several times before folding his hands on his desk. When he spoke, it was with weary agitation, as if he was only at the beginning of what promised to be a lengthy battle. "The Board of Health and Hospitals has agreed to keep the program in next year's budget if we can fund it for the remainder of this fiscal year."

"That's our only option? Raising the money ourselves?"

"I know it's a long shot, Eli, but at least it's something."

In the midst of their debate, Monica found herself focusing not on their words but on their tone. This was not your typical superior-and-subordinate conversation. It was obvious that Dr. Slessinger respected Eli on a deeper level than most chiefs of staff did their attending physicians. It also confirmed what she'd suspected over the past few days: Elijah Holmes had not only made a name for himself in the delivery room, but he'd also earned the admiration of his peers—something Monica knew firsthand was very hard to do.

Eli was shaking his head. "There's no way we can raise the kind of money we would need to keep the center going for the rest of the year. The cost in prenatal vitamins alone is in the thousands. The fate of the center cannot hinge on a banquet that has only pulled in at best five grand. And that's during normal times. With everyone still trying to put their lives back together after Katrina, we would be lucky to bring in our usual amount, let alone enough to fund the center."

"That's why I need the two of you to really put your heads together on this." Slessinger turned to Monica, finally bringing her back into the conversation. "I know this is an awful lot to ask, with you just taking over Dr. Millgram's position, but the Parenting Center is vital to this community. It's all many expectant mothers have around here."

Monica glanced at Eli. He sat slouched in his chair, staring at something on the far wall. His brow had a distinguishable crease, visible evidence of his frustration.

"As a member of this staff, I have a vested interest in the well-being of this community, Dr. Slessinger. I'm confident we can raise enough money to keep the Parenting Center running," Monica said.

Elijah straightened and turned to her. "This is a state-run hospital. We don't have the same donors as the fancy private hospital you probably worked at before coming here."

"I worked at a university hospital that was funded by the state of Missouri," Monica clarified.

A shadow of annoyance floated across his face. "I'm just trying to be realistic here. The event's past supporters have been the people who live in this community, and I can guarantee attending some hospital banquet is not high on their priority list this year."

"Then we take it out of the community. The entire city can be in on it," Monica countered.

"Did I mention the time constraint?" Slessinger interjected. "The Board of Health and Hospitals isn't on the same fiscal calendar as the rest of the state departments. Funding for this year ceases at the end of the fiscal year. We have to have our proof of payment by the end of November. We have a little over three months to pull this off."

"Forget it." Eli bounded from the chair.

"No," Monica said. "This can be done."

The beeper in the breast pocket of his scrubs went off. Eli unclipped it and read the small LCD readout. "It's OB." He looked over at Dr. Slessinger. "I don't know what to tell you, Will. Millgram worked like a dog on this banquet every year, and the amount he cleared would hardly pay for utilities."

"Just think on it, Eli. We can't let the center go down without a fight."

The beeper sounded again. "I have to go," Eli said. "The last thing I want to see is the Parenting Center close, but unless we can pull off a miracle, we need to start informing patients that they'll need to look for alternative care."

He left the office, and a heavy feeling remained, the foreboding scent of doom acrid in the confined space. Dr. Slessinger rested his fingertips on his lips and sighed. "I hate to admit it, but he's right. I need to accept the fact that the center is going to close."

"No, it won't," Monica said.

This banquet was her golden ticket, the opportunity she'd been hoping for. Her skills in the emergency room might get her foot in the door, but after being passed over countless times back in St. Louis, Monica knew that being a good doctor would take her only so far. Those who went the extra mile, who presented the whole package were the doctors who became a part of the team.

So what if her personal life was boring as hell? Being at the top of her profession more than made up for it. And if she really wanted to make the kind of impression that got *her* name on a parking spot, she needed to save the day, or in this case, Methodist Memorial's Parenting Center.

She could do this. She had worked on campaign fundraisers for Patrick's father. Raising money, even during hard times, could be done if you took a clever approach.

Monica refused to let Slessinger's enthusiasm die, not when he'd just delivered her way into the old boy's club on a silver platter. "I don't care what it takes," Monica said, fierce determination etched in her words. "I won't let them shut the door to the Parenting Center."

Chapter Seven

For the third time, Jeffrey placed the cellophane-wrapped roses back in the refrigerated display case, then took them out and put them in his shopping cart. He looked at the price sticker and almost returned them to the cooler again. It was an expense he could not afford, but with so much at stake, he was willing to pay the price.

He'd do just about anything to get Amanda back.

Jeffrey maneuvered his cart around a fresh fruit display and made his way to the refrigerated shelves, picking up a sealed container of fresh melon cubes. It seemed like a healthy dessert. Tonight he wanted to surprise Amanda with a meal she couldn't resist.

The instructions from Dr. Holmes said she needed to increase her iron intake to help with the anemia. He studied packages of plastic-encased meats, trying to decide between beefsteaks and boneless chicken breasts.

Wait. Didn't he hear somewhere that fish was a good source of iron?

He moved over to the seafood department. Studying the selection behind the clear display, Jeffrey asked for a couple of grouper fillets. He would make his special tartar sauce and steam a few fresh vegetables for a side dish.

Carrots.

Amanda loved carrots. She could do amazing things with them when she was in a playful, sexy mood.

Jeffrey nearly broke down in the middle of the grocery store.

God, he missed his wife.

How could two people who had been so crazy in love get to where they were now? They barely spoke. Hell, Amanda could hardly look at him most of the time. How could they have allowed this to happen? How could it have gotten this bad?

Jeffrey stopped the self-deprecation and forced himself to get back to his game plan. Tonight was about wooing Amanda. He wouldn't think about the downward trend of his marriage over this past year and a half. He still loved her. They had a baby on the way. His marriage was *not* over.

When Jeffrey arrived home, Amanda's car was parked in the driveway. It felt good just seeing it in its usual spot. It felt glorious having her back. And it was hell on Earth.

As much as Jeffrey had wanted her here, he was beginning to regret ever making the suggestion. Because it just wasn't the same.

It pained him to no end to walk into their old bedroom and not see her lying in the bed they'd shared for so many years. He'd offered to take the spare room, just to have the chance to see her on their bed.

But Amanda refused. She'd flinched when he had mentioned it, as if she couldn't stomach the sight of the place where they had expressed their love in the most primitive of ways.

Jeffrey opened the door, expecting to find her on the sofa in the den. It was where she spent most of her time, probably because it was the farthest room from their old bedroom.

He was right. She was curled up on the end of the tan-and-green-striped couch, her feet tucked under her.

"Good evening," Jeffrey said.

She turned her attention from whatever she was watching on television, and stared at him. After a long moment, she answered with a soft, "Hello."

It was the first time in months she had addressed him without that tired, cynical drawl, had looked at him without scorn.

Jeffrey balanced the grocery bags in his hands and kicked the door closed.

"I thought you had class tonight?" he asked. He knew she was on a Tuesday- and Thursday-night schedule this semester.

She stared at him, not saying anything, and Jeffrey's hopes plummeted. He was hoping that for once they could have a civil conversation, like a husband and wife were supposed to have at the end of a long day.

"I pulled out of school weeks ago," she finally answered. "It was too much for me to handle right now."

It took all he had not to shout for joy. Ever since Amanda started having the dizzy spells, Jeffrey had been scared to death that she would pass out while heading to class, but he'd been afraid to voice his opinion. Knowing Amanda, she would have continued attending the night courses just to spite him. But she had made the decision to stop on her own, and God, was he grateful. It was one less thing to worry about.

Jeffrey felt a twinge of guilt. He should be at least a little remorseful. Earning a degree in social work and becoming a child advocate had been Amanda's dream. She wanted to be a voice for those too little to speak up for themselves. Expensive fertility treatments had made college out of the question until one day Jeffrey had just said screw it. He'd taken a second job in order to pay for Amanda's education. She'd lost a semester due to Hurricane Katrina, and it was no doubt killing her to have to put school on hold yet again.

"Do you plan on starting back next fall?" he asked.

She shrugged.

Jeffrey went over to the kitchen and deposited the bags on the counter. Dinner could wait. After all, he'd accomplished what he had sought to achieve with his gourmet meal.

His wife was speaking to him again.

He walked back into the den and took a seat on the armchair.

"How are you feeling today?" Jeffrey asked, mentally crossing his fingers that his question didn't set her off. She didn't take too kindly to his inquiring about the baby, but he wanted to know. He'd suffered all those years through the same hell she had as they struggled to get pregnant, and then through last year's miscarriage. He wanted this baby as much as she did, and he deserved to know what was going on with her pregnancy.

"The nausea's been more bothersome than usual," she answered. She looked over at him. "It used to be just in the morning, but for the past few days, it hasn't been going away."

Concern skirted up Jeffrey's back like a thousand pinpricks on his skin. "Do you need to see Dr. Holmes?"

"I doubt it. All the pregnancy books say it's not unusual."

"Are you sure?"

"I'm sure, Jeffrey," she said, a hint of aggravation in her voice. Then it softened, "Don't worry. If it gets too bad, I'll go and see the doctor."

"Promise you'll let me know."

"Why?"

"I want to be there, Amanda."

She stared at him, a solemn, sorrowful expression crowding her eyes.

"But for how long, Jeffrey?"

She unfolded her legs and rose from the couch, leaving him with the same question that had plagued him for the last year and a half.

What had gone wrong?

To say the culinary selections in Methodist Memorial's cafeteria were lacking was a definite understatement.

Monica pulled a bowl of lime Jell-O from beneath the Plexiglas shield and placed it on her tray. She filled a plastic cup with ice from the dispenser and opted for Diet Coke. The caffeine would be a blessed gift.

Monica debated whether to get two glasses of soda. After yesterday's bombshell about the fund-raising, she'd had the hardest time falling asleep, and now she was dead on her feet. All she could think about was the banquet, and how it could be her foot in the door . . . or a nail in her coffin. But there was no way she would allow that to happen.

She wanted to show that she had more to offer than just being a stellar ER physician. This was her chance to prove what she could do outside of the emergency room. And if she could save a vital program to the community in the process . . . well, that was just the chocolate icing on a very sweet cake.

The only sour part of the deal would be working with Dr. Pessimistic, Elijah Holmes.

"Want to know why most of these tables are empty?"

Speak of the devil.

Monica nearly toppled her tray. He had come from out of nowhere, sneaking up behind her like some thief in the night. She had to take several quick breaths before she could speak. The scent of his subtle cologne wafted through her nostrils, spurring a sudden burst of wanting. When her heart returned to a normal rhythm, Monica turned.

"You must get a secret thrill from scaring the living day-lights out of people." Her voice came out more calmly than she'd expected. Good. She didn't want Elijah Holmes catching on to the fact that he could fluster her. Lord knows he could.

"I apologize," he said. "My intention wasn't to frighten but to inform. Most of the people who work here eat at Ethel's, the little shop across the street. At least, those of us who have taste buds do. They sell a good roast beef po'boy."

"Oh, I didn't know."

"Thus I am here right now, telling you," he said, sketching a slight bow, as if he were a faithful servant and she a queen.

Monica looked down at the Jell-O and cold pasta salad that had seemed the lesser of two culinary evils.

"I've already paid for this," she said with a hint of sadness.

"Well, now that you know about Ethel's, you can make this your last meal at the Heartburn Café." He leaned over and whispered conspiringly, "Hopefully, you won't learn firsthand how it got the nickname."

Monica smirked and headed for one of the many empty tables. Eli followed. Somehow she'd known he would.

He pulled out her seat and took the tray from her hands, then placed her pasta, Jell-O, and soda on the table. He walked to the trash bin and slid the tray into the collection crate on top, then came back to her table.

He sat, folded his hands together on the tabletop, and

asked, "So, were you born and raised in St. Louis, or did you move there?"

Monica looked up from the pasta she hadn't yet summoned the courage to taste.

"How did you know I was from St. Louis?" she asked. "I only mentioned that I worked for the state of Missouri. I never specified a city."

He shrugged. "I heard it from someone. This is the South. Don't think you're gonna just walk right in here and not be talked about."

"People are gossiping about me?"

"Not in a bad way. You're new. People are going to talk these first few days. It's unavoidable. So, St. Louis native?"

Monica tried to weigh the advantages and disadvantages of answering his question. How much did she want this man to know about her? Though there couldn't be all that much harm in knowing what city she grew up in, could there?

Besides, if the rumor mill was as active as he claimed it to be, he'd probably find out by the day's end whatever he wanted to know.

"I was born in Kansas City, but we moved to St. Louis when I was five. I've lived there ever since."

"We?"

"My family and I."

He made a circular motion with his hands, urging her on.

"What?" Monica asked.

"That's it?" Eli asked. "Just 'my family and I'? Do you have sisters and brothers, cousins, an old aunt Dot you keep hidden in the back room?"

Monica stuffed her mouth with pasta to keep from smiling. She had to get rid of him fast. She could not deal with drop-dead gorgeous, a good job, *and* a sense of humor.

"So?" he asked.

Despite her efforts to remain unaffected, Monica couldn't stifle the amusement that tipped up the corners of her mouth. "An older brother, a younger sister, and two parents."

"Any nieces or nephews?"

She shook her head.

Monica washed down the tasteless food with a swig of Diet Coke. "So, is there a reason you want to know this, Dr. Holmes?" she asked, dabbing her mouth with a paper napkin.

Another shrug. "Making conversation. Trying to show a little interest in a new colleague. And," he continued, not quite looking at her, "I wanted to apologize for yesterday." He met her gaze. "I've put a lot of blood, sweat, and tears into that center. Slessinger caught me off guard with the news that they're going to shut it down."

"Closing the Parenting Center is not a guarantee."

He shook his head. "In a normal year the banquet brings in enough to provide first aid kits to senior citizens and maybe a few bikes at Christmastime to the local kids. And right now the people around here are already strapped. There's no way we can raise enough to keep the Parenting Center afloat."

Monica rolled her eyes. "Could you give this just a small chance? You're shooting down the entire project without even trying."

"The banquet would have to pull in at the very least three times more than we've ever raised. And that's if we want even a laughable chance at keeping the Parenting Center open."

"I thought that was the point of bringing us together, so we could come up with some ideas."

"The best I can tell you is to find a lamp, and hope like hell a genie pops out when you rub it."

"Nice attitude, Doctor." Monica jammed her fork into a piece of celery and stuffed it in her mouth.

He looked at her with a hint of mocking laughter in his eyes. "You didn't strike me as an idealist. I always thought ER docs were more grounded."

"I'm assuming you meant that as an insult, because I'm taking it as one."

Monica wiped her mouth and tossed the napkin over the barely eaten pasta. She stacked the bowl of Jell-O on top, picked up both dishes and her empty cup, and rose from the table. Elijah rose, too.

"Again, Dr. Gardner, I'm sorry. My mood today has definitely been less than ideal. I don't mean to take it out on you." He tried to relieve her of the bowls, but Monica pulled her hands away.

"At least let me gain back some of my dignity by being a gentleman."

She edged past him. "Thanks, but I've got it."

He stopped her forward movement with a hand to her shoulder and plucked the bowls from her hands. "This is the South," he said. "I would be a disgrace to my forefathers if I did not assist you."

"It's also the twenty-first century."

His smile was more genuine this time. "Indulge me," he said, his voice softer than it had been a minute ago.

Monica followed him to the trash receptacles, where he deposited the plastic containers.

"Why don't you indulge *me* for a minute," Monica said. "I understand your concern about the Parenting Center: You've worked hard for it, and you're upset. That's perfectly understandable. But I truly believe that if we try hard enough, we can come up with something viable."

Eli turned, and Monica could tell by the look on his face that this was going to be a battle. She cut him off before he could voice another negative thought. "Just give it a chance."

He shook his head, a patronizing smile on his lips.

Monica nearly screamed in frustration. How was she supposed to accomplish anything if he wasn't willing to give her even an inch? If there was an ounce of credence to his reputation of aggressively pursuing things he held near and dear to his heart, why was he giving up on the Parenting Center? Why was he being so narrow-minded?

Monica decided to ask him just that. "Why exactly are you being so pigheaded about this?" His head reared back as if she'd slapped him, but Monica wasn't finished. "You're ready to shoot down anything I say before I have the chance to say it. For someone who supposedly cares so much about this community, you're willing to give up on them a little too easily for my taste, Doctor."

His eyes turned glacial. He took a step toward her, and Monica tried hard to stand her ground. "Do not question my concern for the Parenting Center," he said with steely resolve. "If it were not for me, that place would have been closed a long time ago."

Well, duh! Didn't he see her point?

"Then why are you ready to sit back and let it close?" She held her hands out, pleading.

He stared at her for what seemed like forever. An uneasy feeling traveled up her back. It was the same feeling she'd had in Dr. Slessinger's office yesterday.

He said, "Enjoy the rest of your lunch hour, Dr. Gardner," before edging past her and walking out the door.

Chapter Eight

Nothing had changed.

Her grandmother's clock still rested on the mantel over the fireplace, right below the Bernard Stanley Hoyes print Jeffrey had surprised her with a few anniversaries ago. He had known how much she loved the artist's work, and that the painting she had been eyeing in her favorite gallery was the perfect gift to lift her spirits. They'd suffered through another failed attempt at in vitro the week before.

The delight over receiving the painting had been no match for the sickening despair that had wrapped its arms around her. Although she'd convinced Jeffrey she was okay, Amanda had known something was wrong. Long after her husband had come to grips with his disappointment, Amanda had felt as if she were still drowning in it, and soon realized she was sinking into one of her episodes.

The depression had overwhelmed her. She could still remember lying in bed, too weak to move a single muscle. She had been so afraid Jeffrey would sense there was something more to her blues and start to suspect she carried the same mental illness that had stolen her mother. Jeffrey always said how grateful he was that Amanda had not inherited bipolar disorder.

If he only knew.

But he wouldn't know. Amanda had made sure of it. Unlike her mother, she had sought help as soon as she'd suspected something wasn't quite right. The medications had kept her symptoms at bay. Until the baby.

Amanda's heart lifted at the thought of her baby. She cradled her widening girth with her hands, gently massaging the baby from the outside. This little one knew how to make his presence known. He'd kept her up half the night kicking.

A smile touched the edges of her mouth.

She would take a thousand kicks a minute if it meant she'd get a healthy baby in three months.

A baby.

Instant tears welled in her eyes. Not the sad tears, but the ones she craved. Happy tears. A familiar sense of awe overwhelmed her at the thought of the tiny life growing inside of her. She could stare at her protruding belly for hours on end and still not believe she was actually having a baby.

Once she and Jeffrey had made the decision to start a family, Amanda had made sure her bipolar meds were safe to use during pregnancy. But they soon realized it was taking longer than expected to get pregnant.

Even now Amanda's chest constricted with the fear she'd felt when she thought she would have to go off her bipolar medication in order to start fertility treatments. Luckily her doctor had found a drug regimen that was safe to use during fertility treatments, but Amanda had been warned those same drugs might lose their effectiveness once she became pregnant. Hormones did weird things to the body. And to the mind.

Amanda swiped at the escaped tear as those awful memories seized her. When she thought about the excited anticipation of walking through the clinic doors, just knowing they were going to get good news, and then the soul-shattering disappointment of learning that they were yet again unsuccessful, her heart broke all over again. There were no words to describe the elation she'd experienced when their fourth in vitro attempt had proven successful.

Then things had changed.

Her world began to fall apart. Jeffrey seemed to stay out later each night. He'd claimed he was working overtime to cover the extra medical bills, and even though his check stubs proved it to be true, Amanda could not shake the feeling that Jeffrey had been messing around. His clothes began to reek with the smell of cheap perfume, and she was certain it had been his Ford Explorer parked at a motel she passed on her drive home from school. It hadn't mattered that she couldn't explain how he'd made it back to their house before she had.

Amanda's gut told her she had been wrong to accuse Jeffrey of being unfaithful, but her mind told a different story.

Then a visit to her doctor had confirmed Amanda's fears. Her valproic acid levels had fallen dramatically. As predicted, the pregnancy hormones had caused her bipolar meds to lose their effectiveness. That was when Amanda had realized her husband's infidelity had been just a figment of her twisted imagination. She'd known then what she had to do. She had to let him go.

How ironic that the child she and Jeffrey had prayed so hard for during their marriage would be conceived on the same day she met with her lawyer to start divorce proceedings.

An ache settled in her chest. The pain had become a familiar companion, slicing through her heart every time she thought of her and Jeffrey's impending divorce. It had been the hardest decision she'd ever had to make, but after realizing there was a possibility her bipolar medication would no longer control her symptoms, Amanda had known it was only fair. Jeffrey didn't deserve to be stuck in a marriage with a woman who on some days couldn't tell fiction from reality.

Amanda moved to the sofa and slid onto the plush cushions. She hugged one of the throw pillows close to her chest, settling her chin on top of it.

She couldn't take living here again. Not with Jeffrey. Every corner held a memory. Every inch of space marked an event in their lives together. Her gaze roamed their spacious living room and landed on the silver-framed picture that had rested on the built-in bookshelf for eleven years.

She, wearing the off-white fish-tailed dress her mother had been married in nearly forty years before. Jeffrey, looking like a GQ centerfold in his midnight black tuxedo. The smiles beaming on their faces were real. They were happy that day.

But she had killed that happiness, and it was too late to turn back now.

Amanda could not halt the tumultuous deluge of emotion that overcame her. Tears sluiced down her cheeks, darkening the deep green fabric of the throw pillow. Her body heaved from the force of uncontrollable sobs.

She loved him so much!

She would always love him. She'd accepted it as her destiny. But her love was not enough to hold their marriage together. They would never be the happy couple staring at her from the picture. Soon they would not be a couple at all.

Her limbs weak, Amanda lay across the deep sofa cushions and cried herself to sleep.

* * *

The unmistakable aroma of roux wafted through the kitchen window Margo Holmes always left open as she cooked her family's dinner. Although a roux was the basis for any number of his mother's dishes, Eli knew she was making chicken-and-sausage gumbo. He had a sixth sense when it came to Mama's cooking.

Eli made it up the wooden steps and pulled open the door to the screened porch. He battled his way through dozens of potted and hanging plants. Toby had threatened to hang a sign saying MARGO'S JUNGLE on the door. If his younger brother didn't do it, Eli would.

When he opened the back door and walked into his mother's kitchen, Eli almost fell to his knees. The teaser that flowed from the window was nothing compared to the full assault once he walked inside. The rich bouquet of spicy flavors filled his nostrils and set Eli's mouth to watering.

"Well, hello," his mother said, turning from the cast-iron pot. Her gumbo pot. Eli smiled.

He walked over to the stove and planted a kiss on his mother's cheek. "I could smell that gumbo when I turned down the street. You've got the dogs in the neighborhood howling."

"That's when you know it's good." She winked.

"How much longer?" Eli asked, looking over her head and into the pot.

"Just until the chicken gets tender. Reach in the cabinet and get me the rice cooker."

Eli moved the coffeemaker from the counter and set up the electric rice cooker in its place. He took the bag of rice out of the pantry and measured four cups, then brought the pot under the kitchen faucet and filled it until the water came up just above his fingertip. Margo had taught her boys to cook at a young age.

"I've got that," she said, taking the rice pot out of his

hands. "Why don't you go into the living room? Alexander and Jasmine are in there. They're watching the video of her dance recital. You can see the part you missed," she said with her infamous pointed look.

"I guess a regular apology won't cut it, huh?"

"I'm not saying a thing, Elijah." It was his turn for the pointed look. "Remember, her birthday's coming up. You can make it up to your one and only niece then."

"Don't worry, I've already bought her gift."

"That's my boy," Margo said, positioning her cheek for another kiss, which he gave to her. "Now go in the other room. I think there's something for you in there," she finished with a curious smile.

Huh? What's that about?

Eli could hear the music from the recital as he walked through the dining room on his way to the front of the shotgun house, where the living room was now. At one time it had been his and Toby's room, but after their father died, his mother had bought the connecting house and converted that side to bedrooms. The door to the other side of the house swung open, nearly taking him out.

"Uncle Eli!" Jasmine exclaimed. She caught him in the stomach with her head as she wrapped her arms around his hips.

"What's up, Magnolia Blossom."

"When you gonna say my right name, Uncle Eli?"

"Never," he answered, pulling on her ponytail.

"You wanna watch me dance on the stage? Daddy's watching it. I learnt him how to work the DVD player."

"You taught him, baby, not learnt." He was going to have to get this girl *Hooked on Phonics* or something.

Eli followed his niece into the living room and stopped cold. Right there, sitting on his mother's floral brocade sofa, was Tosha Culpepper, his old high school girlfriend.

This must be the *something* Mama had mentioned waiting for him in the living room. What was Mama up to?

"Eli!" Tosha squealed. She ran up to him, capturing him in a huge hug. Eli eyed Alex, who sat on the sofa smiling like a clown. Alex clicked off the DVD and threw the remote onto the coffee table.

"Tosha, what are you doing here? In town, I mean? I thought you were in Philadelphia," Eli asked.

"Actually, I just moved to Atlanta, so I'm back in the South."

"Wow. That's . . . um . . . great. So you visiting your family?"

"I came down for Sienna's graduation."

"That's right. She's finishing up at UNO, right? Mama said she was getting her master's degree?"

"Yep. The last of us."

Back in the day, the Culpepper girls had been as popular as the Holmes brothers. Their father owned a chain of barbershops, so he could afford to send his daughters to St. Mary's Academy, the premier African-American Catholic school for girls. Tosha, the eldest of the girls, was the same age as Eli. The middle sister, Ivana, was a year younger, and the baby, Sienna, was closer to Toby's age.

Of the three, Sienna was probably the sanest. Even though Tosha had a good head on her shoulders bookwise, she had the common sense of a Q-tip. And last Eli had heard, Ivana was a voodoo priestess somewhere in the Quarter.

"How are things going? Are you still working for that pharmaceutical company?"

"No, I work for myself. I'm a certified herbalist. I moved to Atlanta to open up my own practice."

Alex sent Eli the raised-eyebrow look. "An herbalist? Really? That sounds interesting."

"Oh, it is. I think it is horrible the way doctors virtually rape the public of their money."

Alex's interrupting cough sounded suspiciously like a laugh. "I couldn't agree more," his brother said.

"Oh, yes," Tosha continued. "Health care costs are ridiculous these days. And most of the treatments doctors prescribe are totally unnecessary. It's a shame, really."

"You do remember that I am a doctor, don't you, Tosha?"

"I know," she said with a bright smile, as if she hadn't just insulted his profession.

"How's everything going in here?" Margo came into the room with a smile as wide as the Mississippi River. Eli sent her a look over Tosha's head. "Isn't this a wonderful surprise, Elijah? I ran into Sylvia Culpepper last week, and when she told me Tosha would be in New Orleans, I knew I had to invite her over. It's been years since the two of you have seen each other."

"It has been too long, Eli," Tosha proclaimed, running her hand up his arm.

His mother raised her hand and pointed to her wedding finger. She mouthed "no ring" and gave Eli a thumbs-up.

Oh, hell no. He was *not* getting caught up in this.

"Eli, did Tosha mention that she's looking for property down here so that she can open a second medicine shop?"

"Really?" His stomach took a nosedive. "I thought you just relocated to Atlanta. You're thinking of moving again?"

"My partner is going to handle the Atlanta store."

Her *partner*. Please let her be gay.

"Deshawn and her husband have been practicing herbal medicine for nearly five years."

That would have been too easy, wouldn't it? He had some serious karma issues. Eli realized he'd have to get his behind back in church if his luck was going to change.

"Won't that be wonderful, Elijah, to have Tosha back in New Orleans?"

"Oh, yeah. That'd be great." Eli sent Alex a pleading look. *Do something, fool!* Where was Jazzy? Why wasn't she clamoring for everyone to watch that recital video?

Jasmine appeared in the doorway like a gift sent down from heaven. "Grandma, is the food ready yet?" she asked, hand on hip.

"Oh, yes," Margo said, swatting the air with a towel. "I don't know where my mind's going. That's what I came in here to tell you guys. Gumbo's ready. Let's eat." Maybe his luck wasn't so bad after all.

After another half hour of listening to the wonders of herbal remedies, Eli was sure his head would explode. Matchmaking Margo was going to get an earful the next time Eli caught her alone. He should have known she was up to something. The signs were all there. How many times in the past few months had she tried to hook him up with some sweet girl she'd met in church, or at her Ladies' Club meeting, or at the grocery store, for that matter.

It was the exact thing she'd done to Alex, and look how *that* had turned out! His brother had married the most selfish woman on the planet. He was not letting his mother pressure him into doing anything he didn't want to do.

"So, Eli, will you try some?" Tosha had directed her question to him, but Eli had no earthly idea what she was talking about. He'd tuned her out halfway through his second bowl of gumbo.

"Excuse me?" he asked.

"My products. Will you try them on a few of your patients? The sassafras and ginger work wonders at aiding in dilation."

He gave a strained smile. "The hospital frowns on us prescribing anything not approved by the FDA."

"Bastards," Tosha snapped.

Everyone at the table stopped and stared. Alex's spoon halted in midair. Jasmine's eyes were wide as saucers.

"Oh, excuse me," Tosha sputtered.

"That's okay, honey," Margo laughed. "I understand where you're coming from."

She knows where Tosha's coming from? Since when?

Probably since she'd decided Tosha's return to New Orleans was her best shot at getting a daughter-in-law. He had to put a stop to this. If Mama had her way, she'd be ordering wedding invitations by next week.

"I hate to cut out early, but I've got a ton of work to do," Eli said. "I just found out the state plans to close the Parenting Center."

"After all the work you've put into that center?" his mother screeched.

"Budget cuts?" Alex asked.

Eli nodded. "They claim that if we can find funding for the rest of the year, they'll be able to pay for next year, but that's a pipe dream. I'm going to start working on finding affordable alternatives for some of my patients. I'll probably do pro bono for most of them. They just can't afford good health care."

"I've got a number of things they can try," Tosha interjected. "Ginger root is a natural anesthetic—"

"I need to get going, Ma." Eli rose from the table. He couldn't stomach another litany from the Tosha Culpepper School of Herbal Health Care.

"You will be here Sunday, right, Eli?" Tosha asked before he could make a clean exit.

"Barring any emergencies at the thieving money pit that employees me," he answered.

Alex half coughed, half laughed. "Hold on, E. I'll walk you out."

Eli rounded the table and placed a kiss on his mother's

cheek, but not before giving her a look that said he knew exactly what she was doing and he didn't appreciate it.

"Have a good week, baby" she said, not the slightest hint of contriteness on her face.

He gave Tosha a kiss on the cheek, since that was, after all, how old boyfriends treated their high school sweethearts.

"Good night, y'all." He pulled Jasmine's ponytail, "Later, Sunflower."

"My name is Jasmine, Uncle Eli," his niece answered in her most irritated voice. Eli winked at her, then headed out the back door after Alex. His brother didn't make it off of the porch before doubling over with laughter.

"Shut up," Eli said.

"Oh, man. I swear, when I walked into the house and saw her sitting in the living room with Mama, I could barely hold it in."

"You couldn't pick up a phone and call a brother? You could have given me some warning."

"And miss the look on your face when she ran up to you?" he laughed, looking at Eli like he'd lost his mind. "She was a little nutty back when y'all were together in high school, but all the herbal medicine junk is too far out there."

"Alex, what am I going to do? If Tosha moves back to New Orleans, there'll be no stopping Mama."

"That's no lie. She's been trying to get you married for a long time now. And you know she always liked Tosha."

"Because she magically sees past the insanity, for some reason."

"Mama's looking for another daughter-in-law and more grandchildren."

"Why in the hell is she not on you to get married? Or Toby? I'm not the only son."

"Hey," Alex held up his hands. "I already did my part."

"There's no law against a widower getting remarried."

"Not gonna happen, brother. And Toby's her baby. What mother wants to lose her baby?"

"This middle-child bullshit never ends, does it?"

Alex fell out laughing again. "I guess not. Look, man, unless you can produce a girlfriend soon, I suggest you start reading up on herbal medicines. Something tells me your future wife won't stop until she has you prescribing them to your patients."

Eli shook his head. "No way. This is one time Mama is not getting her way."

Alex just laughed harder.

"I'm serious," Eli said.

"Whatever you say, E. But if I were a gambling man, I wouldn't even waste my money on the bet. I'd just use it as a down payment for a tux instead."

"I'm outta here," Eli said.

"Hey," his brother called out. "We're still on for ball Saturday morning?"

"Seven A.M.," Eli called back. "Don't be late."

Chapter Nine

"Be careful, Dr. Gardner," Patty warned in a hushed tone.

"Don't worry. I know a trick." Monica held her breath as she repositioned the two-year-old's head in order to get a better angle with the tracheal tube. "Give me some suction."

Patty quickly swiped the long plastic tube in the little girl's mouth, then stepped out of the way, giving Monica the extra room she needed for the tricky procedure. Monica felt her way around the toddler's swollen glands, and when she discovered the tiny opening she had anticipated, she slipped the tube in and pulled back on the handle.

"It's in. Bag her and get her to the OR. Dr. Blake and his team are waiting."

"Great job." Patty stripped the bed and efficiently draped fresh paper over it.

"Those saves are particularly sweet, aren't they." Monica smiled. She balled up the hospital gown and stuffed it into the disposal bin. She took a satisfying breath as she surveyed the room.

"That little girl has you to thank. If you hadn't found a way to get the trache in, she would be dead. It takes skill to get a tube down such a small throat, especially one as swollen as hers."

"I did a double rotation at the children's hospital back in St. Louis. I like working with kids." She had also needed as much practice as possible after nearly killing a young boy. A familiar weight settled in Monica's stomach as she thought back to that day, how she'd struggled to get the tube down his throat. She quickly pushed those memories aside.

"Just wait until you have a few kids of your own." Patty smiled. "You'll sing a different tune."

An incoming emergency stopped their conversation short. Before she knew it, Monica had seen eight patients, and three hours had passed. She left word with Patty that she was going to lunch, but when she came across the bank of elevators, Monica decided to face her most dreaded ordeal of the day. Why put it off?

After their last confrontation, she did *not* want to see Eli. Monica got off on the fourth floor and, when approached by one of the floor nurses, asked where she could find Dr. Holmes.

She was informed that "Super Doc" had just delivered a set of twins and would probably be in his office in a few minutes.

Monica walked over to Eli's office and tried the door. When she found it unlocked, she pushed it open and entered the office. She was duly impressed with the massive space and rich décor. For one so young, Elijah Holmes had certainly made a name for himself in his profession, and it showed in the perks that were lavished upon him. No doubt Methodist Memorial knew he could be scooped up by a number of hospitals if given the incentive to leave.

Monica felt a twinge of guilt at looking around his office while he was not here, but curiosity got the best of her.

The man could not be more than thirty-five, yet he was already a legend, both in the delivery room and—if what she had heard while sitting around the nurses' station had any truth to it—in the bedroom.

She did not want to think about Eli in the bedroom. The image was too tantalizing, especially for a woman in the middle of a yearlong drought.

One of the most interesting things to run past her ears today was the news that Eli did not date doctors. Hearing it had come as such a shock that Monica had immediately asked the ER nurse to repeat what she had said. She didn't think about how it would look to everyone that she had been eavesdropping, but she couldn't help it.

A man with his reputation would go out with anything in a skirt, right? But not Dr. Holmes. He apparently had no qualms with dating nurses, paramedics, or even the female hospital administration workers, but he drew line when it came to doctors.

Monica could not help but wonder why.

The door opened, and Monica jumped back from the framed picture on top of a mahogany filing cabinet of a pretty little girl with two missing front teeth.

"Dr. Gardner? Can I help you?"

For a moment Monica was taken aback by just how good he looked in scrubs. Wasn't it a rule that all doctors looked goofy when they donned lime green hospital-wear? Somebody forgot to tell Eli.

"Monica?"

"I'm sorry." She shook her head and tried to summon a bit of her common sense. Monica vowed to kick herself as soon as she left his office. "One of the nurses told me I could wait in here while you finished with your delivery."

"Making yourself at home?" He nodded toward the pictures she'd been examining.

"Oh, no, I was just looking. Is she . . . is she yours?" She hoped he didn't notice her stutter.

"She's my niece, Jasmine."

"Oh. So you don't have any children of your own?"

"No, no children. Do you?" he asked.

Her head jerked back. "Of course not. I'm not married."

"Actually, that's no longer a requirement," he said with a grin. There was something about when he smiled that sent her brain's pleasure neurons into overdrive. "It's not like you could keep something that big a secret around here anyway. Remember the rumor mill?"

"Well, if it's not too much to ask, I'd like to keep my personal life as far away from the rumor mill as possible."

"Wouldn't we all," he said, still smiling.

She needed to get this discussion over with and get out of this office. The more space between herself and this man, the better. It was bad enough that they would have to work together on the banquet. She would need all her powers of resistance for the upcoming weeks.

Monica took a deep breath. "We need to talk," she stated, proud that her voice didn't shake.

He gestured to a chair, and she took a seat. He perched on the edge of the desktop and crossed his feet at the ankles.

"You still think the center can be saved?"

"As a matter of fact, I do," Monica replied. He started to speak, but she stopped him. "I know in the past the banquet hasn't been much of a moneymaker, but this year will be different. There's too much riding on it."

He held his hands up. "Dr. Gardner, I doubt there is another person at this hospital who wants to save the Parenting Center more than I do, but the state has backed us up against a wall."

"Would you just hear me out?" She took a deep breath. One way or another, she was going to get this man to listen. "In the past, people paid a certain amount for a ticket to attend the banquet, right?"

"Twenty-five dollars per couple, fifteen for singles." Eli pushed himself off the desk and walked around it, settling into his chair.

"Was that the sole source of revenue?" she asked.

"Some of the local businesses act as sponsors. We've done raffles a few times, and there's a cash bar at the banquet."

Just as she suspected, no real moneymakers.

"Well, this year, I proposed we do things a little differently." Monica stalled, not sure what his reaction to her next words would be.

Eli raised his eyebrows. "Care to elaborate?"

"I was thinking . . . Well, I thought we could put on a bachelor auction." There, she said it.

Eli's brows etched higher. "Excuse me?"

"A bachelor auction. You know, women can bid for dates with single men. Single doctors, to be exact. This *is* a hospital benefit, after all."

"And where do you supposed we find these single doctors?"

Did he really expect an answer, especially when it was so obvious? Monica answered anyway. "I figure we've got more than enough single doctors on staff, and we don't have to peddle one-dollar raffle tickets to our friends and family or waste valuable time soliciting donations from surrounding businesses, which are having a hard enough time these days as it is."

"You'll solicit human beings instead," Elijah stated.

"We'll *seek* volunteers," she clarified. "My best friend,

Nia, has a brother who's a firefighter. His squadron held an auction with some of the firefighters from their company, and they raised an obscene amount of money. Granted, they *are* firemen, but I know the doctors here can do just as well, if not better."

"And exactly how will you convince the single doctors of Methodist Memorial to take part in this auction?"

"Well . . . that's where you come in."

He stared at her. "You're serious, aren't you?" he asked after some time had lapsed.

"I am very serious."

"What makes you think the single docs will agree to something like this?"

"Because everyone at the hospital knows how important the Parenting Center is to this community. I have no doubt the doctors here will be willing to do all they can to keep the center open."

"I have an aversion to being paraded around like cattle."

"*You* don't have to," she said, frustrated. "Just get the rest of them to participate."

Eli picked up a ballpoint pen and tapped it against his well-shaped lips. He gazed at her with shrewd, piercing eyes.

"What is this really about, Dr. Gardner?" Eli tossed the pen back onto the desk and sat up in his chair, folding his hands in front of him. "Why are you so determined to make something of the banquet? You just moved here. You have nothing invested in the Parenting Center."

"Someone needs to rally around it. If it were up to you, who I believe have the most stake in it, the state could just as well close the doors right now."

"Because it's inevitable."

"You want to know what Nia's brother's squadron made on their auction?"

"It wouldn't be—"

"Forty-two thousand dollars," Monica said. That shut him up. But not for long.

"The women in this neighborhood can barely afford to put shoes on their children's feet. They're renovating their houses and trying to replace their flooded-out cars," Eli rationalized. "Do you really think they'll be willing to shuck out thousands to pay for a date with a doctor?"

"Why are you so against this?" Monica asked, holding her hands out in exasperation.

"I'm not. I told you, I want nothing more than to keep the center open, but I've got to be realistic. I have patients to consider, young women who think they are going to have decent health care throughout their pregnancies. I'm more concerned with finding them a suitable alternative than with crossing my fingers and hoping we can raise more money than we've ever been able to raise before. I'm sorry, Dr. Gardner, but I don't think you can pull this off."

"Of course not, at least not by myself. I need help." She was not letting him ruin this for her. Monica took a deep breath, reluctant to admit what she was about to tell him, but nothing else seemed to get through his thick head.

"Consider my position for a minute," she said, hating the pleading tone in her voice. "I'm new here. I want to make a good impression."

Understanding sparkled in his eyes. "And what could be better than the new kid on the block stepping in and saving the center?" he concluded before Monica had the chance to finish. It was all she could do not to grit her teeth.

"Being Super Doc and all, I'm sure you don't find yourself in need very often, but try putting yourself in the shoes of someone who could use a little help." Monica could not believe she was admitting this, especially to him. But she was feeling a little desperate. She liked it here, and she wanted to fit in. She hated playing politics, but it was the way of the world. She would not be left on the outside, looking in.

"It's not totally selfish." Monica rose from the chair and started pacing the floor between the side of his desk and a pair of freshly polished bookshelves. "I believe the Parenting Center is a wonderful, worthwhile asset to the community."

"And if saving it will help you look good, that's just icing on the cake." His words mimicked her own thoughts so closely that it was almost scary.

Too late, Monica realized that admitting her semi-ulterior motive for wanting to pull off a successful banquet was a mistake of gargantuan proportions. Not only would he see her as unrealistic—as he had already inferred—but he would also think all she was looking for were praise and recognition. Yeah, she wanted those things, but her motives were not completely self-serving.

Right, like he would believe that after her proclamation. Monica had a strong urge to hide under the rich mahogany desk until, oh, the year 2045 or so. That should be long enough to get over her embarrassment, or at least for Eli to go senile.

Monica caught the slight smile playing at the corner of his mouth. He *so* was not laughing at her.

"I know what you're thinking," she said.

"You do?" His grin widened.

"Yes, and I do not appreciate it. I'm a damn good doctor, and I can hold my own in any emergency room you put me in. That is not why I'm pushing for this banquet. I have nothing to prove."

"Did I say you did?"

"I know it's what you're thinking."

"Trust me, Dr. Gardner, you have no idea what's going through my mind right now."

Monica caught the laughter in his eyes, but she ignored it. He could go on thinking what he wanted. She was through doubting her ability. Despite what happened in St. Louis. Despite what the nagging little voice that occasionally reared its head whispered to her brain at the most inopportune time: She was a *great* doctor.

But Methodist Memorial was filled with great doctors. She needed something that would set her apart from the rest. Dr. Slessinger had put a lot of stock in her, and doing a good job in the ER wouldn't cut it, at least not by Monica's standards. She wanted to do something that would be remembered throughout the ages, something that would make a lasting impression. She wanted to save their beloved Parenting Center.

But she couldn't do it by herself. She needed help. Eli's help.

His mouth still held that curious lift with just enough lightheartedness to be considered a grin. It was unbelievably sexy.

"Have you finished your workout?" he asked with amusement sparkling in his eyes. Monica had never noticed just how deep-set they were.

"I am so relieved you find such joy in this, Dr. Holmes. How powerful it must feel to have someone admit they need your help, and to know that you can crush all their aspirations with a single word."

He sat back in his chair and steepled his fingers over his chest. "Why do you think I would do that?"

"Because you can. And because you've already voiced your opinion about the banquet. It's a pipe dream. You don't think it will make a difference. So why even bother, right? Why don't we just close the doors now without even trying?"

"But then how would you impress your colleagues?" he asked, the teasing laughter still in his eyes.

"You know what, forget it." Monica headed for the door. She didn't need his condescension or his help.

Eli shot out of his chair. "Wait a minute," he said, grabbing her by the arm. Monica wrenched free.

Eli covered the hand she had wrapped around the door handle. He couldn't let her leave. Not yet. Not in anger. And especially not after the idea that had popped in his mind like a twenty-thousand-watt lightbulb.

Monica Gardner was his salvation, the answer to his fervent prayers.

When his mother had called that morning, asking if he could swing by the Culpepper house on Sunday to pick up Tosha, Eli had thought up the only excuse he could muster on such short notice: He told her he would be bringing his new girlfriend to Sunday dinner. Only problem was, he didn't *have* a girlfriend.

Until now.

Smart and beautiful, Monica was Eli's ticket to getting his matchmaking mama off his back. If he showed up to Sunday dinner with Monica on his arm, his mother could not possibly continue to shove Tosha Culpepper, Herbalist Extraordinaire, down his throat.

Dr. Gardner needed his help, but Eli realized he needed hers just as much. Maybe even more. She simply wanted to look good for her boss, but Eli was fighting for his freedom.

He waited until she was once again seated before taking the chair behind his desk. He folded his hands and rested his lips on them for a minute, contemplating his approach. Convincing Monica to go along with the scheme fermenting in his brain would take more strategizing than Eli had ever had to exert.

He had no doubt he could do it. He had to. There was too much at stake. He had been witness to his mother's handiwork on several occasions. The last time Margo

Holmes tried to hook up one of her sons, the outcome had been disastrous. Disastrous and tragic—although Alex had gotten Jasmine out of the deal.

Still, Eli was not in the market for a wife or a child. If he ever felt the urge to spoil a kid rotten, he had his niece. He did not need his mother pulling out the heavy guns in order to wrestle him into a relationship with a woman.

Eli needed Monica Gardner. Pretty, smart, sane Monica Gardner. *Dr.* Monica Gardner. If his mother was so gung ho about Tosha being an herbalist, she would probably do cartwheels over Monica being a highly revered physician.

As he glanced at the open calendar on his desk, Eli recognized that time was of the essence. If he had any hope of convincing his family that he and Monica were the real deal, he would have to get her onboard as quickly as possible. It would take a lot to pull the wool over Margo Holmes's eyes.

"I've got a proposition for you," Eli started, not willing to waste another second.

Monica eyed him with guarded curiosity. He didn't blame her. What he was about to propose was as unethical as anything he'd ever thought up.

Blackmail. That's what it was. But putting the rightful name to his scheme was not going to stop him. This was too important, and it wasn't as if he would be the only one to benefit. If everything worked out, he, Monica, and the Parenting Center could come out smelling like roses.

"I'm not sure I want to know," Monica said.

"It's nothing to get worried about. I just thought of a way we can be of assistance to each other."

"How is that?" Monica asked, the leery contemplation in her gaze making Eli want to smile. She was perceptive; he'd give her that.

"Are you seeing someone?" he asked.

She barked out a laugh. "That's none of your business."

"Are you or aren't you?" Eli persisted.

"What does that have to do with anything?"

"Like I said, I have a proposition for you."

She crossed her legs and folded her hands over her propped knee. "Just because I haven't been entertained enough today, I'll bite. Exactly what is your proposition, Dr. Holmes?"

Eli looked into her eyes, taking a deep, self-assuring breath. This was not going to be easy, but it was his best chance.

"You want to impress Slessinger, right?"

"I want to help save the Parenting Center," she countered.

Eli waved off her declaration, "Yeah, yeah. That's a given. I'm talking about the little something extra—to use a Louisiana term, the lagniappe. You want to get in good with Slessigner."

"I'm not trying to suck up or anything," she said with that edge he'd heard more than once today.

"Did I say that?" Eli asked, feeling a little defensive. Eli checked himself before continuing. He had to be smart about this. The last thing he wanted to do was antagonize her.

"Look, Monica, there's nothing wrong with trying to make a good impression. It's smart. Doing a brilliant job with the banquet is just the type of thing that can set you apart from the rest."

"You make it sound so calculating. Like a sleazy scheme or something."

No. What he was about to suggest was a sleazy scheme.

"Forgive me. Apparently I'm not getting my point across as eloquently as I had hoped. All I mean to say is that I don't blame you for wanting to stand out, and if you believe pulling off this banquet is the thing that will do it, then I want to help." Her eyes lit up like a candle in a room that had been dark for a hundred years. Eli knew his next statement would dim them a little. "Provided, of course, you help me."

The leeriness returned, along with caution in her voice, when she asked, "How so?"

If he didn't execute the next minute as deftly as possible, he might as well start shopping for a tuxedo and applying for his license as an herbal obstetrician.

"I need a girlfriend."

Eli waited for a reaction, but there was none. She just sat in her chair, legs still crossed, knee bobbing slightly up and down. He was about to ask if she'd heard him when she said, "I'm waiting for the punch line."

Eli shook his head. "No punch line. I'm serious."

"No, you're not."

"Yes, Dr. Gardner, I most definitely am."

"Do I look like a fool? You don't date doctors," she remarked. "I've heard it more than once. You will not be seen in a romantic light with any doctor."

Eli shrugged. "Yeah, so?"

"Yeah, so?" She looked at him as if he'd grown an extra set of limbs. "Then why do you all of a sudden need a girl-friend, especially one who happens to be a doctor?"

Eli decided to tell her the truth. His plan didn't have a chance if Monica was clueless to the motives behind it.

"Because my mother is campaigning for a daughter-in-law," he stated, "And I don't like the candidate she's chosen."

"And exactly what does this have to do with me?"

"I need you to pretend to be my girlfriend." Eli was ready to pull out all the stops.

Monica stared at him for seconds before speaking. "You're not serious."

"You have to know my mother to realize just how serious I am. My old girlfriend from high school is back in town—"

"And your mother has it in her head that the two of you are meant for each other," she finished for him.

"I could be with a fortune-teller; my mother could not care less. As long as one of her sons has a beautiful woman on his arm at my cousin's wedding, she'll be happy."

"If the only requirement is someone who's breathing, why are you asking me? I'm sure you could find someone in your repertoire of women to fit the bill."

"*I* don't want just anyone. I've got a standard."

"I'm flattered," she said, sounding anything but. She stared at him as if she really was considering his proposition. Then she said, "This is crazy. I doubt your mother would believe you were actually dating a doctor, especially if your rule is as steadfast as I've been led to believe."

The added edge to her voice had Eli thinking she was upset by his rule. Now if *that* wasn't interesting.

"My mother doesn't know anything about my rule, which really isn't a rule at all," he lied. "It's a rare occasion that I'll even bring a woman around my mother, so she has no idea who I date. But she's getting tired of it. Mama hates to lose."

"What does your love life have to do with your mother losing?"

Eli sighed. Divulging the ridiculous familial trait might turn her off even more, but he needed to be honest, right? "There is a competitive streak the size of the Mississippi River running through my family," he explained. "My brothers and I have always been in competition, and we get it directly from my mother. When Mama and Aunt Lydia get together, it's like two lionesses. They're constantly bickering over who's got the best new piece of African art, or the flashiest Sunday church hat.

"And don't get me started on whose children are the better successes at both job and family. Mama's winning the battle on the job part, but family is another thing. My cousin Kathleen is the last of Aunt Lydia's children to get married. So you can imagine how Mama feels with three single sons."

"Isn't one of your brothers married? The one with the daughter?" she asked, motioning to Jazzy's picture on his file cabinet.

"Alex is a widow."

"So now your mother is on a mission to see you married?"

Eli nodded. "Or at least with a prospect. The fact that she's trying to push Tosha down my throat is a testament to just how desperate she is."

"But I'm not a true prospect."

"That won't matter. Mama will just be happy to see me with someone. And if she thinks we're serious about each other, that's gravy."

Monica raised her eyebrows. "You're willing to lie to your mother?"

"Yes," Eli answered without compunction. "If it means I won't get suckered into going out with Tosha Culpepper, then yes. I will lie, cheat, and do whatever else is necessary to make sure that does not happen. Including"—he stared into her eyes—"doing all I can to make your banquet a success."

"Can't you just tell your mother no?"

"How badly do you want to impress Slessinger?" He could tell by the look in her eyes that she wanted it *really* badly.

"This is crazy," Monica said. "You cannot be serious."

"Like I said before, I am extremely serious."

"I can't do this," she said after a pause, which made Eli think she'd actually contemplated it.

That was all the incentive he needed. He pressed harder. "Why not? Give me one good reason."

"I don't have to give you anything," she said defensively.

"Think about it, Monica. What would be the harm? We could both get what we want."

She didn't trust him; Eli could tell by the uneasiness radiating from her across the span of his desk. He couldn't blame her. If he were in her shoes, Eli wouldn't trust himself, either.

"How long would we have to pretend?" she asked softly. Impressing Slessinger must be more important to her than he had guessed.

"The wedding is the second weekend in November."

"That's three months."

"It is. Would you be willing to put up with me for that long?" he asked, unable to keep the grin from forming at the corners of his mouth.

"You'll agree to all my plans for the banquet?"

"Absolutely, if you think they'll work. I am your willing servant, Dr. Gardner."

She gave him that look again, the one that said she trusted him about as much as she trusted a politician who moonlighted as a used-car salesman.

"Fine." She stuck out her hand, and Eli almost expired from relief. "You've got yourself a deal, Dr. Holmes."

Chapter Ten

"Watch it!" Monica snapped. "Sorry," she said to the orderly wheeling a very pregnant woman into the elevator.

She had been in such a god-awful mood today. She was suffering from a severe case of crankiness brought on by fatigue. The amount of sleep she'd gotten this past week could be measured in a teaspoon.

Instead of sleeping, she'd spent most of her nights trying to figure out when, exactly, she had turned insane. Only someone delusional would have accepted Elijah Holmes's proposal. It was simply unexplainable.

But now that she had agreed to it, how could she back out? Especially since she had spent the hours when she wasn't contemplating the sudden loss of her good sense thinking about all they could do with the banquet. She'd envisioned the entire night, from the food they would serve to the playlist for the band. They could start with soft jazz for mingling, then move to old-school favorites like Earth, Wind & Fire and Marvin Gaye. Then they could bring in a little Destiny's Child and Kanye West for the younger crowd.

She'd had vivid dreams about the bachelor auction, or, she should say, a certain bachelor. Monica had no doubt Eli Holmes could bring in a thousand dollars with just his smile. Offer up the rest of him for bidding and they could keep the center open for eternity. Too bad he was staunchly against taking part in the actual auction.

Monica spotted him at the nurses' station. He jotted something on a form and handed the clipboard across the desk to the board nurse. Monica tried not to notice the way his scrubs stretched across his well-chiseled chest.

God, she was pitiful.

"We need to discuss the banquet," she said without preamble.

"Hello to you, too, Dr. Gardner."

"Good morning," she said with acceptable contriteness. "Is this a good time to discuss a few of my ideas for the banquet?"

"Do you mind if we do it over lunch?"

Monica's inner alarm automatically went off. She looked at the clock on the wall and took into account the position of the hands. It *was* lunchtime. The man was hungry. That was all. If she continued to read little innuendoes into every suggestion he made, she would drive herself crazy. The safest thing was to keep her mouth shut about anything not concerning the banquet, at least until she had more time to think over all of this.

"I can introduce you to the menu at Ethel's," Eli offered. "I promise it'll be better than the macaroni surprise you had in the hospital's cafeteria."

"The pasta wasn't so bad," she lied.

He initialed his last chart and passed it to the nurse. He crossed his arms over his chest, a playful glint sparkling in his gorgeous brown eyes. "That's because you've never had Ethel's crawfish pie and homemade carrot cake."

"Carrot cake does sound better than green Jell-O."

"You are going to forget the way to the cafeteria."

Ethel's Cajun Café was wall to wall with customers. Tiny but cozy, with oak-paneled walls and mismatched table-and-chair sets. The spicy aroma suffusing the air caused hunger pangs to quake through Monica's empty stomach. She didn't need to see a menu—just bring her one of everything.

The restaurant's customer base seemed to be mostly doctors in white coats and scrubs. Monica recognized a few of the faces. She waved at Patty, who sent her a conspiring wink. Monica shook her head, but Patty had already gone back to her conversation.

"People are going to talk," she said as Eli pulled out her chair.

"They do that already," he answered, sitting opposite her.

"Yes, but now they have reason to."

He rested his forearms on the table and leaned in close. "Actually, they don't, but we could give them something to talk about if you really want to."

Monica found it impossible not to return his grin. "You must have some innate flirting instinct. It just happens automatically, doesn't it?"

He pretended to mull over his answer. "Yeah, pretty much." Eli opened the menu the waitress had just placed in front of him. "So, what ideas do you have for the banquet?"

Monica was momentarily caught off guard at his swift change in attitude. He went from playful flirt to all business in nanoseconds.

"I've been thinking about a venue," she said. "Where was last year's banquet held?"

"One of the downtown hotels, the Sheraton. I can't be sure, but I think it's reopened."

"Well, I had something a little different in mind."

He closed the menu and folded his hands. "Do tell, Doctor," he said, his eyes glistening with interest.

"Okay, don't look at me like that."

"Like what?"

"Like . . . *that*. It looks like we're discussing more than business."

"It really bothers you to be seen with me, doesn't it? I think I'm crushed." His mouth drooped in an affronted pout before curving into a sexy smile.

Monica glared at him before explaining, "I just don't want people getting the wrong impression."

"We're two adults having a conversation over lunch. Exactly what impression do you think people can glean from that? Besides," he continued, not giving her a chance to answer, "we *are* a couple now, or have you already forgotten our deal?"

"We're a couple around your family."

"No, we are a couple all the time," he said slowly, his forehead creasing with his frown.

"But—"

"We can't pretend to date only part-time. It's too risky."

"You are the one with the strict policy about not dating doctors."

A speculative eyebrow lifted. "You've mentioned that an awful lot."

"Is it true?"

He sat back in his chair and folded his arm over his chest. The motion caused his shirt to pull taut over his well-sculpted shoulders. Monica tried not to stare.

"Would it bother you if it were?" Eli asked.

"No," Monica lied. She didn't know why this was such a burning issue with her, but it was. The fact that Eli

Holmes summarily wrote a woman off just because she happened to be a doctor had needled at Monica more than she cared to admit.

But if he held firm to this all-important rule, why was he laying on the heavy charm? Was it just an act? Monica wasn't sure she even wanted to know the answer to *that* question. The implications were more than she could handle right now.

"I thought the playacting was for the sake of your family only," Monica argued, going back to the original subject.

"I never said that."

"Then it looks like we need to revisit the specifics of our deal, but now is not the time. Let's just get back to discussing the banquet."

In an effort to return to the matter at hand, Monica pulled a brochure from her purse and laid it out on the table. She quickly placed her trembling hand back in her lap. The thought of having to pretend in front of her colleagues that she was Eli's girlfriend had her a little on edge.

"Instead of the usual hotel ballroom, why don't we hold this year's banquet at one of the old plantation homes? I've been visiting them on the weekends."

Eli picked up the brochure and perused the glossy accordion-style photo spread.

"Why a plantation?" he asked.

"Why not? They meet all the requirements we need. They're large, and many of them have both indoor and outdoor facilities. We could have the meal inside and hold dancing and the auction on the grounds. It would be different."

His unreadable expression was unnerving.

"So?" Monica asked.

He folded the brochure and placed it in the middle of the table. "I like it," he said with a shrug.

"That's it? You like it?" Monica replied, imitating his shrug.

"Like you said, it's different. I don't know how renting out an entire plantation home compares in price to a ballroom, but if we can pull it off, I say we go for it."

"I had not anticipated it being this easy, Dr. Holmes."

"I don't make a habit out of being difficult, unlike some people." That was a direct shot. "And would you please call me Eli?"

Okay, maybe she deserved that. He had not done anything to warrant her caustic behavior. Monica thought for a minute; was it possible the impact of Patrick's deception had clouded her judgment when it came to men?

Eli wasn't so bad. In fact, he wasn't bad at all. Despite his obvious playboy appeal, and his refusal to include female doctors in his pool of dating candidates, he was a nice guy . . . for the most part. It would take her a long time to forget that encounter over the preclampsia patient.

"Do you have a particular site in mind?" he asked, bringing Monica out of her reverie. "A plantation home? Do you know which one you want?" he continued.

"Not really. I figured I'd visit a few more this weekend."

"That sounds good. Do you mind if I tag along?"

"You want to spend your Saturday looking at plantations?" She had a hard enough time not feeling like a nervous schoolgirl around him while at the hospital. Monica wasn't sure she was ready to handle Eli outside of the safe confines of their workplace.

"What's wrong with that? It's what you'll be doing."

"I just thought a popular guy like you would have more to do with his weekend."

"Your image of me is so wrong. Although you're right, I do have something to do this weekend. I was hoping you could join me."

"What's that?" Monica asked, already feeling uncomfortable.

Eli wiped at the corners of his mouth with a napkin, bunched it up, and threw it over his nearly cleared plate.

"My niece has a birthday party Saturday afternoon. Alex is throwing a small get-together at the house. It'll be the perfect chance to introduce you to my family."

"Oh, God. You mean I'm already meeting the parents?"

"That's the point of this, right? And it's just my mother. My dad died nearly twenty years ago."

"I'm sorry," she said.

"Thanks," he said with another shrug. "There are a few things you should know about Mama. Even though she looks like she could be a resident of Munchkinland in *The Wizard of Oz*, she can be a little intimidating at times. Whatever you do, show no fear."

"She sounds scary."

"She's going to love you."

Monica gave him a skeptical look. "What makes you so sure?"

"You're female and you're breathing," he answered. "The fact that you're talented and beautiful will have her ready to break out into song."

He had just referred to her as talented and beautiful.

With anyone else, Monica would have latched on to the praise of her talent, but for some reason, the fact that Elijah Holmes found her attractive meant a hundred times more. The strangeness of it scared her. His thoughts of her beauty should not mean anything to her. But they did. Flutters of giddy excitement continued to dance around in her stomach.

"So when do you want to meet?" Monica asked.

"Is eleven okay? I'm covering part of Dr. Langois's shift, so I'll be getting in pretty late Friday night and I'm hooking up with my brother for our weekly basketball game Saturday morning. I can handle leaving that a little earlier, but I know you want me fresh and alert for tours," he finished with a grin.

"What time does the party start?"

"Three, I think. I'll have to check with Alex. We can get there around four or so. That should give us enough time to check out some of the closer plantation homes."

"Are you sure about this?" Monica asked. She had resigned herself to being stuck with all the planning details outside of the actual auction. She would never have guessed that he would actually get involved in other aspects of the banquet preparations. If Monica had known mentioning the plantation idea would place her alone in a car with Elijah Holmes, she would have kept her mouth shut.

"Of course I'm sure," Eli answered.

"Okay, then. Eleven it is. Do you want to meet at the hospital?"

"I can pick you up at your place."

"Ah . . . um, well, okay." Did she really want Eli knowing where she lived? Monica looked across the table at his cocoa brown face and mellow copper-colored eyes. Oh, he was dangerous all right.

Before Eli could comment further, Monica rose from the table. "I need to get back to the ER," she explained as she fidgeted with the clasp on her purse.

He rose from his seat, retrieved his wallet from his back pocket, and threw a twenty on the table. "I've got you covered."

Oh, no, he was not footing the bill. Not with half the hospital trying to inconspicuously examine every move they made.

"I'll pay for my own lunch, Dr. Holmes."

"Would you stop calling me that?" His snappish response took Monica by surprise. He lowered his voice an octave, but it did nothing to conceal his agitation. "You don't want anything other than a professional relationship when we're not around my family? Fine. I get it. But even strictly professional colleagues share enough camaraderie to exist on a first-name basis."

"Does this really bother you that much?" she asked, dumbfounded.

"As a matter of fact, it does. In front of patients we should stick to 'Doctor,' but at lunch?"

"If it's that much of an issue, I'll call you Elijah from now on."

"Eli."

"I'll agree to Elijah," Monica said. "Let me work my way to Eli."

He smiled.

Her knees went weak.

Methodist Memorial's psychiatry department needed to take a Polaroid of that smile and pass it to patients suffering from major depression. How could anyone's spirits not be lifted by that man's gorgeous smile?

Monica handed him a ten-dollar bill to cover her half of lunch. He stuffed his hands in his pockets.

"I told you I could take care of my own lunch," she said.

He lifted one shoulder with a halfhearted shrug. "Why should you if I've already paid for it?"

"Because I don't want you paying for it."

"Are you this difficult all the time?"

"When it comes to stuff like this? Yes."

"Why? You want to show the world that you're your own woman, that you don't need a man buying you lunch?"

Monica was a second away from putting her hands on her hips and going off on him.

"That's fine." Eli held up his hands. "Be independent. But don't turn down a free lunch, because, you see, since I paid today, I'll be expecting you to pay for lunch on Saturday. And I can guarantee it will be more expensive than a plate of red beans and rice from Ethel's."

"So this is your way of getting off cheap?"

"Got that right. I know how to take advantage of a good deal when I see one. There's more to me than just a handsome face," he said with a wink.

Okay, Psychiatry could use both the smile and the wink in their therapy. The combination could quite possibly cure every case of depression in America.

They started toward the exit. Patty gave her a sly smile as Monica passed her table. She would have to start devising a plausible explanation for this lunch right now. As innocent as the truth was, there was no way it would fly with Patty.

"I'll pay for lunch on Saturday. I'm sure we can find a McDonald's."

"I've got a strict policy that prevents me from eating at any establishment with a drive-through window," Eli answered. He held the door open for her.

"Then something tells me you are going to be pretty hungry come Saturday," Monica answered.

"Well, if you feed me McDonald's for lunch, that just means I'll have to take you somewhere proper for dinner."

She looked up at him. The ten inches he had on her made him just the right height. Monica desperately needed to find a credible flaw, because as of now, Elijah Holmes seemed perfect. And who in their right mind would say no to the perfect man?

Monica turned fully around in the opened door. She crossed her arms over her chest and said, "You just won't stop until you get me to accept a dinner invitation, will you?"

"Now you're getting the picture," he answered with that smile she was starting to anticipate. Monica had come to accept the fact that few things on this earth were as startling as Eli's smile.

Yet the question remained: Why was he so persistent? She agreed to meet his family on Saturday, which fulfilled part of the obligation of their deal. Why did he insist on dinner Saturday night?

The conflicting stories were starting to confuse her. Either every nurse in the ER was wrong, or Elijah Holmes was throwing everything he'd held strong out the window. But would he really do that just for the chance to have dinner with her?

The thought was too delicious to contemplate.

Just as she was about to walk out the door, Eli caught her by the arm and turned her to face him.

"So?" he asked.

Feminine ego won out over common sense.

"Fine," Monica said. "On Saturday, I pick the lunch venue and you pick where we go for dinner."

The corners of Eli's eyes crinkled with his smile. "Hmm, maybe I won't be lying to Mama, after all. It sounds to me like we're officially dating, Doctor."

Chapter Eleven

Eli laced up his white Nikes, then brought both hands over his head and stretched. He rocked from side to side, loosening his oblique muscles.

"Would you quit with the workout, Jane Fonda," Alex called as he approached him on the outdoor court. His older brother hurled a Spaulding basketball at his midsection. "I've got about an hour before I have to be at the site."

"What's up with you, man? You trying to kill me?" Eli rubbed his stomach. "Why do you have to get there so early? You're the boss. You should have the best hours of anyone on the job."

Eli dribbled the ball, then stepped back and sunk a jump shot.

"Since the storm hit, Holmes Construction has more jobs lined up than we've had since I started the business. And if it's going to grow, I've got to be there to make sure everything's running smoothly. I'm not leaving my livelihood in just anybody's hands. Besides"—Alex faked right and went around Eli, laying the ball up and into the basket—"what else would I be doing?"

Eli caught the ball with both hands. "I'm tired of trying to convince you of what any healthy, *normal* man would be doing."

Alex rolled his eyes, clearly indicating that Eli had better not go there.

"Anyway, I don't have time to worry about your love life," Eli said as he waited for Alex to take another shot. "I've got enough problems with my own."

"What kind of problem? Is Alicia back?"

"No, thank God. I haven't heard from her since the weekend." Eli gripped the ball with his left palm, then switched to his right, swooshing past his brother with a crossover that would have made Allen Iverson proud. "Damn, I'm good," he said when the ball floated through the hoop.

Alexander bent over, his fists resting on the front of his thighs. He was already winded. Eli bounced the ball off his back.

"You need to get in shape, dog."

That, of course, was a lie. With the hard manual labor Alex put into his construction business, Eli couldn't think of anyone in better shape than his brother. It was age that was probably catching up with him, that and his work environment. A thirty-seven-year-old who worked on dusty construction sites all day couldn't have the same lung capacity he did as a seventeen-year-old fresh out of high school.

"Kiss my ass," Alex puffed out. He threw the ball back at Eli. "If Alicia's not bothering you, then what's the problem?"

"We've got a new doc in the ER."

"And?"

"Let me rephrase that," Eli said. His ball rimmed out. Alex beat him to the rebound. "We've got a new Victoria's Secret model–caliber doc in the ER."

"Oh," Alex said. He stood under the goal, balancing the ball on his hip. Eli wasn't falling for it. He knew his brother was just trying to catch his breath.

They played for another twenty minutes. Eli banked his shot and decided to let Alex off the hook. "That's ten. We need to stop it here. I have to get back to the hospital."

"If you really want to stop," Alex puffed out between labored breaths.

They walked toward the nine-foot fence that surrounded the court. Eli retrieved two towels and a couple bottles of water from the gym bag he'd propped against the fence. He passed a towel and bottle to Alex. They both slumped to the ground, their backs against the chain-link fence.

"So what's the deal with the Victoria's Secret model?" Alex asked after taking a huge gulp of water.

Eli took a deep breath, already knowing the reaction his next statement would elicit. "I'm bringing her to Jazzy's party this afternoon. And I told Mama I would bring her for Sunday dinner."

Alex's mouth dropped open.

"Don't look at me like that, man."

"How do you expect me to react when you tell me you're bringing some woman to Sunday dinner? That's serious, E."

"I know . . . I—" Eli wasn't certain whether to confess to Alex, but he needed to confide in somebody. Alex had always been his sounding board. Eli had to make sure he was doing the right thing.

Alex downed half the bottle, then stopped. "Hold up a sec. Something's not right here. What happened to your rule about never dating doctors?"

"It's complicated."

"That does sound serious. Let me finish my water. I don't want to miss a minute of this." Alex drank until the plastic bottle was empty; then he stuffed it into his gym bag and turned to Eli. "Okay, so what's the deal?"

Eli stretched out one leg and bent the other, resting his arm on his knee. "I convinced her to pretend to be my girlfriend for the next few months."

Eli gave him the abbreviated story about the center being in trouble, and Monica's valiant effort to save it while also making a good impression on the senior staff. He told his older brother about the conversation he'd had with their mother and how the idea to feign a relationship with Monica first came about.

Alex listened without interruption, something he had always done when playing the part of the confidant for his younger brothers, who always seemed to get into one bind or another. Eli wouldn't have guessed that at thirty-four he would still be looking to unload on Alex.

"I don't know what to say, man. You've got guts to try to pull something like this over Mama's eyes."

"What else could I do, Alex? Tosha has been back in town all of two weeks and I've seen her more times than I have in the last fifteen years. I needed to do something drastic."

"Which this definitely is," Alex agreed. "What about your rule?"

"Mama never paid attention to my rule."

"Are you crazy? Do you really think Mama wouldn't have been throwing hints about you hooking up with a doctor all these years if she didn't know how you felt about it?"

Eli shrugged. "I can say the rule's been overwritten."

Alex's brows arched skeptically. "And we're supposed to buy that?"

"If you saw Monica Gardner, you would," Eli clarified.

Alex's brows rose even higher. He reached into Eli's gym bag and grabbed another bottle of water. He uncapped it, took a long pull, then draped the towel over his head. "So what do you plan to do? You know Mama's got her heart set on you and Tosha getting back together."

"I'm hoping it's not the idea of me with Tosha, just that I'm with *someone*. I need to convince her that Monica and I are serious about each other."

Alex nudged him with his knee. "You sure you're not?"

Eli shot him an irritated look.

"Hey, man." Alex put his hands up in mock surrender. "I'm just saying. Maybe this shouldn't be pretend. It's not like you couldn't use a steady relationship."

Eli lolled his head to the side and stared at his brother. "Just in case you didn't realize it, you're the pot," he drawled with distinct mockery.

"What?"

"You are the pot calling me, the kettle, black."

"Don't start."

"How are you, a man who hasn't had sex in God knows how long, gonna sit here and tell me that *I* could use a steady relationship? Do you even remember what a naked woman looks like?"

"You finished?"

"Are you?"

"Look, E, you've passed on enough good, fine women simply because they're doctors. Not every female with a white coat is Elizabeth Graves."

"Leave it alone, Alex."

"All right. I'm finished," his brother said, dusting off his hands to make his point.

Eli tilted his head back against the fence and closed his eyes. Monica's image flew to the front of his mind. He had visions of thick, luscious hair the color of deep, dark molasses gliding through his fingers. He could almost feel the soft, baby-smooth skin on his fingertips. And those eyes. They had nearly stopped his heart the few chances he'd had to look directly into them.

Man, he was in trouble.

Eli placed his right palm flat on the gritty asphalt and used it to push himself up. He hauled the towel from Alex's head, along with the one he had used to wipe his face, and stuffed them both back in the black duffel bag. He zipped it up and slung it over his shoulder.

"When's Toby coming?" Eli asked as he stretched his hand out to help his brother up.

Alex's strong grip clutched Eli's palm, and he heaved himself off the ground. "Sometime this week, I think."

"I thought that singer he's been promoting was debuting in the city tonight?"

"She is, but he couldn't be sure when he would be able to get away. Some new group he discovered is cutting a demo."

"Ah, the life of a Quincy Jones wannabe."

"You never know. Old boy may surprise you one of these days."

"You can hold your breath if you want to, but I'll pass."

They walked out the gate, Eli stepping back to let Alex go first. At the curb, they exchanged pats on the shoulder and took off in different directions, Eli for his Range Rover, Alex for his Ford F-150.

By the time Eli arrived back at the hospital, he had time to make only a short run through the maternity ward before heading home to get ready for plantation-hunting.

As he pulled up to the house, his shoulders sunk with relief when he didn't spot the white BMW in his driveway. He could not keep living like this. He paid too much damn money for this house to be afraid to come home to it.

After putting away his basketball gear, Eli went up to his bathroom to take a longer, more thorough shower than the one he'd rushed through at the hospital. He opened the glass door and stepped under the running water.

Eli groaned as the hot water pelted his shoulders and back. He stood still for a moment, letting the pulsing streams work their magic as they shot out from ten separate jets within the shower walls.

His skin was alive with excitement, but it had nothing to do with the invigorating water spray. No, it was anticipation that had Eli ready to climb the walls. He was practically salivating at the thought of seeing Monica.

Eli dipped his head under the stream flowing from the brass showerhead and shook it. Man, he had it bad. When was the last time he'd felt this much eagerness for a woman—one who wasn't even a sure thing?

He would rectify that situation ASAP. He'd decided on the drive home that just because they were pretending to date did not mean they couldn't engage in a little extracurricular activity. A man would be just plain stupid not to at least *try* to get a woman like Monica in bed.

Eli smiled at the thought.

It may take more finessing than he usually had to expend, but one way or another, he would have that woman—every soft, luscious caramel inch of her.

He walked out of the steam-filled shower and wrapped a plush terry cloth towel around his waist.

"Why have you been avoiding me?"

"What the—"

Eli turned to find Alicia Taylor standing in the doorway to his bathroom. "Alicia." He placed his hand over his chest in an effort to calm the chaotic pounding of his heart.

Alicia took another step into the bathroom. The clack of her mile-high stilettos echoed loudly on the marble floor.

"How did you get in here?" Eli wrapped the towel more tightly around his hips, tucking in the edge at his waist.

She took another step. Eli backed up. A ripple of chilling fear raced along the column of his spine as he took in the look in her eyes.

"Alicia, how did you get into my house?" It was hard to keep his voice calm.

She held out a single key and dropped it to the floor. It hit the hard surface with a loud ping.

Eli's jaw dropped. She had made a copy of his house key? This was going too far! "Copying my keys without my permission is illegal, Alicia. I could call the cops on you."

"But you won't," she said with a cold finality that did nothing to alleviate the bad feeling running through Eli's gut. He would have been more comfortable if she was acting a little hysterical. Her cool, unruffled, almost tranquil state raised the hairs on the back of his neck. Only the maladjusted remained unfettered in such situations.

Eli tried to decide if she was crazy enough to have a weapon hidden somewhere beneath the skintight catsuit that clung to her body like a second skin. The sight of her didn't arouse him. Stalkers, no matter how fine they were, just were not enticing.

"I want answers, Elijah. Why haven't you called?" She continued her slow stroll toward him. "I love you and you pretend it doesn't matter."

"We were together for less than a month, Alicia."

"Why are you doing this to us?" She'd backed him up until the back of his legs hit the bathroom counter.

How in the hell was he supposed to talk his way out of this?

Eli took a deep breath. He caught Alicia's forearms in his hands and gave her a firm shake. It was all he could do to keep from strangling her.

"Alicia, go home."

"Just tell me why you ended it, Elijah. I want answers."

Eli's mind fumbled as he tried to think of something to

say. He couldn't come up with a single viable excuse. He couldn't tell her that he *never* dated a woman for more than a month.

Once again, he would have to rely on his old faithful excuse to get him through yet another situation.

"You know I have a very demanding job," Eli said with sincerity he didn't feel. "I couldn't spend as much time with you as you deserved. I was only thinking about you, Alicia. I didn't think it was fair."

It was starting to sound like bull even to his own ears. But it did the trick. Alicia's lips formed a sexy pout, but Eli could tell she had relented. She captured his chin between her thumb and forefinger.

"I knew it had to be something like that. Thanks for being so considerate, but don't let it concern you. I knew working around your schedule would be tough, but that doesn't matter to me. I'm willing to take you anyway I can get you." She leaned forward and planted a soft kiss on his lips. Eli swallowed audibly.

"I'll see you later," she whispered, then turned and headed for the door, stopping to pick up the key she had dropped.

Eli stood motionless for several minutes. He did not take a breath until he heard the click of the front door closing.

"Damn." His low whisper reverberated off the bathroom walls.

Eli covered his face with his hands and slumped back onto the vanity. He took several deep breaths, drawing as much air into his lungs as he possibly could. For a second there, when she had him cornered against the bathroom counter, Eli wasn't sure how many breaths he had left.

What was he going to do?

There was one thing at the top his list: the locks were being changed.

He ripped the electric shaver loose on his jaw and neck,

splashing on aftershave when he was done. He quickly slipped into the clothes he had laid out on the bed and headed out of the house, aware that Alicia probably was lurking somewhere nearby.

It was eleven-thirty before Eli pulled onto I-610. He was going to be so late. Another reason to strangle Alicia.

The Louisiana sun was out in full force, shining down from high above, and turning every surface it touched into a stove top. Eli cranked up the AC another notch as he maneuvered the wide vehicle through the narrow French Quarter streets. He pulled up to the address Monica had given him.

Eli noted the chipped pale pink paint on the building's façade. He knew it was considered part of the charm, but to him the French Quarter was nothing but a bunch of old buildings.

He cut the engine and got out of the car, waiting for a produce truck to pass before he headed for the building's front door. Just as he reached for the handle, the wrought-iron door opened and Monica stepped out.

Eli had to stop himself from letting out a low whistle. He knew enough about her to know she would take offense. Still, he couldn't help but stare as she stood before him in an airy sundress.

She was charmingly petite, with slim arms and legs and an all-around perfect body. He liked it when a woman was smaller than he was. He knew from personal experience that statuesque runway-types were not all they were cracked up to be.

"Good morning," Monica said.

"Good morning." Eli walked her around to the passenger side, opened the door, and made a sweeping motion with his hand.

"Thank you," she said as she slid her slim form onto the leather seat.

Eli rounded the front of the car and slid behind the wheel. He checked his mirrors and adjusted the interior temperature controls.

"Is it too cold for you?"

"I'm from St. Louis, remember? I'm used to the cold. This stifling humidity that everyone seems oblivious to is a different story. I don't know if I can get used to actually feeling the air on my skin."

He chuckled. "We're not oblivious, just used to it. It's one of the few drawbacks to living down here in the very deep South."

"That and the drivers." She sent him a sideways smile.

Eli shook his head. "If it takes standing in the middle of the highway and letting you run me over with your car, I will make up for my past vehicular transgressions."

"Vehicular transgressions? Is that a new way of saying 'hit and run'?" she asked, the smile tugging at the corners of her mouth bringing a matching grin to Eli's lips.

"Will you ever let me off the hook?"

"Nope." The laughter in her voice was contagious. It had been a long time since he'd had the desire to engage in the humorous banter that came naturally whenever he was with Monica. It was comfortable. Effortless.

She reached over and upped the volume on the car stereo. "Who's this?"

"Some new jazz artist. My brother sent it to me. He's an aspiring record producer."

"Really." She looked impressed.

Eli tried not to roll his eyes. "The great Tobias Holmes. He played ball at St. John's, was even drafted by the Wizards. He was in a car accident a few weeks before the pre-season and suffered damage to his spine and knee. Even with physical therapy, it was too much to overcome."

"So he never got the chance to play?" Monica asked.

"Not one professional game."

"That must have been tough."

"For any normal person. But Toby is one of those people who are destined to be in the spotlight. When he realized the basketball career was over, he latched on to music. He's itching to give Sean 'Puffy' Combs a run for his money."

"That's a great attitude. I hope he does well."

They drove along the winding Great River Road that abutted the Mississippi River.

"It doesn't look like this area was hit as hard by Katrina," Monica commented as they passed a string of wood-frame houses that would never have withstood the fierce winds of the storm.

"The storm was too far east to cause much damage here. Your plantation homes should be intact."

Monica sent him a sideways grin, then brought her attention back to the scenery outside the window.

"What made you choose New Orleans?" Eli asked after some time had passed. "Or, should I ask, what made you leave St. Louis?"

Her expression changed, and Eli knew his question had wandered into None-of-Your-Damn-Business Land. Monica surprised him by actually providing an answer.

"They were cutting back at the hospital, so I got out before they could give me the ax."

"A doctor with your reputation? I doubt you would have been included in the cuts."

She shrugged her slim shoulders. "It was time for a change. I'd lived in St. Louis most of my life. It seemed like a good time to try somewhere new, and I wanted to help in the recovery effort going on down here."

"I guess Methodist Memorial lucked out, then."

She looked over at him with genuine gratitude gleaming in her brown eyes. "Thank you," she said.

"You're very welcome," he answered.

For some unfathomable reason, Eli found himself needing to learn more about her. She was hiding something. He could sense it in the way her body tensed whenever he mentioned anything remotely personal. Monica Gardner had secrets, and nothing turned him on more than a woman with a past.

An inner alarm warned Eli to be careful. Alicia was one of many who had caught him with that seductive, mysterious facade.

Well, that and the whipped cream.

But look where that had gotten him. His heart skipped a terrified beat every time he ran across a white car. It didn't even have to be a BMW. No, he needed to leave mystery right where the hell it was—out of his life.

But, Monica's head seemed firmly planted on those delicate, softly curved shoulders. Other than this secret Eli suspected she kept hidden, she was about as normal as any other woman he had dated.

No, that was a lie. Normal didn't do her justice. Normal suggested she was average, and one thing he had learned about Monica Gardner these past few weeks was that she was nowhere near average.

The fact that she was gorgeous was obvious the minute she stepped into a room, but her face was but a small facet of what made her special. Eli saw her true beauty in the soothing touches she shared with frightened patients, the reassurance she imparted to their nervous loved ones. Monica had a calming way about her that beckoned comfort and ease.

As if that wasn't enough, she hid a killer body under her scrubs and white coat. The woman had serious curves. More and more, he felt the desire to explore them.

That was his new goal, to see exactly what she had under those clothes.

After traveling several more miles in comfortable silence, they came upon the first plantation home on their itinerary. Eli turned onto a white graveled road nestled under an awning of towering oaks. A large, ostentatious mansion broke into view from behind a thick covering of trees.

"It looks different from the brochure," Monica commented as they parked in the grassy area a few feet from a wooden gazebo.

Eli cut the engine and made his way to the other side of the car. He held her door as she stepped out.

"The brochure you have is probably an old one. I heard some company from up North bought this plantation a few years ago, and it's starting to lose some of its authenticity."

Eli turned and studied the front facade. The elaborate shiny brass hardware on the doors was definitely not from the late eighteen-hundreds. He was sure the large ceiling fans twirling lazily above the front porch were not there during the Civil War, either.

"It's still very nice. I'm not necessarily looking for a place with historical significance; I just think the character would add something special to the banquet."

Elijah followed Monica to the door and pressed the doorbell. He snorted. Yeah, they had *those* a couple of centuries ago. The door opened and a young woman appeared. She looked from Monica to Eli, then back to Monica. "Can I help you?"

"We were hoping for a tour," Monica said, holding the brochure in front of her.

"Oh, I'm sorry. They stopped giving tours over a year ago. This is a private residence now. You can try San Francisco Plantation just down the river, or cross the bridge and go to Oak Alley. That's one of the more famous ones."

"That one's on my list," Monica answered. "Sorry we bothered you."

They turned and started for the car.

"Just how old *is* that brochure?" Eli asked as he backed the Range Rover away from the gazebo and started back up the driveway.

Monica's head fell back against the seat. "How embarrassing."

"Maybe we should have called first." Eli turned west.

"Can you imagine living in a place like that? I have never had someone ask to tour my house, I can promise you that."

"Would you even want to? It probably takes them ten minutes to walk from the bedroom to the bathroom."

"It's still amazing."

Eli caught the wistfulness in her voice, and wondered about its source. Had she been forced to live in a tiny little apartment while growing up, and had always dreamed of a big, fancy home? Did she just have a love for things old? He knew so little about her.

Usually, that suited him fine. The less he knew about a woman, the easier it was to cut her off at the end of the four-week period. But it was different this time.

A trace of sweat broke out across Eli's brow as something akin to panic lodged in his throat.

The next plantation they visited was up and running, but there were no tours due to a termite infestation.

"You have got to be kidding me!" Monica shouted at the car's ceiling once they were back on the road.

"We're batting oh for two."

"It's depressing."

"I don't think plantation-hunting is in the cards for today."

She sighed, then asked, "Do you want to stop somewhere for a bite to eat before going to your niece's party? I do owe you lunch."

"Nah. There's going to be plenty of food there. You can pick up the tab at dinner tonight."

Monica turned slightly in her seat to face him. "You think you're pretty slick, don't you? Will this dinner cost me a fortune?"

"Nah. I'll take it easy on you this time."

"This time? That makes it sound like a next time is a given."

He lifted his shoulder in a nonchalant shrug. "Pretty much."

"Are you always this sure of yourself, Dr. Holmes?" Her eyes glittered with easy humor.

Eli's mouth eased into a slow, confident smile. "Pretty much."

Chapter Twelve

Amanda waited for a break in traffic, crossing the street after the blue Chrysler rolled by. She walked through the double doors of the nondescript two-story building.

"Good morning, Mrs. Daniels," the receptionist said.

"Hello, Gloria," Amanda answered. "Dr. Berkenshire agreed to see me today."

"Yes, she just went up. You can go ahead to her office."

"Thanks."

Amanda sulked as she pressed the button for the elevator. This no-stair-climbing business caused more drama in her life than Dr. Holmes probably realized when he handed her his guidelines. Amanda turned right after getting off the elevator. Dr. Berkenshire was waiting at her door, the always calm, serene smile pasted on her face.

She could not be human. Real people were not so at peace with themselves all the time.

"You've grown since the last time I saw you," the doctor

said by way of greeting, pointing to Amanda's middle. "How is the pregnancy coming along?"

Amanda sat on one of the soft leather chairs in a setup that looked more like the cozy corner of a coffee shop than a psychiatrist's office. There were books lining the wall to her right and an antique free-standing globe to the left. A smooth instrumental piece played softly from a sleek CD player.

"Do you mind the music?" Dr. Berkenshire asked. "It's usually how I wind down on the weekends."

"Not at all," Amanda answered. She needed something to help her relax. She didn't want to be here. But, then, she was the one who'd asked for this session. Not that she needed an official "session." She just had a few things she needed to work out, and she figured running them by the doctor would be a good idea.

And just who are you trying to convince?

"So," Dr. Berkenshire said, interrupting Amanda's internal debate. "How are you? You didn't say how the pregnancy is going. Any complications?"

"Well, technically, I'm on bed rest. I have a bad case of anemia."

"Ah." The doctor nodded. "I had the same with my pregnancy." She waited a beat, then said smoothly, "And how is everything else?"

Amanda took a heavy breath. Sometimes she really hated the way these shrink types tried to con you into talking about your problems, as if it were just a regular conversation between two friends meeting in the grocery store. Although Amanda had to admit Dr. Berkenshire's technique was more comfortable than what she'd first expected. That stereotypical scene of a patient lying on an uncomfortable couch while an old, stuffy white man in a tweed jacket probed her mind had been etched in her brain. She vastly preferred sitting with a cup of tea and chatting with the petite, soft-spoken Dr. Berkenshire.

"I'm dealing with it." Amanda answered the indirect question. "But it's been more difficult these past few days."

"Why is that?"

"I moved back in with my husband," she replied in a noncommittal murmur.

The doctor's brows rose. "And how are you dealing with that?"

Amanda looked over at the gold-plated clock on the wall, the pendulum almost hypnotic in its steady sway. "It hasn't been easy," she finally admitted. "Some days are better than others, but there are just so many things going through my mind when I'm there."

"Like what?"

"Everything! Having to quit school. Having to quit my job. Even though it paid next to nothing doesn't mean I didn't need it. Then there's Jeffrey."

"What about him?" Dr. Berkenshire asked.

"I don't know. I just have all these feelings coming back. Memories of when we were happy, when *I* was happy."

"Are you starting to question the divorce?"

Amanda shook her head. "No. The divorce is for the best."

"How are you so sure? Have you talked with your husband, Amanda?"

"No. I told you, I can't—" Why was it so hard for this woman to understand that she could never tell Jeffrey about this? "I've told you this before," Amanda lamented. "Jeffrey saw the type of family I came from, and he said early on that he could never endure what my father went through with my crazy mother."

What would Jeffrey do if he ever found out she'd inherited her mother's bipolar disorder? Would he fear her illness would drive him to drink, the way it had done with her father? Would he believe Amanda would take her own life, the way her mother had?

Amanda had vowed never to have Jeffrey plagued by those questions.

"There is a distinct difference between you and your mother, Amanda. You are being medically treated for your illness."

"But you told me yourself, my meds may not work the same after I have the baby."

Dr. Berkenshire sat back in her chair and folded her hands in her lap. "It is not a guarantee that your hormone levels will return to their pre-pregnancy state, so, yes, there is a possibility that your medication will not have the same effect."

"What then?" Amanda asked. "What happens when the pills don't work? I've spent the past eleven years hiding this from Jeffrey. If he finds out I'm bipolar . . ." She brought her trembling fingers to her lips. "You just don't understand," Amanda whispered.

Amanda took a moment to collect herself. "I wasn't always like this, you know?" she said to the doctor, toying with the hem of her maternity top. "I used to laugh."

"And you don't anymore?"

She shook her head. "Not as much as I would like to."

They sat in silence. Then Dr. Berkenshire's eyes took on that knowing, probing look that always raised Amanda's defenses.

"You can be happy again. That's what the medication is for. We've already gone over this. The potential risks to a developing fetus are so marginal that they are hardly worth mentioning."

"You said that the last time."

"Your meds did not cause your previous miscarriage, Amanda," the doctor said.

"You can't be sure of that. Anyway, it doesn't matter." Amanda stopped her before she could reply. "I am not putting my child in danger. I don't care how miniscule the risks."

"And if the delusions return?"

Amanda willed her temper to remain under control. "I'm handling them," she gritted between clenched teeth.

"So they have returned," the doctor accurately assumed.

Amanda closed her eyes in frustration. "I know they're not true, okay? I understand that."

"But?"

"But it doesn't matter," she answered with a sigh. "Even as I'm telling myself he's not cheating, I can't help but believe it. Why did I have to turn out crazy like her?" She threw her hands up in despair.

Dr. Berkenshire scooted to the edge of her chair and took Amanda's hands in hers, giving them a strength-infusing squeeze.

"Delusions are pervasive, Amanda. It's not as simple as telling yourself you don't believe them. If you went back on your medication, all of this would go away. Why would you do this to yourself if you don't have to?"

Amanda pulled her hands free and placed them on her stomach. "I've waited my entire life for this baby. I will carry it full-term. I refuse to take any chances."

Dr. Berkenshire sat back in her chair, a slight, resigned smile on her lips. "As always, it is your choice. You haven't done anything to endanger yourself or your baby, so I cannot force you to go back on medication, but I do urge you to continue talk therapy. Why don't you come to one of our group therapy sessions? You don't have to share the first time. You can just listen. Both sufferers and their families attend." The doctor emphasized the word families.

"If I come, it will be alone. I am not bringing Jeffrey."

She shrugged, the tranquil, composed facade returning. "It's your decision. I can't make you do anything you're uncomfortable doing. So will I see you on Tuesday night?"

Amanda thought about returning to the house and all its memories. She thought about how difficult the past few days had been and how there was no end in sight, at least not for the next few months. If she had even the smallest chance of surviving the upcoming months, she would have to do something.

"I'll see," Amanda finally said, although in her mind, she was already trying to conjure an excuse for having to leave the house on Tuesday.

Elijah pulled in front of a shotgun-style house that Monica thought looked to be the norm around most of the New Orleans neighborhoods she had visited. Cars were lined up and down the street. Monica could see the tip of a red and blue Spacewalk peeking over the back fence.

"Smells like Alex broke out the grill," Eli said as he helped her out of the SUV.

"I thought you said this would be a *small* get-together."

"This is small," he answered. "Believe me, you'll know the difference when we do something big."

Monica followed him up a graveled path along the side of the house. He opened the gate, and she walked in ahead of him. The backyard was packed. There were at least fifty people, and they all seemed to stop when she and Eli came in. Unease, instant and nerve-wracking, rippled down Monica's spine.

A short, small-framed woman with pretty eyes and flawless skin came from around the food-laden picnic table, wiping her hands on a towel, which she threw over one shoulder.

"You made it," she said to Eli, although her eyes were on Monica. Eli bent down and gave her a kiss on her proffered cheek. Her gaze remained on Monica the entire time. "And who might this be?" the woman asked.

"Mama, this is Dr. Monica Gardner. She just moved here from St. Louis. She replaced Dr. Millgram in the ER. Monica, this is my mother, Margo Holmes."

"Nice to meet you, Mrs. Holmes." Monica extended her hand and felt instantly at ease as Margo returned the gesture with a warm smile.

"Same to you, Dr. Gardner."

"Monica."

"Then you must call me Margo," she insisted with Southern charm.

"Uncle Eli!" A little girl, whom Monica instantly recognized from the picture in Eli's office, ran up to them and threw her arms around his knees.

"What's up, Rosebud?"

"My name is Jasmine," she answered. She held out her hand. "Where's my present?"

"Jasmine Sophia, you know better than to ask for gifts," Margo chastised.

"But it's my birthday." Even pouting, to Monica the little girl was too cute for words.

"That doesn't matter," Eli's mother explained, taking Jasmine by the hand and giving her butt a pat. "Now you go back to the Spacewalk and Uncle Eli will give you your gift after you have blown out your candles." With a resigned smile creasing her face, Margo shook her head as her granddaughter ran toward the Spacewalk. "That little girl."

"Did Alex hide the bicycle in the old toolshed?" Eli asked.

"It's in there, though I'm not so sure she deserves such an expensive present. Her mouth is getting sassier by the minute."

"That's because she's a princess, and she knows it."

"It's because she's spoiled rotten." Margo turned curious eyes to Monica. "So, are you looking to make New Orleans your permanent home, or is this just a trial period?"

Monica's antennae instantly perked up as Eli's warning rang through her head. "My contract with the hospital is for two years, so I guess I'll reevaluate at the end of that time period. I love the city so far, though. The resilience of the people here is inspiring."

Margo's eyes brightened. "Wonderful," she said. "Elijah, why don't you see if Alex needs help at the grill, and I'll introduce Monica to the rest of the guests?"

"Okay." Turning to Monica, he asked, "Is that all right with you?"

Well, if it wasn't, it was a little too late. Monica caught the sly gleam in Eli's eyes and realized she'd just been snowballed.

"Sure," she said, sending him a look that said she knew exactly what he was doing. Eli's smile widened. The man was slick as mud on wet cement.

"Wonderful," Margo said again. "Oh, how exactly should I introduce you? Coworkers? Friends?"

Oh, that was subtle. Monica realized she wasn't dealing with your regular run-of-the-mill matchmaker. Margo Holmes was a pro.

"As I told you on the phone the other day, Mama, Dr. Gardner is more than just a coworker," Eli answered.

Monica didn't think Margo's eyebrows could perk up any higher, but she had just been proven wrong. "Well, we didn't have much time to talk, Elijah. I wasn't sure how serious things were."

Monica decided to step in since it was obvious Eli was having too much fun making his mother eek out every detail.

"Eli and I have been seeing each other pretty regularly."
Not a total lie—she did see him nearly everyday at the
hospital.

It was like a ton of fireworks detonated behind Margo's
eyes. "I didn't realize you two were dating. My son used to
share such news with me," Margo said in a stage whisper.

"I thought I used the word 'girlfriend,' " Eli said.

"You did not. I would have distinctly remembered if
you had."

"Well, I'm saying it now. Mama, Monica is my new girlfriend." Eli reached over and took Monica by the hand. As
he placed a gentle kiss on her fingertips, an instant zing of
something Monica did not want to identify shot from her
fingers to every part of her body. They had not discussed
public displays of affection, and she certainly wasn't prepared for the feel of Eli's soft lips on her skin.

"That's just wonderful," Margo said.

Pinpricks of guilt assaulted her conscience as Monica
witnessed the joy shining in Margo's eyes. The woman's
enthusiasm forced Monica to come to grips with the far-
reaching implications of her snap judgment. When she
agreed to Eli's plan, she had not considered how their pretend relationship would affect other people in their lives.

"Let me show you off to the rest of the family," Margo
said. Eli laid it on just a bit too thick by pretending he
didn't want to let go of her arm. They were definitely going to have a discussion the next time they were alone.

"I'll just drop in on Alex, then I'll be with the two of
you, okay?"

"Don't worry about us," Margo said, practically dragging Monica.

A few hours later, Monica felt as if she had known Eli's
family for years. They were boisterous, and sometimes
bawdy, but they were a close family in every sense of the

word. The stories Margo told of her three sons were apparently staples at family gatherings. Nearly everyone could recite them verbatim. But they all laughed at the same parts, too. From what Monica could glean from his mother's tales, Eli and his brothers were a rowdy trio, but always had each other's backs.

When Eli tapped her on the shoulder, interrupting her game of Pitty Pat, Monica realized she wasn't ready to go.

"Are you sure you two can't stay a little while longer, Elijah?" Margo asked as she put her hand of cards down and rose from the table.

"Sorry, Mama. Monica has plans that have been in the works for weeks. She couldn't cancel."

Had they really been dating, Monica would be disturbed by the fact that he could lie so easily.

"Well, I'll see you two tomorrow. And be on time, Elijah Marcus. You know I don't take any excuses when it comes to Sundays," Margo said before either of them could respond.

"I promise," Eli said, his laughing eyes on Monica as he bent to give his mother a kiss.

Margo took Monica's hands and cradled them between her soft, warm palms. "It was a pleasure meeting you."

"For me, too. You have a beautiful family, Mrs. Holmes."

"I told you to call me Margo."

"Margo," Monica amended.

Eli came around and rested his hand on the small of Monica's back. It was a casual gesture, unnerving in its familiarity and in how right it felt. "We've got to get going. I'll see you tomorrow, Mama. Hey, Daffodil," Elijah hollered toward the jungle gym, where his niece was hanging upside down.

"It's Jasmine, Uncle Eli." She jumped to the ground and ran toward them. Elijah scooped her up into his arms.

"What did you say?"

The little girl rolled her eyes. "How many times do I got to tell you? My name is Jasmine."

"How many times do you *have* to tell me?" He blew a raspberry on her cheek. "Enjoy the rest of your birthday."

"Thanks for the big-girl bicycle, Uncle Eli."

"You're welcome, Easter Lily."

Jasmine gave him an exaggerated eye-roll. His deep rumble of laughter sent a pleasant chill down Monica's back. "That little girl," Eli said, shaking his head as they turned onto the sidewalk and headed for his Range Rover.

"She's precious," Monica said.

"She's a trip and a half. Alex has his hands full."

"How awful must it be for a five-year-old to lose her mother," Monica said softly.

Elijah used the remote to turn off the alarm and unlock the door.

"How did she die?" Monica asked after Eli settled into his seat and buckled his seatbelt.

"A car accident last year," he said, checking his rearview mirror, then pulling out.

"That's horrible."

"Not really."

Monica inhaled a shocked breath. "Why would you say such a thing?"

He swerved to miss a basketball that had bounced into the street. He waved at the group of teenaged boys hanging around the basketball court. Eli glanced at her.

"Chantal was smart, beautiful, everything my mother could want in a daughter-in-law. But she was a witch. Toby and I saw it from the bat, but Alex's nose was so wide open you could see that fool's brain cells."

"That's still no reason for you to be so nonchalant about her death."

"Look, I'm not saying I was happy to see her die, but I

didn't break down at her funeral either. That girl put my brother through hell." Eli paused. He took an uneasy breath, then said, "She wasn't alone in the car when she wrapped it around a tree."

"Oh." Understanding brought unease with it, as Monica felt the anger radiating from Eli.

"You want to know the worst of it?" Eli shook his head. "Alex knew all about Chantal's other man. She had been seeing him for more than a year. Chantal had even brought her lover to their house. She had my niece calling him uncle."

Monica wasn't sure why Eli was telling her all of this. It was as if he'd kept it inside and finally had someone to unload on. She could not believe Alex Holmes would tolerate such behavior in a wife. It just didn't gel with his all-brawn, no-nonsense demeanor.

"Forgive me for asking, but why in the world would he stay with someone like her?"

"She'd threatened to take Jasmine away. Alex would walk through fire and back before he let anyone take that little girl away from him."

Monica nodded in understanding. Although she had only spoken to him briefly at the party, it was unquestionable that Alexander Holmes's life revolved around his daughter.

"And you all found out about this after she died?"

"Toby and I did. Alex never told Mama. She still thinks Chantal should be petitioned for sainthood."

"And Jasmine?"

"Her mommy is an angel. Alex would never do anything to mar Jazzy's memory of her mother."

"He's the one who deserves to be sainted."

"I'd be happy if he just went on a date again."

"He doesn't date?" Monica asked, amazement lifting her voice. "But he's gorgeous."

"Any other man would be flattered that you think so,

but the compliment would probably fly right over my brother's head. Alex hasn't dated since before he and Chantal were married."

"He needs a girlfriend."

Eli let out a shout of laughter. "Please do not say that around him. I almost got my head knocked off my shoulders the last time I suggested he get a woman."

"I have a feeling your suggestion was more depraved than mine."

He winked, an easy smile playing across his lips. "You're right."

Monica shook her head. The man was a constant flirt.

"So, what's this about Sunday dinner?" she asked.

"Oh, yeah . . . that. It's sort of a tradition."

"Was I going to hear about it before you came to pick me up tomorrow?"

"I was going to tell you. I just hadn't had the chance."

"Uh huh," she answered with a smirk.

"Are you available?"

"My shift starts at six tomorrow night."

"That's perfect. Church is over about noon. Mama spends about another hour fellowshipping, even longer depending on whose granddaughter dressed like a tramp for church. Dinner usually isn't served until about two o'clock. That's plenty enough time for you to eat and visit before you have to get ready for work."

"Should I get used to these surprises?"

"I'm sorry to just spring this on you. I promise to give you more notice in the future."

They pulled up to the curb in front of her apartment building. Eli got out and it wasn't until he came over to her side to open the door that Monica realized she had waited for him to do just that. Already she'd come to expect it.

She would not let herself get used to his gallantry. She had seen enough women lose their heads over the Cinderella treatment. Before coming to New Orleans, she had been one of them.

"Sorry the plantation-hunting didn't go as well as you'd wanted it to," he said, lending his hand, which Monica accepted as she alighted from the vehicle. "Do you have a plan B?" Eli asked.

"Yes, but I'm not ready to give up on plan A yet. Those were not the only plantation homes on the list."

"Just let me know when you're ready to go again."

Her brows rose. "You are actually willing to spend another day searching for a venue?"

"It's only fair I hold up my end of the bargain. After all, you'll be doing your share, starting with dinner tomorrow."

Before Monica could reply a loud voice from up the street stopped her.

"Well, it's about time!"

Chapter Thirteen

Monica and Eli turned to where the voice had come from.

"Nia?" Monica shrieked, then ran toward her best friend, who was walking up the sidewalk eating a snow cone. The two clasped each other in a hug.

"What are you doing here?"

"Don't look at me like that. It's your fault. You just had to go and mention beignets and jazz music. Next thing I knew, my behind was on a plane headed for New Orleans."

"Girl, you are out of your mind," Monica laughed.

They started toward her apartment, but Nia stopped midstep. "Ooh, child. What do we have here?"

Eli waited where Monica had left him standing. The light afternoon breeze plastered his shirt to his chest, displaying a hint of his incredibly chiseled abdomen and chest. Lord have mercy, but the man was fine.

Monica looked over at Nia and could almost see the wheels turning in her friend's head. Oh, no. She would not let Nia paint her own sordid picture.

"It's not what it looks like," she said.

"You sure? Because *it* looks like he could be draped across a buffet table and drizzled with chocolate."

"Nia!" Monica whispered fiercely, thankful they were still too far from Eli for him to overhear. She wished Nia would, for once, talk like the married woman she was. Granted, marrying Monica's best friend had loosened her brother up, but maybe Phillip was a bit too trusting. Most husbands would have a problem with their wives ogling other men.

As they approached him, she said a silent prayer that Nia would not embarrass her in front of Eli. Given her sister-in-law's track record, Monica knew she was asking a lot.

"Eli, this is my best friend, Nia. Nia, this is Dr. Elijah Holmes. He's an ob-gyn at Methodist Memorial."

Eli took Nia's hand and placed a gallant kiss on the back of it. "A pleasure to meet you."

Nia made stupid, gooey eyes at Monica over his bent head.

"Did I interrupt something?" Nia asked. "Oh, please tell me I interrupted something. I can go back down to Jackson Square." She turned to Eli. "How long should I stay gone? One hour? Two? The rest of the night?"

"Nia!" Monica was going to wring her neck. She needed to get this girl away from civilized people. "We need to go." She grabbed Nia by the arm and pulled her toward her building.

"What about our date?" Eli called out after them.

Monica stopped short. She turned to find Eli smiling. He was having his own brand of fun with this.

"Date?" Nia's eyes lit up. "You go, girl," she whispered in Monica's ear.

"It's not what you think," Monica said under her breath. Gesturing to Nia, she said to Eli, "I didn't realize I would have company. You understand, don't you? Maybe we can—"

"Don't cancel your plans on my account," Nia said.

"No, Monica's right," Eli replied. "You came here to visit her."

"True, but I also came to see the city." Dislodging her arm from the hold Monica had on it, Nia walked over to stand directly in front of Eli. "So, how long have you lived here?"

"All my life," Eli answered.

"Well, then, you must know of some good jazz clubs. You see, my best friend lured me here with the promise of good food and good jazz, and since I'm only in town for a couple of days, I don't want to waste a minute."

"I can show you a few places."

"Umm . . . hello?" Monica waved her hands. "I thought you were here to see me," she said to Nia.

"You're going to be with us. I'm not going to go hopping around the city with your man without you."

"He is not—"

"Why don't I go and change, and be back in an hour to pick the two of you up?" Eli suggested. "We can have dinner at the Praline Connection and then see what's happening at the clubs."

"I've heard of that place," Nia said.

"Best cooking you can find, other than my mother's kitchen, of course."

"Mmmm . . . Southern soul food." Nia smacked her lips. "That sounds wonderful."

"I'll see the two of you in an hour," Eli said. Before Monica knew what he was about, he took her chin in his hand and placed a brief kiss on her cheek. Then he darted around his SUV, hopped behind the wheel, and was gone.

"Giiiirl." Nia dragged the word out. "I should have your behind for not telling me about him."

Monica rolled her eyes. "There's nothing to tell."

"The hell there's not. Were we both looking at the same man? I know the man I just saw was about the finest I've seen in all my life."

"I'm sure Phillip would appreciate hearing you say that."

Nia waved her off. "I have to hear him fantasizing about Tyra Banks."

"Big difference. That snow cone you're eating has a better chance surviving in hell than Phillip has of getting Tyra Banks."

"Don't tell him that, honey. He thinks all it'll take is an introduction. I told him if he's lucky enough to get Tyra to even give him the time of day, go for it."

Monica shook her head. "I will never understand your relationship."

They entered the apartment building, and Nia knocked on the door of the building manager. She retrieved her bags from the holding room and followed Monica upstairs.

"I want to know why this is the first I'm hearing of Dr. Holmes. I cannot believe you've been seeing this man and didn't tell me, Mon."

"I'm not seeing him. Well, not really." Monica unlocked the door to her apartment and held it open for Nia.

"What's that supposed to mean?"

She debated whether to tell Nia the truth about the deal she'd made with Eli, but Monica knew withholding the whole story could be detrimental. If her best friend thought for the slightest minute that Monica and Eli's relationship was even remotely real, Nia would be on her butt like red beans on rice.

She mentally rolled her eyes. She was beginning to think like a New Orleanian.

"Before you go getting any ideas, let me explain what's going on between me and Dr. Holmes."

Nia plopped down on the sofa, crossed her legs, and propped her elbow on her knee. "Explain away."

Monica took a deep breath. "Elijah and I are colleagues, nothing more."

"Hmm . . . well, I didn't realize colleagues saw each other on their days off—you did tell me you were off today, right? That's the reason I flew in, because I distinctly remember you telling me you were going to be off."

"I—"

"And," Nia continued, "I didn't realize colleagues had dates. My ears were not deceiving me when I heard Dr. Fine say the two of you had a date."

"Would you please shut up," Monica sighed. "My goodness, girl. You should have gone to law school instead of getting an MBA."

"My verbal skills come in handy in the boardroom, thank you very much."

"You probably tire everybody out."

"Why are you so cranky? Aren't you supposed to loosen up after getting some?"

"Nia!" Monica picked up a pillow from her armchair and threw it at her.

Nia dodged it, nearly doubling over with laughter. "I'm sorry." She took the pillow and placed it daintily in her lap. "Now, you were telling me how this extremely fine doctor you're dating is just a colleague."

"Really, I'm not dating him. We have an agreement."

Nia's mouth dropped open. "You're using him for sex! You *go*, girl!" she exclaimed, clapping her hands.

Monica threw her hands in the air. "I'm through with you. I don't know why I even bother."

"Well, what then?" Nia groaned.

"Forget it. If I tell you what's really going on, I won't hear the end of it. So just go on thinking whatever you want."

Nia rose from the sofa and came to sit on the edge of the armchair. She brushed a few strands of hair from Monica's face. "Mon, please. Tell me what's going on. If you're not dating him, then what's up?"

"You promise to hold your opinions until the very end." It was a demand.

Nia made the sign of the cross over her chest. "Promise."

By the time Monica finished explaining the deal she'd made with Elijah, she thought she would have to find a bucket for Nia to puke.

"I can't believe this," Nia said in a dazed whisper. "I just cannot believe it."

"What's so hard to believe? We're both benefiting from the situation."

"But look at him, Monica! If I didn't love my husband more than my own life, I'd be going after him. You, on the other hand, have every reason to make a play for him. You're beautiful, single, and in need of a man."

"I am not in need of a man. Goodness, Nia, you make me sound desperate."

"It would get your mind off Patrick."

"I have not thought about Patrick Dangerfield since . . ."

Monica thought it better to shut up while she was ahead. Nia could always tell when she was lying, and if she said she hadn't thought about Patrick since she arrived in New Orleans, Nia would see straight through her. Still, just because she had the occasional thought about her ex-boyfriend didn't mean she needed to jump into another relationship—especially with Elijah Holmes, a man who made it a rule not to date women of his own profession. For some reason, that still irritated her.

Nia crossed her arms over her chest, and Monica knew she was in trouble. "Give me one good reason why you don't want to date Dr. Fine."

"Would you stop calling him that!"

"Okay, give me one good reason why you don't want to date *Dr. Holmes*."

"Because I don't want to. That's all the reason you need."

"Maybe for someone who doesn't care, but that's not gonna cut it with me, baby doll."

"Nia, please." Monica could feel a headache coming on. She knew this would happen if Nia found out about their arrangement. "Even if I wanted this to be real—which I definitely do not want," Monica clarified, "I'm not the only one who has a say in it. Anyway, I'm not the type of woman Dr. Holmes dates."

"Then why would he ask you to pretend?"

"I already told you, because his mother is pressuring him to get back together with his high school sweetheart. He knew if she thought he was dating an upstanding, respectable woman, she'd lay off."

"And of course your only reason for dating him just has to be work-related. I swear, girl, you are just like the rest of your family. I have never seen a set of people more married to their jobs. When are Gardners going to learn that life is not all about work?"

If there was one issue that came between them, this was it. No matter how many times Monica tried to explain, Nia would never understand that for Monica, work *was* all she needed.

"I just want you to be happy, Mon," Nia said, dropping her hands to Monica's shoulders and giving her a light squeeze.

Monica patted her hand. "I am happy. Really. Moving here was a good thing. I'm loving my job and the people I work with, and if it'll make you feel better, I think about Patrick less and less each day."

"I want you to forget his name," Nia said. Her voice

was stern, but Monica could feel the compassion behind her statement. Nia cared.

"I will," Monica promised. "Eventually I will."

The two best friends stood for a moment holding each other. Nia was the first to move.

"Come on, girl. We've got a fine man picking us up in a half hour. I'm ready to have some fun."

Monica shook her head, and said a small prayer for the city of New Orleans. With Nia on the loose, God knew it would need it.

Chapter Fourteen

Eli pulled at the hem of his wheat-colored polo shirt, making sure it was in place. He ran a hand over his head and down his cheeks, then stared at the doorbell labeled M. GARDNER. What was it about this woman that had him acting like a teenager going on his first date?

This dating scheme wasn't going exactly as he'd planned. He hadn't expected this to feel so, well, *right*. There was something about the way she smiled at him when she knew he was trying to pull her leg. Or maybe it was the way she had meshed so well with his family. A couple of times that afternoon when he looked over at the card table and caught her laughing, or when she went over to push Jasmine on the swings, Eli couldn't help but think how much she seemed to belong there.

Just as he was about to ring the bell, the door opened. It was Monica.

"Hi. Sorry I'm late."

"That's all right. Nia's still getting ready." She scooted past him. "I need to get something out of my car."

"Do you need help?"

"No, I think I can handle getting a tube of lipstick by myself." She smiled. "Go on up. I'm in 2B. Maybe you can light a fire under Nia's tail."

Eli looked up and down the street. Even though it was illuminated by the Old World–style streetlamps, this was still the French Quarter at night. He wasn't about to leave her out here alone.

"I'll come with you to your car."

Monica's eyes lit with laughter. "You do realize I go outside alone on a regular basis, right?"

"This city may be safer than it used to be, but it's not Disneyland. A lot can happen to a single woman on these streets."

"Thanks for the concern, Dr. Holmes, but I'm a big girl. I can take care of myself."

To hell with her objections. She was the perfect target for some vagrant or drunken reveler.

"I'm not leaving you out here, so we can either stand in this doorway for another hour or we can get your lipstick."

Monica shook her head, the smile still tilting her lips. "Suit yourself."

As she led the way to her car, Eli noticed for the first time since she opened the door what she was wearing. Her black top was made of a soft, stretchy fabric that clung to her perfectly shaped breasts. It ended right above the top of her jeans, providing a glimpse of smooth mocha-colored skin.

Eli's mouth went dry.

He followed a few steps behind her, focusing his eyes on a nice round butt clad in dark blue jeans. Her hips flared slightly, creating the perfect spot for his hands to grab.

Monica unlocked her car and leaned into the passenger-side doorway, leaving her butt in the air. Eli had to bite down on his lower lip to keep from groaning out loud. He itched to pull her from the car and drape her over the hood. He could have her out of those clothes in a heartbeat.

For a brief second, Eli closed his eyes and imagined what her underwear looked like. She was too fine to wear plain white. No, Monica Gardner looked like a black-lace kind of girl. His body instantly hardened with the thought of peeling silky lingerie from her soft brown skin.

"See," she said, coming up with a peach-and-chrome lipstick tube, "I even managed not to trip on the sidewalk, but having you here to help made all the difference."

"I didn't realize you were such a smart aleck," Eli drawled.

"Only when it's warranted."

"I was wondering where you'd gone off to, girl." Nia came out of the building dressed in a tasteful but definitely sexy hot pink halter top and matching leather pants.

"Are we ready to go?" Eli asked.

"I just need to run upstairs and grab my purse," Monica said.

"Got it," Nia said. A small black bag hung from her fingertips.

"All right, then." Eli led them to his Rover. He opened both doors on the passenger side and waited from them to get in, Monica in the front and Nia in the back. Then he closed the doors, rounded the car, and got behind the wheel.

"Nia, is this your first time in New Orleans?" Eli asked as he pulled away from the curb and headed up Dumaine Street.

"I was here for Mardi Gras my sophomore year of college, but I can't remember a thing."

"Thankfully, I missed that trip," Monica interjected.

"I do remember the city being unique, and that hasn't changed," Nia said as they passed a saxophonist leaning against an ornate streetlamp at the corner of Dumaine and Decatur. The horn's sweet-sounding melody wafted in even through the Rover's closed windows. "It's fascinating."

"That's one thing Katrina couldn't take away," Eli said. "There's no place like New Orleans."

"The city seems to be recovering well," Nia commented.

Eli shrugged. "Depends on where you are. The downtown area is almost back to normal, but some of the outlying neighborhoods look like they did the day after the storm hit. It's all going to come back, though. It would take a lot more than a hurricane to break the city's spirit."

"Amen," Nia said.

"Now how about some New Orleans–style soul food?" he asked.

"Umm . . . sounds wonderful," Nia answered.

"That's okay with you?" he asked Monica.

"Sure. I'm up for anything."

Eli stifled another groan. If she were really up for anything, he would drop her friend off in the middle of the Quarter and head straight for his house.

Eli turned onto Frenchmen Street, and luckily found a parking spot only steps away from the entrance to the Praline Connection.

"I'm warning you, Dr. Holmes, I take my food seriously." Nia stopped in the process of getting out of the car. "Is the food really as good as I've heard?"

"You are about to eat the best cornbread in New Orleans," Eli answered. "You're not watching your weight, are you?"

"Nia doesn't have to," Monica answered for her friend. "She's been naturally skinny her whole life. She can eat an entire buffet and not gain a pound. That's why everyone hates her."

"I am not skinny. I'm fine, sweetheart." Nia wrapped her arm around Monica. "And you know you love me."

It was obvious they were best friends. They exhibited the same camaraderie he shared with his brothers. Eli would bet money they would get in a fight before the end of the night. He, Alex, and Toby couldn't be around each other for more than a few hours before they were ready to kill one another.

Eli opened the door to the legendary restaurant and followed behind Nia and Monica as the hostess showed them to a table. He'd called before leaving his house and had managed to reserve a table even though reservations weren't generally accepted.

"Can I start you off with an appetizer?" the hostess asked after handing out menus and placing glasses of ice water in front of them.

"Ooh, why don't you forget dinner and just bring me some of this homemade bread pudding with praline sauce," Nia said.

"I second that," Monica replied, closing her menu.

"Oh, come on. You two are not eating just dessert. Especially you." Eli nodded in Nia's direction. "Monica can get this kind of food anytime, but you can't get cooking like this in St. Louis." Eli turned to the hostess. "Bring us the Taste of Soul platter and three orders of bread pudding."

"Gumbo, fried catfish, greens, jambalaya. That'll work." Nia passed the waitress her menu, folded her arms on the table, and looked Eli directly in the eyes. "So, you're an obstetrician?"

"Yes," Eli answered after taking a sip of water.

"He's known as Super Doc around the hospital," Monica teasingly interjected.

Eli tried not to stare at Monica, but it was impossible. The soft light above their table glistened off her dark brown hair. The woman had the prettiest hair he'd ever seen. He could say the same about her eyes.

Eli shook his head. This was bad. Here he was sitting across the table from *Dr.* Monica Gardner, and all he could think about was dragging his fingers through her mahogany hair.

Then again, he was a man. And what red-blooded heterosexual male would not fantasize when faced with her luscious smooth skin and womanly curves? He could just envision her naked on his living room couch.

Dragging his mind from the lust-filled tangent it had wandered off on, Eli squeezed a slice of lemon into his ice water and downed the entire glass in an effort to cool himself off. The waitress arrived with the large platter of food. She removed the bud vase and placed their food in the center of the table. "Enjoy," she said after handing out three smaller plates.

"This looks delicious," Monica said.

"You ever thought about going into private practice, or are you content at the hospital?" Nia asked.

"I've been at Methodist Memorial for years. I can't imagine leaving."

"Really? I would think private practice would be more rewarding, at least financially."

Hold up. Eli knew a fishing expedition when he heard one. Nia was trying to scope him out.

"Money isn't everything," Eli responded. He waited for the waitress to refill his water glass. "How long have the two of you been friends?" he asked, trying to gear the conversation away from himself.

"Since the first grade," Monica answered. "She stole my Wonder Woman pencil." She dipped a portion of fish in the tangy tartar sauce and popped it into her mouth.

"I did not," Nia protested. "It was a misunderstanding.

To this day, I still have no idea how that pencil wandered into my book bag. So." Nia rested her elbow on the table and placed her chin in her upturned palm. "How long have you and Monica been dating?"

"Actually—" Eli caught the glare Monica shot Nia's way. "We were returning from our first 'official' date when we drove up earlier this afternoon. I took Monica to my niece's birthday party."

"Oh, I didn't realize that!" she said innocently. There was definitely something going on. If Monica's eyes could shoot fire, Nia would be fried crispier than the catfish on their plates.

"Have you ever been married?" Nia asked. Eli nearly spit his water across the table.

"Nia Gardner!" Monica groused.

"Your last name is Gardner?"

"She's married to my older brother, Phillip," Monica bit out.

"So you two *are* sisters," Eli stated, the picture becoming clearer. Nia was married, so the nosing into his personal life wasn't on her behalf. She was looking for someone for Monica. Interesting. "No, I've never been married," he answered.

"Engaged?"

"Okay, that's enough," Monica said, her lips thin with anger. Nia shrugged her shoulders, an innocent look on her face.

Oh, yeah. There would be a serious fight in a certain French Quarter apartment tonight. Eli realized he would have to be careful around Nia. He wanted his family and friends to believe he and Monica were really dating, but he knew if he went overboard, overzealous relatives could make things a thousand times more complicated. Instinct told him Nia was the matchmaker in Monica's life.

"Fill me in on what's happening back home," Monica said.

"Same old, same old," Nia lifted her shoulder in a half-hearted shrug as she heaped a scoop of jambalaya onto her plate.

"Has my mother convinced my father to come out of retirement yet?"

"No, but not for lack of trying," Nia answered. "She's pressing Phillip to run for a state House of Representatives seat. Arguing before the state supreme court on a regular basis just isn't enough. She thinks he needs loftier goals."

Eli noticed the shadow of annoyance that passed over Monica's face. "That sounds about right where Mother is concerned. Even when you do your best, you can always do better."

"Here's dessert," Nia said. The cheerfulness in her voice seem more forced this time, Eli noticed. The waitress placed three servings of warm bread pudding on the table, effectively putting an end to all conversation.

"Oh my goodness, this is so good," Monica groaned halfway through her dessert. She licked praline sauce from her knuckle and sucked it from the tip of her finger.

As hard as he had tried to keep his thoughts clean, that one act shot his efforts straight to hell. His mind instantly conjured a picture of her tongue wrapped around a part of his anatomy he damn sure shouldn't be thinking about in a crowded restaurant.

Sitting at a table in the Praline Connection, surrounded by dozens of people, Eli couldn't help but imagine running his fingers through Monica's hair as she knelt before him, suckling his body, sending him from one pleasurable peak to another.

Eli had to force his thoughts to change direction. There was only so much of this he could take before embarrassing himself beyond all repair. If he knew it would be this hard to resist her, Eli would have never suggested this whole pretend-dating thing. What in the hell had he gotten himself into?

"I ate that way too fast," Monica said, pushing the empty dish away. "You've hardly touched your dessert. You don't like bread pudding?"

It took Eli a second to realize she was talking to him. "I ate most of the Taste of Soul platter. I forgot to leave room for dessert."

"Well, I'm happy I did," Nia said, stacking her plate atop Monica's. "That was awesome. What's next?" she asked.

"Are you two up for going to a club? Some new R & B singer my younger brother discovered is performing at Snug Harbor."

"Sounds good to me," Nia said as she picked at a sugar-covered pecan she'd left on her dessert plate.

"I'm up for it," Monica replied. "I don't go in until to-morrow evening."

"Well, come on," Nia exclaimed, pushing out of her chair and heading for the door.

Monica rose from the table, shaking her head. "I'm sorry about that."

"Forget it." Eli waved it off. He took two twenties from his wallet and threw them on the table.

"I've got dinner tonight," Monica said, unclasping the tiny black bag.

"No, you don't."

"Paying for my sister-in-law's meal was not a part of the deal," she said, still trying the clasp of her purse.

"Monica." Eli put his hand on her arm and immediately realized his mistake. If he'd wanted to keep thoughts of her body at bay, touching her warm, silky skin was not the way to go about it.

Monica's gaze traveled from where he touched her arm up to his face, and the desire he saw in her eyes was strong enough to knock Eli to his knees.

"Uh ... all right," she uttered, her voice shaky. "I'm ... I'll see where Nia went," she said, disconnecting from his grasp. Without a backward glance, she left Eli standing next to the table contemplating again just what the hell he'd gotten himself into.

Monica had no question as to how Snug Harbor had acquired its name. The place was about the size of a broom closet, but there was something to be said for quaint. The last time Nia had dragged her to a club, there had been hip-hop blasting from speakers the size of redwood trees, and dizzying strobe lights destined to send epileptics into seizures.

Snug Harbor was the polar opposite. Mellow lights shone off the rich wood beams that crisscrossed the high ceilings. Tiny blue oil lamps cast a soft glow over the small round tables. The laid-back atmosphere was a welcome relief.

Although there was nothing Monica wanted more right now than to be locked in her bedroom. Alone. The chaotic thoughts flowing through her mind were more than enough to keep her company tonight.

What had happened back there?

Either she was going crazy, or she and Eli had shared a ... Well, she didn't know what they'd shared, but after the lightening rod that shot through her body as his eyes stared into hers, Monica knew they had shared *something*.

It was not supposed to happen this way. This was a business deal, a strictly platonic mutual agreement. So why was the image of his deep-set eyes burning a permanent mark on her brain?

"Having a good time so far?"

Monica nearly jumped out of her skin as Eli's whispered

words entered her ear, sending a slight tremor down her spine.

"I didn't realize it was also a restaurant," she managed to choke past the lump in her throat.

"We can come back another night for dinner, if you'd like."

He'd gotten even closer. Monica started feeling faint.

"What's this?" Nia asked, pointing to a series of pictures along the brick wall. "A Mardi Gras parade?"

Eli walked over to examine the pictures. "No, a jazz funeral."

Nia shook her head. "Y'all party for everything around here."

"When did they start letting in just anybody?"

A tall, spectacularly built man with light brown skin and eyes like Elijah's stood at a door just beyond the bar. Eli met him halfway, and the two embraced in a hug most men would be ashamed to share in public.

"Boy, what are you doing here? I though you weren't coming until later this week."

"I decided to surprise Mama," the other man answered.

Eli's brother. She should have known just by looking at him. The resemblance was unmistakable. The two disengaged, but Eli kept his arm draped across his brother's shoulder, even though the other man was at least four inches taller.

"And what do we have here?" Eli's brother asked with a voice as smooth as butter on a warm biscuit.

"This is Dr. Monica Gardner, the new ER physician at the hospital, and her sister-in-law, Nia. Nia is visiting from St. Louis. Ladies, this is my baby brother, Tobias."

"Toby," his brother said, extending his hand first to her, then to Nia.

Oh goodness, another one with a killer smile. Monica didn't know what to make of these Holmes brothers.

There should be a signal to warn any woman who came within ten feet of them.

"You're the recording mogul?" Nia asked, taking Toby by the hand and entwining her arm with his.

Toby shrugged. "I wouldn't say mogul yet, but someone has to be responsible for giving people a reason to shake their butts."

"I hear that, honey," Nia flirted.

"I should have expected to find you with a beautiful woman on each arm," Toby said to Eli. "Has my brother been behaving himself?"

"He's been the perfect gentleman," Nia replied.

"As always," Eli added.

Toby shot him a raised eyebrow, "Do you want me to bring up any of the number of stories I can remember of you being anything but a perfect gentleman?"

"Don't even think about it," Eli said. "Why don't we find a table?"

"I've got one. Come on."

Eli took Monica by the arm. Beyond the door revealed another room Monica could only describe as snug. About thirty chairs, all filled with people of various ages and ethnicities, faced a tiny stage. There were more of the blue oil lamps casting shadows on the tables. A sleek black baby grand piano sat in a corner on the left side of the stage. A drum set was in the opposite right corner, with a large base guitar between them.

"Excuse us."

Monica moved to the side as four men, one carrying a trumpet, edged past them and made their way to the stage.

"Up here," Toby said. He guided them up a narrow stairway to an alcove overlooking the main floor.

"Is this okay?" Eli asked as he pulled out a chair for her. That look was in his eyes again. Monica wasn't sure how to describe it. Interest? Awareness? Whatever it was, it was tangible.

"This is perfect," Monica answered. She tried to ignore the tingle that radiated from the spot where his warm hand brushed the space between her shoulders.

"How long will you be in town?" Eli asked Toby.

"I'm not sure," Toby signaled a waitress. He relayed an order for two mai tais for the ladies at the table and beers for Eli and himself. "Actually, I'm thinking about moving back to New Orleans permanently," Toby answered.

Eli's brows shot up. Before he could comment, Toby said, "Don't start, E."

Eli put his hands up in mock surrender. "I'm not saying anything. I just thought Houston was the spot for finding new talent. I definitely didn't think you'd be back in New Orleans anytime soon."

"Yeah, well, Houston's only an hour away by plane," Toby answered.

"It'll be good to have you home, brother." Eli reached across the table to shake his younger brother's hand. The sincerity in his eyes touched Monica's soul.

"Are we supposed to share a cup of flavored coffee now?" Toby joked, lightening the mood once again.

"Shut up, man. Let's get to the important stuff. Who is this newly discovered star?"

"Yeah," Nia said. "Is she good enough to make it to the big time? I'd love to say I saw a big star when they were just a nobody."

"Whoever she is, I doubt she would appreciate being called a nobody," Monica retorted.

"Oh, you know what I mean." Nia stuck her tongue out at her. Monica discreetly scratched her right temple with her middle finger.

"You troll," Nia said, pinching Monica on the arm. "I knew you would do that."

"Do what?" Toby and Eli asked in unison.

"Nothing," Monica answered. "Now, what about this artist, Toby? What's her name?"

"Aria Jordan."

"Is she any good?" Eli asked.

"Would I sign on as her manager if she wasn't?"

"I don't know. Depends on how she looks when she walks out on stage."

"She has a range that goes from Toni Braxton's low alto to Patti Labelle on her best day."

"Uh-huh, and I'll bet she has a behind like J Lo."

Toby spread his hands out in helpless surrender. "Excuse my brother, ladies. As you can see, his ungentlemanly qualities tend to come out as the night wears on."

"And if my brother is true to his reputation, this new talent"—Eli made quotation marks with his fingers—"will be worthy of the *Sports Illustrated* swimsuit edition."

Before Toby could respond, the emcee walked up to the mike and introduced the night's performer. A petite but curvy young woman entered from a door just to the right of the stage. The trumpet player took her by the hand and led her up the three steps to the microphone stand at the center of the stage.

"I rest my case," Eli said, leaning back in his chair and crossing his hands behind his head.

"I never denied she looked good," Toby defended. "But that's not all she has going for her. Just wait."

The performer opened her mouth, and Monica was enthralled by the amazing voice that pelted out a song she'd never heard before. The entire club sat riveted by the sheer beauty of Aria's soulful singing.

When the slow, sexy tune was over, Monica had no qualms joining the rest of Snug Harbor's patrons in a standing ovation.

"That was amazing," she said to Toby.

"Unbelievable," Nia added.

They all looked at Eli. She knew it killed him to have to admit he was wrong. "Okay, so she can sing."

"No way, man, you gotta do better than that. After all the grief you gave me, you need to eat some serious crow."

"Fine. Fine. She's the bomb, all right?" A repentant Eli was way sexier than Monica could handle with a mai tai in her system. "Really, man, you've got yourself something special right there. I hope you're treating her right."

"I'm a professional, E."

"I'm not talking just professionally."

Toby shook his head. "That's all there is."

"Uh-huh," Eli said.

Aria Jordan came over to their table and wrapped her arms around Toby's shoulders, planting a kiss on his cheek.

That was a friendlier greeting than most professionals would share. Monica looked over at Eli, who sported a knowing gleam in his eyes.

"Everybody, this is Aria." Toby introduced each of them by name and the young woman, who had to be no older than twenty, floated around the table, shaking each of their hands.

"You have an amazing voice," Monica told her. "And the song was beautiful."

"Thank you, although Toby gets credit for the song."

"You wrote that?" Eli stole the words from Monica's mouth.

"Yeah, I've been writing a little. You know, just playing around. This is the first one ever to be recorded, though."

Monica was duly impressed.

"It was nice meeting all of you," Aria said. She turned her attention to Toby. There was no mistaking the infatuation in her eyes, though Monica noted it was not returned.

"I want to go around to some of the other tables. I'll catch up with you after the last performance, okay?"

"Sure, and good job." He gave her a wink so similar to Eli's that Monica was certain the elder brother had given Toby lessons.

"Thank you," she said, bending to give him another kiss. That girl was in love. Monica had seen the same starry-eyed look reflected in the mirror when she had first started dating Patrick and fancied herself in love, too.

Now, why did she have to bring him up?

She had actually been enjoying herself. *Really* enjoying herself, for the first time in months. And just like that, her foolish mind had to conjure his image and ruin her good mood.

No way. She would not let thoughts of Patrick dampen her night.

"Anybody up for dancing?" Monica asked, surprising herself.

"Sure," Nia answered, already rising. "Okay, Eli, let me see what you've got." She grabbed Eli by the arm and yanked him up.

Snug Harbor was a little too snug for an actual dance floor, but that didn't stop them. Monica allowed Toby to guide her to the narrow passageway just beyond their table. The old hardwood floor creaked as the four of them along with three other couples tried to maneuver in the small space. A local saxophonist belted out an upbeat tune. Monica had a hard time keeping up with Toby, who might have been good-looking but who couldn't dance to save his life.

"You really need to stick to songwriting," Monica said as he tripped her up again. Toby had about four left feet.

"Eli's the dancer in the family. I do better with slow songs," he said with a good-natured laugh.

As if on cue, the trumpeter began to play the melody to an old Freddie Jackson song.

"Let's switch," Nia said, reaching for Toby. "That one over there thinks he's on *Soul Train*."

Monica turned to find Eli standing scant inches from her, his palm upturned, awaiting her hand. She placed it in his and allowed him to pull her closer than she should have. He placed a hand on her waist, settling it on the ride of her hip. The other hand entwined with hers, just above her shoulder.

Monica closed her eyes for a brief moment, trying desperately to collect her thoughts. When she opened them, the sensual fire radiating from Eli's heated gaze was enough to scorch her.

"Are you enjoying yourself?" Eli asked, his voice a husky whisper against the backdrop of the song's sensual melody.

"Yes," Monica answered softly.

"That's good to hear," Eli said. "I would hate for you to be bored with me already."

"I doubt that would ever happen," she answered with a shaky laugh. She took another unsteady breath, but the lightheadedness wasn't going away.

They swayed to the music, their bodies barely touching. When someone bumped into her back, forcing her breasts into brief contact with Eli's well-sculpted chest, Monica's world nearly exploded. The sensation of his defined muscles against her long-ignored breasts made her ache with need. It had been way too long since she'd had a man.

Monica made the mistake of glancing at Eli again, and the look in his eyes said it all. He was just as affected by the currents of electricity shooting sparks between their bodies.

Again, the couple dancing next to them bumped into Monica, but this time she was pushed flush against Eli's

GET UP TO 4 FREE BOOKS!

You can have the best romance delivered to your door for less than what you'd pay in a bookstore or online. Sign up for one of our book clubs today, and we'll send you **FREE* BOOKS** just for trying it out...**with no obligation to buy, ever!**

HISTORICAL ROMANCE BOOK CLUB

Travel from the Scottish Highlands to the American West, the decadent ballrooms of Regency England to Viking ships. Your shipments will include authors such as CONNIE MASON, CASSIE EDWARDS, LYNSAY SANDS, LEIGH GREENWOOD, and many, many more.

LOVE SPELL BOOK CLUB

Bring a little magic into your life with the romances of Love Spell—fun contemporaries, paranormals, time-travels, futuristics, and more. Your shipments will include authors such as KATIE MACALISTER, SUSAN GRANT, NINA BANGS, SANDRA HILL, and more.

As a book club member you also receive the following special benefits:

- **30% OFF all orders through our website & telecenter!**
  (Plus, you still get 1 book FREE for every 5 books you buy!)
- **Exclusive access to special discounts!**
- **Convenient home delivery and 10 days to return any books you don't want to keep.**

There is no minimum number of books to buy, and you may cancel membership at any time. See back to sign up!

*Please include $2.00 for shipping and handling.

YES! ☐

Sign me up for the **Historical Romance Book Club** and send my THREE FREE BOOKS! If I choose to stay in the club, I will pay only $13.50* each month, a savings of $6.47!

YES! ☐

Sign me up for the **Love Spell Book Club** and send my TWO FREE BOOKS! If I choose to stay in the club, I will pay only $8.50* each month, a savings of $5.48!

NAME: _____

ADDRESS: _____

_____

TELEPHONE: _____

E-MAIL: _____

☐ **I WANT TO PAY BY CREDIT CARD.**

☐ VISA   ☐ MasterCard.   ☐ DISCOVER

ACCOUNT #: _____

EXPIRATION DATE: _____

SIGNATURE: _____

Send this card along with $2.00 shipping & handling for each club you wish to join, to:

**Romance Book Clubs
1 Mechanic Street
Norwalk, CT 06850-3431**

Or fax (must include credit card information!) to: 610.995.9274.
You can also sign up online at www.dorchesterpub.com.

*Plus $2.00 for shipping. Offer open to residents of the U.S. and Canada only.
Canadian residents please call 1.800.481.9191 for pricing information.

If under 18, a parent or guardian must sign. Terms, prices and conditions subject to change. Subscription subject to acceptance. Dorchester Publishing reserves the right to reject any order or cancel any subscription.

body, and there was no mistaking the hardness that pressed into her stomach. She yearned to pull him closer. She was mesmerized by the evidence of his desire, empowered that she could elicit such a response from him.

"I'm sorry," he mouthed, a mixture of contriteness and yearning in his eyes. "I can't help it," Eli whispered against her cheek.

Don't be, Monica wanted to say. She couldn't help her reaction, either, as her body experienced the closest thing to an orgasm a person could have in public.

She should pull away. Remaining in his arms, pressed up close to his body, would only complicate an already complicated situation. But she couldn't tear herself away from his hold.

When the song ended, Eli trailed his finger down her bare arm as he escorted her back to the table. The sensation of his touch remained upon her skin long after he'd let her go.

Toby called for Eli to follow him downstairs to the stage area so he could introduce him to a few of the band members. As soon as they were out of earshot, Nia slapped the table.

"All I have to say is, good riddance Patrick Dangerfield."

"What are you talking about?" Monica said, trying not to watch Eli walk away, but watching all the same.

"Girl, you may not think you and that man are serious about each other, but from what I just saw, you're lying to yourself."

Monica forced herself to look over at Nia. "Don't start. I told you this is just a business deal."

"Honey, I've been in the business world for a few years now, and I have never been hugged up on any of my business partners." Monica attempted to speak, but Nia cut her off. "You didn't see the look in your eyes while you were dancing with him, Monica. This isn't just business for you."

A bead of panic threaded through Monica's bloodstream. Nia was right. She did want him. She didn't just want him—she *burned* for him. But was she setting herself up for heartache?

This was different from what she'd had with Patrick. Although she now realized that what she and Patrick had felt for each other wasn't even close to love, Monica had truly believed it was the real thing at the beginning of their relationship.

But she hadn't gone blind into this thing with Eli. She knew his stand on dating doctors, his reputation for being a player. Forget the message his body had sent while they were dancing; that was purely physical. Monica knew that desire did not reach his heart. And if she didn't take control of this situation soon, it was her own heart that would be in danger of being crushed.

Monica sat at the table in quiet contemplation for nearly the entire hour they remained at the club, getting up only once to dance with Toby during Aria's second performance. When they left the club, Monica sat rigidly in the passenger seat, her mind reeling, her confused emotions feeding the headache that had started forming toward the end of the evening.

"This was so much fun," Nia said from the backseat. "Your brother is a piece of work."

"Yeah, Toby knows how to have a good time," Eli answered.

Monica didn't join in their conversation. Instead she spent the drive home reacquainting herself with her common sense, and all the reasons she could not allow this attraction to consume her. Elijah Holmes was a means to an end. Period. She would not lose sight of her ultimate goal.

Yet Monica was unbearably conscious of every time Eli's sultry gaze fell upon her from his place behind the wheel.

They arrived at her apartment building, and like the perfect gentleman, Eli again opened the door for her and for Nia. Monica clutched his hand tightly, grateful for the support.

"I'll walk the two of you upstairs," he offered. He placed his hand at the small of her back as he followed them upstairs. She had been trying to steel herself from the effects of his heated stares and velvety soft words, but that one touch was enough to make her faint.

"I'm getting too old for this," Nia said. "It's just after midnight and I'm about to drop. That was a joke," she said after neither Monica nor Eli responded to her quip.

Nia looked back, giving them both a curious look.

Monica shot her a wan smile, but she could tell by the slight upward curve of Nia's mouth that her best friend had correctly read the situation.

They arrived at her front door. Monica could have kicked herself for not getting the key out sooner, but her mind was occupied with too much to think about anything so mundane. She searched through her black clutch and came up with the key.

Nia grabbed it out of her hand and quickly opened the door. "I'll be in the shower," she said, closing the door behind her and leaving Monica and Eli in the hallway.

Monica turned to face Eli. "Thanks for putting up with us," she said softly.

She could tell by the look in his eyes that he was nowhere near ready to leave. Monica could not deal with this tonight. Her scattered brain was still too fraught with the dozens of conflicting emotions that had plagued her since the second she chose to take him up on that ill-fated plan. Of all the colossal mistakes and bad judgment calls she had ever made—and she'd made plenty—Monica had a feeling this pretend dating scheme was at the top of the list.

Because she did not want it to be pretend anymore.

Her mind fought against the revelation. She knew better

than to let her heart get involved. It had let her down too many times before. Yet just thinking about how it had felt to be pressed against his decadent body had her heart turning over within her chest.

But she would *not* allow it to be broken again.

"Is that all you're going to say?" Eli asked, his deep voice reverberating off the walls of her brain.

Monica decided to play off the whole thing like it wasn't that big of a deal. He'd said he wasn't looking for a relationship, either. Maybe pretending that her reaction tonight was just a part of the charade was the way to get this situation back on a platonic plane.

Monica shrugged. "It was a fun night."

"That's all it was, a fun night?"

"What else do you want me to say, Dr. Holmes?"

"Don't start with the Dr. Holmes again, Monica."

She stretched her hands out in front of her, putting on her best bewildered act. "What do you expect me to say?" she asked again.

Eli crossed his arms over his muscular chest. "We can't deny what happened tonight," he stated bluntly.

"Nothing happened," Monica replied. She turned, intending to go into her apartment, but Eli stopped her.

"Are you saying you didn't feel anything while we were dancing?"

"Except for the obvious, you mean?"

His expression hardened. "It was a natural reaction brought on by something I know you felt, too." He stared at her, his brown eyes piercing. He stepped in close, his body encasing her. Monica felt her back pressing into the door with each ragged breath she took. "I saw the way you looked at me. I *felt* the way you looked at me," he whispered with fierce intensity. "Do you expect me to believe you didn't feel that, too?"

Monica shuddered, even as her blood began to simmer

at the passion flowing off his body in waves. "Eli, please, I can't handle this right now. Just go home."

"I didn't expect this, either, Monica." His voice dropped to a gentle tone that was nearly her undoing.

"Eli, please," she pleaded. If he didn't leave right now, she was going to lose it.

Everything in his stare said he didn't want to go, but after a moment he stepped back. "We'll talk about this tomorrow," Eli said. "I'll pick you up at noon."

"I thought you said two o'clock."

"That's what time we'll get to Mama's, but you and I need to talk." Without another word, he turned and headed down the hall.

Monica's eyelids slid shut. She pressed the back of her head against the door.

This was more than just a mistake. It was a disaster.

Chapter Fifteen

The tiny back for her earring fell to the hardwood floor with a soft ping.

"Great," Amanda hissed. If she stooped down to look for it, it would take her an hour to get up from the floor. Amanda closed her eyes and took a deep, irritated breath.

She fumbled through her wooden jewelry box, searching for another pair of earrings that would match her dress and shoes, but came up with nothing.

She was being punished. She was convinced.

She crossed the hallway from the guest bedroom to the master suite.

She had kept her distance from this part of the house. The memories were too strong, even though she and Jeffrey had not been man and wife in the true sense of the phrase for some time now. Well, except for the night she had become pregnant.

The door was opened slightly. She pushed it a fraction wider, but stopped at the sight of Jeffrey's naked torso.

He had a gorgeous body. Always had. She still missed snuggling up next to it at night. Even though her bipolar medications carried a risk of sexual side effects, she and Jeffrey had never had a problem in that arena until last year.

She stared wordlessly as Jeffrey pulled a plain white T-shirt over his head. He picked up a salmon-colored button-down from the bed.

"Jeffrey," Amanda said, opening the door all the way and walking into the room.

His head came up, his eyes darting to her stomach, which she cradled in her palms.

"What's wrong?" he asked, his voice etched with concern.

"Oh, nothing like that," Amanda answered, quickly dropping her hands. Now she felt even more of a fool for asking what she was about to ask. "I need your help."

She noticed his head rear back slightly, and there was no mistaking the hint of surprise on his face.

"What do you need?" He slowly drew his arms through the sleeves of his shirt.

"My earring. I dropped the backing. If I try to get it myself, I'll never get up."

The makings of a smile crept onto Jeffrey's face, lifting one corner of his mouth into that sexy grin she had fallen in love with. Suddenly she was filled with regret.

Jeffrey strode to where she stood, stopping only inches in front of her. He was so close that Amanda had to tilt her head up to see his face.

"What does it look like?" he asked. His voice had dropped at least an octave.

It took a second for his question to register. For some reason, her mind had become infatuated with looking into his golden brown eyes.

"Uh . . . like this." Amanda tilted her head to the side and brushed the hair from around her ear. "It's the little gold thing on the back that keeps the earring in place. It should be right around the dresser, if it didn't roll too far when it hit the floor."

Without another word, Jeffrey left the master suite.

Amanda looked around the room. This was the first time she had been back in here since the day she'd packed her bags and left.

Not much had changed. He'd replaced the bedding, but, then, Amanda knew he would. Jeffrey hated the lilac floral comforter she'd purchased. He preferred the old white bedspread that was nearly threadbare.

Amanda tried not to glance at the tall chest of drawers to her right, but as if she'd been told not to think of the white elephant in the room, her eyes went straight to it and to the picture she knew she would find there. It was the one of her and Jeffrey on a beach in Montego Bay. It was encased in a handmade frame decorated with various seashells they had collected from the shore.

That trip had been one of the happiest times in her life, right before they had made the decision to start a family. She wondered how different things would be if they had chosen to remain a childless couple.

She'd had the disease under control. Her doctor had found a drug regimen that kept both the mania and depression in check, even through the years of fertility treatments. It was when she'd actually conceived for the first time, and her chaotic hormones had interfered with the drugs' effectiveness, that things started spiraling out of control.

Amanda placed a reverent hand on her belly. She was willing to pay any price, even her marriage, to have this baby. Dr. Berkenshire had tried to convince her that a divorce was not necessary, but Amanda knew how Jeffrey felt about living with someone with bipolar disorder. She refused to subject him to a life of misery, the way her mother had subjected her father.

But, God, she would miss him.

Jeffrey returned, the tiny gold earring backing between his thumb and forefinger. His shirt was unbuttoned, and the T-shirt underneath clung to his chiseled chest and stomach.

"Do you need help putting it on?" he asked.

Yes. No. She didn't know. When had this deluge of confusion overcome her body? Why did she picture herself all of a sudden in her soon-to-be ex-husband's arms?

Amanda's head started to pound. Looking into his eyes, she fought back tears. An overwhelming flood of dread washed over her, weighing down on her chest, nearly smothering her.

Oh, God, her head hurt. She couldn't breathe.

Why was her head spinning? What was she doing here? Why was she in her old bedroom? And with Jeffrey?

How could she be around him after what he'd done to her? The man had crushed her heart. She'd seen it with her own eyes. He had thrown away eleven years of marriage on a tramp who wasn't worth the fake Jimmy Choo shoes she'd been wearing the day Amanda saw them together.

She had to get away from here. From him.

Stop it, Amanda chided herself. It wasn't true. Jeffrey would never cheat on her.

But she'd seen them together!

"I've got it," Amanda said, snatching the backing from his fingers. She turned to leave, but Jeffrey stopped her, grabbing her shoulder.

"Amanda, wait."

"Let go of me," she growled between clenched teeth. "I need to finish getting ready for church."

"No. We need to talk."

"I said let go of me." Amanda tried to move, but his grasp was firm.

"Dammit, Amanda, I'm tired of this. Would you sit down and talk to me?"

She spun out of his hold, her body shaking in anger.

"Do you think I care about what you're tired of, Jeffrey? Do you think I care about what *you* want? I'm tired of a lot of things, like a lying, cheating husband." His stunned expression didn't register. She could see nothing pass her own fury and confusion. God, she was so confused.

No, she tried to tell herself. Jeffrey wouldn't betray her. *But she saw them!*

"I'm tired of living here with you, pretending everything is okay when we both know it's not," she screamed. "I'm tired of having to look at your face and remember what you did to me. I can't do it anymore, Jeffrey! It's over! I don't care how many flowers you bring or gourmet dinners you prepare. Nothing is going to change. It's *over!*"

Amanda stormed out of the room, barely making it to the guest room before collapsing on the bed in a heap of silent sobs.

When Eli found himself standing before Monica's front door for the second time in twelve hours, he felt better than he had the first time. He'd hardly been able to sleep last night, thoughts about the impending conversation taking precedence over everything, even sleep.

After the explosion of mutual desire they had shared at the club, Eli was determined to take this so-called pretend relationship to another level.

Alex was right. It was stupid to write off all female doctors because of the actions of one. Monica was not Elizabeth. Monica possessed scruples, something that other woman wouldn't know about.

Eli did not deny Monica was using him, just as Elizabeth had, but at least Monica was up front about it. She had not tried to manipulate him into helping her with the banquet. Monica told him exactly why she wanted his help, and agreed to help him in return. She was honest, and one hundred eighty degrees different from Elizabeth Graves.

And Monica was attracted to him. Of that he had no doubt. The minute his eyes had drifted to hers and he'd seen the desire and lust, Eli knew her feelings mirrored his own. She wanted him.

He knocked. Nia opened the door.

"Eli. Hi. Come on in."

"You do that all the time?" Eli asked as he followed her into the apartment's small foyer.

"Do what?" She motioned him to follow her deeper into the apartment, granting Eli his first view inside Monica's private domain.

"Open doors in strange cities without asking who's on the other side of it?" he asked, taking a seat on the blue leather couch.

The room was decorated in warm colors: soft browns, reds, and muted yellows with touches of green and blue. Framed African prints and masks hung on the walls, and several small wooden sculptures sat on end tables and on the mantel over the fake fireplace.

"You sound like my husband," Nia said. "You know, that man sent an intern from his law firm to the house, pretending to be a carpet salesman. Needless to say, Phillip went ballistic when I let him in without question."

"I don't blame him. The world is a scary place. You can't trust people. Is Monica getting ready?" Eli asked, too wired to engage in another second of chitchat.

"She's not here," Nia answered. "And I'm angry because I just found out I have to fly home today, and we haven't spent any real time together."

Eli could feel his blood begin to boil. "Did she say where she was going?"

"Nope. When I woke up this morning, she was already dressed. She said you would probably stop by, and told me to tell you something came up and she had to cancel."

"Do think she went to the hospital?" Eli asked, giving Monica the benefit of the doubt. He hoped whatever her excuse was, it was a good one.

Nia shrugged. "Not sure. She didn't seem dressed for the hospital, though. I was just about to throw some clothes on and walk down to Canal Street for some shopping. I haven't spent nearly enough money here, and now that the knuckleheads I work with have completely screwed up one of our largest accounts, I don't have time to do any real damage to the credit card."

"I'm sure you can put a hurting on it, even with limited time," Eli said, rising from the sofa.

"I'm still going to try to make Sunday dinner at your mom's. You said her cooking was better than the Praline Connection. I'm not taking your word for it, though. I've got to find out for myself."

"You're welcome to come over. You need me to pick you up?"

"No, just give me the address. I'm not sure what part of the city I'll be in, so I'll just grab a cab."

He jotted down his mother's address and gave Nia a parting kiss on the cheek. Eli didn't know whether to feel hurt, anger, or outright rage as he exited the apartment building.

She'd backed out on him.

He had a mind to drive over to the hospital to see if she was there, but decided against it. He wouldn't chase after her. They had a meeting with the banquet committee tomorrow, and she would not be able to run away from him then.

Eli hopped in his SUV and drove out to Armstrong Park. He needed an outlet for his pent-up energy. And since Monica wasn't around, exercise would have to do.

He grabbed his gym bag from the back of the Rover and dipped into a restroom, changing into running shorts and his old pair of cross-trainers. He ran back to his truck, deposited the bag on the front seat, then took off on the concrete path that wound through the park.

Eli started out at a slow jog, grateful the park wasn't crowded. He needed the solitude to clear his mind.

He had to figure out what to do about Monica. Their situation had changed, whether or not she wanted to admit it. When they had first agreed to this pretense, neither could have known this intense craving would surface. But it could not be denied any longer.

The thought of turning their relationship into something more serious scared the hell out of him. He had gone back and forth over all the reasons he should break things off completely. Opening himself up for the pain that could eventually come was just plain stupid. He'd felt that pain before, and he'd made a promise to himself that he would never feel it again.

But he also knew not to let go of a good thing when he found it. And Monica Gardner was a good thing. A *really* good thing.

It was time for a renegotiation of their deal . . . as soon as he could get Monica to sit still long enough to talk to him. This avoidance game she was playing couldn't last forever. That was the beauty of working together.

As the mist from the pond blew across his skin, Eli thought out the conversation he and Monica would have tomorrow. It was a foregone conclusion that she wouldn't show for dinner at Mama's.

He had almost forgotten about dinner. Eli checked his watch, surprised at how much time had elapsed; then he took in his surroundings and realized he had run farther than he'd originally planned. He had to double-time it as he reversed directions and headed back to where he had parked.

Eli stopped over at the hospital anyway. He told himself that it made more sense to come here and shower than to drive all the way to his home in Old Metairie—but if showering was the only thing on his mind, then why did he use the ER entrance instead of the one he usually used?

In the end, it didn't matter. Monica wasn't in the ER, and according to the nurse he questioned, she had not been there all morning.

Where in the hell had she run off to?

Though the more important question was *why* she had run. The answer was obvious: She was afraid of what they'd discovered last night. Unlike Eli, Monica wasn't ready to face this newfound passion.

It was nearly two thirty when Eli pulled in behind Alex's F-150 on the graveled driveway that ran the length of his mother's house. As always, the smell of Margo Holmes's cooking perfumed the air. Smelled like fried okra and baked chicken were on today's menu. Eli could only hope that Mama had some of her creamy mashed potatoes to go with them.

He made his way through the throng of green foliage on the back porch and stopped dead in his tracks when he opened the door and found Monica and Nia sitting at the small kitchen table with his mother and Alex.

"It's about time," Margo said, rising from her seat and giving Eli a kiss on the cheek. "We were about to start eating without you. Let's move to the dining room. Tobias, Jasmine," she called out.

Carrying Jasmine piggyback, Toby came through the

door that led to the side of the house where the bedrooms were.

"It's so nice to finally use this table again," his mother said. "With just the four of us, we usually just eat in the kitchen."

The dining room table was decked out with a lace table-cloth and satin placemats. Mama had broken out her wedding china to set the table, and even had a short vase filled with fresh flowers for a centerpiece.

"Everything looks great, Mama," Eli said, taking a seat directly across from Monica.

She avoided eye contact, choosing to focus her attention on the place setting in front of her.

Toby sat across from Nia, and Alex and his mother sat at the opposite heads of the table. Jasmine sat at the chair Alex had dragged from the kitchen table and placed between his and Eli's spots.

"What's up, my little African Violet," Eli whispered to his niece.

She rolled her eyes. "Hi, Uncle Eli."

"Are we ready to eat?" Margo asked.

Nia's "Yes, indeed" was heard above everyone. "I was told this is the best food in New Orleans, and I've been waiting to find out if it's true."

"I can assure you," Toby said. "It's the truth."

"Well, all right then," Nia said.

"Since Tobias is home, I think he should have the honor of saying grace," Margo said.

"Sure, Mama," Toby answered. "I know E has probably forgotten how to say grace, since it's been so long since he's gone to church."

"Just say the damn prayer," Eli snarled.

"Elijah Marcus! Not at the dinner table, and especially not in front of company. I apologize, ladies." Mama looked over at Nia and Monica. "My sons tend to revert to adolescents when they get together."

"As do most men," Nia remarked, eliciting a laugh from the women at the table.

Eli caught Monica's lame attempt at a smile. If she didn't relax soon, his mother would know something was up. It did not take much to raise Margo Holmes's antennae.

Eli looked at Monica across the table, and—surprise, surprise—she actually looked back. He sent Monica a silent but unmistakable message: *Don't blow this!* Convincing his mother they were a couple was the whole point of their deal. If they didn't start acting like one, Mama would definitely pick up on it.

"Tobias, grace," his mother said. They all held hands and bowed their heads.

"Heavenly Father, bless this food, the cook who slaved over it, and the people who are about to tear it up. Amen."

"That was very adult," Alex commented, tearing his dinner roll and placing half on Jasmine's plate.

"Thank you," Toby responded. "Now can we eat, please? This is the first meal I've had in four months that didn't come from a box."

Ceramic dishes filled with mashed potatoes, baked and fried chicken, smothered greens, fried okra, and buttered corn made their way around the table.

"I've told you about eating that processed garbage, Tobias," Margo chastised.

"It hasn't killed me yet."

"But Mama will," Alex laughed. "You're going to have to get some dry ice and start shipping him meals if you want that fool to eat right."

"She won't have to ship it too far, right, Toby?" Eli asked. Toby gave him a murderous look, which Eli returned, making sure his brother knew that mentioning his possible return to New Orleans was payback for the crack about church. Too bad Mama didn't catch the hint.

"You've been quiet, Monica," Alex said.

Everyone's attention turned to where Monica sat nibbling a piece of chicken. Eli's heart skipped a beat.

"Alex is right, sweetheart. Is everything okay?" his mother asked.

"Oh, I'm fine," Monica answered.

"She couldn't get a word in with all this talking," Toby said in Monica's defense.

"I was just thinking how different this is," Monica said. "My family never ate meals together."

"That's so sad," Margo said. "I cannot imagine sitting at the table without my boys around me."

"And me," Jasmine inserted.

"And you, too, baby girl. Sunday dinner is an institution in this house."

"It really is lovely, even the bickering," Monica said, her smile more genuine this time.

"You haven't heard bickering yet," Alex said. He licked mashed potatoes off his right knuckle and pointed two fingers in Eli and Toby's direction. "Get these two on the golf course. It's like a replay of Tyson versus Holyfield."

"I'm just happy they haven't hurt each other yet, at least not enough to require medical attention," Mama said.

Eli exchanged a smile with Toby, though he still wanted to knock his brother upside the head.

To Eli's surprise, Alex kept Monica engaged even more than Mama. Several times over the course of dinner, he brought Monica into the table's discussion. Nia needed no one's help. She was a natural conversationalist and had charmed the apron strings right off Mama.

It wasn't until Alex started asking more personal questions—seemingly out of the blue—that Eli started to suspect his brother was up to something. Alex tried to play it smooth, addressing both Monica and Nia about how they chose their careers, what part their families had played in their decisions, and whether anyone other than family had influenced them, but Alex wasn't known for his subtlety. Every time his older brother opened his mouth, Eli cringed.

"I always had my heart set on being a doctor," Monica said, her elbows resting on the table, hands folded under her chin.

"It's a hectic job. Even though we live in the same city, E and I can go a week without seeing each other."

"He gets enough complaints from me," Mama chimed in.

"I understand," Monica said, sending Nia a knowing look. "But career goals have always been very important in my family."

"Putting in long hours is second nature to the Gardners," Nia added.

"None of your boyfriends ever complained?" Alex asked Monica.

Eli nearly kicked his brother under the table.

"Well, it did pose a problem a few times, but nothing major," Monica said, glancing uncomfortably around the table.

"It's a good thing you and Eli are together. You understand each other's schedules. It's like a perfect match."

Eli's fists clinched. What was Alex doing? Eli wanted to do this on *his* time. He did not need an older brother, who was as inconspicuous as a brick landing on Monica's head, bombarding her with a bunch of private questions.

His mother blessedly ended the conversation by announcing ice cream and apple pie for dessert.

"Eli, can you help me in the kitchen?" his mother asked as she rose from the table.

Eli wiped his mouth and pushed his seat back. He followed his mother into the kitchen and headed for the freezer to get the ice cream.

"Elijah—"

He closed his eyes briefly and turned. "Look, Mama, I know what you're about to say."

"No, you don't. You see—"

A knock at the door stopped her.

Chapter Sixteen

His mother's eyelids slid shut, and a pained expression came over her face. "I forgot to ask Tosha not to come over for dessert," she finished.

"You what? Mama!"

"I know you all are in there." Eli heard the high-pitched voice coming from the porch and cursed himself for not locking the door behind him. Had the wrongs he'd committed over the years really been bad enough to deserve this?

"There you two are," Tosha said, walking through the back door and into the kitchen. She cradled a dish in her hands. "I brought along a lemon and ginseng pie."

"Oh . . . that's so thoughtful of you, honey," his mother said, taking the pie from Tosha's hands and placing it next to the apple pie on the tray.

"How are you doing, Eli?" Tosha crooned, snuggling entirely too close to him. He didn't want any of her ginseng fumes rubbing onto his clothes.

"I'm good, Tosha," Eli answered.

His mother gave him a *what-do-we-do-now?* look, which Eli returned with a look that said *how-do-you-expect-me-to-know?* Though for Eli, after how the rest of the day had unfolded, Tosha's showing up to the same dinner where both Monica and her sister-in-law were in attendance seemed par for the course.

That instant, Eli made the decision to return to church. He was definitely praying for past sins.

All three heads spun when Monica walked into the kitchen. They were silent for a second, and then both Eli and Mama began speaking at the same time.

"I'm sorry," Mama said, overspeaking her son. "Monica, this is Tosha Culpepper, an old friend of the family."

Eli shot his mother a surprised look. At least her tune had changed.

"Nice to meet you, Tosha," Monica strolled toward them, her hand extended.

Tosha shook Monica's hand. "Are you here with Toby? I heard he was in town."

Monica looked pointedly at Eli.

"Monica and I work together at Methodist Memorial," Eli said. "We've been seeing each other."

"I'm going to serve dessert," Mama said, making a quick exit from the tension-filled kitchen.

"I didn't realize you were attached, Elijah." Tosha's voice had taken on a definite edge.

"Eli," Monica interrupted. "I'd come to tell you and your mother that I have to be going. I need to take a nap before my shift starts tonight."

"Okay," he answered. "We'll talk tomorrow," he added in a tone that could not be misinterpreted.

"Nice meeting you," she said to Tosha, electing not to respond to his statement.

Tosha didn't answer. When Monica was gone, she turned

to him. Eli took an instinctive step back. The woman was geared for attack.

"So, were you not going to tell me you had a girlfriend? Were you going to just play along as if you were single?" Her voice escalated with each question. "Are you two serious, or are you stringing her along like you do every woman you've ever been with? You will never change, Elijah."

The conversation in the other room had stopped. *Damn*. Alex and Toby would rib him for the next five years after this.

"I don't know what I ever saw in you," Tosha continued, her squeal reaching an all-time high. "You are nothing but a conceited, two-timing dog. You're going to get yours, Elijah Holmes. And I hope it hurts like hell!"

She took off like a rocket, slamming both the kitchen and porch doors on her way out. The house was eerily quiet, the only sound coming from the boom of someone's stereo as they cruised down the street.

Eli leaned against the kitchen counter and threw his head back, pinching the bridge of his nose. If this was the turn his life had taken, he would need more than just church to overcome it. He was going to Bible study, too. He might even stay around for the fellowship hour.

"Is everything okay?"

Eli opened his eyes and looked over at his mother standing at the edge of the doorway that led from the kitchen into the dining room.

"I'm not bleeding," he answered. "That's the best that could be expected."

"I don't know how I forgot to call her. It just slipped my mind."

"I hope you don't enjoy the lemon and ginseng pie too much. I doubt you'll be getting another anytime soon." He looked over at her, his eyes probing. Eli crossed his arms over his chest and braced his feet slightly apart. "What did you tell her, Mama?"

He couldn't wait to see how she talked her way out of this one.

"Tell who?" She walked over to the sink and started stacking the pots and pans on the counter.

"Don't start doing those dishes. I want to know what you told her."

"Who?"

"Tosha. What did you tell Tosha?"

"I didn't tell her anything."

Yeah, right. As screwy as Tosha was, even she wouldn't just assume there was something between the two of them after fifteen years.

"Did you tell her there was a chance the two of us would get back together?"

She looked over her shoulder. "Now, you know better than that, Elijah."

"I know *you*," he said, walking toward her. "It would not be the first time you meddled in one of your sons' lives."

She shook her head, refusing to look him in the eye. That told Eli that whatever was about to come out of her mouth was not the whole truth.

"I didn't give her any impression, one way or the other."

"Mm-hmm."

Mama turned and plunked a hand on her hip. *"Mais, ja mais d'la vie."*

Oh, yeah, she was lying. Whenever his mother wasn't telling the truth, she'd revert to the Cajun French she learned growing up in the Acadian section of western Louisiana.

"You don't have to believe me," she mumbled.

"Mama, I'm with Monica."

"And I couldn't be happier," Mama answered, her eyes lighting up. "She is lovely. I agree with Alex—the two of you are perfect together."

"I'm happy you think so, but do me a favor: don't butt in."

Her mouth gaped open. "When do I ever butt—"

Eli caught her open lips between his fingers and closed them. "Don't even finish that statement."

She rolled her eyes at him. "Go and get yourself some dessert."

"Only if you come with me. Your sons will do the dishes."

Mama threw the dish towel she'd just snatched from the drawer onto the counter. "Well, isn't it nice to have all three of my boys home? I could certainly get used to y'all taking care of me for a while."

Eli put his arm around her waist and bent down to give her smooth black hair a peck. "Come on, we've got lemon pie waiting for us."

"You can eat it. I'm not getting near that pie."

"Nia's probably finished it, anyway."

"That girl sure likes her food, doesn't she? Too bad she's married. She would be perfect for Toby."

Eli squeezed her shoulder. "Don't start."

After dessert had been eaten and all the dishes stacked in the kitchen, Alex broke out the Scrabble game. They formed teams: Alex and Mama, Nia and Toby, and Eli and Jasmine, who had the advantage of having none of their words challenged since no one dared tell Jasmine her made-up words were not real.

When it came time for Nia to leave, Eli offered her a ride to the airport, much to the ire of his two brothers, who were left with a mile-high stack of dishes.

They drove back to Monica's apartment, and Eli brought

down Nia's bags, which she admitted numbered more after her earlier shopping expedition.

They headed west on I-10 toward Louis Armstrong International Airport.

"So, did you enjoy your stay in the city?" he asked.

"I loved it. It's good to see the city coming back. I'll definitely remember more from this one than the last time I came down here."

"It's probably best you don't remember that first trip. Most people seem to regret the combination of Mardi Gras and booze. It tends to loosen inhibitions."

"I'm sure I've subconsciously blocked it all out," Nia laughed, then she turned to him. "Okay, enough with the crap."

Eli looked over from the driver side, surprised at her swift change of demeanor.

"I like you. You're cute, you've got a good job, and you seem to have your head on your shoulders. That's why I'm trusting you with my dearest friend." The look on her face could only be described as dead serious. "I'm telling you now, Elijah Holmes, if you break her heart, I will come down here and kick your behind. I've fought a man before. Don't think I wouldn't do it again."

Okay, so Nia was *way* overprotective of Monica. In fact, it seemed as if she was trying to prevent something that had happened once before. She would not be this concerned without good reason. Monica had been hurt, and Nia Gardner knew the story. Now, how could he get it out of her?

It was crucial that he learn who and what had hurt Monica. Well, knowing *who* wasn't really necessary, but Eli wanted to know anyway. He at least wanted the name of the biggest fool on the face of the earth.

Knowing *what*, however, was essential. If he knew what

had hurt her, he had a better chance of not doing the same. But could he get that kind of information out of Nia?

Obviously Monica had not divulged the truth of their arrangement, which surprised him. Women always talked about this kind of stuff, especially two as close as Monica and Nia. It made him feel guilty for spilling his guts to Alex.

The fact that Nia didn't know about their deal worked to his advantage, since he was ready to throw the deal out the window and pursue a serious relationship with Monica anyway. If Nia knew about their bargain, she would be skeptical about sharing anything from Monica's past.

Eli took his right hand off the wheel and placed it over his heart. "I promise, with my whole heart, never to hurt Monica."

"Does this mean you're serious about her?" she asked, a curious raise to her eyebrows.

"Most definitely," he answered without hesitation. More than even Monica knew.

"Good," Nia straightened in her seat and looked forward. "So when Phillip and I come back, you and Monica will still be together." This was a statement, not a question.

Eli caught the note of triumph in her voice, as if she'd orchestrated the entire thing. He flashed her a quick glance. Was he being played?

They arrived at the airport. Eli drove up the ramp to the loading zone and pulled in at the outside check-in kiosk. He opened the door to the back, where her bags were stored, and motioned for a skycap.

Nia alighted from the Rover. "Thanks for the ride." She hefted a small carry-on bag over her shoulder.

"No problem." Eli handed the skycap a ten-dollar bill. He gave Nia a hug. "Don't make yourself a stranger."

"You fed me your mama's cooking. You can't get rid of me now."

Eli chuckled. "Margo Holmes's kitchen is always open."

"You'd better watch what you say. I won't hesitate to hop on a plane and fly down here when the mood for gumbo hits me. I've been known to do some crazy things in the pursuit of good food."

"As I said, you are always welcome." Eli reached into his pocket and retrieved his wallet. He pulled out one of his cards, realizing the first step in getting information out of Nia started with establishing contact apart from Monica. "My office, pager, and cell numbers are on here, along with my e-mail. If you ever want to surprise Monica again, but don't want to get a cab from the airport, give me a ring."

"I just may take you up on that. Hold on a minute." Eli tried to hide his smile as Nia shuffled through her purse. She came up with a business card. "If you need anything, just let me know. Now, you take care of my girl."

"Yes, ma'am." They exchanged another light hug. "Have a good flight."

Eli remained where he stood until Nia walked through the automatic doors. When she was gone, he got in his SUV and headed back for Mama's. He hoped Alex and Toby had already washed the dishes.

Chapter Seventeen

Cheating husband.

Of all the vile, intolerable words to spew from Amanda's mouth during her tirade, *cheat* was the one that continued to ring through Jeffrey's mind.

If there was one thing he had never thought about throughout their eleven years of marriage, it was to cheat on his wife. Even during their estrangement this past year, when she wouldn't so much as look his way while other women practically threw themselves at him, Jeffrey had not considered for one minute sleeping with another woman.

Why would she even suggest it? Was it just to hurt him? Was she trying to catch him off guard? She'd accomplished both.

Jeffrey capped the torch and put his welding tools away. The guys for the night shift were starting to trickle in, and he wanted to be out of here as soon as his relief walked through the shop door.

He and Amanda had a long night ahead of them. He had to get to the bottom of her suspicions.

Jeffrey exchanged the pertinent facts of the business with Raynaud, his counterpart on the night shift, and left the shipyard. Twenty minutes later, he pulled into the driveway, his shoulders sinking in relief at the sight of Amanda's car. All day he had feared he would come home to find her gone.

Instead of pulling alongside it, Jeffrey parked the Explorer behind her Nissan Altima, blocking the car in. He was not giving her an easy escape.

Jeffrey grabbed his lunch kit from the passenger seat and headed for the side door that lead to the utility room. He deposited his steel toe boots and Nomex jumpsuit, changing into the jeans and T-shirt he left hanging on the coat hook behind the door.

Amanda was at the sink, frantically rubbing two potatoes together as she held them under running water.

"Do you think I cheated on you?" Jeffrey asked without preamble.

She jumped, the potatoes falling from her hands. She turned. "My goodness, Jeffrey," she said, putting one still-wet hand to her chest. "Are you crazy?"

"Answer my question?"

"What's your problem?"

"The fact that my wife thinks I screwed around on her."

She turned back to the sink and resumed washing the potatoes, her hands moving in quick, jerky motions. "Jeffrey, I don't have the time or energy for this."

Jeffrey shook his head as he walked up behind her. "No, you are not turning your back on me." He grabbed both of Amanda's wrists in one fist and used his other hand to turn off the water. He turned her around to face him. "I'm not going to let you accuse me of something I didn't do. Why did you say that yesterday?"

"Don't manhandle me." She tried to yank her wrists, but his grasp was too firm. Jeffrey tightened his grip even more.

"Why, Amanda?"

"Do you want me to use big letters and neon lights?" she yelled.

"Yes. Apparently I need you to spell it out for me, since I have no idea what you're talking about."

"Oh, don't give me that, Jeffrey. You know what you did."

"I know for eleven years I went to work every day so I could provide for my wife. And instead of appreciation, I get accused of cheating."

Amanda looked up at him, a mixture of anger and disbelief etched on her face. "Unbelievable. You have the audacity to still deny it." Her voice escalated. "How long did it last, Jeffrey? The relationship, not the individual bouts of sex. I have a rough idea how long those lasted. Unless, of course, she was able to keep you more excited. Is that why you went to her in the first place? Was I not stimulating enough for you?" she said, wrenching her arm away.

Jeffrey stood there in shock. He could hardly comprehend the words escaping his wife's mouth.

"You didn't have to sneak around," she continued. Grabbing a towel, she began wiping the countertop in fast, furious circles. "You should have just told me you were ready for something else. It would have saved us both a lot of time and unnecessary heartache." Her last words came out on a sob.

"Amanda, stop it," he said. "You're acting crazy." He grabbed her and turned her around.

Jeffrey heard her swift intake of breath. A sudden icy contempt flashed in her eyes; then they widened in alarm.

"Get away from me!" she screamed, breaking free from his hold.

He didn't let her get far, catching hold of her arm again before she could exit the kitchen. She sobbed in earnest, covering her face with her free hand. The sound tore at his heart. Jeffrey wrapped his arms around her, tucking her head in the curve of his shoulder and resting his chin on her soft hair.

"Amanda, where is this coming from?"

"Just stop it," she sobbed.

"Stop what?"

"The lies."

Jeffrey raised his head and gently pulled her away so he could look into her eyes. They were wet, luminous, and full of hurt. His heart felt crushed within his chest.

"Why?" he asked on a whisper. He cleared the lump that had formed in his throat. "Why do you think I'm lying, Amanda? How . . . how could you think I would *ever* stray from you?"

She pushed away from him, wrapping her arms around the wide girth of her belly. "Don't you dare talk to me like I'm some stupid child. I saw the two of you, Jeffrey. Don't try to pretend it didn't happen, because I saw you!" Looking wide-eyed and confused, she turned away.

"I have never been with anyone else since the day we starting dating—since the day I first laid eyes on you. Even when I was still dating your sister, I refused to sleep with Regina because I knew from the moment I saw you that you were the woman I would spend the rest of my life with. You are the only one I have ever wanted, Amanda!"

"I. Saw. You," she repeated through gritted teeth. "You had her in my house. In my house, Jeffrey! I'm sorry, but I can't forget that. And I won't forgive you."

She turned, heading for the back bedrooms. This time Jeffrey let her go. Baffled by her accusations, he couldn't think of anything else to say. How could he defend himself for something he had never done?

Anxiety gnawed at his brain. Amanda had it in her mind that he had been with another woman, and not only that he had been with her, but that he had brought her to their house.

How could she even . . .

When she had first filed for divorce, he had agreed without much resistance, knowing it was inevitable after her withdrawal the previous year.

He'd nearly driven himself crazy trying to figure out what had gone wrong. After some time, he simply resigned himself to the fact that Amanda had just grown tired of being married, as some people do. Jeffrey had not thought for a minute that the reason behind her distant behavior had anything to do with infidelity.

They had to straighten this out. Had to. But he'd lived with Amanda for eleven years, and he knew how stubborn she was. It would take an act of God to convince her that what she thought was the case was actually the furthest thing from the truth.

It didn't matter. He wasn't about to let his wife throw away the rest of their lives on some fictitious affair.

Monica lifted one eyebrow and stared at the ringing phone. In order for her to answer it, she would have to reach over to the nightstand. That would require movement, something her mind intensely protested.

It stopped ringing, and Monica's body sank with relief. She nestled further into the covers and buried her head in the plush pillow.

The phone rang again.

"Ugh," Monica groaned. She summed up enough strength to stretch out her arm and retrieve the receiver. "Hello," she moaned with sufficient weariness to let whoever was on the other end of the line know that they had awakened her.

"You still asleep?"

It was Nia. Guilt wouldn't work.

"I had a long night," Monica answered.

"All right, then," Nia teased. "Go, Eli."

Monica groaned again. "He had nothing to do with it. Did I not explain my relationship with Eli to you?"

"Unfortunately," Nia drawled.

"I had to pull a double shift. I've had about two hours' sleep and I have to be back at the hospital for a meeting"— Monica rolled onto her side and looked over at the red numbers on the alarm clock—"in about forty-five minutes."

"Then it's a good thing I called. You would have probably overslept."

"I had the alarm set to go off in another five minutes." Monica reached over and shifted the small dial to the off position. No need to suffer the irritating sound of the alarm if she was already awake. She pushed herself up and rested against her soft leather headboard. "What's up?" she asked Nia.

"I was just calling to make sure you were okay. I hate that we didn't get to spend more time together."

"Me too, but you'll be back soon enough."

"Oh, yes, honey. I discovered the shops on Canal Street. I'm a visitor for life."

"It was still fun, though, the time we did get to catch up. Sometimes I forget how much fun it is to hang out and have a good old-fashioned gab session."

"You seem to forget a lot of things, Monica, like how a good man can be just as valuable as a good friend."

Monica rolled her eyes heavenward. How had she just *known* this conversation would return to Eli?

"Give it a rest, Nia." Monica threw the covers off her legs and rolled out of bed, taking a deep stretch before heading to the closet, the phone tucked between her shoulder and ear.

"He's perfect for you."

"How can you say that? You don't even know him."

"From what I do know—"

"Which is barely anything," Monica interjected.

"—he's everything you need," Nia continued, not missing a beat.

"I already explained this to you—it's a business deal. That's it."

"And I'll bet if you suggested it become more, Eli wouldn't turn you down."

"I'm ending this conversation. I need to get dressed and to the hospital."

"Just think about it, Mon."

"Good-bye, Nia," Monica said, then pressed the button on the phone to end the call. She tossed the phone onto her bed and pulled out blue slacks and a soft yellow sweater. She brought the clothes into the bathroom and hung them on the hook behind the door so she could steam out the wrinkles as she showered.

Monica took a quick shower and brushed out her hair. She went to the kitchen and poured herself a bowl of cornflakes.

Monica rested her butt against the counter as she ate her cereal. She looked out over the bar into the open space of the living room.

This place was too quiet.

With Nia's loud mouth gone, the full effect of living alone hit Monica with the force of a hammer. She missed having someone to come home to, someone to snuggle with on the sofa and share her day. She missed the companionship that came with having a significant other.

Maybe Nia was right. Maybe she should find herself a man.

Monica put that notion right out of her head. If she wanted companionship, she would get another goldfish.

They couldn't cuddle, but at least she wouldn't be alone. And a goldfish had the added benefit of being a lot easier to deal with than a man.

Monica tried to focus on the upcoming meeting with the banquet committee, but her mind continued to steer back to Saturday night and the contentment she had felt, cradled in Eli's arms, as they swayed on the dance floor.

He had a strong embrace, the kind that made you feel safe and protected. It had been so long since she'd felt that kind of security.

Monica didn't know whether to feel excited or afraid. Right now, she was feeling a little of both. She knew all too well that elation could turn into heartache in the blink of an eye. She would not put herself through the trouble.

Even if it means never experiencing the rapture of romance ever again?

Monica wasn't sure she was ready to go that far yet. Never allowing herself to experience love again would give Patrick Dangerfield too much power over her. She refused to let his selfish actions play such a big part in her life.

But she wasn't sure Eli was the man she wanted to give her heart to, either. He had his share of issues. The fact that he didn't date doctors was the most prominent, at least where Monica was concerned. Just because he was physically attracted to her, which had become more than evident Saturday night, did not mean he was willing to disregard his rule.

And even if he was willing, did that mean she was just going to fall into his arms? No! The man was . . . Well, he was funny, and handsome, and successful, and had a wonderful family, and . . .

Nia's assertion that Eli was the perfect man for her resounded through Monica's mind. She could not find one credible flaw, not one thing that would have stopped her from pursuing a relationship with him if this were a different time and there were not so many complications involved.

Monica sighed in frustration.

Why was she doing this to herself? She had a billion other things to worry about, yet she chose to waste the morning lamenting over an ex-boyfriend who'd made a fool out of her and a gorgeous coworker who had no doubt dated dozens of attractive women.

Yet he had gotten pretty excited when he'd danced with her Saturday night.

Goodness, girl, you're a doctor!

She should know a simple biological reaction when she saw one or, in this case, *felt* one. He probably would have had the same reaction if he'd been hugged up with an iguana.

Now that was a deflating thought.

Monica rinsed out the bowl and stacked it in the sink. She would wash dishes when she got home tonight. Right after hooking up her new ten-gallon aquarium.

Monica arrived at the hospital a half-hour before the meeting was scheduled to start. She told herself she needed to leave early just in case traffic was heavy, but in a far corner of her mind, the real reason lay as an idle reminder of what her life had become: a lonely existence in a well-decorated apartment.

"Good morning, Dr. Gardner." Patty whizzed by, holding a full IV bag in each hand.

"Morning, Patty. Looks like things are cooking a bit early today, huh?"

"It's been interesting," Patty called.

Monica pulled the first chart from the rack on the admin desk.

And what was her prize today? A scalp laceration behind curtain two, a simple enough way to pass the time before this morning's meeting.

"What are you doing here?" Patty asked as she came around the desk, sans IV bags, marking up a chart.

Monica stuck a couple of ballpoint pens into her coat pocket. "The banquet committee has a meeting. I thought I'd stop by here to see how things are going."

"You work too much, Dr. Gardner."

"That just shows how much I love my job," Monica smiled. *And how little of a life you have outside of work,* Nia's voice chimed in her head.

The scalp lac was so minor that it took only three stitches. Monica dressed the wound herself instead of bothering one of the physician's assistants. When she emerged from behind the curtain area, Eli was waiting for her.

Monica suppressed a groan. Would it have been too much to ask not to see him this morning? Monica resigned herself to her fate; she had known she couldn't avoid him forever.

"Can we please talk, Mon—Dr. Gardner," he amended.

"Actually, I'm busy," Monica said in a light voice, moving around him toward the admin desk.

Eli followed her. He pointed to the dry-erase board hanging on the wall behind the desk, which clearly showed that she was not one of the physicians on shift this morning.

Busted.

"Fine," Monica sighed, signing the discharge papers for the scalp lac and depositing the chart into the proper bin. "What do you want to talk about, Dr. Holmes?"

Eli looked around. "Not here." He grabbed her hand and took her down the hall into a room Monica didn't know existed.

"What is this?" she asked, stepping over a plastic candy cane.

"Old doctors' lounge. They turned it into a storage closet after the renovations. Can we stop with the chitchat and get to the matter at hand?" Eli glanced at his watch. "We only have a few minutes before the meeting starts."

"And the matter at hand is?" Monica asked, her expression purposely perplexed.

"Don't act cute. You know what this is about. You cannot keep avoiding me, Monica. We have a deal."

"Which I am upholding. Actually, I'm surpassing even my own expectations. Your family adores me," she said with a satisfied smirk.

"You hardly spoke at dinner."

"Not true at all. I turned into a bona fide social butterfly once you left the room."

"Why are you being like this?" Eli asked, the sincerity in his voice knocking the wind from her sails.

Monica's shoulders slumped as her body became suddenly weak with the weight of this entire situation. It was not supposed to happen this way. This was a business agreement, with the admiration of her family and colleagues as her ultimate goal. Now Monica wasn't sure what she wanted as the end result of her deal with Eli. Accolades and praise didn't seem so important anymore, at least not as important as filling this void in her life.

Closing her eyes, Monica massaged her temples in an attempt to stave off the headache she could feel forming. She so did not need this today.

"I don't know what to do," Monica whispered.

She heard Eli take a step closer, could feel the heat radiating from his body. A jolt of electricity raced through her as he reached out and took one of her hands in his. He cradled her hand between his warm palms, brushing his thumb over her knuckles.

"Neither of us expected this," he said. Monica could not trust her voice. She could only nod in response as she swallowed deeply. "But it happened," Eli continued. "Why fight it?"

His voice was as soft as a dusting of snow on a December morning. His words had an equally chilling effect. And, try as she might, Monica could not deny them. It—whatever *it* was—had definitely happened. She couldn't put a name to the tumultuous emotions rioting through her brain, but she knew one thing for sure: Their relationship was evolving.

"But you don't date doctors." Monica tried to insert a dose of reality.

"I changed my mind," Eli answered, a hint of laughter in his voice.

Monica slowly raised the lid of one eye to see if he actually had the nerve to be amused at a time when her emotions were running rampant.

"You are so *not* laughing at me," she stated.

"No, I'm not," Eli answered, though his broadening smile belied his words. "Actually, I'm . . . relieved," he said slowly, as if testing the word to make sure it was the right one. "Relieved and happy. I'm being honest when I say I neither expected nor wanted to be in a relationship, Monica, but I won't turn down a good thing when I see one."

Was she ready for this?

If she said no, she would most likely beat herself up over the fact that she'd pushed away a fine, gorgeous man. If she said yes, she would have to buy a supply of Band-Aids for those months following the moment when he inevitably broke her heart.

Maybe that's what fate had in store for her—a life full of broken hearts. And if that was the case, maybe she should resign herself to her destiny and enjoy the periods of happiness as much as possible. If she accepted the fact that heartache was unavoidable, the blow shouldn't hit as hard as it had when Patrick left.

"Are you willing to give this a chance?" Eli asked.

How could she go against fate?

Still not trusting her voice, Monica nodded.

Eli smiled, and Monica could feel his shudder of relief. "Thank you," he said. "We'll just take it as it comes, all right?" He took her by the hand and led her from the storage room. "Come on. It's time to figure out a way to make this banquet rake in the big bucks."

"How many bachelors would we need?" Adele Collins asked. The head of oncology seemed the most skeptical, though Monica had been warned to expect it.

"Dr. Holmes has already been successful in getting many of the physicians and even some of the male nurses to sign up. I say, the more, the merrier."

"And who will pay for the dinners?" This question, again, from Adele.

Monica slowly counted to five while taking a deep breath. It came with the territory. She would just have to handle this like the adult she was trying very hard to be. Though her inner five-year-old was ready to hold Dr. Collins to the ground while she forced a mud pie down her throat.

"As I stated before, the bachelors have agreed to pay for the dinners. All participants understand this is for charity. No one expects the hospital to foot the bill."

"Are you certain?"

Eli stepped in. "Yes."

Thank goodness. No doubt he had noticed the steam escaping her ears.

"Everyone involved knows the importance this banquet has to the future of the Parenting Center. We're striving to pull off the event at minimum cost."

"Well, I think the work that's been done so far is excellent," William Slessinger commented, rising from his seat toward the back of the small conference room Monica had commandeered for the meeting. "Great work, you two."

He turned to Monica. "Dr. Gardner, I never expected when I hired you that you would take over the way you have. I am more than impressed—I'm astounded."

Monica tried for a nonchalant shrug, even though she was ready to burst inside. That smile on Dr. Slessinger's face was genuine gratitude.

Yes! *This* is what she had been hoping for; this was her goal—recognition for a job well done. Monica had to stifle the elated scream that was dangerously close to escaping.

"All we have to do is get people out there," she said instead. "But don't worry: We have that covered, too. I've been in touch with several of the local radio stations, and I'm waiting to hear back from the CBS affiliate about a spot on the early-morning news."

"Excellent!" Slessinger said, rewarding her with a pat on the shoulder.

The rest of the room's occupants started to file out, and soon she and Elijah were alone in the conference room.

"That went well," he said, perching a hip on the table.

"Except for Doubting Adele."

He brushed that off with a wave of his hands. "If you told her you had Usher singing the national anthem, she'd ask if you were sure he could pull it off."

Monica started to laugh at his quip, then something occurred to her. "Just how connected is Toby to the music industry?" she asked, an idea forming.

"If you asked him, he's in like Flynn. I'm not convinced he knows half the people he claims to, though. Why? What are you thinking?"

"Well, we want to attract people across the entire spectrum, from every age group, ethnicity, and background, right?"

"Yes," Eli answered, nodding his head cautiously.

Monica started pacing as she thought aloud. "That singer Aria Jordan?"

"What about her?"

"I've been hearing her song nonstop on the radio, at night especially during the eight to ten o'clock time slot."

"When most of the teenyboppers are calling in to hear a song that's been played a hundred times already that day? What are you doing listening to the radio then?"

"It's when I work out," Monica explained. "What do you think about having Aria Jordan headlining the entertainment? Even if it's only a couple of ballads, I know she can bring in a good number of people. Her fan base is growing everyday."

Eli shrugged. "We can give it a shot. I'll talk to Toby tonight. And speaking of tonight . . ." he said, moving toward her.

The seductive timbre of his voice made Monica's throat suddenly dry. She had not given much thought to all the elements a relationship entailed, especially when she had not engaged in particular elements in quite some time. She wasn't ready to take that step just yet, and she needed to set the pace before Eli's sexy eyes and stimulating voice had her doing something she would later regret. But no doubt enjoy.

Monica held up one hand, halting his progression. "We haven't had a chance to discuss what our expectations of this . . . this new situation are, but I know what I am willing to do. And what has to wait."

"Monica, I don't expect you to jump into bed with me just because we've decided to make this real."

"You don't?" she asked, not really believing him.

"I'm not saying I would turn you down, but no, I'm not expecting anything to happen. Yet," he made sure to include. "Tonight I just want to hang out. Rent a DVD, pop some popcorn. You know, just chill."

Monica wasn't so sure she was buying the innocent act, but his plan seemed harmless enough.

"Okay," she agreed. "Do you want to come over to my place?"

His bright smile made his handsome face even more devastating. "I'll pick up the movie and snacks. You provide the drinks."

"Deal," Monica said, still questioning the wisdom of "making this real," as Eli had put it.

"I'll see you at seven?" he asked.

"Seven sounds good."

They stood there, unsure of the next move. Monica thought he was going to bend down and kiss her, but he didn't. He only smiled, then walked out of the conference room, leaving her alone with a mixture of anxiety, fear, and—she had to admit—a good bit of excitement.

Chapter Eighteen

Eli should have known better.

In fact, he should have expected it. This wasn't the first time she'd stood him up.

He switched the plastic bag from his right hand to his left and knocked on the door again. Two long minutes later, just as he raised his fist to deliver another round of knocks, Monica turned the corner and came walking up the hallway.

"I'm so sorry," she said. "I got stuck at work."

"But you were not on shift today, were you?" Eli asked, silently acknowledging the spurt of relief that coursed through his veins at the realization that she hadn't stood him up.

"I was on call," Monica explained. "Of course, I didn't find that out until I got paged."

She looked whipped. Eli didn't want her to feel obligated to spend time with him just because she had agreed to it earlier. But he didn't want to leave. He had been thinking about her ever since this morning's meeting.

"Are you sure you still want to do this? We can save it for another time," he said, despite his brain's protest.

"No. I can use the downtime. I've been looking forward to this all day."

Her words caused a delicious shudder to rumble through his veins. Eli moved to the side as she took out a key and inserted it, unlocking the door.

"What did you rent?" She opened the door and led him in.

"Actually, I picked something from my personal collection. You like action movies?"

She turned and placed a hand over her chest. "A man after my own heart," Monica said with exaggerated dramatic flair.

Her words were too close to the truth for Eli to keep his feelings from showing on his face. They stared at each other for long moments as an invisible web of sensual awareness wrapped itself around them. Monica was the first to break free of its magnetic hold.

"I, uh, need to freshen up," she said, slowly backing away from where they still stood in the doorway.

Eli couldn't tear his gaze away as she walked to the apartment's back rooms. He set up the movie and popped the popcorn while Monica showered and changed. He was emptying a bag of peanut M&Ms into a bowl when she walked in dressed in a peach lounging set.

His stomach tightened.

This was going to be a test of his willpower. If he could spend an evening with her and refrain from touching her, Eli knew he could accomplish damn near anything.

"That feels so much better," Monica said, taking a seat on the sofa.

Eli followed. He deposited the bowl of chocolate on

the coffee table and picked up the remote from the arm of the sofa. He'd chosen *Passenger 57*, and was happy, though a little surprised, when Monica said she had never seen it.

"I love DVDs," she said, eating a few M&Ms. "I watch everything, from the director interviews to the deleted scenes."

"The added features are cool," Eli agreed.

"Hey, you won't be disgusted if I mix my popcorn and M&Ms, will you?"

"Do you mean in the bowl?"

"No, just in my hand. Pat—an old friend of mine used to get grossed out whenever I did that."

An old friend, huh? He thought about Nia's card sitting snugly in his wallet. Now he had a name to go on when he contacted her. He was going to find out what part this Pat guy played in Monica's life.

Monica picked out a couple of M&Ms and some of the fluffy popcorn and popped them into her mouth.

"That is kind of strange," Eli said, glancing at her.

"The sweet and salty tastes play upon each other. It's good. You want to try it?" She held out a handful of her strange snack mix.

Eli's head reared back. "I'll pass. But—" He rose from the couch and walked over to the kitchen. He grabbed one of the small soup bowls from the dish rack. "You go ahead and enjoy it." He grabbed a handful of M&Ms and poured the popcorn over them, then gently tossed the concoction around like a salad.

"There you go," Eli said, handing the bowl to Monica.

She took the bowl from his hand, an odd look on her face.

"Why are you looking at me that way? Monica?" he asked again when she didn't answer.

She shook her head. "I . . . umm . . . I'm sorry. Let's watch the movie."

As the night wore on, Eli felt more and more like a teenager on his first date, with tiny bubbles of elation bursting within whenever they got a little closer to each other. They began the night sitting side by side on Monica's love seat. Eli kicked it up a notch by draping his arm over the back of the couch. Then, during an exceptionally suspenseful part of the flick, Monica nudged closer toward him. By the time the credits rolled, her head was resting on his shoulder, and Eli was feeling pretty good about himself.

"Wow, that was good," Monica said, rising from her lounging position.

"I've seen that movie a thousand times," Eli said, ejecting the DVD and placing it back into the slim case.

"I don't know how I missed that one. I love action films."

"Maybe we can have a *Die Hard* marathon one of these days."

"Ah, Bruce Willis jumping out of a skyscraper. Sounds like a plan." Thoughts of the smile her face displayed would keep Eli company for the rest of the night.

Eli dusted his hands on the back of his khakis because he didn't know what else to do with them. He knew what he *wanted* to do. The thought had been at the forefront of his mind from the second she walked out of her bedroom. Visions of his hands running up the inside of her shirt, along the waistband of her pants—it was enough to drive him crazy.

But he had promised Monica they would take it slow, and he was not about to mess this up by pressuring her into something she wasn't ready to do.

When the time was right, they would take it to the next level. And if there was one thing he was certain of, it was that Monica Gardner was worth waiting for.

"We should probably call it a night," Eli said. "You've had a rough day."

"But tonight really helped," she answered, sincere appreciation in her eyes. "It's been a long time since I've just laid back and kicked it, you know? Nia is always looking to go out and do something. Sometimes it's nice to just . . . just *be*."

"I know what you mean," Eli agreed.

And he did. He couldn't remember the last time he'd enjoyed himself as much as he had tonight, just relaxing on a couch watching one of his favorite movies with someone who wanted to be with him, not because he was a doctor or because of how he looked. Monica wanted to be with him because she had seen something *in* him. That meant more to him than Eli had ever thought possible.

"Well, I guess this is good night," Monica said. She walked him to the door.

"I probably won't see you tomorrow. I've got a C-section scheduled about ten minutes before your shift ends."

Wait. Was that . . . *disappointment* he noted in her downcast eyes?

A few weeks ago, if anyone had suggested that Monica Gardner would have been disappointed at the thought of not seeing him, Eli would have had him admitted to the psych ward.

"I need to visit a couple of bakeries anyway," Monica said. "The pastry chef that usually works with the caterer has a prior engagement scheduled for the night of the banquet."

"How unfair is that? You drag me along to look at dusty old plantations, but when it's time to sample pastries, you leave me out."

"Hmm, now that you mention it, you did get the raw end of the deal," Monica replied, a mischievous grin creating a dimple Eli had never noticed before in her cheek. The effects of her smile were heart-stopping. An overwhelming rush of desire cloaked itself around Eli's body. Suddenly all he could think about was covering Monica's lips with his own.

Eli lost all sense of time and place as he stared into a pair of the most seductive eyes ever known to man. When her tongue darted out to nervously lick her lips, the fledging willpower Eli had been clinging to vanished as his body erupted in a blaze of raging need.

"I have to do this," was all he managed before dipping his head low and capturing her soft, lush lips. He moved his mouth over hers, savoring the sweet tenderness of her kiss. The sensation was mind-boggling. His legs could barely support him as wave upon wave of aching want crashed through him.

His hands came up to grip Monica's shoulders as he plied her mouth with his kiss, gently running his tongue along the seam of her lips, urging her mouth open.

She moaned, and he lost it.

Eli crushed her body against the door and plunged into her open mouth. Their tongues engaged in a spirited dance, instinctively finding each other again and again. He sucked at her bottom lip, growling at how good she tasted.

"No," she purred. "No . . . not yet." Monica pushed at his chest.

Eli reluctantly released her lips. The instant ache of not being connected to her nearly crippled him.

"I'm sorry," he said through a battered sigh.

Monica stepped back, rubbing her hands up and down her arms as if she was cold.

"Monica, I'm—"

"It's okay," she said, though Eli could tell it was anything but okay. She looked confused and afraid. The one thing he did not want to do was frighten her.

"No, it's not okay. I said I would not go there with

you until you were ready, and . . ." He shook his head. There was no excuse for his behavior. "All I can do is apologize and promise not to touch you until you say it's okay."

She raised her head. The sight of her doelike eyes caused his chest to tighten.

"Thank you," she said, her voice a mere whisper. All traces of the fear he'd glimpsed gone, she moved back to where he stood near the door.

Monica brought her hand up and placed a warm palm on his cheek. Eli melted into her hand, relishing the sensation of her delicate caress.

"I won't make you wait forever. I'm just not ready yet."

Eli captured the hand that covered his cheek. He brought it to his lips and gave the crest of her fingers a light kiss.

"It will never happen again, Monica. I swear to you."

"Never?" The makings of a smile graced her face, softening her features and making her even more alluring in the dim light of the foyer.

"Well, not until you make the call."

"Thank you for being so understanding."

She was thanking *him* for being understanding?

It was at that moment Eli realized the person standing before him was no ordinary woman. She was a rare jewel, a being so precious it would be a sin to let her go without exploring all she had to offer to his life.

"I'm going to try to see you tomorrow."

"Of course you will." She grinned. "You want that éclair."

"You caught me." Eli winked.

He turned and opened the door, dreading the fact that he had to leave her. He wanted to stay right where he was, even if it meant fighting the unrelenting surge of almost painful lust. Just being near her was enough to assuage all hurt.

But it was not meant to be. Not tonight. They would take it slow. She was worth waiting for.

"Good night, Eli." Monica rested on the edge of the door. Her sorrowful expression made him feel marginally better. She didn't want him to go, either.

He ran his hand down the length of her hair, capturing her upper arm and giving it a light squeeze. "Get some sleep."

"I will. Drive safely."

"See you tomorrow."

"See you."

As she closed the door, a strange sensation tugged at Eli's heart. He had never felt this sudden flood of longing after leaving a woman. He'd never felt any of these emotions before, at least not to this extent. This was new territory.

Proving yet again that Monica Gardner was rare indeed.

Amanda was numb.

For the past ten minutes, as she sat in the increasingly uncomfortable chair, she had dithered between stages of shock, outrage, panic, and now . . . nothing. She could barely understand the words coming from the handsome doctor's mouth. From the moment he said the Parenting Center might be closing, her brain had shut down.

It would have been easier to handle if her first errand of the day had gone differently. The visit to the bank was a lesson in fortitude. Not many people would have been able to maintain a straight face as they learned their bank account was nearly depleted. Of course, with the technology of online banking, Amanda had had the advantage of knowing that tidbit before her meeting with the bank's customer service representative.

She'd spent it all. Every last cent.

The spending sprees had gotten her in trouble once before, when she'd run out of her bipolar meds and sky-rocketed into a volatile manic episode. Jeffrey had been out of town, thank goodness, and she had been able to cash in her life insurance policy to cover her tracks. But how would she pay off the debt this time?

She was broke. The restricted activity to which Dr. Holmes had consigned her required that Amanda start her leave nearly two months earlier than originally planned, so there was no extra money coming in. And, if what Dr. Holmes just told her was true and not a figment of her admittedly overactive imagination, there was a possibility she wouldn't have the free medical care she depended on.

"We are trying everything we can to make sure the center stays open, Mrs. Daniels. We won't let it go down without a fight." He folded his hands on the desk. "I just wanted to warn my patients of what could happen," Dr. Holmes finished.

"So." Amanda cleared her throat, still trying to wrap her mind around everything she'd heard in the past half hour. "So there's still a chance the Parenting Center will remain open?"

He hunched his shoulders. "Like I said, we're trying. I don't want you to worry, though. In fact, I've grown so confident that the center will remain open that I held off telling you. I don't want you needlessly upset. You concentrate on keeping yourself healthy. You need as much rest and relaxation as possible."

He rose from behind the desk and came to help her from her chair. How unsettling that she would accept assistance from a virtual stranger, yet she balked when her husband so much as touched her. Emotion lodged in her throat.

"I'm going to see you in a few days, but I'll warn you now, if your anemia doesn't improve, you are going to have to go on restrictive bed rest. That means being in bed all the time, literally, until this baby arrives."

"Is it really that serious, Dr. Holmes?"

"Your case borders on severe. It's a very real possibility, Amanda."

Lord help her. She would *really* go insane. How would she survive being confined to her bed for eight weeks?

"How much sleep have you been getting lately?" he asked, his shrewd eyes homing in on her, making her feel as though she'd just been caught skipping school.

"Not much," Amanda admitted.

"I'm not a mental health professional, Mrs. Daniels, but I know enough about your condition to know that lack of sleep will only exacerbate your symptoms."

"I know," she said.

"You need to remain well rested and free of stress," he cautioned.

"Telling me I may not have free medical care is not the best stress reducer," she said under her breath.

A smile pulled across Dr. Holmes's face. He covered her hand with his. "Don't worry about the Parenting Center. Just make sure you take care of yourself."

She left the hospital, thinking the only way her day could get any worse was if she walked in front of a bus. By the time she pulled into the driveway behind Jeffrey's truck, Amanda wasn't so sure getting hit by a ten-ton moving vehicle was a bad idea. She was being tested; that was the only explanation she could devise. And Amanda had a feeling she was failing horribly.

After an entire day of running the road, all she could think about was soaking in a tub of steaming lavender-scented water with a good book and a glass of wine. The wine would have to wait a few more months, but a hot bath and a book were readily available.

With more effort than usual, Amanda pulled herself from behind the Altima's steering wheel. Soon she would not be able to fit behind it. Of course, if Dr. Holmes followed through on his threat of restrictive bed rest, it would not make much of a difference whether she could fit behind the wheel. She wouldn't be able to drive anyway.

Amanda shook off the depressing thought and made her way up the footpath. She went through the front door and froze at the site before her.

There were boxes everywhere. Stacked on the table. Shoved against the wall. Strewn across the sofa.

Jeffrey was leaving.

An ache settled in her chest at the thought that he could so effortlessly walk away from the life they shared, but after the accusations she'd wailed at him, there was not much he could say or do—except leave.

This *was* what she wanted, wasn't it?

"Oh no," Amanda moaned as the familiar throbbing sensation started behind her eyes. Her senses heightened. The light hanging from the ceiling fan became brighter, too bright. The air began to weigh down on her skin. Amanda tried to shut out the onslaught of sensation, but she was just too tired. She could feel what was happening to her, but she was powerless to fight it.

Looking around the living room and dining area, an eerie sense of wariness crept up Amanda's spine. Something about this was not right.

The black lamp sitting on the dining room table was familiar, but it seemed out of place. The same went for the framed lithograph leaning against the wall. Wait . . . these were her things. From her apartment.

"You're here," Jeffrey said, coming from the kitchen. He was still dressed in his blue coveralls.

"What have you done?" Amanda growled low in her throat.

"I cleaned out your apartment, and I cancelled the lease."

"You did what?" If the pictures had not been so securely

fastened to the wall, they would have shook from the force of her bellowed scream.

"I won't let you do this, Amanda," he said firmly. "I refuse to lose you over a misunderstanding."

"Jeffrey, if you do not put every single piece of furniture back in my apartment—"

He shook his head. "No. Your stubbornness is not winning out this time." He took a step toward her, and she took a step back. Jeffrey wasn't deterred. "I have spent over a decade of my life loving you. Eleven years ago, I vowed before God and family that I would spend the rest of my life loving you. I plan to honor that vow."

Amanda took a labored breath. She wanted to respond, but words escaped her. To her horror, she felt tears welling in her eyes, and before she could stifle it, a heart-wrenching sob tore from deep within Amanda's soul.

When Jeffrey rushed to her side and put his arms around her, she was too weak to pull away. A flurry of emotions went through her as she wept for what her marriage had once been and what it had now become. She wept over the love she still held for her husband, and acknowledged that her heart was still undeniably attached to the man whose arms surrounded her.

"Don't cry, baby," Jeffrey whispered soothingly. "Please don't cry."

"Why?" Amanda swallowed another sob. "Why are you doing this to me?"

"Because I love you. I love you, Amanda," he said again.

She wrung free of his hold and pushed him a good foot away from her. The hurt in his eyes caused her physical pain. This was so unfair. She shouldn't be the one hurting here. *He's the one who did wrong!*

No, he didn't, Amanda pleaded with her own mind to understand.

Yes, he did. She'd seen them together.

"Don't tell me you love me," she growled. "If you loved me, we wouldn't be in the situation we're in right now."

"And just why are we in this situation, Amanda? In all this time, you never once told me why you wanted out. You just left."

"I don't have to tell you."

"Yes, you do. Because if it's for the reason I'm starting to suspect, I'm calling the lawyers tomorrow to contest this divorce."

"Just try it," Amanda challenged. She crossed her arms over her ever-increasing breasts, primed for his reply.

But Jeffrey didn't take the bait. His response held no anger, only anguish and exhaustion. "You can fight it all you want. I'm not giving you up for something I didn't do."

Amanda had to take another deep breath before she could speak again. "I cannot believe you can look me in the face after telling that lie," she said.

Jeffrey held his hands out to her. "Where is the lie, Amanda? What is it you think I'm holding back from you?"

"I. Saw. You." She could barely get the words past the lump in her throat. She was so confused, she could barely think. The lights overhead became even more intense. Everything seemed to be coming at her at once.

"That's what I've been trying to figure out," Jeffrey said. "What did you see?"

"I saw *you*! You and your whore! You had her in my house, most likely in my bed. You have no respect for our marriage or for me. You threw it all away, Jeffrey. Eleven years of shared laughter, and heartache, and love."

If she hadn't known better, Amanda would have believed that was genuine confusion she saw on his face. Jeffrey shook his head, his expression one of bewilderment.

"I don't know what you saw."

His voice was raspy and raw, and Amanda was hard-pressed not to slap him across the face for attempting to play games with her. His secret was out now. There was no need for the lies to continue.

"You are unbelievable. I've just told you that I saw you with my own two eyes, and you're still playing dumb?"

"Whatever you think you saw, it had nothing to do with me cheating on you."

"Why deny it, Jeffrey?" Amanda asked laconically, growing tired of the conversation.

Jeffrey stalked up to her, his tall, broad frame looming above her. "I'm denying it because I've never done it. I have never given you reason to doubt me, and it hurts like hell that you could even think I'd do something like this."

Amanda was suddenly struck with a bout of fatigue that made it hard to stand. A pulsating rhythm beat like a drum at the base of her skull. She could practically hear the blood rushing to her head.

She had to lie down. And she had to get away from Jeffrey and his denials. She didn't have the energy to keep up this battle. It was time they both accepted what lay ahead of them.

Amanda had to force her tongue into action. It, along with the rest of her body, had become unbelievably weak.

"Look, Jeffrey," she managed to mutter. "The divorce is inevitable. We just need—"

Before she could finish, everything in her world went black.

Chapter Nineteen

"This was not what I had in mind for our first date as an official couple."

Eli pushed the bright orange oversized shopping cart up the paint aisle.

"I know," Monica said. She entwined her arm with his, thrilled that he was willing to change his well-made plans without hesitation. Simply because she'd asked him to.

Over these past few weeks his easygoing demeanor and flexibility had been a pleasant surprise. When she was with Patrick, Monica had always found herself apologizing for her crazy hours. But that wasn't the case with her and Eli. They understood each other's hectic schedules, so there were never hurt feelings when dates had to be cancelled or pushed back an hour or two.

"I'm just so tired of those white walls. They take away from the rest of the décor. It needs color. I want to make the apartment my own."

"You pay rent. That's about as much ownership as your landlord expects you to take."

She pinched him on the arm. "Don't be smart. It's just that I never painted the walls in any of my other apartments before, because I knew I wouldn't stay for long. This time, it's different."

"So this is a commitment thing, then?"

"Sorta," Monica admitted. "I like New Orleans. I think I'm going to hang around here for a while."

"Did I have any bearing on this decision?"

"I'm not telling," she laughed. "Your ego is big enough as it is."

Whether or not he knew it, Eli had more of an impact on her decision to make New Orleans her permanent home than Monica was willing to share with him, lest he use the knowledge to take advantage of her. Although she was starting to suspect Eli wouldn't do what she had come to believe was typical of all men. He would not use her words to hurt her.

She thought back on the various elements that had factored into her decision to set roots in this city. There was a spirit here that had seeped into her bones. Despite the crushing blow New Orleans had suffered, the will to rebuild remained strong. The resilience of the people she served every day in the ER was inspiring.

The fact that the staff at Methodist Memorial had made her feel at home had also played a huge part in her decision to stay in New Orleans. Monica loved her job more than she had ever thought possible. And the charity banquet preparations were going even better than she could have hoped for.

She had Eli to thank for much of that.

He had taken his role seriously, and since their relationship had escalated to this new level, he seemed to work even harder.

"Are you sure you like this color?" Eli asked, holding up the color sample Monica had handed to him on the way to Home Depot.

"The Venetian red is perfect for the kitchen and living room." She took the color palette and held it up to the tiny fabric sample she'd cut from the under hem of the chair in her living room. "Don't you see how well it goes with the rest of the décor?"

"I guess," Eli shrugged.

Monica snorted. "As if you know anything about style. I'll bet your house is still sporting colors from the eighties."

He leaned over and whispered in her ear, "Why don't you come on over and find out?"

A tingle of excitement swept across Monica's skin. "Eventually," she promised with a shy smile.

"From your beautiful lips to God's ears." He nipped playfully at her nose.

If he continued with this pursuit of the Most Charming Man in America award, Monica would find herself in his bed earlier then she had anticipated. Elijah Holmes was becoming impossible to resist.

When was the last time she had engaged in love play in public? Monica could barely recall even kissing Patrick outside of the bedroom. He'd told her they were under constant scrutiny because of his father's position in the community, and needed to avoid anything the media could turn into a scandal. His rule had changed after he got married. The few times Monica had run into him and his wife, they'd looked to be on the verge of getting a motel room.

Apparently Patrick wasn't against public displays of affection, as long as they were not with *her*.

Eli had no qualms with allowing the world to see how he felt about her. Whether they were at Ethel's, his mother's, or even in the hospital halls, Eli constantly bestowed light touches and soft kisses.

Monica was still unsure of the decision to make their relationship known at the hospital, but to her chagrin, no one seemed surprised. In fact, when she finally imparted the news to some of the ER nurses who had become more than just coworkers, but friends, many asked why it had taken so long. The nursing staff claimed to have seen the sparks between Eli and Monica ever since their first encounter.

Eli wrapped his arms around her, and Monica nestled her back against his chest, melting into the solid strength of his arms. They rocked slightly side to side as they waited for the sales associate to mix the paint combination.

"Do you want Chinese or pizza?" Eli inquired softly in her ear. His sensual voice could make even the most mundane question erotic.

"Why don't you choose?" Monica answered.

"Hmm . . . well, I say we forgo painting for tonight, make another stop—this time at the grocery store—and I cook dinner for you at my place."

Monica turned around so sharply she nearly bumped his chin. "You cook?"

"Of course I cook. You've met my mother. Do you honestly think I could grow up in that house and not learn my way around a kitchen?"

"Dr. Holmes, you continue to surprise me." She grinned.

"That's a good thing. I've heard dullness has a bad effect on relationships."

He let her go and deposited the three paint cans into the basket. "So, what do you say? Do you think you can live with those depressing white walls until next weekend?"

Monica hesitated. She knew accepting this invitation might lead to more than just dinner, but she was willing to take the risk. Sleeping with him was inevitable. Eli had left to her the decision of when it would happen, but Monica knew that, sooner or later, it definitely *would* happen.

A mixture of excitement and fear spread through her belly at the thought of it possibly happening tonight.

"I'm in the mood for steak," she said, her eyes gleaming with amusement.

Although Eli said he had T-bones in his freezer, they stopped at the grocery store since the meat would have to defrost. In addition to the steaks, they bought baking potatoes, a bag of Caesar salad mix, and a bottle of Merlot.

Standing in his kitchen, Monica had to admit she was impressed. The layout was worthy of a gourmet chef, and the rest of the open living, dining, and kitchen areas looked to be straight out of the pages of *Architectural Digest*.

"What's with the face?" Eli asked.

Monica doubted he realized how sexy he looked with the cream-colored apron tied around his waist. He sprinkled cayenne pepper on the steaks and rubbed the two pieces of meat together, then set the glass dish aside.

"Just admiring your house," she answered. "It's gorgeous."

"Why don't I give you a tour while the steaks marinate," he said, untying the apron at the back.

Wrapping her arms around him, Monica stilled his hands. "Leave it on. I like this look on you."

The grin on his face spread from his mouth up to his eyes. "Far be it for me to go against the lady's wishes. You're not going to attack me in a fit of passion when I pick up the grilling tools, will you?"

She raised a brow. "And you would have a problem with that?"

"Hell no."

Laughing, Monica grabbed him by the hand. "Come on. I want to see the rest of this place."

Impressive didn't begin to describe the house. The décor was both rich and inviting, and even though he used more neutral colors than the bold ones she gravitated to, the soft browns, muted golds, and pale yellows suited him. The intricate woodwork on the banister and crown molding must have taken months to complete.

"Eli, this is beautiful," Monica called out as she stood in his granite-and-marble bathroom. "You can fit my entire apartment in this shower." She turned to where he stood in the doorway, and sent him a teasing smile. "I guess this is what you get when you're Super Doc, huh?" She turned back to admire the chrome- and gold-plated fixtures.

"This is what you get when you learn to appreciate the finer things in life," he said, his voice hushed, sensual.

Monica had the feeling he was no longer talking about the house. She became aware of him right behind her. The massive bathroom suddenly became too small. Slowly she turned to face him, and the smoldering look in his eyes confirmed her thoughts.

Eli continued. "I treat my home the way I treat everything else in life."

"And how's that?" Monica panted, mesmerized by the intoxicating timbre of his softly spoken words.

He stepped an inch closer until their bodies were nearly touching. Eli's voice was almost a whisper as he said, "When I see something I want, I go for it. No matter the cost."

Elijah Holmes had the power to tear down her defenses. After an entire year behind the wall she'd erected around her heart, Monica could feel the barrier slowly crumbling. She didn't want to shield herself any longer. She wanted to give herself fully, freely over to him.

"I used to worry about paying the price for what I wanted," Monica admitted.

"And now?"

"Now . . . now it doesn't matter. I don't care about the price anymore, Eli. I want to go for what I want."

He trailed a finger down the length of her jaw. "And what do you want?"

She swallowed. "You," Monica answered truthfully. She refused to hold back any longer. She was tired of denying herself, tired of living in fear of what would happen tomorrow. She was ready to live for today—for this very moment.

"I want you, Eli," Monica said more forcefully. "Right now."

"I want you, too," he said. Taking her by the hand, Eli led her out of the bathroom and into his master bedroom. The large wrought-iron bed presented a picture of down-filled heaven, with mountains of stuffed pillows in various shades and sizes.

"Wait." Monica stopped him. "Before we go one step further, I want you to tell me the truth." She saw the dejection on his face. Monica smiled inwardly. "You didn't decorate this house by yourself, did you?"

The sexy grin upon his lips lit a fire deep within Monica's belly. "I didn't decorate it at all. My cousin Indina is an interior designer. This is all her doing."

"I knew it was too good to be true." She returned his grin.

"Give me a couple of minutes. I'll show you something that's really too good to be true."

The excited rush that flashed through her body was enough to weaken her knees. It didn't matter, since Eli swooped her into his arms and carried her to the bed.

With painstaking slowness, he undid the buttons of her blouse and peeled the silky fabric from her fevered skin. He trailed light kisses upon her flesh as he revealed more of it to his gaze.

She lay against the backdrop of pillows, clad only in a lace bra and panty set Nia had bought her as a gag gift. She had not worn it in ages. Monica wondered if she'd unconsciously known this would happen today.

She reclined languidly against the plush pillows as she watched Eli undress. He stripped out of his shirt and khakis, then hooked his thumbs in the waistband of his silk boxers and drew them down his legs.

Monica's eyes widened.

He was gorgeous.

And he was hers.

"Come here," she said, sitting up. Eli crawled to meet her in the center of the massive bed, their lips the first part of their anatomies to meet.

Monica moaned as Eli's tongue invaded her mouth. An onslaught of hedonistic pleasure coursed through her body as he plunged into the deep recesses of her mouth, lavishing her in an erotic rhythm Monica could only hope was a precursor to what was to come.

Her back arched instinctively as his fingers traveled along her spine, finding the clasp of her bra and releasing her breasts from their lacy confinement.

Monica sighed in ecstasy as Eli's hands closed over her aching breasts. He cupped them, sending sparks of white-hot pleasure streaming through her body as his thumbs played upon her sensitized nipples.

"You feel so good," he breathed against her neck. He trailed his tongue across her collarbone, nipping her skin with his teeth. "Lie down," Eli commanded.

Monica felt like floating as he lowered her onto the mound of pillows and covered her body with his. His tongue skimmed her shoulder on its way to the valley between her breasts. He traveled down the length of her body, punctuating her flesh with hot, moist kisses.

Monica moaned in satisfaction as he found his way to her stomach. Her lower muscles tightened as Eli burrowed his face against her abdomen; then he caught the edge of her lace panties between his teeth and tugged.

She lifted slightly off the bed so he could pull the flimsy garment down her legs. Monica lay before him completely naked and, to her astonishment, totally unself-conscious.

The embarrassment that had usually overwhelmed her whenever she'd made love to Patrick was absent. She didn't feel shy or awkward in Eli's arms. She felt womanly. Alive. Wanted.

Reclaiming her lips, Eli crushed her to him. Monica's body responded violently to the sensation of Eli's muscled form flush against her naked skin, her limbs shaking in stark excitement.

"Give me a minute, baby," he whispered hoarsely in her ear. "I'll give you a reason to tremble."

Capturing her knees, Eli spread her legs open and plunged deep into her quivering flesh. Monica's head reared back as her entire body arched off the bed. She clutched the silk sheets in her hands, lifting her hips to meet his insistent thrusts.

The sensation started deep in the pit of her belly, rapidly escalating as Eli repeatedly drove into her with his hard body. Monica opened her legs wider, wrapping them around his hips as they pumped in a rhythm that reverberated throughout her being. She ran her hands up and down his back, gripping the solid muscles and squeezing.

His pace quickened.

Surrendering to her body's demands, Monica started to tremble as waves of passion spiraled through her.

The pleasure was pure and explosive. She cried out in exquisite release, her inner muscles clutching Eli's flesh as it continued to pulsate inside of her.

Taking shallow breaths, Monica tried to bring herself back to a place she recognized. Eli had just taken her to unparalleled heights, and for many moments after they were done, Monica was unsure of what to say or do.

In the end, all she could do was slip into blissful sleep, wrapped in the warmth of Eli's strong embrace.

Every time Amanda tried to open her eyes, a piercing pain shot from the back of her head. So she decided to keep them closed for as long as she could.

The insistent beeping made the task impossible.

With agonizing slowness, Amanda raised her eyelids from their resting position. The first person she saw was Jeffrey.

"Let me get the doctor," he said, and was gone before Amanda could form a word.

Less than a minute later, a young woman who looked as if she should still be in high school followed Jeffrey into the room. The green scrubs and white coat indicated she was the doctor, but Amanda was skeptical. When did they start giving medical degrees to teenagers?

"Well, we're certainly happy you're awake," the young doctor said. She raised Amanda's eyelids and shone a pen-light into her eyes.

Amanda winced. "What happened?" she managed to ask through the pain pounding in her head.

"You blacked out for a little while. You have a severe case of anemia, Mrs. Daniels. My thought is that you overextended yourself today, and your body was just unable to keep up."

"Is the baby . . . okay?" A tear formed in her eye and rolled down her cheek. If her baby was hurt . . .

"We have you on a monitor as a precaution, but it looks like the baby fared just fine. I can't say the same for you, however. I'm going to consult with Dr. Holmes, but I believe you will be on more restrictive bed rest for the remainder of your pregnancy."

"He mentioned the possibility earlier today."

"You saw Dr. Holmes today?" Jeffrey asked. Amanda

had forgotten he was in the room. Her head began to pound in earnest. She was not up for another argument. "You never told me you had an appointment with the doctor today."

"You had to work. I needed answers to a few questions. It was nothing important."

"But he said he was putting you on restrictive bed rest, right?"

"He said it was a possibility," Amanda clarified.

"I think it just went from a possibility to a certainty," the doctor interjected. "We'll be keeping you overnight for observation, and I'll make sure Dr. Holmes sees you bright and early tomorrow morning to go over everything."

The doctor smiled and left the room.

To Amanda's utter relief, the other bed in the semi-private room was unoccupied. She didn't want the world to witness the clash that was about to commence. She knew Jeffrey had been waiting for the doctor's departure so that he could pounce on her for not telling him about today's visit.

"Don't start," Amanda warned before he could say anything. "I'm not in the mood to argue."

"I don't want to argue with you, Amanda. I want to *talk* to you."

"Talking leads to arguing."

"It doesn't have to. That's my point." He took her hand and held it. "It wasn't always this way between us. We used to talk to one another. We used to laugh. I want that back, baby."

Amanda refused to let any more of the tears welling in her eyes escape.

"You have no right to do this to me." She choked on a sob. "I'm not the one to blame for the state of our marriage."

"Neither am I," he argued, though he kept his voice at a whisper's pitch. But he was still defending himself to her, and Amanda had had enough. It was time for him to own up to what he had done.

"You sleep with another woman, Jeffrey. How can you say you're not to blame?"

"Why don't you believe me when I tell you I have *never* been with anyone else? I've been in love with you since the very first moment I laid eyes on you."

The tears she'd tried valiantly to suppress came down. She shouldn't believe him, but God knew she wanted to. With all her heart she wanted to believe the man she married had never strayed. But how could she doubt something she'd seen with her own eyes? She *had* seen them together. It was not her imagination. Was it?

She couldn't be sure of anything anymore.

Jeffrey brought her hand up to his lips and dusted her knuckles with featherlight kisses.

"I promise you, Amanda, I have never even thought of being with another woman. I don't know what you think you saw, but it was not that. It's never been about that."

Amanda closed her eyes, hoping to blot out the sight of his face. Because when she looked at him, she saw sincerity. And honesty.

Deep in her heart, Amanda knew he was telling the truth.

But her mind refused to believe it.

Chapter Twenty

Standing at the stove, which sat in the middle of the island in his kitchen, Eli flipped several strips of bacon with a fork and turned down the heat. He searched through the utensil drawer for the wire whisk he knew was hidden away somewhere. He pulled it out and used the whisk to beat the eggs into a fluffy, light yellow froth.

Eli passed his hand over the skillet of melting butter to ensure it was properly heated, then poured in the eggs, using the whisk to scramble them.

He looked up to find Monica lounging against one of the marble columns that marked the entryway from the living room to the kitchen.

She'd thrown on one of his scrub shirts. With the early morning sun streaming through the floor-to-ceiling windows, Eli could see her naked body silhouetted through the lightweight material. His body instantly hardened.

"Good morning," Eli said, smiling. After last night, he would probably smile for the rest of his life.

Since the moment his eyes opened, Eli's thoughts had been fixated on the time they'd shared in bed the night before. He would have never imagined the ardor she possessed. Hidden behind her straitlaced outward appearance was an inherent passion that had both surprised and encouraged Eli to try things he had only dreamed of doing to a woman. From the satisfied look on her face as she stared languidly at him from across the room, Eli could only conclude Monica had enjoyed last night's experimenting as much as he did.

Her enthusiasm had spurred him to go on for hours. He had never experienced anything like it. Even as a horny teenager it had taken his body a good half hour to recover before he was ready to go again.

Not last night. Last night, he had been going for Olympic gold. Just one look at her this morning, and Eli was ready to defend his medal.

"You hungry?" he asked, motioning to her with his head. He piled the fluffy eggs, bacon, and seasoned potatoes onto a platter and walked over to the glass-top table nestled into a bay window. He went back to the kitchen counter and grabbed the carafe of hot chicory coffee and a small basket of croissants and flaky pastries.

"Where did you get all this?" Monica asked.

"The bakery down the street. I passed it on my morning jog, so I decided to stop in and pick up a few things."

"It's just after seven o'clock. What time did you go jogging?"

"Five thirty. I like to get in at least five miles in the morning."

"I feel like such a slacker compared to you."

Eli leaned over and gently pressed his lips to hers. "You have no need to work out," he said in a deep voice. "You have the perfect body."

Her brows rose. "You still think so after doing it with the lights on?"

"Baby, I know so," Eli murmured against her neck. "You are exquisite."

Monica blew out a haggard breath. "You sure know how to start a girl's day off on the right foot."

"If only we had the time, sweetheart, I would have you singing for the rest of the day."

Monica took a seat on the edge of the table and crossed her legs.

Eli started to salivate at the sight of her delicate brown thighs peeking from underneath the hem of his shirt. Once again, his mind traveled back to last night. He could feel those soft thighs cradling his head as he consumed her sweet flavor. Eli closed his eyes, desperately fighting the urge to drape Monica over the table and fill her body with his own.

She rose from her perch on the table, took a seat, and started filling a plate.

Eli snapped his fingers, remembering the carton of orange juice in the fridge. He got up and snatched it, along with two small juice glasses. He returned to the breakfast table and took his seat at Monica's right.

"What time do you have to be at the hospital?" he asked.

Her eyes went to the digital clock on the microwave. "In about another hour. I need to stop at my place so I can shower and change."

Eli's heart fell. There went his hopes for an abbreviated repeat of last night.

"Does your shift end at six?" he asked.

She nodded as she swallowed a forkful of potatoes. "Yeah, but I've got a ton of things to take care of after work for the banquet. I need to stop at the caterer to finalize the menu. Then there's the decorating company, who I swear to you has no idea what they're doing. I asked for ecru balloons, and the woman pulls out this awful eggshell."

"Monica, you do realize you have subcommittees to take care of these things, don't you? You've been running yourself ragged tending to each tiny detail, when there really is no need. Is there anything left for the rest of the banquet committee to handle?"

"I just want to make sure everything goes well," she answered defensively.

He'd single-handedly ruined the mood of the morning. All her sexy playfulness had vanished.

Since the damage was done, Eli decided to go for broke. It had been on his mind, and now was as good a time as any to bring it up.

"Why do you insist on doing it all?" he asked.

"I do not."

"Yes, you do. You've got your hand in everything. Do you think the banquet will fall apart if you're not the one to finalize the menu, or if someone else makes sure the decorator has the right color balloons? And what the hell kind of color is ecru, anyway?"

She wiped the sides of her mouth with a napkin and tossed it on the empty plate. "You don't know what you're talking about." Monica pushed her chair from the table and rose.

"Whether you admit it or not, you're a control freak."

She turned around, and Eli could physically feel the heat emanating from her glare. He'd messed up big-time with that one.

Her eyes creased in anger. In a slow, steady voice that belied the fury in her stare, she said, "I left the catering details to Dr. Moore and had to find another pastry chef because he gave them the wrong date. Nurse Cannon from Pediatrics was in charge of getting the tickets printed, and we now have five hundred tickets with Memorial Methodist Hospital instead of Methodist Memorial. If I don't step in now, we're liable to have fluorescent pink tablecloths and chicken from Popeyes as our dinner.

"There is a lot riding on this banquet's success. I have too much at stake, and I'm not trusting just anyone to do it."

"They are not eleven-year-olds, Monica! These are professionals."

"Who can't remember the correct name of the hospital where they have worked for years!"

This was hopeless.

Grabbing her hands, Eli brought them to his lips and kissed her fingers. "Look, the last thing I wanted to do was argue."

"Well, something in your plan went awry." She jerked her hands away and crossed her arms over her chest.

Eli threw his head back in frustration. The scent from the roses he'd also picked up on his jog was starting to give him a headache. The only reason he'd bought the damn flowers was because Monica had said yellow roses were her favorite. He pinched the bridge of his nose and tried to think of a way to salvage their morning.

"All I'm trying to say is that you don't have to kill yourself by doing everything," he stated, hoping she didn't take off on another tirade. "People are not going to give the center less money if the balloons are eggshell instead of ivory."

"Ecru," Monica answered.

"Ecru," Eli conceded. "Are we okay?" he asked, opening his arms.

She hesitated for a moment before stepping into his embrace and Eli sent up a silent prayer of thanks. He wrapped his arms around her and squeezed. He loved the feel of her soft body against him. He could stay like this for the rest of his life. Too bad they both had to earn a living.

As if she had read his mind, Monica gently disengaged. "I need to go," she said on a deep sigh. "I want to catch Patty before she's relieved by the day shift."

"Do you need me to come with you to the caterer tonight?"

"Don't worry about it. I'm starting to reconsider whether or not I need to go."

Yeah, right. Eli would bet money that she would be at the caterer as soon as her shift ended.

"Just in case you change your mind, beep me. I'm sure I'll still be at the hospital."

With a forlorn sigh, she said, "I really need to be going." Monica reached up on her tiptoes and planted a loud kiss on his lips. "Thank you for the lovely breakfast."

He reluctantly released her, but held on to her hand for a second longer. "Wait. Just breakfast?"

Monica looked back at him over her shoulder. "Well, I left fifty bucks on the nightstand for the services you provided last night."

He gave her a healthy tap on her butt. Monica covered her rear end with her hands and scooted out of the kitchen.

Eli settled against the counter with his coffee mug, shaking his head as he watched her ascend the stairs. There was no mistaking it: He had it bad for this woman.

When he arrived at the hospital a few hours later, after first stopping in to check on Mama, Eli discovered that Amanda Daniels had been admitted the past evening. Her chart stated a fainting spell brought on by her anemia, but Eli wasn't so sure the medical condition was the only cause. Mrs. Daniels's blackouts could very well be stress-induced.

Given her mental illness, the strained relationship between her and her husband, and the news Eli had laid on her regarding the possible closing of the center, Amanda Daniels had several reasons to block out the world.

Eli lightly tapped on the door before entering.

Both Daniels were there and—what?—they were holding hands. Well, he wouldn't say Amanda was reciprocating the gesture, but the fact that she allowed her hand to rest in her husband's palm was extremely telling. Maybe the two were on the track to reconciliation.

"Good morning," Eli said from the foot of the bed.

"Dr. Holmes." Jeffrey Daniels rose from the uncomfortable chair he had apparently slept in.

Eli tucked the clipboard under his arm and returned his handshake. "I heard you two had an eventful night."

"It wasn't too bad," Amanda replied in a weak voice.

"The good news is that the baby is fine. He or she," Eli said, respecting the fact that the couple did not want to know their baby's sex, "is perfectly healthy. Unfortunately I cannot say the same for the mother. You know what this means, right, Amanda?"

She nodded, a regretful look clouding her face.

Out of the corner of his eye, Eli noticed Jeffrey's head volleying back and forth as if he were watching a tennis match. Eli didn't have to be psychic to know that Amanda had not clued her husband in on yesterday's discussion.

"When will I be able to leave?" Her voice was so faint that Eli could barely hear her.

"I'll be back to see you in a few minutes," Eli said, patting Amanda's covered feet. "The phlebotomist will be in to take a little blood. I want to run a few more tests, then we'll talk about releasing you, okay?"

At her nod, he turned to Jeffrey. "Mr. Daniels, I'll let you bear the burden of all the paperwork. Follow me. The sooner you get started, that's the sooner you and your wife will be able to leave once she's medically released."

In the hallway, he stopped Jeffrey, saying, "I think we need to go to my office for a few minutes."

"There's something wrong, isn't there? Something happened to the baby that you were too afraid to say in front of Amanda."

"No, nothing like that." Okay, he could have handled this better, Eli admitted to himself. He'd been in this business long enough to know he should not make such a vague statement to a man whose wife was lying in a hospital bed. Eli decided on a more direct approach.

"Did you know of your wife's visit to the hospital yesterday?" he asked.

Jeffrey leaned back against the wall, dropped his head, and sighed. "I found out she came to see you after she was admitted to the hospital last night. I thought I had a list of all of her scheduled visits."

"Yesterday's visit wasn't scheduled. Amanda called with a few concerns typical of a first-time mother. It wasn't anything too serious, but I did impart some important news that I have a feeling she has not shared. It's something that concerns you both. Can we go to my office to discuss it?"

Jeffrey took another deep breath, and nodded. Eli could tell the man was still concerned for the health of his wife and baby, and thought that Eli wasn't telling him everything. He would have to do a better job at setting his mind at ease before he told him about the center's possible closing.

To Eli's relief, Jeffrey Daniels took the news about the center rather well.

"As I said," Eli continued as he sat behind his desk back in his office, "we are giving it our best effort to keep the facility open. I just want to make sure my patients have alternate care lined up."

"I'm not worried about that," Jeffrey answered. "The benefits with my new job will take care of Amanda's hospital bills."

Eli's eyebrows lifted. "You have a new job? Congratulations."

"Yeah, I got on with the company I've been contracting with. It comes with benefits, and I don't have to worry as much about getting laid off. It happened at the best possible time, too. This new job is going to free up a lot of my time. I won't have to take as many odd jobs, and I can give up my part-time job."

"You were working a full-time and part-time job?" And Eli thought *he* put in long hours.

Jeffrey Daniels bit nervously on his fingernails. He glanced up at Eli, chewed a second longer, then asked, "Can I get your opinion on something, Doc?"

Eli wasn't sure he wanted to hear this. He had a suspicion it had something to do with the state of the couple's marriage, and with the brand-new relationship he and Monica had just embarked upon, Eli did not want to think that people who were once in love could end up like the Danielses.

But it came with the job. He had counseled frightened, uncertain husbands before. He wouldn't leave Jeffrey Daniels up a creek without a paddle. Besides, Eli was curious as hell about what had gone wrong in this marriage. He didn't want to repeat the same mistakes with Monica.

"What's on your mind?" Eli picked up his favorite pen and rolled it between his thumb and forefinger as he watched the man settle uncomfortably in his seat.

"I'm sure you've noticed the relationship between my wife and me is somewhat . . . umm . . . strained."

"I perceived some distance between the two of you," he said simply. "Women experience many levels of emotion during pregnancy. I thought maybe that had something to do with it."

"No." Jeffrey shook his head. "The problems started before Amanda got pregnant. In fact, she'd filed for divorce the day the baby was conceived. It was one of those, you know, for-old-time's-sake kind of things." He paused for a moment. "As I think about it, things started going downhill around the time of the first pregnancy. You do know that Amanda miscarried once before?"

"We discussed her miscarriage on her first visit."

"Yeah, I guess you would know, being her doctor. You seem to know more about my wife than I do," Jeffrey said with a grunt.

"Mr. Daniels—"

"No, that's okay." He waved Eli off. "The important thing is keeping Amanda healthy, and that's what you're doing. I just . . . I wish she would talk to me."

The look Jeffrey gave him made Eli feel ten kinds of sorry for the poor guy.

"I love my wife, Dr. Holmes. This divorce was her idea, and for the longest time I had no idea why she wanted out. Then the other day she accused me of cheating on her. I have never been with another woman the entire time we've been married. I don't know where she got the idea that I cheated.

"I can't lose my wife," he said pleadingly. "She and that baby mean everything to me."

Jeffrey Daniels's face had taken on a desperate expression. His eyes were wide and bright, like a man with nothing to lose but everything.

"Mr. Daniels, I . . ."

"I'm only asking you to talk to her," he stated. "She listens to you, respects you."

Okay, here was one situation Eli had never found himself in before. This was not included in his job description. The hospital provided marriage counselors for things like this.

"You know, we have a great counseling center."

Jeffrey shook his head, the defeated look on his face turning into one of determination. "I know Amanda. She wouldn't go for that."

"What makes you think my talking to her will make a difference?"

"You got her to move back into our house," he stated simply. "It's a feat I could not accomplish with months of begging. I can't pinpoint what it is, but there's something about you that, I don't know, calms her."

He'd heard this before. Back in med school, his classmates used to say he had the magic touch when it came to pregnant women. His "gift" had aided him through a number of eventful births, but right now, Eli was ready to give the gift back to wherever it had come from. He did not want to be caught in the middle of this couple's marriage.

"Just think about it, Doc," Jeffrey said. No doubt he sensed his discomfort. At this point, Eli was doing very little to hide it.

"I can't promise you anything," Eli said, rising from his desk, hoping Jeffrey Daniels would get the hint.

The man rose from his chair and waited for Eli to round his desk. He grasped Eli's hand between both of his, and shook vigorously. The genuine hope and sincerity on his face created a feeling of dread in the pit of Eli's stomach. No use fighting it now; he was already in the middle of this. Eli resisted the urge to roll his eyes. How did he get caught up in these situations?

"I'll see what I can do," he said, pulling his hand free. He looked up at the clock on the wall. He had about twenty minutes before he had to start preparations for his first C-section, one of five scheduled today.

If he got Jeffrey Daniels out right now, he could sneak to the ER for a few minutes to see Monica.

Eli had a feeling working at the same hospital with his girlfriend would get him in trouble. Maybe that was the real reason he never wanted to date doctors. Maybe it had nothing to do with Elizabeth Graves.

Nah, that wasn't it. He had dated his share of nurses

who worked here, and he had never broken his neck to see them while at the job.

This time it was about the woman. Pure and simple.

Eli followed Jeffrey out of his office, closing the door behind him.

"Hey, Dr. Holmes." An RN walked up beside him on the way to the elevator. "You hear about the strike?"

"What strike?" Eli asked.

"In Mississippi. Where have you been all morning? It's all anyone is talking about."

Eli glanced at his watch. He was down to seventeen minutes.

"Nearly all the physicians have walked out of the hospitals or closed their practices," the nurse continued.

Okay, that sounded serious. Eli could only imagine the chaos that would ensue if something similar were to happen to the health care system in this city. Like those in New Orleans, Mississippi's hospitals had been painfully understaffed since Katrina.

"What caused the walkout," he asked, keeping in mind his ticking wristwatch.

"Insurance premiums."

Figures.

"I heard that some specialists are paying as much as two hundred thousand dollars a year in malpractice insurance," she said in awe. "As much as I gripe about the difference in pay between doctors and nurses, even I have to agree that's ridiculous."

Eli nodded. He empathized with the Mississippi doctors. He could have paid for his house three times over if so much of his salary didn't go for insurance. It was the price for practicing in the litigious land of mass tort lawsuits.

"I also heard they're asking for docs from neighboring states to help out until everything is resolved."

A sense of foreboding traveled down Eli's spine at the

potential implications of the nurse's statement. He only hoped neither he nor Monica were called out.

"Eli!"

His chin dropped to his chest at the sound of William Slessinger's jovial voice.

"I've been looking for you all morning. I'm happy I caught you before the marathon of Cesareans you have planned for today," Slessinger said, draping his arm across Eli's shoulders. "I've got a really big favor to ask. Why don't we go to your office for a few minutes?"

The sense of foreboding evolved into all-out dread. Eli already knew what would happen next.

He was on his way to Mississippi.

Chapter Twenty-one

As she threw her overnight bag on the backseat, Monica asked herself once again just what she was doing. She didn't even know how to get to Hattiesburg, Mississippi. Relying on directions she downloaded from the Internet, Monica could not believe she was actually about to get in her car and drive to another state.

For a man!

Okay, so things had not gone according to plan. Instead of staying man-free for another year or so, she had gone ahead and fallen in love.

Was she in love?

No. Love didn't happen this quickly. So what if the man cooked her breakfast, opened car doors, and looked spectacular in the buff? It took more than a couple of cozy dates, good food, and great sex to make her fall in love. Didn't it?

Monica pulled away from the curb and headed for the interstate. She drove through Slidell, crossed the state line into

Mississippi, and felt confident she wouldn't get lost when she saw the I-59 sign.

Peter Banyon, who was filling in for Eli, told her that most of the replacement doctors were staying at a hotel close to the hospital in Hattiesburg.

Two and a half hours after leaving New Orleans, Monica pulled into the parking lot of the hotel and smiled as she spotted Eli's SUV.

She parked, grabbed her bag from the backseat, and headed for the lobby. The front desk clerk sat behind the counter, thumbing through a magazine.

"Can I have the room number for Elijah Holmes," Monica asked. "He's expecting me."

Big lie. Actually, she had hoped he wouldn't be there. It would have been a nice surprise to be waiting in his bed when he returned. Naked.

"Monica?"

Monica turned at the sound of Eli's voice. She ran to him, wrapping her arms around his neck and slathering his face with kisses.

"Don't ask me what I'm doing here. I have no idea."

"I thought you had things to take care of for the banquet."

"I blew them off," Monica admitted, nearly giddy with the excitement of seeing him. How had she fallen so hard, so fast?

"I don't believe it," Eli said.

"I know. It's so not like me. I don't know what's happened to me, Eli. I think I'm addicted to you."

The smug smile that drew across his face made Monica wish she had the willpower to turn around and leave. Lord knows the man had a big enough ego. But she wasn't about to deny herself. There was something about him that she was powerless to fight, and if that made her weak where he was concerned, so be it. As long as she was in his arms once again, that was all that mattered.

Eli nibbled her neck, pulling her closer, his body's response to her boldly pressing against her stomach. Monica shivered.

"You know," Eli said, "some doctors prescribe going cold turkey in order to overcome an addiction. But I've always been of the mind-set that if you really want to cure it, you need to feed it."

Monica moaned. He felt so good. "What if I'm not looking for a cure?"

"Feed it anyway," he whispered against her neck, causing a trail of goose bumps to travel across her flesh.

"Can we go up to your room," Monica asked, remembering for the first time since she'd ran into Eli's arms that they were standing in the middle of the hotel lobby.

"Yes," Eli answered. "Food can definitely wait."

Monica lifted her head from where it rested against his chest. "I'm sorry. I don't want to stop you from eating dinner," she said, untangling from his embrace. "Go and get something to eat. I can wait."

"I can't."

"Eli, you need to eat something."

He cocked a brow.

Monica's entire body blushed. "I mean food."

He looked to the girl behind the desk. She was still engrossed in her magazine and, to Monica's relief, was not paying them any attention.

"How late does room service deliver?" Eli asked.

"Ten," she answered, not raising her head.

"Dinner is solved."

He grabbed Monica by the hand and led her up the flight of stairs to the second floor. Monica nearly shivered in anticipation.

She didn't know what was happening to her. She enjoyed sex as much as any healthy heterosexual female, but she'd never been champing at the bit. Eli was turning her into a sex fiend.

And, my goodness, was she loving it!

As soon as she crossed the threshold, Eli picked her up, kicked the door closed, and carried her to the bed. He laid her gently onto the soft bedding and covered her body with his.

This time they took it slow and easy, lavishing each other with moist kisses. Tasting each other with languid tongues. Loving each other with full hearts.

Monica closed her eyes and held on tight as Eli explored her body. She took pleasure in every soft, reverent stroke, relishing the great care he employed as he worshipfully made love to her.

When their pleasurable journey ended, Monica wrapped herself in a sheet and went to stand on the balcony while Eli ordered room service. A few minutes later, he joined her.

A million stars twinkled in the darkened sky, like a swarm of lightning bugs in a pitch-black rain forest. The night was quiet and peaceful, as if everyone had turned in early, leaving nothing but the crickets to beautify the night with their music.

With a deep breath, Monica took in the clean air.

"Something wrong?" Eli asked. He came up from behind and wrapped his arms around her shoulders. He kissed the top of her head and squeezed tighter.

Monica shook her head.

"You're not talking much," he commented, running his hands up and down her arms.

She smiled inwardly. "I'm speechless," she finally said.

Elijah threw his head back, his deep laughter rumbling through the quiet darkness. "That's about the best compliment I've ever received."

Monica sobered. "Have you had many?"

"Many what?"

"Compliments. For . . . you know . . ."

She felt him sigh against her back. "Why would you pick right now to ask me something like that?"

She turned to face him. "Because I want to know."

"You'll just get upset and stop talking to me, and it'll take the rest of the night for me to get back in your good graces. I had other plans for our night."

"I won't get upset." She drew a cross over her chest with her finger. "I promise."

"Yeah, right," Eli muttered. After a few moments he said, "I'll make a deal with you. I'll tell you what you want to know, if you do the same for me."

She laughed. "I don't have much to tell, but fine."

"Okay. So what do you want to know?"

"How many serious girlfriends have you had?"

"Two."

"Does this include the woman who came to your mother's last Sunday?"

"Three," he corrected.

Monica chewed on that piece of information for a bit. She pretended to look for dirt underneath her fingernails. With feigned casualness she knew Eli would see right through, she asked, "How many women have you slept with?"

"You don't want to know. Next question."

"Give me an estimate."

"No."

Monica crossed her arms over her chest. He uncrossed them and brought her hands to his lips, giving each of her fingers a light peck.

"Have you ever heard that sex is different for men and women?" he asked.

She nodded.

"It's true," Eli stated. "I will be the first to admit that during those years when I was not in a serious relationship, sex meant nothing more than physical relief. It was like eating and drinking, just a basic, everyday necessity."

"You're right; I don't want to hear this." Monica tried to pull away, but he held on to her hands.

"I now know the difference between having sex and making love." His eyes became serious. "Making love to you is a hundred times more meaningful than it has ever been before."

A rush of warmth washed over her, skating across her skin with sensual awareness. Her legs felt weak, as if they wouldn't hold her up. It was the most beautiful thing anyone had ever said to her.

"Now it's your turn," Eli said.

Monica had to clear her throat before she could speak again. "I told you, I don't have anything you would really want to know," she said, her emotions reeling from his heartfelt proclamation.

"I beg to differ." He grabbed her hands and kissed them. "I want to know who hurt you."

Monica frowned in confusion. "What do you mean?"

"I know you've been hurt, Monica. The signs are all there."

And all this time she thought she had done a pretty good job of keeping her feelings shielded. It was scary to think Eli could see through her so easily.

"His name was Patrick," Monica said, resigned to the fact that he would eventually find out. "I dated him for six years." She shifted uncomfortably. "We talked about marriage on and off, but Patrick always said he wasn't ready."

"He was a coward," Eli said.

"No, he was right," Monica asserted. "If Patrick and I had married, it would have been the biggest mistake of both our lives. I didn't love him," she admitted. "Not like you're supposed to love the person you're going to spend the rest of your life with."

"Why did you stay with him for so long?" Eli asked.

"He was safe," she said simply.

"I don't understand."

"I needed to be with someone who could live up to my parents' high standards and make me look good in their eyes, for once." She tipped her head up. "You see, I'm considered the slacker in my family."

"You? Miss Top Five Percent in Her Class?"

"That's four percentage points from the number one spot. And for Catherine and Garrett Gardner, nothing but number one will do."

"What does this have to do with you and the jerk you dated?"

She shrugged. "Patrick comes from a prominent family. He was the type of guy my parents expected me to end up with. So I convinced myself I was happy. Well, happy enough."

He gave her arm a gentle squeeze, and Monica nearly faltered. She expected ridicule. She had never imagined Eli would offer her comfort, nor had she expected the soothing reassurance it would bring.

Spurred by his encouraging embrace, Monica continued. "In a way, I don't fault Patrick for leaving. Everyone deserves to find true love, and maybe that's what he's found. It's the way he left that I can't forgive."

Monica took another deep, reassuring breath.

"About a year ago, I came in from a terrible day at work to find Patrick sitting at the table with another woman. His bags and boxes of his stuff were stacked next to the door. He introduced the woman as Elaina and told me she was pregnant and that he was leaving me. They had been married earlier that morning."

"Oh, baby." Eli wrapped his arms around her and held

her head against his chest. His compassion was nearly her undoing, but Monica refused to shed a single tear over past mistakes with Patrick, especially in the arms of the man she was beginning to love.

Eli pulled back and dipped down to her eye level. "I knew you were in pain, but I never would have guessed how much he hurt you."

"Not anymore. Really," Monica assured him when he gave her a skeptical look. "I'm better off without him," she said, and for the first time in over a year, she actually believed the words. As of this moment, as she stood surrounded by Eli's strong arms, she knew for certain she no longer needed Patrick Dangerfield in her life. Eli was all the man she needed.

He captured her by the shoulders and turned her around. He resumed their previous position with her back against his chest. He rested his chin on her head and held her in his arms as they swayed side to side, surrounded by the silent, peaceful night.

Happiness bubbling over within her at the thought of how Eli had freed her heart, Monica smiled contently, relishing his warm embrace. She felt as if a thousand-pound boulder had been lifted from her shoulders.

"Now I have another question for you," she said.

"I thought I'd already had my turn," he murmured.

"The counsel has rebuttal rights."

Eli let out an exaggerated sigh. "Fine. Whatever you say, Counselor." He dragged out the last word. "What else do you want to know?"

"How did your rule of not dating doctors come about?" she asked. It had been a burning issue since the moment Monica had heard the nurses discussing Dr. Holmes's hard, fast rule. Even before she had any romantic intentions toward him, Monica would admit she had been miffed about his unwillingness to date a woman simply because she was a doctor.

There was a knock at the door.

"Saved by the bell," Eli said. "Stay here, I'll get that." He winked as he left her standing on the balcony while he collected their dinner.

"The pasta looks good," Eli said, coming up to the sliding door. "You better get back in here before it gets cold."

"Not so fast, Mr. Slick." Monica caught him by the waistband of the pajama bottoms he'd pulled on over his silk boxers when he went to answer the door.

Eli closed his eyes, and his head fell forward. He looked as though he was headed to the guillotine.

Monica giggled, but she was not letting him off the hook. "You still have to answer my question. The food can wait."

"But I'm hungry," he complained.

"All the more reason for you to start talking." This time Monica was the one to pull him into her embrace. She wrapped her arms around his waist and laid her head against his warm, naked back. He felt so strong and oh so good.

"Okay, what's the deal with the rule?" she asked.

"You are asking the tough questions tonight, aren't you?" He took a deep breath and began. "Back when I was young and extremely stupid, I got mixed up in an affair with one of my professors."

"Not the wisest move," Monica said.

"I've definitely had better moments," Eli concurred. "Someone caught us in a compromising position in her office. Instead of owning up to our relationship, she started spreading rumors that I tried to seduce her to get ahead because I didn't have the skills to make it as an ob-gyn. It wasn't until later that I found out she was up for the head of obstetrics position. She pretty much fed me to the wolves to save her own hide."

"Oh, Eli, I'm so sorry." She paused. "Is this why you have such an aversion to being auctioned at the banquet?"

"I never really thought about it, but I guess in a way, yeah. I doubt anyone will bid based on what they think of a doctor's professional skills."

"I think it's an accurate assumption that professional skills will mean squat to the bidders," Monica grinned. She gave him a light kiss on his back. "I guess I can't blame you for having that rule."

He shrugged. "The rule was never written in stone, but I was so leery of being accused of trying to sleep my way to the top that I decided to cross doctors off my list of eligible love interests. There are millions of women around the world who are not doctors; I thought I could surely find my soul mate in one of them."

"Do you still see it that way?" Monica asked, wrapping her arms tighter around his waist. Eli dislodged himself from her hold, turned around, and pulled her into his arms. He kissed her deeply, and Monica arched her neck to give him better access to the sensitive spot that craved his kiss.

"No," he answered after trailing a string of kisses along her proffered neck. "I think I've found my soul mate, and she happens to be a brilliant doctor."

A ripple of excitement fluttered through her. "I think I've found my soul mate, too."

"Is he a *brilliant* doctor?" Eli asked, an irresistible grin lighting up his face.

"I wouldn't say brilliant, but he's okay."

He bit her shoulder. "Just for that, you're going to be punished." He bent down and scooped her up in his arms. The bedsheet opened at her neck, and Eli dipped his head and ran his tongue between the valley of her exposed breasts.

Monica gasped, then moaned as his mouth moved to her nipple. "Mmm . . . but I like your form of punishment," she purred. "So is it really punishment at all?"

"Yes, it is," Eli said. He brought her back into the room and deposited her on the mattress. Standing at the foot of the bed, Eli relieved Monica of the sheet, throwing it over the room's lone chair. He pushed the pajamas and boxers from his hips and down his legs. "You see," Eli said in a silky voice, "this time I'm going to make you scream for hours before I let you sleep."

A smiled curved up the corners of Monica's mouth as a shiver of heated excitement ran down her spine. She held out her hands and parted her thighs.

"Let the punishment begin."

Chapter Twenty-two

Monica tried to concentrate on the caterer's words, but her brain was having none of that. Instead it was fixated on the man whose bed she had left in the wee hours of the morning.

Monica had never been more tempted to call in sick than when the alarm had gone off at four o'clock that morning. Eli had set it after their long bout of lovemaking, when Monica told him she would need to be back in New Orleans by seven A.M. She had switched to an earlier shift so that she could tend to banquet issues that afternoon.

As she tried to keep herself awake long enough to understand the caterer, her heart overflowed with regret. She did not want to be here. She wanted to be in Hattiesburg, waiting in Eli's bed.

Monica cursed the Mississippi insurance commission. They had no clue of the far-reaching implications of their actions. If not for them, Eli would be only a few minutes from her grasp, not hours.

Monica nodded at the caterer, shook his hand, and prepared to leave. She would speak to Dr. Moore about entrusting the catering details to the subcommittee once again. Eli was right: She didn't have to do it all by herself. Monica had other ways to spend her time, like in bed with her man.

Tragically, she would not be in his bed for another couple of days. Since the strike in Mississippi seemed nowhere near its end, Eli was stuck there for the remainder of the week until one of the other OB docs returned from vacation.

Although Eli was over a hundred miles away, Monica would not be alone tonight. She'd accepted a dinner invitation from Alex. Apparently Eli's niece had accomplished something outstanding in school today and wanted to celebrate with dinner at her grandmother's. Alex said it would only be a few people, but Monica already knew what the Holmes family considered a "few." She was prepared for a houseful.

When she pulled up to the curb in front of the wood-frame house, Monica smiled at her accurate assumption. There were three cars in the driveway and four parked along the street. She could hear the myriad of voices as soon as she stepped out of her car.

Bypassing the front door, Monica walked to the back of the house and, knocking lightly, entered through the kitchen door. Many of the people she had met at Jasmine's birthday party were gathered in the kitchen, though there were a few unfamiliar faces. Monica did, however, notice the woman Eli considered one of his past serious relationships. She tried to keep her teeth from clenching.

Goodness, when had she become so possessive?

Monica spotted Alex among the fray and motioned for him.

"Hey, I'm glad you could make it." Alex bent over and gave her a light peck on the cheek. She would have to get used to these freely-given offers of affection. Her family had never been the touchy-feely type; they'd been too wrapped up in their own pursuits to form a true family bond.

"I bought a little something for Jasmine," she said, holding up the doll with the huge lips and big eyes that seemed to be all the rage with little girls Jasmine's age.

"You didn't have to do that," Alex said, ushering her in and closing the door behind her.

"It's what Eli would have done." Monica tried to speak above the noise. "I didn't want her to be disappointed."

Alex waved away the notion. "Eli had me store a closetful of toys for those occasions when he can't get away from the hospital. My little Jazzy Bean is never without a little something special from her uncle Elijah."

That didn't surprise Monica one bit. She knew how much Eli loved his niece. He doted on her as if she were his own. He would make a wonderful father one day.

A warm sensation formed in the pit of her belly. Monica wanted to close her eyes for just a second to imagine herself and Eli welcoming a baby into the world, but just as she was about to, Margo came up to greet her with a big hug.

Monica's presence and her position as Eli's girlfriend were summarily announced to the entire room. She was then introduced on a more intimate level to the people whom she had yet to meet.

Monica got her first real look at Tosha Culpepper, who made sure to mention at least five times in the first five minutes of conversation that she and Eli had dated throughout high school. She was also introduced to Tosha's younger sister, Sienna, who seemed much more down-to-earth than her high-strung sister, and who was celebrating a new job she had landed with one of the city's premier marketing agencies.

"You and my best friend, Nia, should talk," Monica told Sienna after hearing about the multimillion-dollar account the young executive had landed her first month on the job. "The two of you could go into business together."

Sienna laughed. "I'm not sure I'm ready to take my show on the road yet. Maybe after I've established a few clients and made a name for myself, I'll consider branching out on my own."

"She had better kick butt at her day job, because her basketball game is weak," Toby said, coming over to where they were standing just to the right of the stove. His arm was draped across Aria Jordan's shoulders.

Monica noticed Sienna stiffen at Toby and Aria's intrusion. Her previously relaxed expression turned to one of discomfort.

Quickly recovering her gaiety, Sienna responded to Toby's jibe. "Even though I could kick his butt in basketball even before his accident, Toby still thinks he's the better player." She hunched her shoulders in helpless surrender. "I begged him to get help for his delusions, but he just won't listen."

"Let's bring it outside," Toby demanded. "We can handle this right now."

"Are you sure you want the wrath of St. Mary's Academy's all-district and all-state player?" Sienna asked. "You do remember there was only one player—me—with that distinction during senior year, right?"

Toby shook his head in agitation. "There you go bringing that up again. You know I had a bad flu that season and my school's coach wouldn't let me play."

"Yeah, yeah. Always an excuse."

Monica laughed at their sparring and wondered again about the look that had flashed briefly across Sienna's face when Toby walked over with his arm around Aria Jordan. It was obvious the two had been friends for a long time.

Sienna's reaction caused Monica to wonder if they had ever been more than just friends.

A few minutes later, everyone sat for an informal dinner of hot dogs and potato chips. Because this special dinner was in honor of Jasmine's having a perfect report card, she was given the honor of picking tonight's menu.

Monica could not decide whether the Holmeses just loved getting together or if she'd had a lacking childhood. She had received straight As from kindergarten through twelfth grade, but since the same could be said for her older brother, that accomplishment had gone unnoticed by her family. Jasmine Holmes made all As and the entire block showed up to celebrate.

Monica felt a twinge of disgust with herself. Was she really jealous of a five-year-old? How pathetic!

No. It wasn't just the five-year-old that struck an envious cord; it was the entire family. Monica had never experienced such closeness. She wondered if the Holmeses realized just how lucky they were. And she couldn't help but pray she would become a more permanent fixture in their family.

Monica nibbled on a piece of chocolate cake—yes, there was even a "Congratulations, Jasmine" cake for the occasion—and perused the scene before her. She tried to ignore Tosha, who had come to stand next to her. Tosha leaned against the wall, mimicking Monica's stance.

"So, how long have you and Elijah been together?"

Well, she certainly didn't waste any time, did she?

"For a while," Monica answered. That was about as specific as she cared to get. She did not owe this woman a play-by-play recap of her and Eli's relationship.

"We were together throughout high school. We were so in love," Tosha sang sweetly.

"Yes, you mentioned that already." Monica could not

control her clipped tone. She felt ridiculous resenting the ex-lover. How clichéd.

But she didn't like this woman.

Tosha Culpepper had purposely injected her and Eli's high school romance into the conversation every chance she got. She had tried every trick known to man to make Monica feel left out.

"I'm not sure what he's told you, but when Elijah and I decided to end our relationship, it was not as amicable as he makes it out to be. I was the one who ended it."

Monica turned her head to the side and ran her gaze up and down the other woman, hoping she achieved the uninterested look she was going for.

"I was tired of his lies," Tosha continued. She turned her body fully toward Monica. "You see, no matter how much he tells you he loves you and that you're the only woman for him, Eli will always be attracted to other women. He is incapable of being committed to one woman." She shrugged. "Of course, some women are willing to let him get away with it. For what you get in return, letting Eli have a little something on the side isn't much to pay."

Monica lifted a brow.

Tosha patted her on the shoulder and said with a half-hearted laugh, "Don't even try it, honey. I had him long before you did. I know how good he is."

She *had* him? Just the thought of Eli with this woman had Monica ready to throw up. Or throw a punch upside Tosha's head. Either one sounded good at the moment.

"His roaming eye gets old," Tosha continued. "And no matter how good he is in bed, the fact that he's giving it to countless other women will start to get to you. I just thought I'd warn you," she said, then smiled as if they had just spent the past five minutes trading recipes.

Monica stared at Tosha's retreating back and fought the

urge to tackle her like a football player. She refused to give an ounce of credence to what she'd said. Monica knew envy when she heard it. Tosha Culpepper wanted Eli for herself. The woman could not be more transparent if she were made of sheer lace.

Alex had already explained that Tosha's being here tonight was unavoidable since she answered the phone when he'd called to invite Sienna, but he promised to keep her as far away from future Holmes family functions as possible. That, at least, brought Monica a bit of relief.

By the time she arrived at her apartment, Monica was ready to crash on the floor of her foyer. The ten steps to the sofa seemed like a mile.

It had taken a half hour to say good-bye. Of course, every time Monica tried to leave, Margo dragged her into another conversation.

Even in her tired state Monica managed to smile. She liked Margo. She was the polar opposite of Monica's own mother, who ruled her children with an iron fist and was as cold as Antarctica in the dead of winter. No matter how hard she tried, Monica could never please her mother. But with Margo, just being there seemed to be enough for her.

The telephone rang, and Monica groaned. In order to answer it she would have to walk, and that was just a little too much to ask of her aching body at the moment.

She managed to shuffle to the phone on the end table. She picked up on the fifth ring. "Hello."

"You miss me?" came a deep, decadent voice.

A warm glow started from within her chest and spread throughout her body. It was amazing what just the sound of this man's voice did to her.

"I was going to lie, but what's the point? I miss you terribly."

"Good."

"Shut up," she laughed. "I had a great time with your family. Your uncle Jake put a hole in your mother's kitchen wall, trying to open a jar of pickles."

"Never a dull moment at the Holmeses."

"Want to know the most interesting portion of my night?"

"What's that?" Eli asked.

"My little heart-to-heart with one Ms. Tosha Culpepper," Monica answered sweetly.

He waited a beat, then cursed. Monica could barely hear the whispered reply. "That girl."

"She sure is a piece of work."

"She's a basket case, Monica. I don't even want to know the things she told you."

"Oh, you certainly don't want to know, but I'll tell you anyway."

She heard his sigh over the phone.

"According to Tosha, if I'm smart, I'll get out while my heart's still intact. I have to warn you, I pride myself on being a pretty smart cookie."

"I swear she was not this way in high school. Maybe a little off, but nothing compared to the fruitcake she's turned out to be. Don't believe a word she says."

"It's forgotten, Eli. I know a jealous ex-girlfriend when I see one. Now, her sister, Sienna, seems really sweet."

"She is. Sienna is the only sane one in that family. I think their mother found her on the doorstep or something."

"Stop that," Monica laughed. "By the way, Alex wanted me to tell you they've decided to take your mom to Ruth's Chris Steak House for her birthday dinner. I was surprised when he told me it would be just the five of you. That seems a little small for a Holmes family gathering."

"Mama loves throwing big parties for everybody else,

but she never wants us to make a fuss over her birthday. My brothers and I have talked about doing something big for her sixtieth birthday next year, though."

"Well, this year, it'll be just a cozy dinner with Margo and her boys."

"You're invited, too."

"Am I?"

"Of course."

"Thank you," Monica answered, unable to wipe the smile from her face. "Do you have any idea when you'll be back?" she asked.

"That's why I called." She heard the disappointment in his voice. Monica's heart fell.

"What happened? I thought Dr. Lewis would take over for you?" Was she actually whining? She never whined.

"His father is worse off than they realized. He's taking an extended leave. He'll be in Minnesota for at least the next three weeks."

"*Three weeks!* I can't drive up to Hattiesburg for the next three weeks. Do you know how expensive gasoline is? There has got to be another ob-gyn they can bring out there."

"What can I say? They want the best," he said in an exaggeratedly cocky tone.

"This is so not the time to try out the new comedy act. We need to think of something. I miss you," she said softly.

"I know, baby. Let's hope the Mississippi legislature can come up with a plan when their emergency session reconvenes tomorrow."

"They had better," Monica said. "I may just have to go up there and lobby myself."

Eli chuckled. "I'll warn them." In a more serious tone, he said, "I'm sorry I have to be away from you for so long."

"I'm sorry, too."

"And I'm sorry I'm not doing my part for the banquet."

"You've done an amazing job already. So many bachelors have volunteered, thanks to your arm-twisting. And now that you've convinced Toby to let Aria Jordan perform, I know we're going to make more than enough to keep the center open. You just concentrate on getting back here."

"I promise I'll try."

It took everything Monica possessed not to say the words she was dying to say. But until Eli made a proclamation of love, she would not reveal what was in her heart.

She had told Patrick she loved him very early in their relationship, and Monica was now convinced that was when he had tied the puppet strings to her back. Once she made her feelings known, he knew he could manipulate her. Monica refused to be put in that position again.

"Don't let them work you too hard," she said instead.

"Same with you. Although the only person who would work you too hard is you."

"Ha, ha," she mocked, rolling her eyes, although he couldn't see her. "Good night."

"Good night, Monica."

Say it, Monica silently pleaded. But he didn't.

"Talk to you tomorrow," Eli said, then he hung up the phone.

Monica listened to the steady hum of the dial tone for several moments while she mulled over the multitude of questions rolling through her mind. Had Eli fallen as hard for her as she had for him? Would he be willing to take their relationship to the next level? Would he ever tell her he loved her?

She was too exhausted to make sense out of it all.

Monica deposited the handset back into its cradle. She stripped away her clothes on the way to her bedroom and, once there, fell face-first onto the bed.

Chapter Twenty-three

The doorbell's incessant ringing had Amanda near the edge. She smoothed the covers around her and tried to ignore the diabolical chiming, focusing instead on the made-for-TV movie she had been struggling to watch for the past half hour. She still had no idea what the movie was about.

The doorbell rang again, and Amanda fought the urge to waddle to the front door and punch the hell out of whoever had been there for the past five minutes. Probably a bill collector.

Whoever it was, they could press the bell until their fingers fell off. The last thing Dr. Holmes told her was that she had to remain in bed if she didn't want to endanger herself or the baby. She would heed her doctor's warning.

The ringing stopped, and Amanda exhaled a sigh of relief.

Lying in bed all day had her crazy enough as it was; she

did not need additional contributions to her impending insanity.

The doorbell sounded again, followed by rapid knocking.

Oh, for goodness's sake. She would just have to seek Dr. Holmes's forgiveness.

Amanda threw the covers off and struggled to get her legs over the side of the bed. She had been on her back so long that she wasn't sure her limbs would be able to hold her up.

Knowing what she was doing was wrong, Amanda felt a twinge of guilt settle deep in her stomach as she lifted herself up from the bed and headed toward the front door. She said a silent prayer that the dizziness would not return.

She unlatched the chain, opened the door, and froze. Her breath caught in her throat as she stared at the face of the one person she hated more than any other in the world. A person she had never officially met, but who had turned her life upside down.

The other woman.

Like film on a movie reel, her mind raced back to the day she saw Jeffrey and this woman walking out of their house together, hand in hand. At first she had been willing to write it off as harmless, something that could easily be explained. Until the two of them embraced. They'd held each other, then Jeffrey had opened her car door and helped her inside.

That was when Amanda knew this stranger her husband had brought into her house was anything but harmless. She was a home wrecker.

And now she was standing on her doorstep.

"Is Jeffrey Daniels here?" the woman asked.

Amanda was about to tell her to go to hell when she looked down and noticed the woman's very pregnant belly.

Her world imploded.

She lifted her hand to her forehead as sudden dizziness overwhelmed her. The reality of Jeffrey's betrayal hit with the force of a Mack truck. Her heart pounded frantically in her chest, the blood rushing in her ears like a raging river. Breathing became difficult, almost impossible. Unbidden, images of her husband lying with this woman, impregnating her in their own bedroom, flashed through Amanda's mind.

A mass of hurt encircled her heart. Pain. Anger. Fury. Deep, profound, unmitigated fury. It spiraled through her body as the realization of what stood before her dawned with mind-blowing clarity.

Amanda could not give Jeffrey what he wanted, so he'd found someone who could.

"Jeffrey Daniels?" the woman asked. "He still lives here, doesn't he?"

Amanda tried to find her voice. It was lodged behind a lump of resentment. This was the woman who had ruined her marriage, who had coldly stolen her husband.

"Is everything okay?" the woman asked. She flattened her palm over her belly and rubbed.

Amanda saw red. Was she taunting her? Had Jeffrey discussed their infertility struggles?

Even as she felt her own baby flutter inside of her, Amanda was hit with a wave of inferiority. She felt second-rate to the woman whom Jeffrey had easily gotten pregnant.

"Could you please tell Jeffrey I need to speak with him?"

With sereneness completely contradictory to the turmoil roiling inside, Amanda calmly warned, "If you don't get away from my door, I will hurt you."

The woman's eyes widened. "I'm sorry?" she said, confusion contorting her face.

"You heard me," Amanda annunciated through clenched

teeth. At her sides, her hands balled into fists of their own accord.

"Look, I really need to see Jeffrey Daniels. It is very important. It's about work he did on my patio. . . ."

The rest of the woman's words faded into a distant background. Amanda could feel herself losing it. The humming in her ears worsened as her head began to pound.

Then Jeffrey arrived.

His Explorer pulled into the driveway, and he jumped out. Seeing him race toward his lover pushed Amanda over the edge.

"You still want him?" she screamed. "There he is, running to your side like a knight in shining armor. You can have the son of bitch, because I don't want him."

"Amanda! What are you doing out of bed?" Jeffrey tried to grab her arm, but she flung his hand away. She stomped onto the front lawn with measured steps, screaming every inch of the way.

"She came looking for you." Amanda focused her venom on her husband. "I guess you were paying too much attention to me, and your whore didn't like it. Are you planning to introduce your children to each other? Maybe they can be playpen pals?"

"What is she talking about?" The woman looked at Jeffrey. "I only came to pay the rest of the balance for the brickwork you did on my patio." At her husband's mistress's feigned bewilderment and flimsy lie, Amanda felt the frayed threads of her sanity unravel.

"Get away from my house!" she yelled as she hurled herself at the other woman.

Jeffrey stopped her and wrapped his hands around Amanda's wrists. "Dammit, Amanda! What in the hell are you doing?"

"Get your hands off of me! I hate you! I *hate* you!" She choked on the bone-wracking sobs that escaped from deep within her soul. Amanda closed her eyes tightly and fought against his hold. "It wasn't my fault! I wanted a baby as much as you did; it wasn't my fault I couldn't get pregnant. It wasn't my fault that I lost the other baby. But I didn't run out and have one with someone else."

Still holding on to her wrists, Jeffrey turned to his other woman. "Mrs. Patterson, I'll get the payment when I come to finish up the brickwork."

"Go to her! You can have her right now. I don't want anything to do with you." She wrenched her hands free. "I want you gone. No!" she gasped when he tried to capture her wrists again. "Get away from me!"

"Amanda, stop this!"

"Leave me alone." A searing pain gripped her stomach. Clutching it in her hands, Amanda screamed, "I hate you! I *hate* you!" The sharp pain shot through her stomach like a lightening rod, bringing Amanda instantly to her knees. "God, no," she cried, cradling her belly, willing her baby to be okay.

"Amanda!"

Faintly, she heard Jeffrey speaking into his cellular phone to the 911 operator. Another shock of pain ripped through her, and Amanda fell all the way to the ground, the dampness from the earlier rain shower seeping through her lightweight dress.

She felt the rush of liquid flow out of her, and instant tears sprung to her eyes, tears that had nothing to do with the paralyzing pain.

Her water had just broken.

Her baby was coming. Five weeks too soon.

Monica rummaged frantically through the mountain of invoices and receipts. She'd just had the contract for the ice sculpture a minute ago. It had to be in here. But it wasn't. Monica pounded both fists on the table, sending papers flying.

She had to get a grip. The banquet was less than a week away, but her nervous breakdown was less than a second away. If she did not calm down, she was going to go postal on the next person to walk through the door, which would likely be Dr. Moore, since she had commandeered the head of the food subcommittee's office without his knowledge.

She wasn't used to being at the hospital and not being in the ER, but since it was her day off, she'd had to find somewhere else to work. Right now Monica was contemplating bringing everything to the bar down the street. She would probably be in a better mood after a few drinks.

What had she been thinking, taking on this banquet, knowing so much was riding on it? When she first agreed to chair the fund-raiser, all Monica could see were the accolades she would receive after saving the day. She had not thought about what would happen if the banquet flopped.

Fear of the banquet having less than stellar success was giving her an ulcer. Though she must admit the praise already trickling in felt *really* good.

Monica was still on cloud nine after running into Dr. Slessinger in the hallway. News of the record number of presold tickets had made its way back to the chief of staff. The praises he sang would be enough of an incentive to get her through the next few days.

Monica gathered the papers that had flown from the desk and stacked them in a neat pile. Finding this receipt was the last thing on her plate. Once she reviewed it and sent Dr. Moore her approval, she could head to the plantation in Destrehan and make sure everything was in order for Saturday.

Monica heard the door open but didn't bother looking up from her rummaging. "I'll be out of your office in a minute, Dr. Moore."

Yes. Monica breathed a sigh of relief as she came up with the receipt. She had not gone crazy . . . yet.

"Dr. Moore couldn't make it." Her head flew up at the sound of the familiar, sensual voice.

"Eli," she whispered. She bounded from the chair and rushed into his arms, showering his faintly stubble-covered chin with a rain of kisses. "What are you doing here?"

"I've promised to cover a month's worth of weekends for Dr. Bailey, but I don't care. I had to see you."

Monica's heart soared. God, she loved this man.

"I can't believe you went through all that trouble."

"Well, I did. So you can imagine how disappointed I was to find your apartment empty. You messed up my surprise."

"I'm sorry. There was just so much to do here today."

"On your day off?"

"The banquet is in less than a week, Eli."

"And as I've said before, there are other people to take care of this stuff. You've done a wonderful job delegating, Monica. You should be in administration instead of the ER."

She feigned an affronted gasp. "Bite your tongue."

"I know you'd never leave the ER. But seriously, you've done everything you can do for this banquet."

"But I just want to make sure everything is lined up—"

"No!" he said. "You're going to drive yourself crazy if you don't stop."

"I'm already there," she said with a sad laugh. In the relatively short time she had known him, Monica had already learned fighting Eli on something like this was a losing battle. "Fine," she said, conceding before he found out just how involved she had once again become in the banquet preparations. "What is this surprise?"

The devilish grin that curved up the corners of his

mouth sent a tiny shiver up her spine. "We're going to enjoy my number one hobby."

Monica's eyes widened. Teasingly, she said, "In the middle of the day?"

"My second favorite hobby," Eli amended.

"And just what is that?"

"Nuh-uh." He shook his head. "Just in case you don't like it, I'm not telling you until we get there."

"No fair," Monica laughingly protested. "Really, Eli, I need to drive out to St. Charles Parish. I'm scheduled to meet with the coordinator in about an hour."

"Cancel."

"I can't cancel."

"Then send someone in your place."

"I—"

She could send someone else. In fact, she *had* sent someone else. Kenya James, an RN on the site subcommittee, was already at Destrehan Plantation. Monica had no real reason to be there; she just wanted to make sure everything was up to her standards.

"You were saying?"

"Forget it," Monica replied. "Let's go. The capable site committee can take care of the details."

"You see, if you would just accept everything I say as law, you could save yourself so much time."

"Get out of here," Monica laughed, pushing Eli out the door.

"You have *got* to be kidding me."

Eli maneuvered his SUV into the first empty parking slot he could find, sending her a smile.

"Miniature golf?" Monica asked, dismay making her voice hike up like a soprano's.

"I couldn't get a tee time at any of the courses that are

up and running." Eli stepped down from the SUV and went around her side. "Besides, I figured you didn't play, so I thought I'd start you off on something a little simpler than the front nine at English Turn."

Monica halted in the act of getting out of the car. "Please don't tell me you spend all your free time on the golf course. That's so clichéd."

"Hey, I've got to be prepared for early retirement."

She rolled her eyes and finally allowed him to assist her. Placing her hand in his, she stepped down from the front seat. She brushed past him, and Eli nearly died as he caught a noseful of her delicious, delicate scent. Maybe he *should* have opted for his number one hobby.

"You're right," Monica said. "I have no idea how to golf. I've never even held a club."

As she crossed her arms over her chest, Eli's eyes automatically zoomed in on her luscious breasts. He envisioned trailing his tongue along their delicate slopes before taking her taut nipple between his teeth. His groin tightened unmercifully.

"Forget the golf," he said, taking her by the arm. "We've got better things to do."

"No," Monica pulled away. "You brought me out here. I'm ready to hit a home run." She made a swinging motion, as if holding a baseball bat.

"Wrong sport." He rolled his eyes.

"It was a joke."

"Fine. Ha, ha. Now let's go." He reached for her arm, and once again she pulled away.

"Why are you in such a hurry to go?"

Eli looked into her eyes, making sure his smoldering gaze left no question as to what he wanted. Her eyes traveled down to his crotch, where the evidence of his arousal was more than obvious.

When he noticed the devious smile creeping up the sides

of her mouth, Eli knew he was in trouble. Monica took a step back and crossed her arms over her chest again, but this time she rested them just under her breasts. They stood out as if they were being served on a platter. Eli groaned.

"I guess that's a pretty good reason," she finally answered. "But, umm, I think I'd rather golf."

Oh, the woman was heartless.

Eli closed his eyes and dropped his chin to his chest. "You're doing this just to torture me, aren't you?"

"What?" she asked with angel-eyed innocence. Just the thought of all the unangel-like things they could be doing right now was enough to drive him crazy.

"Monica, please." His raspy voice was filled with desire. He *so* needed to get her out of this parking lot and into a bed. He didn't even care whose bed, as long as they were horizontal.

Monica tipped her head to the side and taped her finger against her chin. She squinted her eyes as if thinking really hard. "Uh . . . no. I say we golf."

"Woman, you are so evil."

She was barely able to keep the laughter from her voice. "And you, Dr. Holmes, are way too used to getting what you want. I think someone needs to knock you down a peg or two."

"Can't you do that another night? In fact, I'll let you. You can deny me anything you want tomorrow, but I really, *really* want you right now, Monica." The last part came out like a man pleading for his life, though it was only fair since Eli was sure he would die if he didn't have her in the next five minutes.

"Nope." Monica shook her head. She grabbed him by his sleeve and dragged him toward the colorful entrance to the miniature-golf course, purposely swaying her hips from side to side.

"Stop that," Eli warned.

"Stop what?"

"You know what. If you don't want to go at it between two parked cars, you'll stop shaking your behind like that."

She stuck her nose in the air. "I have no idea what you're talking about." Her hips rocked even more.

Eli reluctantly followed her to the cashier's booth, trying like hell not to look at her firm backside. It was impossible.

When he took his wallet out of his back pocket to pay for the round of golf and the club rental, he pulled his shirt from his pants, hoping to conceal his erection. Obviously his little man wasn't going down anytime soon.

For a sport he enjoyed almost as much as breathing, this was the most frustrating round of golf Eli had ever played. Monica did her best to distract him. She took her sweet time bending over and situating the ball on the tee, leaving her saucy butt in the air a few moments longer than necessary.

She was going to pay for this. He might not let her get any sleep at all tonight.

"Though you say you spend most of your spare time playing golf, you sure are missing a lot of putts," Monica remarked after Eli missed a three-footer he could normally sink with his eyes closed.

"I'm usually not this distracted," he said in his own defense.

"Distracted? Why ever would you be distracted?" There was the doe-eyed innocence again.

"Keep it up," he warned. Unable to guard against her infectious smile, Eli could not help the grin spreading across his face. That was okay. He would be grinning a hell of a lot more in a few hours.

"So what's your handicap?"

"Depends on who I'm playing with."

She stopped in the middle of her putt and looked back at him. "How so?"

Eli shrugged. "I tend to play better with Alex, but Toby brings my game down."

"In what way?" She looked at him with genuine interest.

Eli thought about it for a minute. He'd asked himself the same question time and time again. "I don't know," he finally answered, because truthfully he didn't. "Toby and I have always been in competition with each other, especially after my dad died. Alex fell into the father role, and Toby and I were like the two kids who always wanted to impress him.

"It's not a secret that Toby is the most athletic of the three of us, so when it comes to sports, my game always falters when I'm around him. It's like I break under the pressure of trying to compete with someone I know is better than I am."

"That's the story of my life," Monica said.

"What is?"

"Competition. I'm stuck in the middle of two geniuses. I told you about my brother, Phillip, whom I spent my entire life trying to live up to. Then my little sister, Ashley, came out of the womb playing Beethoven's Fifth Symphony. She's at Juilliard now, probably teaching some of the teachers." A smile touched the edges of her mouth.

"I tried to measure up"—she hunched her shoulders in helpless defeat—"but what can you do?"

"My brothers and I are always trying to one-up each other, but it's all in fun."

"Wish I could say the same," she said with a dry laugh. "It went far beyond just Phillip and Ashley, though. The competitiveness seeped into every part of my life, and just like you said, I would crumble under the pressure of working beside someone I knew was better than me.

"The worst instance happened back in St. Louis, at my old job."

Eli dropped his club and walked over to her, taking her hand. He sensed the unease in her voice, but he had to ask, "What happened?"

She looked down at their clasped hands and gave him another of those sweet but sad smiles. "It was during my second year of residency. A new doctor, Mark Festerling, started in the ER. He was a trauma surgeon who wanted to change to emergency medicine, so he was put on a residency rotation. Of course he blew all of the other residents out of the water.

"I studied my butt off that year. Went so far as to practice my incisions and suturing on raw chickens. I was determined to win even more accolades than Dr. Festerling. But my plan backfired."

She was no longer looking at him but instead focused on something over his shoulder.

"A six-year-old came in with an obstructed airway. Something so simple," she said with a derisive laugh. "But, you see, the toughest part of my entire residency was my peds rotation. I had a hard time intubating small children. The narrower breathing passage," she explained, taking a deep swallow. Eli could tell this was hard for her, but he would let her continue. She obviously needed to talk through the ordeal. He squeezed her hand, a silent message of encouragement.

"I was doing really well until Dr. Festerling invaded the trauma. As soon as he walked into the room, I froze."

"Did the child die?" Eli asked, stroking his thumb over the back of her hand.

Monica shook her head. After another deep breath, she said, "Festerling stepped in and saved the day. I was devastated. I contemplated quitting."

"Oh, Monica," Eli grabbed her shoulders and brought her to his chest, cradling her head against him.

"Someone who would put some stupid competitive streak over the life of a child should not practice medicine."

"It was a mistake."

"Would you want to be the one to explain it to that child's mother if he had died?" She shook her head against his chest. "It's this drive to be perfect. Do you know, every decision I've ever made in life has been to prove that I'm better? I've got to get over this, Eli. No one is perfect."

"You'll get no argument from me there. I've told you more than once that there are other capable people on the planet. You do not have to do it all."

She looked up at him, the tears shimmering in her brown eyes making them even more luminous.

"You've done wonders for me, do you know that? I can guarantee that if I didn't have you to . . . umm . . . distract me, I would have put on this entire banquet by myself. I would not have even bothered to set up subcommittees."

Eli pulled her tighter against him and bent down to kiss the tip of her nose. "You really need to learn to relax, woman."

"I'm sure there are a number of ways you can teach me how to do that," she murmured.

"Baby, I'm ready and willing. Right now."

A couple passed them on the golf course, giving them the evil eye. Probably because they had hogged this hole for the past twenty minutes.

"Can we please get out of here?" Eli whispered into her ear.

"Yes," came Monica's husky reply.

"Thank God. Finally."

"Finally?" she laughed. "Must I remind you that you

are the one who brought me here? You wanted me to learn your second-favorite hobby, remember?"

"Forget my second-favorite hobby."

Eli made quick work of returning the rented clubs. He grabbed Monica by the hand and nearly dragged her to the parking lot like a caveman hauling in his day's catch. He helped her into the SUV and kissed her deeply as he drew the seat belt across her torso and buckled her in.

"It's time for me to show you how my number one hobby earned its prestigious place on the list."

Chapter Twenty-four

Jeffrey tried but could not manage to lower his hand from the thin pane of Plexiglas separating him from his new-born daughter. He wasn't sure how long he had been staring at her. One thing he did know: He could stay in this exact spot, doing this exact thing, for the rest of his life.

Another tear slid down his cheek. He had stopped trying to hide them hours ago. He didn't care who saw him; he was more than proud to say that his daughter brought tears to her father's eyes.

She punched her tiny fist in the air, and Jeffrey's heart lurched. He reached out for her, his palm coming up with hard plastic.

She was so fragile, so incredibly delicate. Just the thought of anything happening to her caused his chest to grow uncomfortably tight. His breath hitched at the knowledge that he was now responsible for the tiny human being lying on the other side of the glass. He held her precious life in his hands.

The awesomeness of his new responsibility crashed through him like a three-ton boulder.

One of the pediatric nurses walked up to the incubator, opened it, and gently pulled out his daughter. She turned to Jeffrey and mouthed, "Feeding time."

He nodded. He didn't want her to go, but his baby had to eat.

"Do you want to feed her?" The nurse pronounced each word slowly so he could read her lips.

"Can I?" he mouthed back.

The nurse motioned with her head. Jeffrey waited while she buzzed him through the electronically locked double doors.

"You'll need to scrub and put on a gown before you can come any farther," the nurse explained after he had taken a couple of steps into the nursery. It had the faint scent of talcum powder and that special newborn baby smell.

Jeffrey turned toward the wash area she had indicated. Taking one of the plastic packages from the shelf, he ripped it open and used the presoaped pad to scrub his fingers and forearms. Watching all those episodes of *ER* had paid off. He could scrub down with the best of them.

The nurse waited next to a white wicker rocking chair covered with a blue-and-yellow seat cushion. She motioned him over, and once he was seated, she tenderly placed his daughter in the cradle of his arms.

The overwhelming rush of emotion was enough to choke on.

Jeffrey accepted the small bottle from the nurse and ever so gently worked the rubber nipple into his baby girl's mouth.

"You're already a pro," the nurse commented with a smile. "No one would believe this was your first baby."

"She is," Jeffrey replied. "She's been a long time coming."

"Does she have a name yet?"

He shook his head. "Not yet. Not until her mother wakes up."

They had tossed around a few names years ago, but he didn't know what the trendy name was nowadays. Besides, he couldn't name their baby without Amanda's knowledge.

"Don't worry," the nurse said, placing her hand on his shoulder and giving it a squeeze. "Your wife is going to pull through."

The knot that had already formed the moment he took his daughter into his arms tripled in size. Jeffrey tried to swallow but failed.

Amanda had to wake up. *Had* to. He could not fathom himself and his daughter going through life without her.

All the future moments he was so anticipating—going to recitals, kissing scraped knees, his daughter dancing with her feet on top of his—had Amanda right there at his side. To think of raising this baby without her . . .

"Think you can handle burping her?" the nurse asked as his daughter sucked the last of the contents of her bottle. She had a healthy appetite. It had come from his side of the family.

"Actually, I think I'll let you show me how it's done," Jeffrey said. Holding a bottle as he rocked back and forth was one thing; burping a baby was an entirely different ball game.

"It's not hard. Put that blanket over your lap." Jeffrey did as instructed. "Now," the nurse continued, "I'm going to lay her across your lap. Just rub her back gently and wait for her to burp."

The baby made a sound worthy of a drunken sailor in a bar.

"That was a good one," the nurse laughed. "We won't have to worry about a fussy baby when it comes to this little one. She makes sure she gets everything out."

"Mr. Daniels?" Another nurse came from the other side of the nursery. "I just got a call from Recovery. Your wife just woke up."

Deep down, in a far-off corner of Monica's mind, something told her that more civilized human beings would have waited until they were in a comfortable bed.

Tonight no one would accuse either her or Eli of being civilized. Tonight they were down right primitive.

Monica brought her legs up and planted her feet more firmly on the coffee table. Her glazed-over eyes barely registered the chandelier high above them as her head swam from the mind-numbing pleasure ricocheting through her body.

Eli buried his face against her neck, and she gripped his bare backside and pulled him tighter against her. They were as close as two people could possibly be, fused almost into one. He quickened his already frantic pace, and Monica felt herself tiptoeing the edges of sanity. She was on the verge of exploding, each fevered thrust bringing her closer to the brink.

Eli crashed into her again, and her body ignited.

Her cries echoed off the cavernous walls and twenty-foot ceilings. She clenched the solid muscles of his back and wrapped her legs around him, cradling his slick body against her.

They lay in the middle of the living room, their labored breathing the only sound in the empty house.

"That was nice," Monica panted between breaths.

Eli's head reared back. "Nice? Woman, you better say that was the best sex you ever had."

"Or what?" Monica asked. She ran her hands up and down his sweat-slicked back.

His dark eyebrows arched mischievously. "Or . . . I'm

going to make you go through it again," he finished, the beginnings of a sexy smile curling the edges of his mouth.

Monica returned his grin. Her heated body burned even more at the knowing gleam in his eye.

"In that case, it bored me to tears."

"It did, did it? Well"—he pushed himself off the table, reached down, and scooped her into his arms—"it looks like I'll have to try again. One way or another, I'm going to make you admit this is the best any man has ever given it to you."

He carried her up the stairs and proceeded to wring a confession from her after all.

Hours later, the doorbell's whimsical chiming roused Monica from her pleasant daydreaming. She groaned and rolled over. It felt too good lying among the plush linens. She could hardly move, much less get out of bed. But, darn it, Eli was still in the shower.

Monica managed to lift herself from the cottony cocoon of pillows. She looked around for a robe but didn't see one.

The bell sounded again. Monica slipped into a pair of scrubs Eli had thrown over a chair. She picked up a T-shirt from atop his dresser and pulled it over her head.

She bounded down the stairs with a satisfied smile. The delicious ache coursing through her body was a stark reminder of her activities over the past two hours. But now she was ravenous, and her mouth watered at the thought of diving into the pizza Eli had ordered.

A rapid series of rings sounded from the doorbell.

"I'm coming," Monica called out. She stopped in the living room on the way to the door and pulled a twenty from her purse.

She pushed a wayward lock of hair from her eyes and opened the door.

Monica froze.

"Who are you?" A woman she had never seen before stood just outside the threshold. She was six feet tall if she was an inch, and glamorous enough to be on a New York runway. "Where is Elijah?"

"In the shower," Monica answered. "Who are you?"

"That's none of your business, but you can tell me what the hell you're doing in my man's house."

"Excuse me?"

The woman trailed her gaze from the top of Monica's head to the tips of her toes. "How dare he disrespect me, and with a piece of trash. You tell Elijah he will hear from me," she said before turning and stalking down the driveway.

Monica stood, suspended in disbelief as the woman stomped—in stilettos, at that—to a white BMW convertible. As Monica watched her peel out of the driveway, the significance of the previous sixty seconds began to sink in.

Eli had another woman.

An overwhelming sense of betrayal gripped her stomach, nearly bringing her to her knees.

It was Patrick all over again.

The time they had shared, the love they had made—it had been a lie. He'd had another woman. He'd made of fool of her, had used her like a piece of . . . trash, just like the woman had said.

Monica forced back the tears threatening to fall from her eyes. She would not cry over this man—over *any* man. She'd prepared herself for this, hadn't she? She knew it would come eventually. But never had she expected it to hurt so much.

Monica fumbled into the living room, where her clothes still lay scattered across the sofa and hardwood floors. She gathered her slacks, sweater, and underwear, and searched around for her shoes.

"Is the pizza here yet?"

Eli. He was out of the shower.

She would be gone before he set foot downstairs.

Monica tugged her shoes from under the upholstered chair and slipped both onto her feet. She grabbed her purse, reached in and pulled out her cell phone, and punched in the numbers for directory assistance, instructing them to send a cab to the major street corner nearest Eli's house.

She closed the door behind her without a backward glance.

It was the hardest thing she'd ever had to do.

The answering service picked up his call after the fifth ring. Eli closed the refrigerator door with enough force to rattle the shelves within. He snatched a glass from the cupboard and poured himself some orange juice.

He punched in the numbers to Monica's cell phone again. Nothing.

He was trying hard not to worry. She wasn't on call tonight, but an ER doc was never really not on call. It was the nature of their business.

Eli finished his juice and picked up the phone again. He called the ER and was told Monica was not scheduled to be on until tomorrow morning.

If she wasn't at home, wasn't at the hospital, and wasn't answering her cell phone, then just where the hell was she?

With the dawn of a grim realization, stark panic crashed through Eli's chest. Something had happened to her.

He tried to stave off the fear that was in danger of crippling him. He needed to focus, not lose his head. He would call the police department of each district Monica had to drive through to get to her apartment.

Wait. Monica couldn't drive to her apartment. Monica didn't have a car. It was at the hospital, where they left it when he surprised her earlier this afternoon.

What was going on?

Eli grabbed his wallet and plucked out the card Nia had given him. It was late, but he didn't give a damn. This was important.

She answered on the second ring.

"Nia, I'm sorry to call so late, but I think something has happened to Monica."

"I hope you can explain it, because that heifer would not say two words to me."

"You talked to her?" Eli's heart jumped to his throat.

"I talked. She didn't."

"When was this?"

"About five minutes ago."

Relief crashed over his body like a tidal wave, making Eli weak. "Thank God," Eli breathed. "Did you get her on her cell?"

"No, at her apartment. Look, I don't know what's going on, but I'm not used to my best friend giving me the cold shoulder. You remember my warning, don't you?"

Despite his worry, Eli managed to smile. "Yes, I remember very clearly."

"Okay, now," Nia answered. "I'll be there in a few days for the banquet. Don't make me have to work a beating into my schedule."

"I made you a promise," Eli said. "You can keep your schedule open for more important things, like eating."

"Now you're talking. Tell that mother of yours to make the gumbo extra spicy."

"I will," Eli answered. "Thanks, Nia."

"You just make sure my girl is okay. I'll see you in a few days."

He disconnected and immediately dialed Monica's home number. Nia had just talked to her. If she was home, why hadn't she answered his call?

Eli felt his temperature escalate with each ring. He hung

up and debated whether to hop in the Rover and drive over there.

He glanced at the oval clock on the counter. It was after midnight. He had a C-section scheduled for seven A.M. He needed to get to bed. Getting answers to his questions would have to wait until tomorrow. Monica would be at the hospital. She might be able to run from his house, but she could not—*would* not—run from her responsibilities at work.

Leaving only the light above his stove illuminated, Eli made sure the doors were locked and went upstairs to bed.

The next morning, he was waiting at the nurses' station in Methodist Memorial's ER. One of the nurses informed him that Monica was in with a stab wound. She came out of emergency room one, shucking latex gloves from her hands.

"Monica," Eli called. She looked over and headed in the other direction. He took off after her. When he caught up with her, he grabbed her arm. Monica flung off his hand. She turned to face him, her usually warm brown eyes as cold as ice.

"I'm working," she snapped, and tried to turn away.

Eli caught her by the elbow. "Monica, what the hell is the matter with you? Why did you leave last night without saying anything? And why haven't you answered my calls? I called a dozen times last night."

She looked down at where his hand still held her elbow, but Eli refused to relinquish his hold.

"This isn't working," she finally said.

"What isn't working?"

"This. Me. You. This whole dating thing."

After the nightly telephone calls the entire time he was in Mississippi? After the hours they'd spent in bed the day before?

"What do you mean, it isn't working? Everything about it

works." This was the closest he had ever allowed a woman to get, and she thought it wasn't working?

"For you, maybe, but not for me. I didn't realize you expected me to be one of several. That is one thing I am not willing to do." The double doors swung open, and two paramedics wheeled in a gurney with a large man strapped to it. "Now if you will excuse me, I have work to do."

For a minute, shock had him rooted where he stood. It wasn't until one of the nurses nudged him with a crash cart that Eli was able to move.

He had no idea what to make of the past few minutes—no, scratch that—of the past few hours. Eli felt as though he were in some alternate universe. Everything seemed out of whack. The Monica he had been with just a day before was nothing like the woman who had just left him standing in the middle of the ER.

And what the hell did she mean when she said he expected her to be one of several? Several what?

It made no sense.

The beeper on Eli's hip began to vibrate. He unclipped it and checked the reading. Damn. If he didn't leave right now, he would be late for his scheduled C-section. Eli looked down the corridor at the door where Monica had disappeared with the patient. He couldn't wait for her, but he would be back.

The day turned out to be more hectic than Eli could ever have imagined. What were the odds of delivering three sets of twins in the span of ten hours?

By the time he got back to the ER, Monica had already left. Without a second thought, he got into his SUV and drove down to the French Quarter. He didn't bother to call; she wouldn't have answered anyway.

Eli spotted Monica's Honda. He waited for a horse-drawn carriage to pass before he pulled up to the curb and parked behind her car. His heart beat triple time as he jumped out and headed for her building. Eli bounded up two steps at a time, making it to her door in ten seconds flat.

"Monica, open up." He rapped on the door with his knuckles. "We need to talk."

Nothing.

"Monica!" Eli pounded harder. Someone down the hall opened a door, but he didn't bother to look back. His only concern was the woman behind this door, and getting an explanation for her actions last night and this morning.

Eli could not fathom what had gotten into her. The statement she'd made this morning continued to whirl through his mind.

I didn't realize you expected me to be one of several.

Since taking their relationship to a more serious level, Eli had banished all other women from his mind and his life. He'd explained about Tosha and, thank God, had not heard from Alicia in weeks. What made her think he wanted her to be one of several . . . ?

Eli knocked again.

He knew she was in there. He pulled his cell phone from the clip on his hip and hit the speed dial for her number. From outside the door, he heard the phone ringing, but she didn't answer.

Maybe she was in the shower. He was willing to give her the benefit of the doubt.

As Eli stood outside, waiting impatiently to give Monica sufficient time to shower if, in fact, that was what she was doing, he allowed his mind to roam to some of the other crises occupying his life right now.

Amanda Daniels, for one. She had opened her eyes for a few minutes but had slipped back into a semiconscious state.

Guilt tore at Eli's gut. Not saying that Amanda would not have lost the same amount of blood during delivery in any case, but Eli would have felt better if he had been here. He had let his patient down.

She had given birth to a beautiful baby girl, though, and Eli hoped the words he'd softly spoken in Amanda's ear about holding her baby would penetrate the new mother's subconscious.

Eli looked at this watch. If Monica was in the shower, she would be out by now. He pounded on the door again.

"Monica, stop ignoring me. Open this door."

Chapter Twenty-five

Nestled among the plush throw pillows, Monica picked one up from the sofa and held it to her chest, resting her chin on it. It took every bit of willpower she possessed not to run to that door. She wanted so badly to open it.

God, had she not learned anything?

How many signs had she had that Patrick had been cheating on her? But she'd chosen to turn a blind eye. With Eli there was no need to interpret any signs. The proof was smack-dab in front of her face—at his front door, as a matter of fact.

How could she have been so stupid as to fall victim again to a lying, cheating man? The threat of tears resurfaced, but Monica tamped them down. She would not cry for him.

Determination setting her shoulders rigid, Monica rose and went into the kitchen. She tried to ignore the knocking.

Her instinct was to head for the freezer and the pint of

Ben & Jerry's Phish Food ice cream, but she opted for an apple and a handful of granola instead. She would not be the typical grieving woman who, after a breakup, stuffed her face with junk food and couldn't fit into her jeans the next week. Oh, no. She would go to the gym every day, just to show Elijah Holmes exactly what he had lost by being a two-timing asshole.

"Monica, stop ignoring me. Open this door."

If he didn't stop soon, someone was going to call the police. She didn't want him to get himself arrested.

Wait a minute. Why should she care? Had he cared about her feelings?

Monica continued peeling the skin from her apple, letting it fall into the sink. When she was done, she cut the fruit and put it into a bowl, then scooped up the skin and deposited it in the trash can. She grabbed her bowl of cubed apple, sprinkled the granola on top, and mixed in a carton of fat-free French vanilla yogurt.

There—now that was much healthier than Phish Food, though one teaspoonful of ice cream wouldn't hurt. Monica stopped at the freezer and retrieved the carton.

Eli hammered with such force that Monica was sure the door would have splintered if it were not made of such solid wood. She ignored his pleas as she skimmed a spoonful of ice cream, capped the container, and returned it to the freezer.

The phone rang.

Monica picked up the bowl and went back over to the sofa, expecting to see Eli's number on the caller ID. Instead it was her brother's cell phone.

Why was he calling her? Monica picked up the phone. "Phillip?"

"No, it's me."

"Nia, why are you calling from Phillip's cell phone?"

"Because he mistakenly took mine with him to the store."

"What's going on?" Monica asked as she settled back on the sofa. She spooned a helping of the apple, yogurt, and granola mix into her mouth.

"That's what I want to know," Nia said. "I got a call from Eli."

Monica let out a loud sigh. Even though she knew Nia would be on her side, she was not up to telling the story of how Eli's other girlfriend had showed up the previous night. She was still in a bit of shock and not at all in the mood to hear Nia's ranting. Her friend would definitely rant.

"Start talking, girl," Nia said.

Nia was also not going to let her off the hook.

With another sigh, Monica relayed the events from when she opened the door at Eli's, expecting to find a pizza delivery guy. Ever mindful of the pair of ears on the other side of the door, she kept her voice level at a minimum.

"I told him I would kick his behind," Nia growled. "I *told* him. Did he not believe me? So what did he say when you confronted him?"

"I haven't confronted him," Monica answered. "I don't want to hear anything he has to say."

"You at least have to listen to his excuses. They always have an excuse."

"I should have known better, Nia. His reputation is legendary. The nurses are constantly talking about which woman he has on his arm any given week. Did I think things would be different because he was seeing me?" Monica shook her head. "I walked right into this, blindly stupid, as always."

"Don't you dare start berating yourself, or I'll kick your behind, too."

In spite of herself, Monica laughed. "I know, I know. It's not my fault, although to be honest, it's not Eli's, either. He never actually said we were exclusive. I assumed it."

"He's the one who should be making the excuses, Monica."

She rested her forehead in her palm. "You're right." She had made excuses for Patrick's behavior, too.

"Well, the two of you are still working on the banquet, right? What do you plan to do about that?"

"I'm going about my work the way I have from the beginning. I don't care what he does."

"It's going to be uncomfortable to work side by side with him."

"No, it won't, at least not for me. I didn't do anything wrong."

"You sure as hell didn't. If anyone is embarrassed, it should be him. He's the one who cheated."

Monica suddenly got a feeling of déjà vu. Didn't she and Nia have this same conversation the day she found out about Patrick's cheating? At the time, she just knew he would come begging on his hands and knees. Instead he had left with his perfect wife. She wondered if Eli now planned to flaunt his girlfriend in her face the way Patrick had. Monica wasn't sure she could take it.

"I'll be there in a few days to give you a big hug," Nia said.

"Thanks, girl. I need it."

"I'll talk to you later, honey," Nia said. "I love you."

"I love you, too."

Monica hung up. She listened for more knocks, and after fifteen minutes went by without a sound from the other side of the door, she concluded that Eli had left. She checked her cell phone for any missed messages. There were none.

Well, it didn't take him very long to give up, did it? He

was probably on his way to Miss Legs-as-Tall-as-a-Tree right now.

That was just as well. It was time for her to focus on more important things, anyway. Whatever she'd had with Eli—Monica refused to call it a relationship—was starting to get in the way of what she valued most, her job. The little diversion had kept her occupied, but from the moment she handed over her first task for the banquet, Monica should have known something was wrong. She never shirked her responsibilities, especially those so important to her career. It was probably better that things ended when they did.

So why was her heart breaking?

There was another knock at the door. She jumped. "Monica, please just open up so we can talk."

He was still out there? *Are you kidding me?* Maybe she should . . .

Shaking her head, Monica picked up her bowl and brought it to the kitchen. She scraped most of the healthy concoction into the garbage, rinsed out the bowl, and stacked it next to the sink with the other dirty dishes. She would do some housecleaning this weekend. For now, it was time to sleep.

Giving the door a passing glance, Monica turned off the kitchen and living room lights and headed for her bedroom.

When she arrived at the hospital the next morning, Monica went straight to Dr. Slessinger's office, but was informed by his administrative assistant that the chief of staff was in surgery. He would not be out for another three hours, so she made her way to the conference room where the final prebanquet meeting was being held.

Monica pushed the door open. Eli was the first person she spotted. He sat at the table, engrossed in conversation with Dr. Moore. Monica was momentarily stunned by how good he looked. Wearing an unadorned polo shirt and khakis, the man was simply scrumptious. But she could and *would* ignore him, no matter how delicious he appeared.

She walked over to an empty seat at the table.

"Thank you all for meeting me this morning," she began. "I promise to keep this short and sweet." She retrieved a small stack of papers from the canvas bag she had brought in with her. "Dr. Walker could not make the meeting, but sends great news. The banquet is a sellout." She smiled as applause erupted around the table.

"Now that we know we're going to be playing to a full house, let's talk about where we stand on the rest of the details."

Monica went down her checklist, receiving confirmation on the status of everything from tent rentals to the food.

"I apologize for not making the meeting with the plantation's curator and the decorator," she said after the nurse relayed the details of the meeting.

Monica refused to look down the table where Eli sat. Her surprise trip to Hattiesburg was the reason she had missed the meeting. Just thinking about all they'd done in his hotel room made her temperature rise to astronomical heights. She had to stop thinking about him. She would go crazy if she didn't.

"That's about it," Monica said, grateful to bring the meeting to a close. The sooner she removed herself from Eli's presence, the better. "If there is anything that pops up, feel free to call my home or cell number if you're not able to get a hold of me in the ER."

"What about the entertainment, Dr. Gardner?" someone asked.

Monica inwardly cringed. She was hoping to get through this meeting without having to address Eli. Taking a steadying breath, Monica trained her gaze on him. He didn't look at her; instead his eyes focused on his hands, which rested on the table in front of him.

"Dr. Holmes?" Monica said. "You took over the entertainment portion. Is Aria Jordan still scheduled to perform?"

Finally he looked up and nodded. "I'll confirm with her manager when I see him tonight, but as far as I know, she's still on tap for Saturday."

"Thank you for all your hard work," Monica managed to get out. She needed to leave right now. She was dangerously close to losing it.

"Any more questions?" Monica asked. She made the mistake of looking at Eli. His expression stated more clearly than words that he was full of questions for her, questions that had nothing to do with the banquet.

"If that's it, then I'll see all of you on Saturday."

The doctors, nurses, and administrators filed out of the conference room. As she had expected, Eli lingered. Monica tried to leave, but he stopped her with a hand on her arm.

"Dr. Gardner, could I see you a minute, please?"

Monica's eyelids slid shut. Her insides trembled as she waited for the last of the people to make their way out of the room. Drawing herself up, she turned and faced him.

"Yes?" she asked.

He hunched his shoulders and raised his hands, total confusion clouding his handsome face. "What happened?"

As if he didn't know. "I told you—it wasn't working for me."

"That's bull, Monica. There was nothing wrong with our relationship. Now, why in the hell did you leave like that?"

"Your girlfriend showed up."

"My what?" Worries about Alicia entered his mind.

Annoyance cut through her. "I am so not in the mood

for playing the dumb routine. I've been through this be-fore, and I have no intentions of going through it again."

"I don't have a girlfriend—besides you, that is."

"You had it right the first time: You don't have a girl-friend."

"Dammit, Monica, would you stop talking in riddles?"

"Do not take that tone with me. I don't owe you any-thing. I told you I wanted out, and that's the end of it."

"The hell it is." He grabbed her by the back of her head and crushed his lips to hers. Monica's entire being melted at the sensation of that decadent mouth her body had been screaming for these past few days. It amazed her how ad-dicted she had become to his kisses. Living without them had been torture.

She opened her mouth, and he plunged his tongue in-side. He kissed her until her knees were weak. When Eli fi-nally dislodged his mouth from hers, it took all Monica had just to remain standing.

"What part of that doesn't work for you?" he asked.

She could not put herself through this again. Despite how much her body cried out for him, her heart could not bear the pain.

"I can't do this." Monica barely choked out the words. "It's over, Eli."

The intensity of his stare nearly burned a hole through her. His eyes went cold. With a rigid shrug, he said, "Fine. You want to throw away everything we had—everything we *could* have had—that's up to you." He moved in closer, his voice at a chilling timbre. "Months from now, when you're thinking about what you gave up, just remember who made this choice." He straightened his shoulders. "I won't bother you again."

As he brushed past her, Monica's eyelids dropped along with her head as despair overwhelmed her. She was unable to stop the tears from cascading down her cheeks. Her body shuddered, but she refused to give way to the sobs she so wanted to let out. She would save them for later, when she was at home. Alone.

Wiping her tears with the sleeve of her white coat, Monica turned, checked her reflection in the door's slim window, and headed out to face the rest of her day.

She had survived a heart-wrenching breakup before. She would do it again.

Chapter Twenty-six

Eli mentally prepared for the confrontation that would commence as soon as he stepped into his mother's house.

He deserved to be shot.

It wasn't until he'd listened to his voice mail that he realized he'd missed his mother's birthday dinner. He had seriously considered packing a couple of bags and running away. He could still do it. He could send Mama the deed to his house as a belated birthday present.

Eli parked in front of his mother's house and got out. At least Mama's ranting would divert his mind from Monica for a little while. Eli winced as a familiar ache pierced his chest. It had been a constant companion these past few days, brought on simply by thinking about her.

Jazzy came up the driveway, pedaling her new bike. She jumped off, ran up to him, and wrapped her arms around his thigh.

"Hey, Uncle Eli."

"Hey there, Jasmine." He patted her on the head and extricated himself from her grip. "I need to go inside and talk to Grandma." He continued to the house, using the front door instead of going around the back. He found his mother snapping the tips off freshly picked green beans.

"Hey, Mama." He kissed her cheek. "I'm so sorry I missed your birthday."

His mother used the towel that was draped over her shoulder to wipe her hands. She pushed the bowl of beans toward the center of the table and started peeling the skin from one of the three potatoes that were sitting on top of a brown paper bag.

"I know my sons are grown men," she stated. "And I know you all have lives of your own. But I don't think it's too much to ask to have you call every now and then."

"I know."

She put down the knife and potato, concern etched across her face. "It's not that you missed my birthday, or Sunday dinner, for that matter. But I called and called, Elijah. I worry about all of you. Alexander is not much younger than your father was when he dropped dead of a heart attack. And Chantal? Do you think she expected to run her car into a tree when she left the house that day?"

"I know, Mama." God, he felt horrible for putting her through all those memories.

"Two minutes. A two-minute call to let me know you're okay. That's all I ask for."

Eli bent down and pulled her into a hug. "Mama, I am so sorry. The last thing I meant to do was make you worry."

She gave him a squeeze and patted him on the back. "It's over now, honey."

Her words caused another bout of hurt to run through him. *It's over.* That was what Monica had said to him.

"Now," his mother said, patting the chair next to hers. Eli took a seat. "Why don't you tell me what's been bothering you?"

He should have expected this. His mother had a sixth sense when it came to her boys. Eli tried to play it off.

"Nothing's bothering me."

"Don't you lie to me, Elijah Marcus. There's been enough of that, don't you think?"

Uh-oh. She'd used the full name. He'd best just come out with it.

"Monica and I broke it off."

Saying the words out loud was more painful than he could have ever imagined. It made it all so real, not like the nightmare he had been hoping to wake up from soon.

"Oh, Elijah. What happened?" Her disappointment was genuine, as he'd known it would be. In the short time since he'd first introduced her to his family, Monica had wormed her way into the tightly woven bunch. His mother, brothers, and even little Jazzy seemed to be charmed by her.

"To tell you the truth, I don't know, Mama. I'm not sure if Tosha had anything to do with it."

"Please don't tell me she's still upset over Tosha showing up for Sunday dinner that time?"

"No, Ma, I don't think it's that." Eli picked up a green bean and idly started breaking it into pieces. "Things had been wonderful even after that Sunday. But all of a sudden she said it wasn't working for her. Then the other day she told me my girlfriend showed up."

"Which one?"

Eli's head popped up. "What do you mean, 'which one?' It's not like I have a trail of women lined up. I have no idea who she's talking about."

"Well, talk to her."

"I've tried. She won't listen. She says it's over." Eli shrugged. "What more can I do but accept her decision? I can't force her to continue dating me."

"Dammit, Elijah, I liked her."

His eyes nearly popped out of their sockets at his mother's language.

"Had you already started picking out the wedding china?" he asked, forcing a grin.

"Almost," she grunted.

"It's not like we had been seeing each other that long, Mama."

"But the two of you were so perfect together."

That they were.

Eli struggled to stave off the agonizing pain that came with the thought of just how good things were with Monica. Although his mind hadn't gone down the marriage path yet, he had seen the road in the distance. If things had continued the way they were, who knows where the two of them would have been a year from now.

It was over. Monica could not have been clearer if she had painted a sign and knocked him over the head with it. All he needed to do was get through the damn banquet and then stay as far away from her as he possibly could.

If God was merciful, Monica and her ex would get back together and she would move back to St. Louis.

A sharp ache shot through his chest. He didn't want her back with her ex. He didn't want her with anyone other than himself. Eli wasn't sure he would be able to handle the first time he saw her with another man. Surely life wouldn't be that cruel.

"I guess this means all three of my sons will be going stag to Kathleen's wedding."

"Maybe not. Toby may take Aria Jordan."

"Hmmm . . . I don't know about her. She has a nice voice and all, but she's seems a little flighty, don't you think?"

"This from a woman who thought Tosha Culpepper was a good catch."

"Well," his mother sighed. "Looks like I'll have to wait

until Jazzy gets a little older. Maybe then I'll get a great-grandchild. It doesn't look like I'll be getting another grandbaby courtesy of any of my sons."

"If Alex has anything to say about it, you won't have any great-grandchildren either."

She leaned over and took Eli's chin in her hand. "What am I going to do with my boys?"

"Feed us."

They both turned as Toby walked through the kitchen door, followed by Alex.

"What happened to you Saturday night?" Alex asked. He deposited two plastic grocery bags on the table.

"Eli was needed at the hospital, so he had to miss my birthday dinner," Mama quickly injected.

Could he love this woman more?

"What's up with you two?" Eli asked.

"Nothing much," Toby answered.

"That's not true," Alex countered. "I got that contract with the city."

Eli rose from the table to give his brother a well-deserved pat on the back. "Congratulations, man."

"Oh, Alexander, that's wonderful," his mother said, jumping from her seat and wrapping her arms around Alex. "This is the really big one, isn't it?"

"Yep. We're in for three of the new magnet schools, and rebuilding nearly twenty of the schools damaged during Katrina."

Eli clamped his hand on his brother's back. Alex needed this. In fact, the news couldn't have come at a better time. What would have been his and Chantal's sixth wedding anniversary was next week.

"To celebrate, I'm treating everybody to dinner tonight."

Oh, no. He wasn't up for this. Tonight Eli wanted to do nothing more than stretch out on his sofa with a movie on the flat-screen and a bottle of Heineken in his hand.

"Thanks for the invite, man, but I really need to head home. I'm beat."

"Yeah, right," Toby said in a stage whisper that was loud enough for the entire neighborhood to hear.

"Are you sure?" his mother asked.

"Yes, Mama." Eli sent her a silent look, pleading with his eyes that what they talked about remain between the two of them. She returned a nearly imperceptible nod.

"We're still on for English Turn tomorrow, right?" Alex asked.

"Of course," Eli answered. Whenever the three of them were together, the Holmes brothers had to spend at least one afternoon on the golf course. "I owe this boy over here a butt-whipping."

"Whatever," Toby said.

" 'Bye, Mama." Placing a perfunctory kiss on her cheek, Eli grabbed the Tupperware container of leftover red beans his mother had given him for his dinner and headed out of the house.

As he drove home in silence, Eli reconsidered going out with the family. He really didn't want to be alone tonight. If he was at home, he would think about her.

Of course, if he was not home, he would *still* think about her. There had not been a single minute these past few days when his mind had not drifted to Monica in some way or another. Eli had the sinking feeling he would be thinking about her every day for the rest of his life.

Amanda stared at the baby in her arms. Her precious, completely healthy baby.

"Mrs. Daniels, I'll need to borrow her for a little while." Looking down at her, the nurse said, "I understand why you don't want to let her go. She's an angel."

"My little angel," Amanda said softly, finally relinquishing hold of Madelyn. They'd decided to name her after her grandmother. "Bring her back soon. I missed the first few days of her life. I don't want to waste a moment more."

"I'll have her back for her two o'clock feeding."

"Thank you," Amanda said. "See you, baby girl." She waved as the nurse exited. A few minutes later, the door opened and Jeffrey walked in.

Jeffrey.

He had been by her side throughout it all. Despite everything she'd put him though, the accusations, the misery—her husband had stuck by her.

"How are you feeling?" Jeffrey asked. He was pensive, and Amanda felt ten times worse. Her husband was afraid to speak to her.

"I'm tired, but it's not so bad. Did you see Madelyn on her way out?"

He nodded. "She's beautiful, Amanda. I still can't believe . . . after all this time . . ." She watched him struggle to swallow back tears. She reached for his hand, and after hesitating slightly, he entwined his with hers and gave a heartfelt squeeze.

"She's a gift from God," Amanda said, rubbing her thumb over the back of his hand.

"She's the most precious thing in my life." He stared into her eyes. "So are you."

Tears flowed down her cheeks like a dam had burst open. Amanda could barely catch a breath.

"I know you're not up for it yet, but when you're better, we need to have a serious discussion. We are not getting a divorce," he said with finality. "I don't know why I ever agreed to it. We are going to work through whatever our problem is, because I am not about to lose you."

"Oh, Jeffrey," Amanda whispered. She pulled him down to her, wrapping her arms around him.

"Oh, baby," he moaned, cradling her.

"Jeffrey, sit down."

"No." He pushed himself up, shaking his head. "Not right now. This can wait until you're better."

"No, it can't," Amanda said. "I've kept something from you, and I don't want our new family to start out with this secret hanging over it."

The apprehension on his face sent another stab of guilt down her spine.

He hooked his foot around the leg of the chair and brought it next to her bed, never releasing her hand. Taking a deep breath, Jeffrey sat beside her. He squeezed her hands and brought her fingers to his lips.

"Thanks for letting me touch you," he said.

Amanda closed her eyes to the hurt. God, she didn't deserve this man. Anyone else would have been long gone after the turmoil she'd caused.

"I'm bipolar," she said with a rush, before she lost her nerve.

His eyes widened. He stared at her for long moments, the silence stretching between them.

"How long have you known?" he asked.

Amanda swallowed past the guilt lodged in her throat. "About ten years," she answered.

"What?" His fierce whisper sliced through her. Jeffrey rose from the chair. He raked his hands down his face and began pacing the short length of her hospital room. "Why did you keep this from me? How could I not know my own wife is bipolar?"

"I've been on medication."

"For ten years?"

She nodded. "I started to sense that something wasn't quite right about a year after we were married. I suspected I was possibly bipolar when I recognized I was doing some of those same things my mom used to do—staying up for days at a time, cleaning the house from top to bottom several times a week."

"I just thought you were trying to impress me." He shook his head.

"No, Jeffrey, they were manic episodes. I found out about a clinic through an online message board for families dealing with mental illness."

"Why didn't you tell me?"

"I couldn't." She choked. "You know what happened to my parents, to my mother."

"Because she refused treatment," Jeffrey said. "Because she shut out the rest of her family. Why would you follow in her footsteps?"

"I didn't want to follow in her footsteps. That's why I sought help. I didn't want to end up like her."

He shook his head, visibly upset. "I cannot believe you kept this from me. That you would go through this alone instead of trusting me."

Amanda bit her trembling bottom lip, her heart sinking at Jeffrey's disappointment. "I know how you felt about living with a bipolar. You told me you never wanted to live the type of life my father lived. I was afraid you would leave if you found out."

"Goodness, Amanda." He ran his hands down his face again. "Did you really think I would leave you to suffer alone?"

"I'm sorry." She covered her mouth, unable to quell her sobs. "Jeffrey, I'm *so* sorry. I've put you through so much, and you didn't deserve any of it."

"Wait." He halted his methodical pacing. "You told me your mother used to accuse your father of being unfaithful."

"She suffered from paranoid delusions," she said in a broken whisper.

"That's what this is about, isn't it? That's why you think I've been cheating on you."

She tried to explain. "I had everything under control, but my hormones screwed with my medication once I became pregnant," she sniffed. "That's when the delusions started."

"I never cheated," Jeffrey argued. "The only other women were people I did odd jobs for."

"I know. Jeffrey, I know. Even when I was accusing you, I knew you would never do that. I just couldn't help what my mind believed to be true. That's why, when I realized there was a chance the medication would no longer control the bipolar disorder, I decided to set you free. I knew you didn't want to be married to a crazy person."

"You never gave me the chance to say what I wanted. How could you decide the fate of our marriage without even consulting me?"

"You didn't deserve to be stuck in the kind of marriage my parents had."

"Would you forget your damn parents? I am not your father. And you're not your mother. You faced your sickness where she never could. You are so much stronger than she is."

Amanda's throat ached with guilt, shame, and hope. "Jeffrey, I don't want a divorce," she said, emotion choking her words. "I want to get back on my medications, and if they don't work, I'll just find a combination that does. But I want you to be there with me. I want to raise Madelyn with you as my husband, not just as our baby's father."

"Oh, baby." He leaned over her, placing a heartbreakingly gentle kiss upon her lips. "There's nothing I want more."

Tears rolled down her eyes. "I am so sorry I put you through this," Amanda whispered.

"I'm sorry you tried to face it on your own." Jeffrey brought her hand to his lips. "But you don't have to anymore. I'm going to be with you in every single way I can.

You and Madelyn are my life. You're the reason I breathe. I'm never letting anything come between us again."

Amanda looked to the heavens, laughing through her tears, and she realized that for the first time in months—possibly years—she felt happiness. It was like finding an old friend. "Thank you," she said to her husband, clutching his hand like a lifeline. "Thank you for not giving up on me."

"Never," he answered in a fierce whisper. "And I won't let *you* give up on you, either."

Chapter Twenty-seven

"I thought you were gonna kick my butt." Unsheathing his four-iron, Toby took practice swings at the teed ball.

Eli rolled his eyes. "Would you take your shot so we can finish this damn round?"

"Kinda testy, huh?" Toby sent the ball soaring down the fairway. Dang, he must have been practicing these past few months.

"What happened at the grocery store?" Eli asked, picking up the conversation they'd started over lunch.

"Oh, man. You will not believe this! We're standing in the frozen food section, and this hottie walks past us. At first I thought she was looking at me, but no, she's checking out the monk over here."

"Must we relive this?" Alex asked, shielding his eyes from the sun and leaning on his bag of clubs.

Toby ignored him. "She's sending him serious sex eyes. And, let me tell you, babygirl was kickin'. She had a butt made for grabbing, and remember, we're in frozen foods, so the nipples were standing at attention like they were saluting the flag."

"I wish Mama could hear you right now," Alex said.

"Would you shut up and let me finish the story?" Toby shot back. "Anyway, after giving homeboy over here every kind of signal under the sun, she comes right out and tells him her name. You want to know his reply?"

"I can only imagine," Eli mused.

"He says, 'I'm Alexander, and I'm not interested.' " Toby tried to mimic Alex's deeper baritone. "I'm thinking to myself, *What the hell?* The girl was ready to invite him back to her car for a quickie, and that's how he answers her."

"She was a teenager, Toby."

"She was at least twenty."

"What am I supposed to do with a twenty-year-old?"

Both Eli and Toby turned and looked at their brother.

Toby shook his head. "This is so sad. How could you let this man go so long without getting some? He's so far gone, he doesn't even know what to do with it when it's staring him in the face!"

"I have to hear enough of this from Eli. Don't you start, too," Alex said. "Besides, from what I hear, it'll be a while before the good doctor here gets any himself."

"E?" Toby pointed his thumb toward him. "What's he got to complain about? He's elbow-deep in it every day."

Eli threw a wooden golf tee at Toby's head. "That's my job, fool. And whether or not I'm getting any is beside the point," he said to Alex. "I could go without sex for a year, and I would still be a year up on you."

"Hold up." Toby pulled off his glove with his teeth. "You're going out with one of the finest women I've ever seen. Is she against sex before marriage or something?"

Eli looked over at Alex, who stared back at him with a look that said, *If you don't say anything, I will.*

"I'm not seeing Monica anymore," Eli admitted. Damn, but Mama had a big mouth.

"What did you do, man?" Toby asked.

"Why do I have to be the bad guy?"

"She wouldn't have left if you hadn't done something to foul things up."

"What makes you think she left? Maybe I dumped her."

"You're not that stupid," Toby answered. "At least I didn't think you were that stupid. *Please* tell me you're not that stupid, E."

"He's not that stupid," Alex answered for him. "I don't know what it is about you this week, but you've managed to piss off every female you've come in contact with."

Eli shook his head. "You're right. First I miss Mama's birthday dinner, then for some reason Monica freaks out on me."

"And don't forget your niece," Alex said.

"My niece? What did I do to her?"

"Apparently you called her by her name."

"I did what?"

"You called her Jasmine. You would have thought the sun dropped out of the sky or something. It took going out for ice cream and to that Build-a-Bear place in the mall to cheer her up. You owe me thirty-five bucks, by the way."

Eli cursed under his breath. Even his Jazzy Bean was mad at him.

"What are you going to do about Monica?" Toby asked.

How many times had he asked himself that question? The answer remained the same. "Nothing," Eli declared. "There's nothing I can do. She said it's over."

"Does she still want Aria to perform for the banquet to-morrow night?"

"Yes. Definitely. It's still about saving the Parenting

Center. We've used Aria Jordan's name to sell most of the tickets."

"Damn, E. She was good for you. I really thought you'd found Mama's next daughter-in-law."

If only . . .

"Sorry to cut the round short, but I need to bail out. I need to check on a few patients."

"I have to go, too," Alex said.

"Aww, man. You two are a couple of suckers," Toby said. "You're only leaving because I'm winning."

Eli and Alex passed each other knowing grins.

"Next time you're in town, man. We're going the whole round," Eli said.

"Yeah," Alex called. "I'm gonna bring my A game."

"If you had an A game," Toby replied.

Eli hooked his towel on his bag and pulled the strap onto his shoulder. "I'll catch you guys tomorrow night."

"Take it easy, man."

"You, too," he called to Alex. "And tell Jazzy I'm sorry."

"I'll tell her, but she's not letting you off the hook that easy. She's a vengeful little thing. That girl's got more of her mama in her than I care to think about."

"Please don't say that," Toby said, still practicing his swing. A quartet was making its way to the ninth hole.

"Don't worry, I'm going to get it out of her before it's too late."

"Tell her Uncle Eli is bringing a special surprise to Sunday dinner. I'll see y'all later."

When Eli arrived at the hospital, he stopped in on Amanda Daniels. She was sitting up in bed, cradling her daughter. The smile on her face was one of pure, unadulterated happiness.

"You were made to have a baby in your arms," Eli said by way of greeting.

Amanda beamed up at him. "Isn't she the most precious baby in the world?"

"Probably the universe. Does she have a name yet?" he asked, walking over to the bed.

"Madelyn Rose."

"Hello, little Madelyn," Eli said, letting the baby wrap her hand around his pinkie finger.

"Thank you, Dr. Holmes." Amanda covered both his and the baby's hands with her own. "Thank you for everything you've done. I could not have asked for a better doctor."

"You're welcome," he answered. "Now, you do realize my special services are not free. I expect an invite to her first birthday party, and school pictures."

"Of course," Amanda laughed.

Jeffrey walked in. "Hey, Dr. Holmes."

Eli shook his hand. "Congratulations once again on your beautiful little girl."

"I don't know how to repay you, Doc," Jeffrey said with sincere appreciation.

"Just take care of your wife and little Madelyn. I'll see you guys later."

"Have fun at the banquet tomorrow," Amanda called out. Eli waved in reply and headed down the hallway. He would look in on a few other patients, then pick up some paperwork from his office and head home. He didn't want to be in this hospital a minute longer than necessary.

It was a disheartening realization. Methodist Memorial was like a second home. He loved his work, and he loved the place where he practiced. But it just wasn't the same anymore. Knowing Monica was just a few floors below left a pall over the hospital.

Eli made his rounds, stopped in the lounge to say hello to Otis, then headed for his office. He was stuffing charts into an old backpack he kept in the closet when there was a knock on the door.

"Come in."

"Are you ready for your whipping?"

"Hello to you too, Nia."

"Don't give me any hello. I'm coming to make good on my promise."

Eli put his head down on the desk. He motioned her in with his hand and mumbled, "Would you please close the door."

"Did you not think I was serious?"

Eli raised his head. He held out his hands, pleading. "Nia, I don't know what happened."

"You broke her heart, hence the impending butt-whipping."

"But I didn't do anything."

"You must have done something. I have never seen Monica so devastated."

"I'm telling you, one minute we're making love—"

She held up a hand. "Okay, I *so* do not want details."

"—and the next she's out the door. She said my girlfriend showed up, but I don't have a girlfriend. I have no idea what she's talking about."

"So you don't have a tall, gorgeous girlfriend who drives a white BMW?"

"White BMW?" he whispered.

"Monica told me about Miss Thang's visit the other night. Who is she?"

"Alicia," Eli said, unable to believe that woman was still wreaking havoc in his life. "Alicia Taylor."

Nia crossed her arms over her chest. "Was she supposed to show up only on Tuesdays and Thursdays?"

"She wasn't supposed to show up at all. I'm not with Alicia anymore."

"Maybe you should have told *her* that."

"I have not seen Alicia since Monica and I started dating."

"Then why was she at your house?"

"Because she's freaking crazy. Nia, you have got to convince Monica to talk to me. If Alicia is the cause of this . . ." He was going to kill her; that was what he would do. He would hunt her down and *kill* her!

Nia looked skeptical.

"Please." He was prepared to get down on his knees and beg.

"I don't know. I love Monica like a sister, and I don't know if I can take seeing her go through this again."

"Nia, I love her, too. I *love* her. I would never do anything to hurt her. You have got to believe me. If I had known this was all because of Alicia . . ."

Nia shook her head, then sighed. "I'm not sure it will make a difference. When you've been burned, you're not too eager to get close to the fire again. And Monica has been burned badly."

"She told me about Patrick Dangerfield."

Nia's eyes widened in surprise before she said, "Well, you're in the same boat with him, buddy."

Eli got up from his chair, crossing over to where she stood just inside the doorway. "No. I am not like him. Nia, you have got to help me."

"I don't know why I believe you."

"Because you know I'm good for her."

"I'm not convinced of that yet."

Eli sent her another pleading look.

She held up her hands. "I'll see what I can do, but I'm not making any promises. I hope you know how lucky you are."

Eli captured her hands. "Thank you, Nia."

"Don't thank me yet. More than likely, Monica's going to put both me and my husband out for arguing on your behalf. I hope you've got an extra room at your house. On second thought, I'd rather stay at your mama's. At least I'd have decent food to look forward to."

"I'll have Mama feed you for the rest of your life. Just get Monica to talk to me."

"I'll see what I can do," she said again. "You need to go home and get some sleep. You won't get a single bid tomorrow if you walk onstage looking like a sick dog."

Eli winced. "You do have a colorful way of putting things." He didn't bother correcting her inaccurate assumption that he would be up for bidding at tomorrow's auction.

"It's my trademark." Nia smiled.

"Please, do all you can," Eli said, more seriously. "I . . . I need to talk to her. I have to straighten this out."

She sighed, shook her head. "I'll see you tomorrow. Hopefully you'll be hearing from her tonight."

When she closed the door, Eli instantly sank to his knees, praying Nia's influence would buy him a few minutes of Monica's time. That was all he needed.

Chapter Twenty-eight

The rental company was late.

Monica took a deep breath and tried to calm her nerves. It wasn't the end of the world. If she was lucky, this would be the only mishap of the day. What a blessing that would be.

"They just called, Dr. Gardner." It was Patty, who was not on the banquet committee but had graciously volunteered her time.

"What's the problem?" Monica snapped. She checked herself. It wasn't Patty's fault the tent was not up yet. Along with the tables and chairs. Five hours before the start of the freaking banquet!

"You're not going to like what they had to say," Patty warned.

Monica closed her eyes.

Breathe. Just breathe.

"What?" she asked, unclenching her teeth.

"They double-booked the tent. They said we either have

to settle for a smaller one, or push our start time back by about an hour."

"Give me that number."

Monica pulled out her cell phone and punched in the number Patty handed to her. Waiting for someone to pick up, she started on a tour of the grounds, supervising the work being done around the massive house.

Despite the current calamity with the rental company, most things were running smoothly. The decorator had done an outstanding job and was patiently waiting in the wings until the tent arrived so she could finish.

The aroma coming from the kitchen smelled good enough to make Monica's stomach rumble, especially since she had skipped breakfast. As soon as she finished ripping into the idiots from the rental company, she would try to sneak a couple of samples from the kitchen.

Finally someone picked up. Monica let loose on the salesman.

Holding up a finger to tell Patty to wait a minute, Monica finished with the threat, "If you want to remain in business, you will have the correct tent here within the hour." She snapped the phone closed.

"I'm scared of you," Patty said with a look of feigned horror mixed with a little admiration.

"Not yet," she answered. "But if anything else goes wrong today, watch out."

"Thanks for the warning," she laughed. "The caterers need to know where to set up the ice sculpture."

"Ah, that's my fault. I was supposed give them that information last week. I'll take care of it," Monica told her.

After informing the caterer, Monica went in search of Dr. Miller, who was in charge of getting the stage set up for tonight's musical performance and the auction that would follow.

Before she knew it, the entire afternoon had flown by. The banquet would be starting in a little more than an hour. Monica spotted Nia and Phillip coming from around the foliage on the far side of the house.

Oh, great. She had too many things on her mind to deal with Nia right now. The traitor.

If Monica could have wagered on who would be on her side in this fiasco between her and Eli, she would have placed every last cent on Nia. If it had been a real bet, she'd be broke.

She could not believe her ears last night as she listened to her best friend—her *sister*—expound on the qualities Eli possessed and give reasons why Monica should allow him to explain.

Give him a chance?

What was that about? Nia had always been her staunchest supporter. For her best friend suddenly to switch sides was not only surprising but also hurtful. Monica had never felt more betrayed and alone.

As Nia and her brother approached, Monica forced herself to keep her face expressionless.

Nia held her hands up in surrender. "I come in peace," she said.

Monica couldn't trust herself to speak.

"I know you're upset, honey."

"Actually, I'd use a stronger word." Monica crossed her arms over her chest. "You see, my best friend stabbed me in the back."

"What else can I say but that I'm sorry?"

"You can admit you were wrong."

"Am I forgiven?" Nia asked. She did not admit to being wrong. Typical.

Still, the makings of a grin tugged at Monica's lips. She could never stay angry where Nia was concerned. "Only because I'm too wound up to fight with you," Monica said, giving her best friend a short embrace so not to wrinkle her elegant silk suit.

Looking at Nia in the knockout-gorgeous cream-colored ensemble reminded Monica that she needed to change pretty soon.

"So, are you nervous about pulling this off?"

"Not at all," Monica answered. It wasn't a total lie. Her nerves had calmed down considerably once she'd settled things with the tent rental company. The increasing gray clouds off in the distance were raising the hair on the back of her neck just a little, though.

"This thing tonight isn't going to put me to sleep, is it?" her brother asked.

"Oh, shut up, Phillip," Nia said. "Don't worry, I won't let him embarrass you by snoring halfway through the auction."

"I just won't claim to know him," Monica said, pinching her brother's arm.

"It all looks wonderful," Nia commented, making a slow circle as she took in her surroundings.

"Thank you. Everyone has worked so hard. I'm just hoping we pull in enough to keep the center open."

And knock the socks off her fellow colleagues, of course. Although the desire to impress the other doctors at Methodist Memorial was not as strong as it had been when she had first begun this project. The more Monica worked on it, the more important it became that the banquet and auction meet their original intent—to save the Parenting Center. That's what it was all about.

"Okay, I know I said I wouldn't mention his name again, but has *he* shown up yet?" Nia asked.

If Nia were not her best friend, Monica would have punched her. It took every ounce of control she had to keep her hands to her sides, though they still balled into fists.

"He doesn't have to be here until the start of the banquet," Monica answered. "His job was securing the entertainment, which is already setting up, and getting the guys for the auction."

To be honest, Monica had been a little upset when Toby arrived with Aria Jordan in tow but no Eli. Her mind kept telling her that she didn't need to see him, but a large portion of her heart rebelled against the thought. Her body was craving him, even if only for a few brief moments.

"Now," Monica said, facing Nia. "We can either change the subject, or you can find someone else to talk to."

"I'm going to look around a little more," Phillip interjected. "I don't think I want to be around for the rest of this conversation."

"Coward," both Monica and Nia said to his retreating back.

"I'm sorry," Nia said, extending her arms.

Monica grasped her hands. "I'm not going to hug you again, because I don't want to mess up your clothes, but your apology is accepted."

"I just think—"

"I'm being very generous, Nia. Don't push it."

"Fine," her best friend said, holding her hands up in surrender again. "You know what you're doing."

"Yes, I do. And right now I'm going to get dressed. People are already showing up."

"You go get pretty. I'll catch up with my husband. He's probably snatching a sneak peek at tonight's desserts."

"If you can, try the crème brûlée cheesecake. It is divine."

"Girl, you don't have to tell me but once," Nia said, heading for the caterer's tent.

Despite the small threat of rain, which passed quickly,

and a misprint on the program, Monica was able to get through the rest of the evening's preparations without having to down a bottle of aspirin or chug Mylanta.

She went in search of the plantation caretaker to inquire about a place where she could change.

"We have the dressing room that bridal parties use. Go up the stairs and take a left. It's the last door on your left."

"Thank you," Monica answered. She grabbed the hanging bag from her car and quickly made it to the dressing room. When she stepped into the spacious area, Monica's heart gave a small tug.

Brides had readied themselves for their husbands in this very room. She could just imagine them in their wedding finery, preening in front of the mirrored wall, preparing for a lifetime of happiness.

All she was preparing for was a banquet.

She closed her eyes for a moment, giving herself the chance to reflect on the abysmal outlook of her romantic future.

Her eyes popped open. She had a job to do tonight, and she was never one to shirk her responsibilities. She could moan tomorrow about being lonely.

Monica changed quickly. She stuffed the clothes she'd taken off into the garment bag, zipped it up, and left the confines of the depressingly cheerful dressing room. By the time she went down to put the bag in her car, half the guests had shown up.

After weeks of planning, the hour was finally here. Time to show them all what she was made of. Time to save Methodist Memorial's Parenting Center.

Eli jerked the black silk tie from his neck, then tried to retie it. If he couldn't make a simple knot for his tie, he should just throw in the towel and plan to spend the night at home. He probably shouldn't drive in the state he was in.

Monica never called.

He'd been waiting at the phone like a love-struck teenager. Checking his pager and cell phone on an hourly basis. Calling his voice mail at the hospital to see if she'd tried to contact him there. But he'd heard nothing.

Either Nia had decided he wasn't worth the hassle of potentially harming her friendship with Monica, or she didn't have as much influence as Eli had originally thought. Whatever the case, he had not heard from Monica in days.

This overwhelming ache in his chest was new to him. He'd broken it off with women before, but he'd never experienced the bone-deep hurt, the true physical pain he now felt. The thought of having to go the rest of his life without ever seeing her face beside him when he woke in the morning, or her smile across the table as they ate breakfast . . .

It stole his breath and caused his chest to tighten unmercifully.

And that was when Eli knew. He was in love with her. He was unbelievably, without a doubt, give-up-everything-he-possessed-just-to-see-her-face-again in love.

It was a feeling unlike any he'd ever had before. In this short amount of time, she'd come to mean the world to him.

And now she wouldn't even speak to him.

Grabbing the tie, Eli made his fourth attempt at making a knot. Somehow, someway he was going to get through tonight. But God only knew how.

Monica joined in the applause as Aria Jordan finished a soulful remake of a Roberta Flack classic. That girl had a set of pipes on her.

Monica's nature had always been overly cautious, which was why she wasn't ready to give herself a pat on the back just yet. But as the night drew on, the urge was there. Everything so far had gone off without a hitch.

The food was absolutely marvelous. The entertainment was outstanding. Even Mother Nature was on her side tonight; the magnolia blossoms gave off a light scent that perfumed the air, wrapping around the grounds of the plantation.

She caught Dr. Slessinger's wink and returned it with a thumbs-up. It looked as if she'd impressed her colleagues, anyway.

Aria started another song, this one a soft, mellow ballad. Monica closed her eyes and let the soothing music drift over her. Standing on the outer perimeter of the grounds with her eyes closed, she felt a semblance of peace for the first time in nearly two hours.

Since the moment Elijah Holmes had arrived, Monica had not been able to stop herself from seeking him out.

It was as if he were a magnet and she a sheet of metal. Throughout the night, whenever she looked in his direction, Eli's eyes were on her. It was the reason she'd left her seat to stand back here in no-man's-land. From where she stood, she could not even see Eli's table.

Monica stifled a small moan. She *wanted* to see him.

She gave herself a mental shake. There were things to do. She needed to check out the preparations taking place backstage. The auction would be starting soon.

"Dr. Gardner?" It was Patty.

Monica opened her eyes and felt an immediate sense of dread at the look on the nurse's usually serene face.

"I'm feeling really good right now, and I have a feeling you're about to ruin my mood."

"I think that's an accurate assumption," Patty answered.

Oh, great. As if she needed this, whatever *this* was.

"On a scale of one to five, how bad is it?" Monica asked.

"Which means really bad?"

"A five."

"Okay, then this is a fifty."

An instant headache formed between Monica's eyes. She brought her hand up and squeezed the bridge of her nose. She was afraid to ask.

"What is it?"

"There was an ammonia leak at one of the chemical plants in Mississippi."

"Uh, Patty, I know that's not necessarily good for some people in Mississippi, but to be honest, I couldn't care less."

"Well, you need to start caring, because half of your eligible bachelors for tonight's auction are stuck in Hattiesburg."

"No, they're not," Monica said, dragging the words out slowly.

"When was the last time you went backstage?" Patty asked.

"Right after the meal was served. Dr. Johnson and Dr. Banyon had just changed into their tuxes."

Patty's head went up and down with exaggerated nods. "Yes, they were. Along with Dr. Myers and Dr. Jackson. But everyone else . . ."

Monica's eyelids slid shut. "Tell me this is your sick, twisted idea of a practical joke. I'm going to kill you if it is, but—"

Patty shook her head. "This is very, very real, Dr. Gardner. What are we going to do?"

This isn't happening. This is so not happening.

"The auction starts in twenty minutes. How many bachelors do we have?"

"Five," the nurse answered.

If there had been a wall close by, Monica would have banged her head against it. Of all the things that could ruin this night, losing the majority of her bachelors had never entered her mind.

"Why am I just finding out about this?"

"The hospital received several calls, but no one bothered to pass on the information."

"You have got to be kidding me!" Monica pointed at her watch. "Nineteen minutes! We've got nineteen minutes, and instead of a dozen bachelors I have five?"

Her mind was a jumble of wet knots. How in the hell was she supposed to handle this? The bully tactics that had worked for the tent rental company wouldn't do a bit of good here. And unfortunately crawling up in a fetal position and crying her eyes out—which was what she felt like doing—wouldn't help, either.

"We need to find some emergency bachelors. I can make my brother, Phillip, join in. Quick, Patty, go to the head table and get Dr. Slessinger."

Patty held up a finger. "One problem—neither of them are bachelors."

Monica opened her mouth, then shut it. "I . . . I don't care. We need some warm bodies, whether they're single or not."

"I'll tell Dr. Slessinger. You find Dr. Holmes," Patty said, leaving before Monica could form a protest. The bottom dropped out of her stomach.

Eli fit the bill to a T. He was both a bachelor and a doctor. But he had adamantly refused to take part in the auction.

Well, they both had to suck it up. Desperate times called for desperate measures. And a hell of a lot of sacrificing.

Swallowing the forty-eight emotions lodged in her throat, Monica whispered to herself, "You can do this."

That positive self-talk crap never did a bit of good. Her heart still beat like a tambourine. Dread filled her chest, but when she rounded the tables where Eli had been all night, he was nowhere to be found.

The emcee announced the first bachelor.

Frantic, Monica looked over to the head table and caught Dr. Slessinger's wide-eyed expression.

Oh, goodness. This was so, so bad.

Anxiety clawed at her skin. She searched the crowd desperately for anyone who could fill in, but she was still too new at the hospital to know all of the doctors. And many who were supposed to be in attendance were either in Mississippi or covering for the doctors who were covering the strike.

On the verge of breaking down in tears, Monica could only watch as the first bachelor strutted across the stage. A night at Delmonico's with Dr. Johnson from Cardiology went for a whopping eighteen hundred dollars.

Monica said a silent prayer of thanks. She had estimated how much each bachelor would go for and had put Dr. Johnson at about only a thousand. If the other four went for more than she'd projected, maybe the night wouldn't be so bad after all.

Except there was no way five doctors would fetch as much as twelve would have. This was such a nightmare.

The second and third bachelors each went for less than she had estimated. Apparently radiologists were not as sexy as some of the other specialties.

Monica stood over to the side and watched as the emcee tried to cajole the ladies in the audience to raise their bids as Dr. Peter Banyon strolled across the platform.

"Twenty-two hundred. Do we have twenty-two fifty?"

"Twenty-two fifty," came a shout from the audience. Was that Nia? Monica craned her neck. Yep, that was her sister-in-law.

"Do we have twenty-three?" the auctioneer asked.

"Twenty-three," someone in the back called.

Yes. Yes. Yes.

Monica crossed her fingers, silently praying the doctor's youth and good looks would hike up his asking price.

Several minutes later, after another round of bidding, including another bid from Nia, the auctioneer finally concluded with, "Sold for three thousand one hundred fifty dollars."

Applause erupted for both Peter and for the woman who'd purchased him. Bless Peter's heart, his date had to be at least seventy years old. When he walked over to her table, the older woman gave him a big kiss on the lips, which the young doctor took in stride, dipping the woman and giving her another kiss.

Monica was ready to kiss him, too. She would owe Peter big-time.

They were up to six thousand three hundred dollars, way short of what she had estimated.

"The fifth bachelor"—and last, Monica thought, closing her eyes in dread—"is Alexander Holmes." Her head shot up. "He's not a doctor, ladies, but he does own one of the fastest-growing construction companies in New Orleans."

What?

Alex sauntered across the stage, dressed in a sleek tuxedo. The bids were already up to a thousand dollars. He flashed a smile, and female hands shot into the air.

Monica stood in a daze, unable to comprehend what was happening as Alex, Toby, and someone named Jonathan, whom she had never seen before, each promenaded as if they'd been scheduled from the very beginning to be onstage.

Eli was behind this. He had saved her.

Monica held back tears as she looked over the crowd once again, searching for him.

"And our last bachelor of the night is Methodist Memorial's one and only Super Doc, Elijah Holmes."

Monica's heart practically stopped as Eli walked onto the stage. He was divine, dressed all in black. He smiled at the crowd, a smile that did not reach his eyes.

Women were bidding faster than the auctioneer could call them out. With each turn Eli made, the price went up.

Nia bid twenty-five hundred, which was quickly followed by a bid for twenty-six.

Monica's heart swelled. She knew he was not comfortable being auctioned off like a piece of cattle; he'd told her those very words. Yet there he was. For her.

"Ten thousand," Monica said, stepping out of the shadows.

A collective gasp swept over the crowd as heads turned her way. But Monica had eyes for no one but the man on the stage.

The look Eli gave her sent a tremor of fear, hurt, and anticipation down her spine. His piercing eyes shot through her like a flaming arrow.

"Do we have ten thousand one hundred," the auctioneer asked. Silence followed. "Sold for ten thousand dollars."

Through the resounding applause, Monica heard a whoop she was sure came from Nia's table, but she refused to look anywhere but at Eli. He stepped down from the stage, never taking his eyes off her.

Monica was at a lost for words.

"That was very generous of you," Eli said, taking her hand and planting a light kiss on the crest of her fingers. "The Parenting Center appreciates it."

"Do you?" she managed to whisper.

He gazed into her eyes. The breath Monica was about to take lodged in her throat. His bold stare sent chills down her spine, Eli slowly nodded. "Yes," he finally said.

"Oh, God," Monica gasped, throwing her arms around him. "Eli, I'm so sorry."

He pulled her away slightly, his stare intense. "There's no one but you, Monica. I need you to know that."

"Shh." She put her fingers to his lips. "No explanation is necessary. I'm sorry I ever doubted you." She stared into his eyes, her heart filled with sorrow and hope. "Can you forgive me?"

The sexy smile she'd missed more than air crept upon his lips. "I guess," Eli answered with a shrug.

She burst out laughing, relief washing over her in waves. "Are you always this forgiving?" she teased, planting a kiss on his mouth.

"For the woman I love? Pretty much." His words reverberated against her lips. An intense burst of joy echoed throughout her entire being.

Monica caught the mischievous crook of his mouth, and the glint in his eyes she'd come to know all too well.

"Wait a minute. Will I have to pay a special price for this forgiveness?" she asked.

Eli's sensual smile broadened.

"Pretty much."

Remember the Alimony

Bethany True

Tips from Delaney Davis-Daniels, former Miss Texas:

Avoid sleeping with the enemy. Even if your ex's attorney is the most luscious man ever and you had no idea who he was when he gave you the most incredible night of your life.

Never let 'em catch you crying. When your slimeball former husband turns up dead and you're suspect #1, stay strong. After all, you have a gorgeous lawyer willing to do anything to help you prove your innocence—as long as he doesn't get disbarred first.

And remember: *Love never follows the rules.*

A MOMENT ON THE LIPS

PHYLLIS BOURNE WILLIAMS

Grant Price wants old classmate Melody Mason to work for his family's Boston investment company. Melody has retired from big business and is hiding. It is Grant's assignment to lure her back to the fast life. But when he arrives at her door, she doesn't look like the woman he remembers....

Melody has hidden herself away in rural Tennessee for a reason: she desperately needed a life change. So she has no intention of returning to a fast-paced lifestyle. Instead, she makes Grant an offer: stay, relax and find out what life is like without a hectic pace. Unfortunately, real life calls and Grant must return to Boston. Can Grant and Melody agree on what a good life truly means?

Dorchester Publishing Co., Inc.
P.O. Box 6640
Wayne, PA 19087-8640

_____5659-3
$6.99 US/$8.99 CAN

STRONGER THAN YESTERDAY

NICOLE KNIGHT

Faith's marriage is the kind written in fairy tales. Her husband, Gerard, is passionate, attentive and all hers. Then everything changes when Gerard's ex-wife tells him he is the father of her eight-year-old son—a child he never knew about. Now, the baby conceived on Faith's honeymoon seems unimportant—and Faith feels the same way.

Gerard is stunned at the news of his son's existence—and he's thrilled. After being abandoned by his own mother, he vows to be a real father to his child. What he can't understand is Faith's jealousy and insecurity. It will take all his patience to convince his beautiful wife that he has enough love for everyone in their new family—and especially her.

Dorchester Publishing Co., Inc.
P.O. Box 6640   ___5660-7
Wayne, PA 19087-8640 $6.99 US/$8.99 CAN

Please add $2.50 for shipping and handling for the first book and $.75 for each additional book. NY and PA residents, add appropriate sales tax. No cash, stamps, or CODs. Canadian orders require $2.00 for shipping and handling and must be paid in U.S. dollars. Prices and availability subject to change. **Payment must accompany all orders.**

Name: _____

Address: _____

City: _____ State: _____ Zip: _____

E-mail: _____

I have enclosed $_____ in payment for the checked book(s).

For more information on these books, check out our website at www.dorchesterpub.com.
_____ *Please send me a free catalog.*